Surface Tension

Also by Joanna Hines

Surface Tension

Joanna Hines

SIMON & SCHUSTER
A VIACOM COMPANY

First published in Great Britain by Simon & Schuster UK Ltd, 2002
A Viacom company

1 3 5 7 9 10 8 6 4 2

Simon & Schuster UK Ltd
Africa House
64–78 Kingsway
London WC2B 6AH

www.simonsays.co.uk

Simon & Schuster Australia
Sydney

A CIP catalogue record for this book
is available from the British Library

Hardback ISBN 0-684-86053-8
Trade paperback ISBN 0-684-86046-5

Typeset in Stempel Schneidler by
SX Composing DTP, Rayleigh, Essex
Printed and bound in Great Britain by
Clays Ltd, St Ives plc

Acknowledgements

Thanks are due to all the friends who took time to answer my questions: Dee, for the building; Ken for the survival course; Russell for the electrics; Kate for the medicine and my cousin Chris for all the invaluable information and literature about new religious movements.

For Hilary,
Luke and Sam

Back Then

August 1976

That was the summer when the lush green of the English landscape was bleached pale as parchment. Streams dwindled to a trickle, then dried up entirely. Reservoirs were barren and fissured like elephant hide. Blue skies above and sunshine, day after day for weeks, weeks that stretched into months.

That was 1976, the summer of the drought.

For the six friends who had taken up residence in the lofty rooms of Grays Orchard, those summer days of heat were a long indulgence. The biscuit-coloured lawns round the house were permanently dotted with rugs and pillows, and a hammock slung between two apple trees was hardly ever empty. At night they lay on their backs on the grass and searched the heavens for shooting stars.

One morning in late August, a morning hazed with gold like all the other mornings of that endless summer, Gus Ridley woke late. The air drifting through the open window was sweet with pollen and hay. From outside came the murmur of voices and, far off, the steady drone of a combine harvester. Another flawless day.

He planted both feet firmly on the wooden floor, squatted on the edge of the double mattress he mostly shared with Katie and ran his fingers through his tangled thatch of dark hair. Then he coughed, reached for the packet beside the anglepoise lamp and tapped out the first cigarette of the day. Pausing only to pull on a pair of threadbare shorts, he padded barefoot down to the kitchen, where he plugged in the electric kettle and spooned Nescafé from an enormous jar into a mug. There were tomatoes and new potatoes heaped on the table: Pauline had taken advantage of the early-morning coolness to work in the garden.

Gus headed towards the door to go out and join the others on the lawn, then thought better of it and retreated into the cool gloom of the house. Today he wanted to observe, without being seen.

Quietly, he padded from room to room, pausing each time to gaze out of the window at the group on the lawn. He went into the drawing room, the morning room, the library, the smoking room, the dining room – grand names, all of them, for rooms whose function was interchangeable, since all were equally bare of furniture. A few cushions, perhaps, a battered armchair, a rickety table. A pile of magazines or a plate with an ancient meal congealing round its rim. The room most used was the breakfast room, which had a gramophone on the floor in one corner with a heap of records fanned out beside it.

Gus loved these rooms; he loved their echoing purity and the way the dust spun through them in shafts of sunlight. His love for the house at Grays Orchard, and all it represented, had become a fierce pain in his chest now he knew their tenure was running out.

He tossed the stub of his cigarette into the grate, where

it snagged on a cobweb and remained hanging above the pile of cinders and old butts, then he went upstairs. From the bow window on the landing he looked down again at the group on the lawn.

Raymond, as usual, was sitting a little apart from the others. Feet tucked up on opposite thighs in a full lotus position, he looked like a small Indian god with his dark, exquisite features . . . Gus never knew, with Raymond, where the pose ended and reality began, and he had a hunch Raymond wasn't sure, either.

Katie and Harriet were the centre of the group. Of course. Two such beautiful women were bound to be the centre of attention wherever they went. Harriet's brown hair was bleached by the sun. Tall and strong and regal – Gus had always wanted to paint her as a warrior or an archer. Boadicea must have looked like Harriet, he thought. Boadicea in a flowered dress. By contrast, Katie under her straw hat was all blue-eyed, pink and blonde femininity. As he watched them, Katie laughed and leaned over to press her ear against Harriet's stomach. Harriet smiled and shoved her gently away. Too soon, she must be saying; it's far too soon to feel the baby move.

From opposite sides, Pauline and Andrew looked on. Gus knew that, although their mouths were smiling, their eyes would be cautious, holding back.

He felt a piercing sadness. Already this unborn child of Harriet's had become the most important member of their group. Raymond, cross-legged under his tree, was no doubt reciting a mantra designed to ensure its spiritual pre-eminence. The first Grays Orchard baby. Since Harriet's pregnancy had been confirmed, they'd devoted their spare time – and most of their time was spare, that summer – to discussing how the child was to be reared. 'Not like we were' was the common theme. Andrew had already started looking out wood for a crib, Katie and Harriet discussed names endlessly, and Pauline, God help her, had bought knitting needles and a ball of lemon-coloured wool.

Gus could have wept. They honestly believed this present contentment was to be the foundation of all their future happiness; he could have told them that time was running out and their best times were already in the past.

A little later he was in his studio, the high, vaulted space that used to be the apple loft and was still permeated with the acid scent of old apples. All the canvases for his next exhibition were propped against the walls, on chairs and easels. They showed the members of the Grays Orchard group doing all those vaguely pastoral activities they delighted in: Andrew chopping wood; Pauline scattering corn for her brown hens; Harriet hoeing her vegetables.

His first exhibition, a year ago, had been a runaway success. Dealers and galleries and private buyers fell over themselves to purchase those first twenty pictures of his friends at Grays. The Grays Orchard style. The paintings had been described as 'dreamlike', 'mesmerising', 'luminous'.

If he could, Gus would buy back every one and destroy them all. The light that had so enchanted the public was phoney, he saw that now.

Stepping back, he narrowed his eyes to examine the painting on the easel. It was one he'd done in the spring: a figure lying in the hammock, a blinding shimmer of appleblossom and radiance all around. A waterfall of light.

A treacherous lie.

He took a soft brush and loaded it with a wash of paint, weighed down like a fat bumble bee with pollen. Then, concentrating hard, he began to apply the shadows.

Disaster was approaching. He didn't know how or when, but he knew it was coming.

It had to.

Chapter 1

Their faces materialised suddenly in the fog, an instant snapshot in the gloom. The girl wasn't at all what I'd expected, but I recognised her right away.

She looked younger than her age, could easily have passed for seventeen or eighteen, though I knew she was in her twenties. She had lank blond hair and a stick-thin body wrapped in several layers of clothing. Her features were pinched and angular. They might have been attractive if she'd been smiling, but she wasn't. In fact, her expression was glacial.

And she was about to go into the Turk's Head with my husband.

The traffic in Sturford High Street had slowed almost to a standstill, allowing me plenty of time to examine them both. It's always odd when you unexpectedly glimpse someone you know well, like catching your brain unawares. There's a moment when you see them the way a stranger would. In that brief flash, I saw Gus as a man of almost fifty, tall and distinguished-looking, sure, but with more grey than black in his hair and with a care-worn, almost haggard face and untidy clothes. The next moment, knowing it was Gus, I rejigged my view to fit the man I loved: those features so full of character – he was far more attractive than most men half his age; his battered tweed jacket and rumpled cords the mark of his bohemian lifestyle. After all, no one dresses in a suit and tie to paint pictures. And it was hardly surprising if he looked worried. Gus had a lot on his plate right now.

To be precise, he had Jenny Sayer.

It would have been hard enough for him to deal with his stranger niece even if she'd been diplomatic about it all, but she hadn't. In the first place, she'd been over from Australia for six months before she got in touch. Then she refused to come and stay at Grays Orchard with us, saying she'd prefer to stay at the Travelodge four miles away. Two days before her arrival yesterday, she'd insisted on having some time alone with her uncle before she'd so much as consider meeting up with me.

'Who does she think she is, for God's sake?' Gus had demanded when the letter arrived bearing her final condition. 'It feels as if we're on trial. I'll tell her not to come. Either she sees us both together or not at all.'

But I persuaded him to see it from her point of view. Scary enough to meet an uncle you've never clapped eyes on before; much worse when that uncle is an extremely successful painter. If she thought it was going to be easier this way, what was the problem?

'Okay,' Gus conceded finally, though it was obvious he wanted me along to help out, 'we'll humour her. God, Carol, what would I do without you?'

He thought it was kindness that made me smooth the path for this unknown girl, but mostly it was plain curiosity. Jenny was a link with the world he'd lived in before we were married. Long before. In the days when I was still a child and Jenny hadn't even been born.

I was still wedged in the traffic when they reached the entrance to the Turk's Head. Gus stood aside to let his niece precede him. She seemed uncertain how to deal with this courtesy and her narrow face was pinched with tension. Either she wasn't used to men who let her go through doors first, or else she saw it as a sexist put-down. When he put his hand on her elbow, she shook him off. And then, as she went ahead into the pub, she stumbled on its uneven threshold and Gus had to grab her by the arm to stop her falling headlong.

Poor old Gus, I thought ruefully. It doesn't look as though his long-lost niece is giving him much joy. The traffic began moving again. I glanced back towards the Turk's Head. Gus's long back was framed by the pub's eighteenth-century doorway, then he was swallowed up by the darkness inside and vanished from sight.

For a moment I thought of trying to find somewhere to park so I could go and join them. Given half a chance I was confident there'd be no difficulty persuading Jenny to see me as an ally, and Gus would welcome the support. I checked my watch. Damn. I'd promised Brian to be at the site when the buyers came round at one.

On the outskirts of Sturford, just past the roundabout where the bypass joins the main road near the Travelodge and the new Superstore, the traffic picked up speed, although the fog was getting denser. I switched on my headlights. Outside the dingy Elim chapel a sign hand-written on neon orange paper proclaimed: *Give your worries to Jesus: He'll be up all night anyway*; it made me smile and I made a mental note to tell Gus that evening. Poor old Jesus, I thought, having to wait up all night listening to people's moans. For a moment I felt quite sorry for Him. Still, at least He wouldn't have to put up with mine.

*

'What a shame it's foggy for your first visit to Grays. It's such a beautiful house.'

Her eyes were unflinching. 'So? Doesn't bother me. It's just a house, isn't it? Nothing special.'

'We-ell . . .' I glanced at Gus but he avoided my eye. 'It must have meant a lot to your mother.'

Jenny shrugged. 'Nothing to do with me, though.'

I'd been back at the house only twenty minutes and already I was on the point of giving up. Normally I can thaw out the most icy of guests, but Jenny was determined not to play. Small talk obviously wasn't her thing. I wondered what the opposite of small talk was – big talk, presumably – but I had a hunch that wouldn't be right, either. You had to feel sorry for the poor girl, coming all this way from Australia to find her roots and with the shadow of that tragedy looming in the background: hardly surprising if she was making heavy weather of it all. Her resistance made me more determined than ever. Later, when I remembered my efforts to make her welcome at Grays Orchard I didn't know whether to laugh or cry. I ought to have hammered a 'No Trespassing' notice at the bottom of the lane and barred all the doors, but of course I didn't.

I tried again. Shoving the chicken in the oven, I said, 'Anyway, you're here at last, that's the main thing. Gus and I were afraid you might not come down at all.'

There wasn't a flicker of warmth in response to my smile as Jenny said, 'I wasn't going to, but the cards made me change my mind.'

'Cards?'

'You know, tarot cards?' Her Australian inflections blurred the distinction between statement and question. 'I had a reading a couple of weeks ago and the woman came up with this really weird combination. She couldn't work it out until I told her about this place and my dad and . . . well, you know, everything. She said me coming down here was meant to happen.'

I laughed. 'You don't really believe in all that fortune-telling nonsense, do you?' It was the wrong thing to say, but I thought I'd better get in before Gus crushed her with his scepticism. To my surprise he didn't respond, merely regarded her thoughtfully. Trying to make amends, I added, 'I suppose it's fun as a game, but it doesn't mean anything.'

'How do you know?' she demanded. 'Just because it's not scientific.' She turned to Gus for support. 'You don't think it's nonsense, do you, Gus? Your friend Raymond would have known what I was talking about. I bet you used to do all that stuff here in the old days: tarot and I Ching and ouija boards. Didn't you?'

'We may have done, but I'm afraid I can't really remember. It was all such a long time ago.'

Jenny looked disappointed and no wonder: Gus, normally the most generous of hosts, was going out of his way to be super-formal and polite. Each time he spoke to his niece – and that was only when he had to – it was as though he was using long-handled tongs: rigorously correct but keeping her at arm's length. It seemed to be up to me to set her at her ease.

So I said lightly, 'Oh, Raymond Tucker, he was always off with the fairies. You can tell from those paintings Gus did of him, can't you, Gus?'

Without even a glance in my direction, Gus said coolly, 'I don't know, Carol. I never really thought about it.' Which was just plain ridiculous, as well as making me look like a fool.

I was beginning to get annoyed. Not only was I working overtime to make Jenny feel at home, but I was also doing all the preparation for supper. Normally on Friday evenings Gus took me out for a meal, or else he rented a video and cooked pasta to eat at home. I work hard, and by the end of the week I enjoy a bit of spoiling, but either Gus had forgotten what day it was or he was too disoriented by the arrival of his long-lost niece to function properly. And Jenny clearly wasn't the type to offer assistance. So I washed and chopped vegetables and tried not to feel resentful.

Jenny said to Gus, 'That tarot reading was all about you. Well, you and me, obviously.' She slid me a defiant glance. 'No one else.'

'Really,' said Gus.

I said, 'What does your mother think of all that?'

'We never talk about it,' said Jenny flatly. She leaned across the kitchen table towards Gus, turning her back on me. 'Gus, do you still have any of those portraits you used to do?'

'No. Unfortunately both exhibitions sold out.'

'Why's that unfortunate?'

'I would have liked to destroy them all.'

Jenny tilted back in her chair. She looked shocked. I said swiftly, 'Both the exhibitions were a huge success. Gus's dealer said he could have sold all the paintings five times over.' I knew that because Gus still dealt with the same dealer, who kept saying, even though after twenty-five years he must have known it was pointless, 'Shame you don't do portraits any more, Gus. I could have sold those first two exhibitions five times over,' or anything up to ten times over, depending on his mood. Oliver always went on to qualify his remarks with 'Of course, someone with your gift's got to do what comes naturally. Can't be expected to paint to order.' But he invariably said it wistfully, as though painting to order was precisely what he wished Gus would do. The still lifes and abstracts he did nowadays sold well enough, but nothing since had matched the success of those first two exhibitions.

I said, 'You've seen the reproductions, though.'

Jenny looked cagey. 'Well, some of them, in magazines, that sort of thing, but it was ages ago and to be honest I wasn't all that interested.'

'Surely Harriet showed you the catalogues?' I asked.

'She may have done. I can't remember. She doesn't like to be reminded of all that. You can understand why.'

'All the same . . .' I dried my hands. 'Oliver did Gus proud with the catalogues. Apparently they're collector's items now. We've got them both. I'll get them for you.'

Gus stood up. I thought maybe he was going to volunteer to fetch them himself, but instead he remarked, 'Don't bother now, Carol. I don't suppose Jenny's interested.' There was the shadow of a warning in his voice. I ignored it, because I could see that, though she'd never admit it in a hundred years, Jenny was consumed by curiosity.

So I said cheerily, 'Of course she is. Aren't you, Jenny?'

'I don't mind either way.' But her grey eyes were desperate.

'Maybe tomorrow,' insisted Gus.

'No, no, I'll get them now. I know where they are.'

I couldn't think why Gus didn't want me to show Jenny the catalogues, and I was amazed by the fury on his face as I went past him to the door. I was undeterred. The girl might be rude and awkward, but she still had the right to see the paintings that had made Gus and her parents famous, however briefly. Probably Gus was just being modest.

Fog creates a denser kind of silence. The apple loft, which Gus still uses as a studio, is just across the courtyard from the kitchen where we'd been sitting, but on this particular April evening, it felt a mile away. It's a tall building; the ground floor is used as a garage and general store, and there are outside steps leading diagonally up to the loft door. They were slippery with damp, and moisture was dripping from the eaves. It felt more like November than April and even the birds were silent.

I pushed open the loft door and went in, realising as I did so how rare it was for me to be alone there. I took my time: Jenny was hardly going to miss me and I could use a few moments of solitude to prepare for the evening ahead, which was clearly going to be hard work.

A rustle – maybe a mouse in the roof space – made me turn round suddenly, almost as though I was expecting to see one of the Grays Orchard group standing by the window. It always catches me unawares that way, like an echo left on the air. Maybe that's all ghosts are, just echoes on the air.

Sometimes I wonder if it is possible to miss what you've never known; if it is, then I think I must miss the years when Grays was full of the sound of laughter and argument and song. The house is too big for just me and Gus, though we'd never dream of selling it. Sometimes I fantasise about inviting the Grays Orchard group back, so they can see how happy Gus is again, with me. I'd make them all so welcome, Harriet and Raymond and Pauline. Even Katie. But not Jenny's father. Never Andrew.

I turned back and took the two catalogues down from the shelf. The first one was called simply *Gus Ridley at Grays Orchard*. On the front cover was a portrait of Jenny's mother, Harriet, carrying a long-necked white goose. Even I, who have no pretensions to artistic appreciation, could see why that first exhibition had been such a knock-out success. Gus had depicted his friends enjoying their make-believe pastoral idyll – *Andrew Cleaning his Gun*, or *Pauline Feeding her Chickens* – but had done so with an ethereal, otherworldly quality which saved the paintings from being chocolate-box attractive. Sometimes, when I was living my less glamorous life, I imagined Gus doing a whole new series of portraits: *Carol Scoops Gloop out of the Drain* or *Carol Nods Off in front of the Telly*. But that wasn't going to happen, not ever, even though I'd look good in a picture. Gus hadn't painted a single portrait since the group broke up.

The second catalogue had the most famous of Gus's paintings on the cover: *Being Katie*. It has been called one of the great celebrations of erotic love in the twentieth century: Katie had obviously been stunning, and she and Gus must have been very much in love. So much so that Gus had never really settled with anyone else until he met me.

This second exhibition was called *Shadows in Eden* and you could see why. The light was different in these paintings. There was an ominous quality even in the sunshine, a shadow darkening the radiance. Still, when he was under pressure Gus sometimes darkened his paintings. Once, in New York, a few years after the Grays Orchard group broke up, he'd blacked out a whole series of paintings just before they were due to go off to an exhibition. It was the reason dealers were still wary of him. I wondered if he was doing it now: he'd certainly been different since Jenny got in touch with us, though it was difficult to pinpoint exactly how.

There were canvases stacked against the wall, one or two finished works on a shelf at the far end. Semi-abstract flower paintings were his speciality these days. They did look darker, but it was hard to tell.

Just as I was about to leave I noticed there was a canvas on the easel, covered with an old sheet. Gus always encouraged me to see his work in progress, so I had no hesitation about lifting the corner of the sheet and hooking it over the apex of the easel.

I gasped and stepped back suddenly.

It was a portrait, a portrait of his niece, the first portrait he'd attempted in nearly a quarter of a century but totally unlike anything he'd ever done before. This was a quick sketch, with all the power and intensity of first impressions.

Poor Jenny. If she was aware of how her uncle saw her, no wonder she had veered away from him outside the Turk's Head.

Nearly the whole canvas was taken up with a huge, funnel-shaped flower; it might have been a hibiscus or an amaryllis or a mysterious jungle bloom. It was a deep browny red, the dark red of liver or drying blood or the swollen lips of a woman's sex. Emerging from its fleshy petals were the head and torso of a young woman – Jenny, obviously – though if I hadn't seen her at the Turk's Head at lunchtime I'd have thought this was a demon figure from one of Gus's nightmares. Her skin wasn't a normal human colour at all; it was pale, almost blue, like the skin of a corpse, and it was pulled back so tightly over her skull and the bones of her body that it made her look like a hideous caricature. Her cheeks and breasts were grey shadows. She was pathetic and repellent at the same time. She was in pain, but it was the kind of suffering that made you want to run away, because nothing you did would make any difference. Most obscene of all, at the point where her body emerged from the mouth of the flower, the girl's torso ended in the half-formed curled legs of a foetus. It was grotesque, like being forced to witness the exposure of some foul secret that should have been left in darkness.

'What's kept you so long?'

I spun round. I'd been so absorbed in the hideous portrait that I hadn't heard Gus come into the studio. He strode across the room, unhooked the cloth and draped it back over the canvas.

'Spying, Carol?'

His accusation was so outrageous that for a moment I was speechless. Gus always encouraged me to look at his work in progress and he welcomed my comments. Why should this painting be any different?

'Did you paint that?'

'Of course I did. Do you think I'm inviting guests in to use my studio? Don't be ridiculous, Carol.'

'I thought you didn't do portraits any more.'

'That's just a sketch. It doesn't count. Have you got the catalogues?' He smiled down at me, but it was a phoney smile: he was already regretting that I'd seen his anger. 'Come along, let's show them to Jenny: she's determined to have a look.' And when I still didn't respond he said in a voice that was falsely casual, 'Look, it's not a big deal, Carol. Just an idea I was playing around with. I'll probably go over it tomorrow.'

He was trying, clumsily, to make out that the portrait wasn't important, but he must have known I wouldn't believe him. *Not a big deal*, when it was only the first portrait he'd done in a quarter of a century. *Just a sketch*, when the power of that hideous figure was so strong I could feel it still, even though it was covered by the cloth.

He said, 'You can stay here if you like, but I'm going back to the house.'

As he turned to go I asked, 'Why's that girl had such an effect on you?'

'It's nothing to do with her.'

Another lie. Before I could protest again there was the sound of a car coming to a halt in the yard. Gus looked towards the window. 'Who on earth can that be?'

'I expect it's Brian. He said he'd drop off some costings for me to work on over the weekend.'

'Brian, eh? I wonder if he'd like to stay for a drink.' And without waiting for my answer, Gus ran down the steps to the courtyard.

His eagerness to invite Brian to join us confirmed my suspicions. Usually Gus regards my business partner as a necessary nuisance: he's as friendly as he has to be in order not to be rude, but he never encourages Brian to visit Grays. Gus must be truly desperate for a diversion if he was inviting him to stay now.

Thoughtfully, I closed the studio door behind me, went down the steps and across the courtyard in the dripping mist, and followed the two men back into the kitchen.

Brian and Gus have absolutely nothing in common except me, so when the three of us are together I always end up feeling like a rickety rope bridge, trying desperately to span the gap between them.

Gus is fifteen years older than me; Brian five years younger. Gus is tall and dark and craggily handsome; Brian is thickset and strong, with ginger hair and freckles. Gus is a painter and Brian is a builder. Gus has travelled all over the world and led an interesting and exotic life; Brian has lived and worked his entire thirty years within a three-mile radius of Sturford. I could carry on listing the differences between them indefinitely, but there's no need.

Gus had obviously decided that Brian, being a neutral outsider, was going to make this first evening with Jenny a lot easier to manage. I wasn't so sure, but there was no way Brian was going to turn down Gus's invitation to stay for a drink and then for supper as well: after all, it was only curiosity about Jenny that had prompted Brian to drop the costings off in the first place. He was always curious about anything concerning me.

To begin with it did seem as though Gus was right: Brian was open and cheerful and forthright and he went out of his way to be friendly to Jenny. Like me, he probably felt sorry for her. She responded with her usual grudging chill, but the three of us were able to chat about work and local matters for quite a while, which presumably was what Gus had intended. I was still puzzled by that hideous picture, and longing for the moment when he and I were alone again and I could ask him about it, but in the meantime it looked as though we were going to get through the evening, thanks to Brian and copious lashings of alcohol.

Gus, who hardly ever drinks more than a couple of glasses of wine these days, had poured himself a large whisky and Jenny said she'd have the same. I don't know if whisky was her normal tipple or if it was the stress of this first visit to Grays, but she drank it in record time and had a couple more before I served the meal. Then the wine flowed. I had more than my usual quota, though nothing to compete with Gus and Jenny. Only Brian, nursing his driver's solitary beer, stayed stone cold sober.

Too late, I remembered Jenny had driven herself here from the Travelodge. There was no way she was going to be able to drive back this evening and I no longer felt inclined to invite her to stay with us. I couldn't look at her without being reminded of that portrait.

We were halfway through the chicken tagine and Gus was beginning to relax. He and Brian had been discussing the projected closure of the Sturford cattle market and the council's plans to allow a supermarket to be built on the site.

'Christ,' said Gus angrily, 'the last thing Sturford needs is a new supermarket. Why can't they turn the site into a park, or something really useful?'

'Of course,' said Brian, who never allowed himself to get heated in a debate, 'the main losers will be the Bank Holiday Fair. They've been using that piece of ground for ever.'

'The fair?' Jenny, who had been scowling at her food as she pushed it around her plate, latched on to the conversation with interest. 'Is that the same fair that . . .?'

She didn't finish. Gus frowned. Jenny took another swig of wine and said, 'I mean, is that the fair where the man worked . . . you know, when my father . . .?'

We must have all known it was coming, but Gus thought he was going to be let off.

Brian said helpfully, 'Andrew Forester was your father, wasn't he? I expect Gus has been telling you all about him.'

Gus shot him a vengeful look before saying smoothly, 'The topic has never come up. I'm sure Jenny's mother has told her everything she wants to know.'

'She doesn't tell me anything!' Jenny blurted out, too loud, too vehement. She instantly qualified it by mumbling, 'I never listen to her, anyway.'

'Carol,' said Gus, 'this tagine is delicious.'

Jenny's cheeks were flushed and her eyes were glistening: it might have been the alcohol. She said doggedly, 'I want to know about my father.'

'Of course you do,' said Gus, his voice so falsely helpful it made me cringe. 'I'm happy to tell you anything you want to hear. Andrew was very good with his hands, brilliant at mending things. I wonder if you take after him at all.'

Jenny was looking increasingly frustrated. 'No, not that. Not what he was like. I mean, I do want to know that, but . . .'

Brian came to her rescue. 'Is there anything in particular you're curious about, Jenny?'

'Well, yes, as a matter of fact there is. I mean, I'm interested in him as a man, but I've got an idea about that. But Mum never told me how he died. She did tell me, when I was little, but she said he'd been killed in a car crash.'

'Maybe she thought it was better that way,' I offered gently, and was rewarded with a filthy look.

'She only told me the truth when she knew I was coming to England. She said she didn't want me to get a shock when I found out. But she should have told me years ago. And she wouldn't go into details. She said it upset her too much to talk about it.'

'Well, you can understand why it would.' This time I was braced and waiting for the inevitable glare.

Gus remained silent, so it was Brian who said gently, 'You must be curious about how he died.'

'Yes. I mean, I know he was murdered, but no one's ever really told me how it happened. I've never understood. And I thought' – she turned to Gus and for a moment her hostile defence slipped and she appealed to him directly – 'I thought you could tell me, Gus. I mean, you were there when it happened. You can tell me how my father was murdered.'

Chapter 2

Anybody who'd grown up in Sturford – and that included me and Brian – had been reared on the story of the Grays Orchard murder. No one had talked about anything else for six months at least and, though the adults resented the negative publicity, we children revelled in it and loved seeing familiar names and faces in the papers. We followed the inquest with fascination and were heartily disappointed when the prime suspect was killed in a fight a few months later and the case was closed, though that didn't damp down the rumours. Everyone had a pet theory, but the facts were straightforward enough.

Gus Ridley, his half-sister Harriet and four friends had been living at Grays Orchard for nearly two years, the nearest Sturford had got to a hippie commune ('We weren't hippies and it wasn't a commune,' Gus always said in disgust, but inevitably the tag had stuck), and we'd heard about the scandalous goings-on there ('All wild exaggeration,' Gus insisted. 'The way people talked, you'd think we'd spent our time re-enacting the last days of

Sodom and Gomorrah'). Every August the Bank Holiday
Fair came to Sturford and all the Grays Orchard group
decided to go, but at the last minute Harriet stayed behind.
She said she wasn't feeling well. She was asleep when the
intruder broke into the house: it was assumed his motive
was burglary, but he changed his mind when he saw her
sleeping there. Andrew Forester came back unexpectedly
just in time to tackle the intruder, who pulled a knife and
stabbed him. He was dead when the ambulance arrived, by
which time Gus had also returned. Though a boy from the
fair was thought to be the murderer, Harriet was never
able to make a conclusive identification. Within six months
he'd been killed in a fight anyway.

Those were the facts: that was what everyone knew.
When I first got together with Gus I thought he'd tell me
about it in his own good time, but he never did. In fact, he
made me feel uncomfortable about even mentioning it, as
though there was something unhealthy in my interest, so I
learned not to. And then I pretty well forgot about it.

Until this evening. No one could accuse Jenny of
showing an unhealthy interest, because Andrew Forester,
dead before she was born, had been her father. Of course
she wanted details about his death, but for a while she and
Gus circled round the subject. Gus told her Andrew had
always been impetuous, but he'd been a valued member of
their group because he was practical and liked doing
things. In all the portraits Gus had painted of him he was
busy, chopping wood or mending a fence or cleaning his
gun.

Jenny wasn't the only person listening with interest.
Brian said, apparently casual, 'Someone pointed out afterwards that in all your paintings of him he was carrying a
weapon. Shame he hadn't got one when he needed it most.'

Gus said, 'It wouldn't have made any difference.
Andrew was hot-headed but he wasn't aggressive.'

'What about the fight he had in the Turk's Head the week before?'

'What about it?' Gus looked as though he was beginning to regret having invited Brian to stay for supper.

Jenny said, 'When he was killed, he was trying to protect my mum, wasn't he? He must have been very brave to defend her against a man with a knife.'

No one spoke straight away. It was obvious that Jenny wanted us to confirm her image of her father as a hero. Her eyes were shining. At moments like that, when she forgot her aggressive pose, she had a vulnerable charm, and my heart went out to her.

Eventually Brian looked directly across the table at Gus and said, 'You're the only person who can tell her exactly what happened. After all, you were there.'

'You were there?' echoed Jenny.

'Not when he was stabbed.' Gus shot Brian a furious look. 'But yes, I was the first on the scene. Your father was already dying when I got there. Tom Longman, our doctor, said he would have died even if he'd been just outside an emergency ward when the attack happened. He said one of the stab wounds had punctured his lungs and there was another at the base of his throat. Tom said no one could have survived an attack like that. I think he meant to comfort me, but I've always wondered if there wasn't more that could have been done. If I'd got back sooner. If I'd known more about first aid. If, if . . .'

Brian said calmly, 'Isn't that how people always feel when someone dies? That they didn't do enough?'

When Gus is very stressed, or when he's drunk too much, his left eyelid droops, half closing that eye. This evening the tension was coming off him in waves and he'd already drunk more than he usually did in a week, so his lazy eye was making him look distinctly piratical. He shrugged, as if he didn't care how other people felt, only knew his own feelings and they were pain enough. He said, 'All I know is it's haunted me.'

'Did you see the man who did it?' asked Jenny.

'Not properly. Not well enough to make a positive identification.'

'Is that why he was never charged?'

'I suppose so.' Gus was silent for a little while. We waited. Then he seemed to make a decision. I guess he must have decided that Jenny deserved to hear the story of her father's death. He said, 'You really want me to tell you?'

Jenny's habitual refusal to admit any kind of vulnerability was battling with her curiosity. Curiosity won and 'Yes,' she said.

'Okay, then, I'll tell you.' Gus poured himself some more wine, then pushed the glass into the centre of the table, as though indicating that he needed to be as sober as possible to tell this tale. He began carefully. 'It was the day of the Sturford Fair. At the last moment Harriet decided not to come. She said she felt unwell. I suppose it was because she was in the first weeks of her pregnancy, though she hadn't, as far as I know, experienced any actual sickness. The afternoon was hot. She was planning to read her book in the hammock. She joked as we set off, gave us strict instructions to bring her back a plastic duck for the baby.'

I'd seen enough portraits and photographs of Gus's half-sister for me to picture the scene clearly. Harriet had been tall and strong, with long sunburned legs and long brown hair, and she would have moved with that easy grace women always have in the first weeks of pregnancy, before any swelling shows. I imagined her crossing the wide lawn to the hammock slung between the trees. I imagined her starting to read, then letting the open book fall across her stomach as she closed her eyes and her head filled with the drowsy scents and sounds of Grays Orchard on a hot summer's afternoon.

'So my mother was there all the time,' said Jenny, her eyes round with fascination. 'She must have seen it all. She never told me.'

'No,' said Gus with distaste, 'I expect she prefers to forget.'

'So it's up to you to tell me, then, isn't it?'

For a moment, I thought Gus was going to refuse, but he went on in a deliberately neutral voice, 'It was always assumed the man's original motive was robbery. In those days we had little enough worth stealing, but he wouldn't have known that. He might have seen the others coming across the fields and assumed the house was empty. When he entered the garden he saw Harriet lying in the hammock. During the summer she and Katie went around half naked most of the time. Pauline was always more conservative, but Harriet and Katie liked to wear just a pair of shorts or underpants, with a scarf tied over their breasts. Harriet's breasts had already begun to swell with the pregnancy and a cotton scarf wasn't really adequate any more. Not that she cared. She told me later it must have slipped undone while she was asleep.'

He paused. His eyes were dark with pain as the memories came back. I thought how desirable Harriet must have looked, lying there in the dappled shade of the apple tree, her full breasts spilling free of that flimsy cotton scarf.

'So did he . . .?' Jenny whispered.

Gus ignored her. 'Harriet said she woke up to find a total stranger standing over her. He reached down to grab her, but the moment he touched her she tipped out of the hammock and ran screaming towards the house. She was a fast runner, and I dare say she ran faster that afternoon than she ever had done in her life. Andrew must have heard her screaming even before he reached the garden. Luckily for Harriet, he had got bored with the fair and was already on his way home. Otherwise . . . Well, who knows what would have happened.' He stopped abruptly.

No one spoke. I glanced across at Brian and saw he was as mesmerised as I was. We'd heard the story many times before, but only at second hand in the bland language of the coroner's report or the more sensational words of the national press. Now, as Gus took us slowly through the events of that sultry August afternoon, the tragedy was unfolding afresh.

'She didn't go straight into the house,' Gus went on. 'She ran past the kitchen door and up the steps into the apple loft, which I was using as my studio. Afterwards she explained that all the doors and windows in the house were wide open, so she thought she had a better chance of barricading herself in the loft, but my guess is she just panicked. The man followed her. There was no way of locking the studio door – we didn't believe in things like locks and bolts in those days. Harriet must have put up quite a fight. My easel was smashed and all the chairs and canvases had been hurled across the room. Everything had been trashed. By the time Andrew arrived, the man had knocked her down and was punching the daylights out of her.' He stopped, and for the first time he looked at Jenny directly, the beginnings of a smile hovering around his mouth. In the context of what he'd been saying, that smile was horribly incongruous. 'Do you want me to go on?' he asked.

Jenny couldn't speak; she just nodded.

Gus said, 'Andrew must have heard the noise coming from the loft. He ran up the steps only to see Harriet, semi-naked and semi-conscious, being beaten up by a stranger. Andrew had played a lot of rugger in his time. He hurled himself at the man and dragged him off. That must have been when Jago pulled out his knife and stabbed him. Seven times, to be precise. The fatal blow was the one that severed the main artery in his neck. He lived for a few minutes, but it must have been obvious he was dying. The man fled.'

'You saw him running away, didn't you?' I broke the silence.

Gus threw me a vicious look for daring to ask for yet more detail, but said calmly, 'as I was returning through the lower orchard I saw a figure running down the lane. It was obvious something was wrong. He was running too fast. On a hot afternoon like that, nobody in their right mind was going to sprint. But I didn't see him well enough to make an identification.'

'You called him Jago,' said Jenny, mouthing the word carefully, as if it was dangerous. I wondered what it must be like, tasting the name of your father's murderer on your lips for the very first time.

'That's right,' said Gus. 'Jago was one of the boys attached to the fair and he'd been in trouble before. Burglaries and fights mostly – there'd certainly never been anything like a murder. He was the main suspect right from the start.'

'Yet Harriet couldn't identify him,' said Brian thoughtfully.

'No.'

'That part's always struck me as strange,' Brian persisted. In spite of the expression on Gus's face, which was caustic enough to strip paint, Brian kept to his normal speaking voice, as though he was discussing types of brick or load-bearing beams. He went on, 'After all, the man had tried to rape her. She'd been about as close to him as you can get to another human being and it was the middle of the afternoon. You'd think his details would have been burned into her memory.'

'Really, Brian? And are you speaking from personal experience?' asked Gus with cold fury. 'Harriet was hysterical and extremely frightened. She'd just endured a beating and an attempted rape and she'd seen the father of her child murdered right in front of her eyes. Hardly the ideal circumstances for a cool assessment of the situation, one might think.'

'All the same . . .' said Brian.

I couldn't think why Brian was pursuing this. Being the kind of man who reacts to any crisis by becoming even more phlegmatic than usual, he was unable to understand how the tragedy must have affected someone as sensitive as Harriet. What I found hardest was imagining the Harriet of the portraits, so serene and self-assured, reacting to any event, even such horrors, with hysterics.

Gus said, 'At the identity parade she was ninety per cent certain, but she didn't want to risk a mistake.'

'And there was no other evidence,' asked Brian, 'linking it with the man from the fair?'

'None. This was before the days of DNA testing, remember.'

'Still,' said Brian, 'it's odd there weren't any fingerprints or anything like that.'

'Maybe, but that's the way it was,' said Gus flatly.

'Not even on the murder weapon,' said Brian.

Jenny was looking from one to the other with increasing puzzlement. 'What are you driving at?' she asked.

No doubt about it, Brian was deliberately provoking Gus. It had been a mistake to invite him to stay to supper. I was furious with him for his persistence. He said, 'Remember all the rumours, Carol? Most people around here were convinced someone from Grays committed the murder. They reckoned that story about the fairground worker was cobbled together to throw the police off track.'

'Oh, God,' said Gus with a groan, 'here we go again. Listen, Harriet was nine months pregnant by the time they got hold of Jago and did the identity parade. She was in no state to risk sending an innocent man for trial and she'd been trying to blot out the memory of what had happened. She believed that what you think about during pregnancy affects the way your child turns out, so she hardly wanted to screw her baby up with negative thoughts about psychotic strangers. She kept herself busy with plans for a new life in Australia. She avoided all contact with anyone connected with Grays or the murder. Besides, the police were in no doubt about who did it. They closed the case once Jago was dead.' Seeing Jenny's surprise, he explained, 'The man was killed in a knife fight about the time you were born. He must have tangled with someone who was better able to defend himself than Andrew had been.'

I thought that now surely Brian would let the matter drop, but he didn't. He said, 'The police never closed the case completely.'

Jenny's grey eyes were wide as she asked, 'Why did local people think it might have been someone from this house?'

'It wasn't just local people,' said Brian. 'The police thought so, too. They took Raymond Tucker in for questioning.'

'Routine,' said Gus impatiently. 'That was just routine. Everyone was questioned for days, but the fact is Harriet was there when Andrew was murdered and she saw the maniac who did it. And I saw him running away and I can assure you it wasn't Raymond.'

'But—'

'Oh, for Christ's sake, Brian,' Gus burst out, 'the police questioned your father, didn't they? Does that make him a suspect, too?'

This was news to me. 'Why did they question Brian's father?' I asked.

'Because he used to come up here sometimes to do odd jobs,' said Gus. 'He got into the habit of hanging around the place when he didn't have anything better to do. Somewhere like Grays Orchard attracts all sorts.'

Brian laughed. I was the only person there who knew the fury that lay behind Brian's easy-sounding laughter. 'That's not quite the way Dad used to tell it. He said this place couldn't have functioned properly without him. He said your lot always used to talk about being self-sufficient, but you could hardly bang a nail into the wall without ringing him up for advice.'

'That may be what he told your mother,' said Gus, 'but the truth was Jack loved coming up here. He was convinced this place was a festering heap of sex, drugs and rock 'n' roll and he was forever hanging around waiting for a piece of the action. I thought he was a bloody nuisance, frankly, but the others were more tolerant.'

I hadn't realised until that moment how intensely Gus and Brian disliked each other. Oh, I'd known they didn't have much in common and that they only made the effort to get along because of me, but they'd always managed to keep their antagonism under control. Now, suddenly, it was out in the open and they were snarling at each other like a couple of mastiffs. Gus was furious at Brian for dredging up the old rumours about Raymond, and Brian, for all his smiling calm, was equally angry at hearing his father disparaged. Brian's father had been the local drunk by the time he died of cirrhosis of the liver at forty-seven and he had caused endless trouble for Brian and his mother, but they still defended his memory fiercely.

Brian opened his mouth to retaliate, but I said swiftly, 'It must have been that boy from the fair, or the police would never have closed the case after he died. That's the worst thing about a murder, it stirs up such a pile of mud and everybody starts suspecting everybody else. Who wants some coffee?'

'None for me,' said Brian, but like the good friend he

was he took the hint. 'I ought to be getting back, anyway.'
He turned to Jenny. 'Can I give you a lift?'

She started to insist that she was perfectly capable of
driving herself, but then she must have realised how stupid
that was, or maybe she had identified Brian as a useful
source of information, because she agreed to let him drive
her back to the Travelodge.

When they'd left, and Gus and I were clearing up, I said
casually, 'You've never talked to me about the murder
before.'

'No,' said Gus, just as casually. 'No reason to go over
old ground. It's all dead and buried, thank God. No pun
intended.' Then he added with a smile, 'Nothing to do with
you and me, is it?'

And, like a fool, I believed him.

Chapter 3

The next morning, Saturday, Gus was up first. He brought me tea with a spray of cherry blossom beside the cup. From Gus, the gesture was both peace offering and apology, and that was fine by me.

Later, we lingered over breakfast. The kitchen is one of the glories of Grays Orchard and a triumph of neglect over improvement. Because of the strange history of the house, it has resolutely evaded being brought up to date. There's an ancient rough-tiled floor, the original vaulted ceiling with a variety of lethal-looking hooks, a fine old scrubbed-pine table in the middle and a temperamental solid-fuel cooker which expires on special occasions and threatens to burn the house down when it's not needed. There's not a fitted cupboard or laminated work surface in sight, but, once you're used to it, the whole thing works quite well, and it's the best place in the world in which to drink a lazy mug of Saturday-morning coffee.

The previous day's fog had almost cleared and the sun was breaking through, filling the kitchen with hazy light.

There was a jug of daffodils in the middle of the table, their petals glowing like yellow suns. I could see Gus eyeing them pensively. One of the drawbacks of living with a painter is that objects of beauty tend to vanish studiowards in the cause of art.

'Uh uh,' I warned him. 'Buy your own flowers. These stay here.'

He smiled across at me. 'I thought maybe I'd borrow them. Half an hour?'

'Twenty minutes, tops.' I attempted a smile, but it probably came out more of a grimace. Gus and I were both suffering the effects of our wine-fuelled evening, so although we were working hard to make this a normal Saturday morning our hangovers didn't help at all.

'Do you have to go in to work today?' he asked.

'I ought to do an hour or two some time over the weekend.'

'Tomorrow? I thought we could get away from here for a bit. Why don't we go and have lunch in Bath and—Oh!'

Jenny had slipped in through the back door; no car to announce her arrival and she hadn't knocked, either. Gus stiffened with annoyance, then made an effort to relax his face into a welcoming smile. I don't suppose either of us felt much like dealing with Jenny right then, but there wasn't any choice.

'Have you walked all the way from Sturford?' I asked, while Gus put the kettle on for fresh coffee.

'No, I got a lift to the bottom of your drive,' she said.

If Gus and I were feeling fragile, Jenny looked a hell of a lot worse. Her shoulders were hunched and miserable and there were dark shadows ringing her eyes. It was more than just a hangover. The poor girl looked as if she hadn't slept at all – I dare say the revelations over supper had not been conducive to a good night's sleep. The effect of all this was to make her look more than ever like the semi-human figure in Gus's portrait. He was staring at her in the impersonal way he has sometimes, as though he's seeing surfaces and colours and paint, rather than an individual human being, which didn't help matters at all.

I was sorry I'd let her go back to the Travelodge the previous evening, so I said, as brightly as I could, 'Why don't you come and stay here? You'd be very welcome and it would save you spending money at the Travelodge. Gus would like it, wouldn't you, Gus?'

'Yes.' But he was still regarding her like a rare specimen of butterfly. I hoped her sleepless night meant she was too numb to notice.

She looked at me warily, a tentative smile transforming her face. 'That's really kind of you, Carol,' she said, 'but I don't want to be any trouble.'

'No trouble at all,' I told her. 'We'd love to have you.'

'Oh well, in that case, I could get my stuff and be back in half an hour.'

'Maybe later,' said Gus firmly, before I had a chance to say yes, fine. 'Carol and I have to be in Bath today.'

The smile died on her face. Inwardly cursing Gus, I said, 'But we'll be back by late afternoon. Why don't you come over then?'

But it was already too late.

'Don't bother,' she said, sulkily. 'The Travelodge is fine and I like the freedom to come and go.'

Her face had crumpled with disappointment. 'What about lunch tomorrow?' I asked.

'Sorry.' She stuck her pointy little chin in the air to show she wasn't sorry at all. 'I can't make it tomorrow.'

I was exasperated. Between Gus's inexplicable coldness and Jenny's hypersensitivity, making her feel welcome was going to be an uphill struggle.

I said, 'Well, sit down and have some coffee now. We're

all a bit the worse for wear after last night. But at least the fog has lifted. It might brighten up this afternoon.'

She ignored me and turned to Gus in a purposeful way. 'I only came back to get the car and because I wanted to ask you about Raymond Tucker.'

'Raymond?' Gus made it seem as though this was an eccentric interest. 'Why do you want to know about him?'

'Brian says Raymond was always weird.'

'Really? Unfortunately Brian was an infant when Ray lived here so he was hardly in a position to judge.'

'But his reputation . . . And why did the police single Raymond out as a suspect?'

'Because they were a bunch of idiots, that's why.'

Jenny put her fingers to her forehead. She half closed her eyes and said, 'I can't get his picture out of my mind. You know, that one you did of him, *Gone to Atlantis*. All night, every time I shut my eyes, I saw him. Saw him killing my father. And he got away with it.'

Before Gus could fob her off again, I asked him, 'Did the police really think it was Raymond?'

Gus smiled. 'They called him a Paki bastard and yes, I'm sure they would have been delighted to pin the murder on him if they could have, but fortunately they didn't have a chance. You see, Raymond's mother was Persian and in 1976 the local police force was not the bastion of enlightenment it undoubtedly is today. So yes, they gave him a hard time.'

I hadn't known that, but it explained a lot. It explained his lustrous dark eyes and his exquisite, hawk-like features. Maybe it even explained the otherworldly quality Gus had conveyed in all his portraits of his friend. One picture was different from all the others. It showed Raymond sitting under a holly tree in the lotus position, hands laid on his knees, eyes closed. All around his head was a rainbow of strange shapes and colours. It was generally interpreted as a representation of an acid trip, but Gus had titled it simply *Raymond Meditates: Gone to Atlantis*.

Jenny said, 'According to Brian that wasn't the only reason the police targeted him. Apparently he'd been in a fight with Andrew Forester just a few days before the murder. Several people witnessed it.' I noticed she called him 'Andrew Forester' and not 'Dad' or 'my father'. It must be so awkward for her, trying to find out the truth, when even the language she used was fraught with problems. 'Brian says the witnesses thought they were arguing about Harriet. About my mum.'

'As far as I know, Andrew and Raymond were always the best of friends,' said Gus smoothly. Then he sighed and went on, 'Look, Jenny, Brian has obviously been recycling all the local gossip, but he's not doing you any favours, believe me. I can understand your curiosity. If I was in your shoes I'd probably feel the same. But it's a false trail, Jenny, don't go down it. Andrew's death was a terrible, random, pointless accident. Listen, I saw the man running away – not well enough to be certain who it was, but I'd have known if it was Ray. It was just a burglary that went horribly wrong and destroyed a life. Raymond was nowhere near Grays Orchard at the time – plenty of people saw him at the fair. Take it from me, Jenny, there's no mystery to uncover. You'll waste a lot of time and energy if you dwell any more on what Brian said.'

Gus has a deep and attractive voice. It's also, when he chooses, an extremely persuasive voice. I've seen gallery owners seduced into buying double the number of paintings they intended, and I've seen absolute strangers allow Gus to set up his easel in their garden when light falling in a certain way across a lawn or wall has made him slam on the car brakes and knock on unknown doors. Now Jenny was struggling against its seductive power.

She said, 'But why would people say those things if there wasn't any problem?'

'I know how it looks,' Gus agreed calmly. 'No smoke without fire, and all that. Whoever thought of that one didn't know Sturford. You've no idea how the rumour machine operates in a small place like this. It was inevitable they'd blame us for the disaster. As far as the locals were concerned we were just a bunch of no good hippie layabouts who spent all day and every day in an orgy of sex and drugs. Honestly, Jenny, their attitude was positively medieval. I'm surprised they didn't accuse Harriet of witchcraft every time one of their cows fell sick. Maybe they did. I wouldn't put it past them. So they were bound to think it was one of us. That justified all the sick little fantasies they'd been having about us right from the beginning. And of course they singled Raymond out for special hatred because he was foreign-looking and they didn't like foreigners. Anyone who knew Raymond will tell you he couldn't squash a fly, let alone kill someone. It isn't in his nature. You'd only have to spend half an hour with him and you'd know I'm right.'

Jenny remained pensive. 'Are you still in touch with each other? Does that mean you could arrange for me to meet him?'

'No, we lost contact years ago when Ray decided to transform himself into a guru. You must have heard of that group he and Pauline started, the Heirs of Akasha, they call it. All mad, of course, but probably harmless. Still, you can't go down the pub or swap dirty stories with a man who thinks he's the incarnation of the divine whose sole purpose on earth is to save mankind. Especially as he took a vow of silence and hasn't spoken in years. And he probably wouldn't take kindly to old friends turning up and reminding him of the very ordinary bloke he is underneath.'

'Don't you know any way I can meet him?'

'You don't want to, not unless you intend parting company with your intelligence and becoming one of their crazy members. But it's a false trail: there's nothing he can tell you about Andrew. Let it go, Jenny. Honestly, it's better that way.'

As I said, Gus can be very convincing when he tries and it looked as though he'd convinced Jenny. He'd convinced me, too – almost.

Jenny wrapped her bony fingers round the mug. She was still scowling. She changed tack and said bluntly, 'Why did you lose touch with my mother?'

'What?' Gus looked genuinely surprised.

'You were the only family she had and you should have stuck by her, not pushed off to America like you did.'

Gus sighed heavily. 'Sorry, Jenny, but you've got it all wrong. Harriet made it perfectly plain she wanted nothing to do with anything which reminded her of what had happened. She refused to see any of us, refused to have anything to do with this place. She just wanted to close the door on all of us. And you can understand why. I mean, it wasn't as though we'd grown up together so we weren't close the way brothers and sisters usually are. Anyway, she'd pushed off for a new life in Australia long before I left for the States.'

'You never wrote.'

'Nor did she. And no, I don't count those hideous Christmas circulars all about her new house and where she'd been for her holidays. If she'd wanted to be in touch with me, she'd have written a proper letter.'

'But she did!' Jenny burst out. 'She wrote to you a year ago, I know she did.'

'What?' I was amazed by this information. Gus had never said a word to me about hearing from his Australian sister.

'Maybe she did,' he shrugged it off. 'I honestly can't remember now. You see, the trouble is, it's too late. Our lives have gone in separate directions. There's simply no point in Harriet and me trying to cobble our friendship back together again now.' His voice remained calm, as deeply persuasive as it had been from the beginning, but his hands were shaking. I wondered if Jenny had noticed.

Probably not, because she was too incensed. 'How can you say that?' she blazed. 'She might have had a reason for getting in touch. Didn't you think of that?'

'She would have said.'

'Why? Maybe she thought she'd better test you out first to see if you could be trusted. Just as well, really. You didn't even bother to reply so she knew she was on her own again. Just like always.'

Gus said, 'Don't be melodramatic. Harriet's never been on her own. What about Ian?'

'That man's hopeless. All he cares about is money and material things. He doesn't understand any of the things Mum and I care about.' Suddenly, Jenny was on the verge of tears.

'What is it, Jenny?' I asked. 'Is Harriet in trouble? Does she need help?'

She rounded on me, her dark-ringed eyes furious. 'No! And if she did you'd be the last to know. Why can't you mind your own business? It's nothing to do with you.' She leaped to her feet, almost knocking the mug of coffee over on the table. 'All right, all right, I'm going. I don't know why I bothered to come. It's always the same old bullshit. No one's ever straight with me and I'm fucking tired of being lied to. I'm going to find that Tucker fellow. Maybe he's mad enough to tell me the truth.'

Gus was so relieved she was going he didn't bother arguing about Raymond any more, and nor did I. I don't think either of us really thought she'd take the trouble to seek out Raymond Tucker, which is a shame, looking back, because it wouldn't have taken much to throw her off the scent: a few soothing words from Gus, a few sympathetic questions about why Harriet had wanted to make contact. But, fools that we were, we missed the opportunity.

And paid for it, bitterly, later on.

'We'll go to Bath,' announced Gus after Jenny had left. 'Let's hit the shops.'

One of the great revelations in the early days with Gus had been his love of shopping. I'd assumed a well-respected painter would be far too high-minded to hang around shops, but he loved them. Most of all, he liked helping me find clothes. He was instantly critical of anything that fell short of his high standards, but lavish in his praise when an item was right, and his instinct was unerring.

So to Bath we went. A couple of times en route I floated a reference to Jenny along the lines of 'She must have been devastated to hear how her father died,' or 'I wonder if she'll turn up again,' but each time Gus just grunted or changed the subject. Nor did I ask him about the portrait of her. Maybe I should have insisted, but I was confused by everything that had happened, starting with that hideous picture, and I dreaded being fobbed off with half-truths the way I was certain Jenny had been. Better to hear nothing at all than to hear fictions. That was my reasoning, anyway. The downside was that the whole outing was brittle with false cheeriness, the way it always is when two people talk about everything except the one topic that's on both their minds.

After lunch at our favourite restaurant, Gus insisted on buying me a silvery dress that was backless – and practically sideless and frontless as well. With my brown hair and eyes and creamy skin I always used to favour the warm shades recommended for my colour type, but Gus saw it differently. Also, as a married woman, I would have minimised my long legs and warm-hearted-barmaid's ample bosom, but once again Gus had other ideas.

'The next private view we go to, you'll knock 'em dead,' he said appreciatively as I prowled barefoot round the shop and tried not to feel as if part of my dress had been left in the changing room. 'The pictures won't stand a chance.'

'You don't think it's tarty?' I stood sideways to the mirror and raised my arm, observing the curved shadow of my breast against the silver edge of the dress.

'No way,' he said, and the assistants all grinned the way they do when something is absolutely right.

It didn't stop there. Our haul included a jacket, two pairs of shoes and a handbag made from such soft leather that I kept holding it up to my cheek. And for Gus we bought a designer shirt and six pairs of Argyle socks. So it should have been fun, but it wasn't. We were both trying too hard, and the more we tried to establish our usual closeness, the further apart we seemed to be.

It was a relief to get back into the car with loud music playing so we didn't have to keep up the pretence any more. I was driving and Gus put on a tape, first a Bach cantata and then later, when we were on the home stretch, a Mamas and Papas tape I'd bought at a service station a few weeks ago because it reminded me of my primary school in Sturford. Our collection of music was always varied, but for once I didn't mind what was on the player, so long as it provided a wall of sound between me and Gus.

'Isn't that Brian's car?' The traffic had slowed by the time we reached the outskirts of Sturford. I followed the direction of Gus's gaze and caught sight of Brian's weekend car, a maroon Vauxhall saloon, heading back into town ahead of us. 'Looks like he's found a girlfriend,' said Gus, adding, 'About bloody time.'

We were gathering speed again. 'No,' I said, 'that was Jenny. How odd. I can't think they have much in common.' Brian's car had turned off ahead of us and was going down a side road. I wondered where he was taking her.

'Damn,' said Gus. 'I was hoping she'd push off.'

'Is it that bad having her around?'

'Of course it is. The girl's impossible.'

'Poor Jenny. This can't be easy for her.'

He grunted. 'I don't know why she came.'

'She's bound to be curious.' I hesitated, then, 'Does she remind you of Harriet?'

He didn't answer for a long time. I was afraid my question had offended him, but after a while he said thoughtfully, 'I suppose she must do. She looks more like Andrew.'

I thought of Andrew and his love of weapons. I could imagine Jenny happily toting a loaded six-shooter. Maybe her touchiness was hereditary.

Since my first question had gone down okay, I took a chance on another. 'How come you and Harriet never saw each other till you were grown up?'

'Separate families.' Gus answered easily. The music must have put him in a reminiscent mood. 'Harriet's about three years older than me. My father divorced her mother soon after she was born. Then he married my mother, but they split up when I was about seven. There was never any contact between the two families. He was a difficult man and after the second divorce he became a bit of a recluse.'

'So you and Harriet never saw each other until his funeral?'

'Hm?' He was smiling, humming along to the tape. 'No, I didn't get back in time for the funeral. I was in India, fresh out of art school and doing the backpacking thing with Raymond. Ray was searching for enlightenment. God knows what I was looking for, though I wouldn't have said

no to a bit of enlightenment if there'd been any on offer.'
To my amazement he was talking quite freely. 'We were
staying in some grotty ashram when I got the solicitor's
letter saying I was now joint owner of Grays Orchard with
this sister I'd never set eyes on before. It was weird. But
Ray and I had pretty well run out of money, so we saw the
letter as a sign we were supposed to carry on with our
spiritual journey. We actually believed all that crap in
those days – you know, the idea that certain things are
"meant" to happen. Very convenient, naturally. You'd
think we'd have got things a bit more into perspective after
six months surrounded by the teeming masses of the Indian
subcontinent, but we were hideously arrogant. As if the
deity was going to bother about the finances of a couple of
English backpackers!'

He smiled at the memory. I thought of mentioning the
sign I'd seen the day before, the one about giving all your
troubles to Jesus because He'll be up all night anyway, but
he talked about his early life so seldom that I didn't want
to interrupt the flow of his memories. All I said was 'You
came back to England?'

'That's right. Our plan was I'd come down to Sturford
and arrange for the house to be sold as quickly as possible.
Then Ray and I would head straight back to India and use
my money to finance the rest of our life-changing quest.'

'Is that when you met Harriet, then?'

He nodded. 'In the solicitor's office in Sturford. Hardly
the ideal spot for a first encounter with your long-lost
sibling.'

'What was that like?'

'Horribly embarrassing at first. Chalk and cheese. I
marked her down as a conventional horsey type who'd be
bundled up in tweed skirts and velvet headbands by the
time she was thirty. She must have thought I was a walking
disaster area. We'd probably have sold the house, divided

up the money and gone our separate ways if we hadn't
done a quick tour of Grays first.'

'What happened?'

'We said we wanted to look round the house. The
solicitor drove us out and insisted on showing us the place.
He was a bouncy little man, like someone out of Dickens.
It was May, and all the apple trees were in blossom – you
know how magical it can be. The whole place was awash
with white and pink and green. There'd been rain in the
morning, but by the time we got to the house it had
stopped. You can't imagine the impact of its incredible
Englishness after all those months in India.

'I think I must have been suffering from reverse culture
shock. Everything in England was so drab and grey and
solid and dull. India was full of the most hideous poverty,
but here it was a different kind of poverty: a lack of light
and colour and spirit. Then I came to Grays and the first
thing that struck me was how beautiful the house was, so
empty and huge and elegant. And while we were clumping
around in the upstairs rooms, the sun came out. That light
pouring through all the dust in those empty rooms was
incredible, like a Dutch still life. And all the time the
solicitor was banging on about estate agents and rates and
property values. Harriet and I didn't speak much: I think
by then we'd stopped trying to impress each other. And
then, suddenly, I knew exactly what was on her mind. It
was uncanny, as if her thoughts had got under my skin. It
made me uncomfortable.

'When we'd finished the tour and were starting to go
down the stairs, I said, "Hang on a minute," and I went
back to the top and sat on the highest part of the banister
and slid all the way down to the bottom. The solicitor
was squawking that it hadn't been tested for woodworm
and it wasn't strong enough, but Harriet was watching
me and I knew she was thinking exactly what I was: that

we ought to have been there together as kids, that our parents had denied us a whole precious part of our lives. I told the solicitor to give us the keys and we'd go round the orchards and the gardens on our own, then walk back to Sturford. He didn't like the idea, but he couldn't really argue. After all, it was ours. And when he'd gone we just ran out into the fresh air and across the lawn, like a couple of kids let out of school. And then we were in the orchard—'

He broke off. I waited a moment or two before asking gently, 'Was that when you made the decision to keep Grays?'

'Yes, of course, but it was more than that.'

'More?'

'I remember lying on the grass and looking up at the sky through all the branches and the blossom. I can't explain. It was as though I was seeing blueness and white for the first time in my life. It was what Ray and I had been searching for, all those months in India. And I'd found it in the last place I ever expected: my grandfather's house. An English orchard in May. Simple as that.'

'But that's incredible.'

'No, it wasn't,' he said ruefully. 'It was a delusion. I'd been hunting for some kind of revelation, so I persuaded myself I'd found one. It was probably just a combination of jet lag and hunger, plus excitement because I'd got some bricks and mortar to my name at last. Hardly a very spiritual emotion.'

'No, I meant that bit about the banisters. It's like the first time we met.'

He turned to me, his expression blank. 'Sorry, Carol, but I'm afraid I don't see the similarity.'

'Don't you remember?'

He smiled kindly. 'I do remember thinking you were a stunner, even in that dreadful air hostess outfit. I didn't know you were trying to look middle-aged and responsible so I'd sell you the house.'

'But you showed me round. And you were standing at the bottom of the stairs.'

'Was I? Are you sure we're thinking about the same occasion?'

I couldn't bring myself to answer. Every moment of my first visit to Grays was engraved on my mind because it was the first time Gus and I met. The Sturford grapevine had been saying Gus Ridley had returned from America. He'd bought out his sister's share of the property years before and now he was going to put Grays on the market. Brian and I had done our sums and decided to put in an offer right away. The house could be brought up to standard and sold on and the far orchard, the one that was already surrounded on three sides by development, was likely to get planning permission for six dwellings. It would mean a hefty loan from the bank, so it was bound to be risky, but if it came off the firm of Brewster and Dray would be financially rock solid for the first time. It was true I'd worn my sober, bank-manager-visiting suit, but that was to convince the mysterious absentee owner of Grays Orchard that I was a solid citizen in spite of being not yet thirty.

I'd been incredibly nervous. Every day, during secondary school, I'd seen Grays Orchard from the school bus and now, at last, I was going to meet its mysterious owner, who already had an aura of the exotic and unknown. Gus showed me round the house. Or rather, we'd explored it together, because he'd just driven down from London and hadn't been back to the place for nearly twenty years and the house had been shut up and empty for most of that time. There was lots of 'I wonder if this door is locked? No, here we go – God, another mausoleum for flies.' The tour had ended on the first floor, by which time Gus had fallen silent. Maybe the memories he'd been trying to keep at arm's length with his running commentary and banter had become overwhelming. I sensed that he needed a moment or two on his own, so I pretended I wanted to double-check the dimensions of one of the bedrooms. When I came out he'd vanished. I started going down the stairs, but then, just as he had done that first time he visited with Harriet, I went back to the top and perched on the banister. Given the staircase at Grays Orchard, it's not really such a coincidence. The stairs are one of the main features of the house: they sweep round in a long curve, and the dark wood banisters simply beg to be slid down. Just before I got to the bottom Gus stepped out of the drawing room and looked up at me with a great smile of recognition. He reached out his hands and caught mine, steadying me as my feet touched down on the wooden floor of the hall. That first moment of contact was more powerful than an electric shock. I think I must have fallen in love with him right then. What he felt exactly I don't know – I've never asked – but there must have been some attraction because within five minutes we'd arranged to meet for dinner that evening 'to talk over some of the details'. We were lovers by the end of the week and married a month later.

The car was bumping slowly down the long driveway between the orchards, bringing me back to the present. From the tape deck, Mama Cass reminded someone to say a prayer for her when they were far apart.

I said, 'That first time we went round the house and I slid down the banisters. Surely you remember?'

'Did you, darling? I haven't done it in years.'

We had reached the space between the side of the house and the apple loft and I brought the car to a halt. It was hard to believe he had forgotten an occasion that meant everything to me. I switched off the engine and the tape fell silent.

Gus sat beside me in the stationary car; the back seat was

heaped with carrier bags full of the things we'd bought together. I'd have happily traded them all for the knowledge that it was me he was thinking about now with that far-away expression in his eyes. There had been only one great love in Gus's life, before he met me.

I asked quietly, 'Did you already know Katie when you decided to come and live down here?'

'Katie?' He smiled, a smile so tender and affectionate that I felt the first stirrings of jealousy. 'Oh yes,' he said, 'I knew Katie all along.' I don't think I'd ever seen that expression in his eyes before, not that precise combination of remembered warmth and regret.

I said, 'Why did you and Katie split up? Was it because of the murder?'

It was like watching a light being extinguished. He said shortly, 'Not really. It was just one of those things.'

I'd never felt jealous in my life before, not like I did then. It was shocking, like a sudden injection of poison into my veins, a blinding flash of resentment and hate. His paintings of her paraded through my mind – *Katie Sunbathing, Katie in a Straw Hat, Being Katie* – and in each one she was more beautiful than before. I'd always been so sure that when he met and married me he'd found true love for the first time since he lost her, but now, horribly, I was filled with doubt.

Frowning, he got out of the car and walked towards the house. I had to force myself to follow. I told myself it was a stupid waste of time being jealous, especially of someone who'd stopped being part of his life nearly twenty-five years before, but I was finding that jealousy doesn't listen to reason.

Chapter 4

The site meeting had gone on for nearly an hour, everyone was cold, and tempers were wearing thin. Brian's face had that heavy-jawed, bulldog look he gets when he's preparing to dig in for a long siege, and Phil Reeves, our local planning officer, looked irritated enough to remember Clause F, subsection 81, paragraph 9, or some equally obscure bylaw no one else had ever heard of. As for Samantha Piper, whose dithering had caused most of the trouble in the first place, she seemed to be about to move her bathroom wall for the fifth time. I decided to step in and wrap business up for the day.

'Right then,' I announced, cheerful but firm. 'That covers everything. We'll carry the cost of the extra drainage your department requires, Phil. The original survey underestimated the problems on the lower ground, we're agreed on that. We'll have to charge you for moving your bathroom wall again, Mrs Piper, but we'll do it at cost. That means you stay within budget so long as the plans aren't altered again. Next time you come down you may even have a roof.' As the wind was whipping across the site, this ought to have been a cheering prospect.

'We-ell,' Samantha Piper began in her irritating nasal whine, her bright little eyes beady with suspicion. 'Can I have that in writing?'

There was a rumbling from Brian's throat, the sort of noise that is said to precede earthquakes. Before he could say anything about not bloody likely or over his dead body, I said loudly, 'Don't you worry, Mrs Piper. I'll keep a close eye on everything for you.' And I gave her my most reassuring, woman-to-woman smile. As I anticipated, that did the trick.

Ten minutes later we'd seen them both safely to their cars. When Brian began grumbling about blood and stones and women with too much time on their hands, I interrupted him: 'Is there time for the longer view?'

'Always time for that,' he said with a grin, his irritation falling away at once. 'Number three's the highest.'

I followed him up the ladders and scaffolding that had been erected around the half-built house. The first time we'd taken the longer view had been after my father's funeral. Brian had been working for our family company since he left school and was already the unofficial foreman on the new sites, but he was only twenty-three and had no real status in the company. Nor did I, unless you counted being the boss's daughter and being liable for his debts now he was dead. It was generally assumed the men would be laid off and contracts would be broken. My dad had stuck his neck out on that final job and it wasn't going well. Some people thought the worry was what caused his fatal heart attack at sixty-three, though others said he'd never got over my mother leaving the year I was due to go to university. It was probably a combination of the two, though I'd done my best to make up for my mother's absence and had stayed at home and played a larger part in the business than she had ever done. The solicitor was already muttering darkly about voluntary liquidation and our accountant looked more gloomy each time we met.

It was Brian who had suggested taking a look at the longer view that first afternoon. We climbed to the top of the only house of the group that was anywhere near completion, sat on the ridge of the roof and looked down on the cemetery where they'd just put my dad's ashes. Brian produced a quarter-bottle of brandy, and while we drank it he told me he was prepared to oversee completion of the work on the four houses if I could square it with the bank and keep track of the finances. I was so relieved not to have to lay anyone off that I told him I could do better than that: I'd help with the building as well. We finished the brandy and shook hands on the deal. A pair of magpies, flying close to the rooftop, squawked noisily at us, which we chose to interpret as a good omen.

A year later, Brian and I set up a formal partnership, in spite of all the doomsters who were still saying we were far too inexperienced to make it work. By then Brian was twenty-four and I was nearly thirty. People were beginning to regard us as a couple, which suited Brian fine. Because we were business partners, we were both cautious, with the result that we embarked on an old-fashioned kind of courtship: Brian took me out for meals and brought me flowers and occasionally we'd kiss and cuddle, but that was as far as it went. I think at the time I accepted our relationship was inevitable, yet held back. I still had hopes of travelling, doing something unexpected with my life, whereas once I settled with Brian my future would be entirely predictable. Then Gus Ridley came back to Grays Orchard and turned my life upside down.

Since then, Brian and I had always made the big decisions, or just talked over our worries, either on a roof or as near to one as we could get. We'd been clinging to a

chimney pot in a force-eight gale when we decided to buy
this piece of land on Gander Hill and build six decent
homes which local people could afford. Trouble was, local
people included women like Samantha Piper, who caused
problems whenever they could.

'There she goes,' said Brian, with some satisfaction,
when we were standing on the roof joists and watching her
small blue car heading towards Sturford. 'That woman's
done nothing but whinge since the day she signed up. I
can't stand her type.'

'She's unhappy. That's why she's making such a fuss.'

'And just how do you work that out?'

'She's desperate to start a family and she hasn't managed
to conceive yet. Underneath all that nit-picking and
aggression she's really just insecure. She also thinks her
husband might be having an affair.'

'Bully for him. When did she tell you that lot?'

'Oh, while you and Phil were doing the drains test. She
didn't tell me outright – she's far too proud – but it was
obvious from the way she talked.'

'Bloody hell, Carol. You can get someone's life story in
the time I take to watch water run downhill. We ought to
charge extra for the bleeding-hearts' service.'

'Our Mrs Piper would never pay.'

'She'd want it in writing.'

'She'd want a reduction.'

We both grinned. Brian's red-gold hair was beaded with
moisture and his eyebrows, always prominent, were
glistening. I leaned my forearms on the cross bars and
looked out towards Grays Orchard, still just visible
through the bare branches of spring.

I asked, 'How was your weekend?'

'All right.'

It was a standing joke that you could set your watch by
Brian's weekends. On Saturday mornings he went to the

supermarket and did the cleaning: he'd kept one in the first groups of houses we built and it still looked like a show house. Then he dropped his laundry over to his mother's. In the afternoon he played five-a-side football with a group of mates, followed by a drink at the Turk's Head. He went back to his mother's for dinner unless he was going out, in which case she cooked him Sunday lunch and gave him back his clean, crisply ironed laundry. I wondered how Jenny had fitted into this time-honoured routine.

I told him briefly about my trip to Bath with Gus. Normally, this would have prompted a reciprocal account of his activities, but not today. Since he'd obviously taken pity on Jenny and spent some time with her, I was curious about how they'd got on.

I said, 'I tried ringing Jenny at the Travelodge yesterday morning but they said she'd checked out. I suppose she must have gone back to London.'

Brian grunted. I'd suggested we take the longer view because I thought we'd be able to share our impressions of Gus's niece, but no doubt about it, he was definitely holding information back, which of course only fuelled my curiosity. I wondered what account she had given of the row over coffee on Saturday morning. Had she told him I was an interfering old cow, and was that why he refused to mention her?

I said, 'Oh, by the way, thanks for driving Jenny home on Friday.'

'That's okay.'

'She came over again on Saturday morning. She managed to pick a quarrel over nothing at all. This situation can't be easy for her, but all the same, she makes it hard for everyone.'

'Mm. She's got her troubles, that one.'

So how much had they talked? Brian's reluctance to confide in me was so unusual that I said, 'Why were you

winding Gus up on Friday night? You could see he didn't
want to talk about the murder.'

'I wasn't winding him up,' said Brian. 'I just thought
Jenny needed a bit of help finding out the truth about her
dad. And I guess I was curious, too. There've always been
so many loose ends about what happened.' He yawned. It
occurred to me he had the rumpled look of a man who's
been missing sleep in a good cause. He said, 'I thought
she'd like to talk to my mum about it. Mum's always been
fascinated by that murder.'

'Did you see Jenny again, then?'

He grinned. 'Go on, Carol. You and Gus saw us coming
back from football on Saturday afternoon.'

'I wasn't sure who it was.'

'No? What about all the leading questions?'

Annoyed, I said, 'I wouldn't have thought five-a-side
was Jenny's thing.'

'She enjoyed watching. Then we went for a drink and
then she came back to Mum's for supper and a video.
Black Narcissus. Mum always shows it to people on their
first visit – it's a kind of test – but I don't think Jenny cared
for it much. Do you want to know about Sunday?'

I wouldn't have minded knowing about the rest of
Saturday night, but Brian was enjoying himself too much
for me to admit it, so I said, 'It's none of my business.'

'I thought you might be curious.'

'No, not really.'

Brian just laughed and said he'd better get back to the
yard. I had to go over to Shorter's Barn, the conversion I
was working on with Walter, the oldest of our team.

As soon as Brian and I had parted I wished I'd come out
with it and asked him what was going on. For years I'd
been hoping he'd find a girlfriend, but the kind of woman
I had in mind was someone familiar, maybe someone a bit
like his mum, not an unknown quantity like Jenny. I drove

slowly to the barn, where old Walter was already hard at work and Sean, the lad we'd taken on a couple of months before, was skittering around the place like a clockwork toy and getting in the way.

Brian and Jenny were such an unlikely pairing that my imagination went into overdrive. Had I missed something on Friday evening? Had there been sparks of attraction zipping backwards and forwards across the kitchen table that I hadn't noticed? Did she fancy his earthy, dependable qualities, and was he drawn to her zany vulnerability?

Brian had kissed me only once. That was on the evening when he'd booked us a table at the steakhouse carvery to celebrate our purchase of Grays Orchard and I'd told him the deal was off because Gus Ridley was staying in Sturford after all. Brian had told me I was the only woman he'd ever really cared for and he hoped I might feel the same about him. I'd told him I was already in love with Gus Ridley. We spent the rest of the meal talking about other possible sites for building, then drove home in miserable silence. Just before he dropped me off, he kissed me. It felt like his final attempt to make me care more for him than for Gus. I didn't have to be psychic to know that kiss meant a hell of a lot to him, just as he must have known it meant nothing at all to me.

Remembering all that dammed up passion, I wondered if he'd kissed Jenny and how she'd responded. Did they have sex? It was only natural to be curious.

I told myself sternly that an afternoon standing in a windy field watching a handful of men kick a ball around, followed by *Black Narcissus* with Brian's mum, hardly sounded like the prelude to a night of steamy passion, but all the same . . . I told myself I was concerned for Brian and didn't want him to get hurt. I told myself it was nothing to do with me and I should forget all about it.

Which I did, more or less, that morning as I banged

hundreds of nails into the restored floorboards. The work was satisfying and exhausting. When we gutted the barn in the autumn we'd saved as many of the old oak boards as we could, trimmed them and sanded them and treated them for worm, and now each one was beautiful, a work of art in itself. We'd had to get in a few extras to make up for waste, but I'd tracked down some that nearly matched at an architectural salvage merchant, though their price had been outrageous. As I hammered the boards in place I vowed that if the purchasers of Shorter's Barn laid fitted carpets over my handiwork I'd come back and rip them up with my bare hands.

I decided to nip back to Grays Orchard for lunch. I usually did this once or twice each week, so I can't say there was any special reason for doing so that Monday. Gus had said he was going to set out all the pictures for his next exhibition and I was eager to see which ones he was choosing.

On the car radio, the soothing voice of the man from Classic FM was burbling about pension plans and old age. The road home passed along the edge of our lower orchard, where the apple trees were getting that fuzzy green look which meant the buds were swelling and the leaves would soon start to unfold. A few more days and the magic would begin. Jenny's visit had obviously stirred terrible memories for Gus, but spring at Grays Orchard was a healing time: in a few days we'd be as close again as we'd ever been.

It was a tricky patch of road. The traffic was speeding up for the fast stretch ahead, so one had to slow down and indicate well in advance before turning into the lane to the house. A metallic blue Saab had been riding on my bumper for the past half mile. I glanced in my mirror just as he pulled out to overtake.

'Go on, then,' I muttered, 'if you're in such a hurry.'

There was a scream of tyres and the Saab vanished from my rear-view mirror. Just as I was about to make the turn, a white hatchback rocketed out of the lane. It missed my front bumper by inches and careered into the thick of the traffic. Horns blared. A Transit van coming in the other direction was forced up on to the far verge and almost crashed on to its side.

'Jenny!'

She was hunched over the wheel of the hatchback. Her cheeks were white as chalk and her mouth was open. Shoulders pumping, she was sobbing. She must be blinded by tears.

'*Jenny!*'

Stupid to call out, but I did all the same. I had to stop her – someone had to stop her before she killed herself. 'Jenny, *stop*!' My voice blanked against the windscreen.

I was off the road now, all four wheels in the rutted lane leading to Grays. I slammed my foot down on the brake and looked round, terrified of what I'd see, but I was just in time to make out the light glinting off the rear window of her car as it wove through the traffic, then vanished from sight.

My hands gripped the steering wheel as I drove up the lane. The voice on the radio was still muttering about old age. I felt sick. That stupid, *stupid* girl – she'd nearly been killed. There might have been a horrendous pile-up with half a dozen people dead or maimed. She wasn't fit to drive: I had to stop her. But how? It was too late to turn around and try to follow, and the state she was in, chasing her would be a disaster.

What had happened? Had she and Gus rowed again? Or was it something she had done?

I was shaking when I got out of the car. The silence was profound. Ominous. I pushed open the back door but the kitchen was deserted.

'Gus?'

No reply.

I called through the house. 'Gus! Where are you?' Still no reply.

I hurried across the yard and up the stone steps leading to the door of the apple loft.

'Gus? Are you there?'

Silence.

I pushed the studio door open. 'Gus?' For a moment, I hesitated, afraid to go in. I took a deep breath and stepped inside.

He wasn't there. The shutters had been closed and it took my eyes a few moments to adjust to the gloom. Gus wasn't in any of his usual places, not at his easel or leaning over the table where his drawings were spread.

It was the ragged sound of an indrawn breath that guided me to the shadowy figure standing in the far corner of the room.

Only when I heard that sound did I realise how dark my fears had been. 'Oh, Gus!' My voice was shaking with relief. 'What's happened? I just saw Jenny driving like a maniac. Are you all right?'

He didn't answer, but turned slightly and moved towards the window.

I said, 'That idiot girl was nearly killed.'

'Look,' he said, his voice breaking on the single word, and he pulled back the shutters, flooding the room with light.

I looked. All the furniture in the room was just as it always was: chair, easel, chaise longue, canvases propped against the wall. And then I saw. Where once there had been paintings, now there were just spears of hard paint and canvas hanging in the still air. I took a step across the room and my foot crunched on broken glass.

'Oh, no!'

He was leaning against the wall, his arms hanging at his sides. Slowly he slid down until he was hunched in the corner. He gasped, as though someone had punched him in the stomach, and then he sobbed, dry, painful, racking sobs.

'Oh, Gus.' I crossed the room and knelt at his side. He turned and pressed his face into my shoulder. 'What happened? How could she?'

It didn't take me long to work out the sequence. All the paintings had been damaged beyond repair, but the one reduced to ribbons was the oil sketch of Jenny's naked torso emerging from that lurid flower. She must have lifted its covering when Gus was out of the room and been so shocked by its raw power that she'd attacked it. After that, she must have been possessed by a frenzy of destruction until she heard Gus. Then she would have fled down the steps to her car, leaving him to find what she had done. For a split second I was so angry with her I wished she had driven straight into that oncoming Transit and been killed. It would have served her right.

I looked around for the weapon, and caught sight of the orange handle of a Stanley knife lying near the foot of the easel. 'Excellent,' I said grimly. 'There'll be plenty of fingerprints for the police to work on.'

'Police?' It was only the second word Gus had uttered since I entered the room.

'I'll ring them now. That girl has to be stopped.'

Gus shook his head slowly from side to side, like a bull. 'No police.'

'It's for her own safety,' I told him. 'She needs help.'

'No.'

I wasn't going to argue with him, not then. Always, in a crisis, my instinct is to grasp hold of the familiar and that's what I tried to do now. I wanted to get Gus away from the wreckage of his work, but he wouldn't budge. His sobbing had eased; he shook off my attempts at comfort and stood up. For what seemed like hours he kept wandering round the room, picking up one canvas after another and fingering the frayed edges of their wounds. After a while I realised he was smiling. A little later, to my horror, he began to laugh.

'Gus, stop it. It's not funny.'

'No, of course not.' He didn't sound as though he agreed, but at least he stopped.

'Let's go in the house. I'll clear this up later. You're just torturing yourself.'

He turned to face me and his expression was luminous. He said quietly, 'You're free to leave, Carol. You know that, don't you?'

'It's too late to go back to work today. And anyway, I'm not leaving you here on your own.'

'That's not what I meant.' The quiet way he spoke was chilling, as though he was giving instructions to a stranger. 'I'm telling you to bale out now, before it's too late. You don't have to stay with me. You can go.'

'What are you talking about?' I was so shocked that I, in my turn, felt myself teetering on the brink of hysterical laughter.

Gus continued calmly, 'Or I'll leave if you want to stay here. I can always go back to New York. I'll think of something.'

'Gus, stop it, you're not making any sense. No one's leaving. You're in shock because of the pictures and—'

'No! You're missing the point. I don't care a damn about the pictures. I'm glad they've gone. They weren't any good, anyway. They were a hideous lie. Don't you see, Carol? I'm trying to protect you. It's over between us. I'm finished.'

'You mustn't say that.' The only way I could deal with this was to tell myself that he didn't know what he was saying, that he'd been temporarily unhinged by the loss of his pictures. I said, 'Please, Gus, come back to the house. Let me clear this up later.'

He was shaking. This time, when I put my arms round him, he didn't protest. I told him I wasn't planning on leaving him, not now, not ever, and I told him why. I could be strong enough for both of us, I knew that, and as I held him I willed my strength to pass across to him. I wasn't going to let Jenny's mad assault destroy my marriage as well as Gus's paintings.

Eventually, I coaxed him back to the house. Later, when he was resting, I went back and cleared the worst of the mess into plastic sacks. I told myself we'd face this horror together and maybe even end up closer than before, but I think even then I had my doubts. It was only natural that Gus should retreat into himself, but this was more serious.

Afterwards, as Gus slipped further and further away during the months that followed, I told myself it was because of the trauma of seeing his work destroyed. I told myself to give him time and everything would be just as it had always been. But deep down I think I must have known it was more than that, because his withdrawal had begun the moment Jenny got in touch. The gulf opening between us was only partly because of the pictures, and much, much more to do with Harriet and those other friends who'd been so close when they shared the house, but who had been excised from his life since that summer, which remained for ever out of my reach.

Chapter 5

The shock waves from the loss of Gus's paintings reverberated through the next few weeks. There were practical things to be done, like clearing away all the mess and letting the gallery owner know the show was cancelled, which reminded me of the whole sad business of clearing out cupboards and dealing with undertakers and solicitors after my father's death. It would have been easier if Gus and I had grieved together, but his response was so different from mine that we seemed to move further and further apart. I couldn't understand his lack of anger with Jenny. Each time I suggested trying to track her down, maybe even reporting her missing, he insisted, 'No police. We don't want them involved. What's done is done.' Finally I lost my cool. 'Terrific!' I stormed. 'Why don't we send the bitch a medal and be done with it?' He didn't bother to answer, just shrugged and disappeared back to his studio.

My anger had nowhere to go. Even moaning to his friends was impossible because Gus had made me promise, on the day Jenny left, not to tell anyone what had happened. As far as he was concerned it was a private matter, and however badly Jenny had behaved she was still his sister's only child and he had a duty to protect her. He said there was nothing to be gained from all the publicity that would follow. The pictures were gone and hounding Jenny wouldn't bring them back. Because he was still in shock that day I gave my promise, but I regretted it afterwards. I couldn't even complain to Brian, and it galled me to think he might still regard Jenny as a tragic little victim whereas in fact she'd proved herself to be a raging she-devil.

After that day, the shutters came down. There was no repeat of his extraordinary outburst in the studio. If I tried to get him to talk he became formal and correct, as he had been with Jenny, letting me know in no uncertain terms that the topic was closed, just as all talk of Andrew's death had always been off-limits in the past. My own feelings about Jenny were hopelessly tangled. Part of the time I fantasised about forcing her to face up to the damage she'd done, or simply venting my frustration by yelling at her for a bit. But sometimes I felt bad about her, too.

When she turned up at Grays Orchard I had realised the situation was awkward for her and I'd done my best to make her welcome, but obviously I'd underestimated the strain she was under, or how vulnerable she was. The destruction of Gus's paintings was an act of infantile rage, and right now, in my opinion, the girl needed help. At the very least we ought to contact someone who knew her and make them aware of the situation, but each time I suggested doing so Gus rejected the idea outright and retreated still further into his shell. I told myself ruefully that at this rate he'd soon be spending the nights in his studio, too.

A week later, he did just that.

*

The stranger must have been shouting, but I hadn't heard him above the noise of the machinery. A flicker of movement to my left caught my attention. I released the trigger bar on the chainsaw and laid it down, then removed my goggles. There was a humming in my ears as I shook out my hair.

'Hi, there,' I said.

'Hi. I'm looking for Gus Ridley.' The Aussie twang to his voice suggested this visit was something to do with Jenny and I was interested at once.

'I expect he's in his studio. I'll show you where it is. I'm Carol, by the way.'

'Pleased to meet you, Carol. I'm Ian, Jen's dad.' My guess had been right. He said, 'Hope I'm not disturbing you. I tried the house but there wasn't anyone there.'

'That's okay. I'm glad of the excuse to stop for a bit.'

It was a fine, windy Saturday in May, about six weeks after Jenny's visit, and I was taking the opportunity to pollard some of the willows behind the pond at the end of the garden. It was a job that should have been done in the winter, but was more enjoyable now when the hedge was waist-deep in white parasols of cow parsley. Besides, I was running out of tasks at Grays Orchard to take my mind off my loneliness. If Gus carried on blocking me out much longer, we'd be able to enter for Best Kept Garden in Sturford.

As we walked across the lawn towards the house, I asked, 'How's Jenny?'

'We-ell . . . that's why I'm here.'

'She's not in trouble, is she?'

'That's hard to say, exactly. Let's just say she's giving us cause for concern.'

He didn't elaborate and I guessed he wanted to keep his news for Gus. He said, 'Nice place you've got here, Carol.'

'Yes, isn't it.'

'Grays Orchard. My wife used to live here, you know. She still talks about it sometimes. I always wondered what it was like.'

Harriet. I was trying to imagine what Harriet, the handsome woman Gus had painted so often, had seen in Ian Sayer. Jenny had spoken his name with contempt, but I'd put that down to her mixed-up bitterness; now I wasn't so sure. My first impression was that he was the kind of man you want to edge away from. He must have been in his early fifties, with thinning black hair and a coppery tan. He had long thin eyes and a long thin mouth. There was something distinctly reptilian about that wide, almost lipless smile; you half expected to see the legs of a stick insect dangling over his chin.

I said, 'You're seeing it at its best. It was foggy when Jenny visited.'

'Poor old Jen. Never has much luck, that girl.' He grinned as he spoke, but his eyes remained watchful. He was sizing me up and it made me uncomfortable.

I led him into the kitchen and offered him a chair while I went to fetch Gus, but no sooner had he sat down than he bobbed up again, shoes squeaking. 'Gus is in his studio? Hat told me he was some kind of an artist.' He pronounced her name 'Het' and it was a couple of seconds before I realised he was referring to Harriet. 'Still at it, eh? I'll come with you. I've never seen a real artist's studio before.'

'Maybe he'll show you round later. He doesn't like visitors when he's working.'

'He won't mind me,' said Ian, his thin lips smiling while his eyes observed me coolly. I got the impression he was acting a part. 'I've been house-trained for at least six weeks.' The odd barking noise he made after this statement showed it was intended as a joke. He followed close on my heels as I crossed the yard and went up the steps to the studio.

As a matter of fact Gus did mind, he minded very much indeed, not that Ian Sayer let on that he noticed. No sooner had I introduced them than Ian began prowling round the studio, picking things up at random and setting them down again.

'Good to meet you, Gus, after all these years. Still painting, are you? Hat told me you used to be pretty successful at it. Where are all the pictures, then? I thought you'd have them all on display.'

'I sell through a gallery in London.'

'You do?' Ian raised his eyebrows. 'Don't you sell direct when you can? Always cut out the middle man, that's my belief. I might take one back to Hat as a surprise. D'you have any of this place?'

'No.'

'Shame.' Ian turned away, plucked a brush from a jar and smoothed it against the back of his hand before replacing it upside-down. Gus shot me a look, as if to ask how I could inflict this man on him, and I said, 'Shall we go back to the kitchen? I'll make some tea.'

'This is fascinating,' said Ian. 'Are you sure you haven't got any paintings tucked away?' He reached down and pulled a piece of board out from behind the easel. There was a dark spiral sketched on it. He raised it to his nose and sniffed. 'Paint's still fresh. Hm. A bit abstract for my taste, but Hat might like it. What does something like this go for?'

'It's just a sketch. It's not for sale.'

'Don't be coy, Gus. Everything has its price, isn't that right? What do you want for it? Couple of hundred? Can't have taken you more than an hour or so. Three hundred? Go on, Gus, that's not bad for an afternoon's work.'

Gus stepped forward, removed the canvas from Ian's hand and tossed it angrily into a corner. 'I told you, it's not for sale. If I thought Harriet wanted one of my paintings

I'd give it to her, but she'd hate it. You know she would. Now, how about tea?'

'Okay, a nice English cuppa will do me fine. Mind you, I only flew in from Melbourne this morning and I'll probably start nodding off in a couple of hours. Just point me at one of your spare beds. You must have plenty of those in a place this size.'

Gus looked appalled at the prospect of his new-found brother-in-law still being around at the end of the day.

'Nice place you've got here,' Ian continued as we all trooped down the steps and across the courtyard. 'How many bedrooms are there? And only the two of you living here. Six, eh? Each with bathroom en suite, I presume. Oh well, can't be helped. It's going to cost you a bit to bring it up to standard, isn't it?'

'We like it how it is,' said Gus stiffly and Ian's eyes narrowed still further. I could see him pigeon-holing Gus as a typical uptight Brit, but the next moment he had burst into a roar of laughter.

'That could've been Hat speaking! Except she never does like things the way they are. Between you and me, she's a bit of a moaner, that sister of yours, Gus. Never happy with what she's got.'

Gus was beginning to look as if homicide was the only solution. 'Ian's worried about Jenny,' I said swiftly as I put the kettle on the stove. 'She's in some kind of trouble.'

'That's right,' said Ian. He watched me as I removed the canvas jacket I'd put on to work outside, revealing my white T-shirt and jeans. He glanced at Gus, then back at me. I knew that expression, had seen it on the faces of Gus's middle-aged friends when they met me for the first time. It was a mixture of admiration and envy and disapproval and lust all rolled into one. I still hadn't quite got used to it.

Gus said, 'What's the problem?'

'Jen's the problem, if you want my opinion. Not that anyone asks me. She's been hard work from the beginning. I mean, I raised her as if she was my own. That girl's always had the best of everything, but she's got a contrary streak. Nothing's ever right for her. To be honest with you – no sugar for me, thanks – I heaved a sigh of relief when she said she was going to try her luck in London for a while. Thought she was finally off our hands and about time. Then we heard she was coming down here to see you, Gus. Can't say Hat was thrilled about that, but I thought, great, let the rest of the family deal with her for a while. Then the next thing we hear the bloody stupid girl's gone off and joined this lunatic cult—'

'What?'

'That's right. The Heirs of bloody Akasha, would you believe. You must have heard of them, Gus, they're run by an old mate of yours.'

'Yes, I've heard of them.'

'You have?' Ian's voice was affable enough, but he was subjecting Gus to the same calculating stare he'd given me. You didn't have to be clairvoyant to sense the hostility behind his words. I wondered if Gus had played a part in his marriage, just as Harriet and the other members of the Grays community had played a part in mine, even though I'd never met any of them. 'Nice company you and Hat used to keep, I must say. I suppose you know this Tucker character is a crook – just in it for what he can get. Still, if it was up to me I'd let the girl find out the hard way what the crazies are up to, but Hat doesn't see it quite like that. Mother love and all that, though she's never been exactly what you'd call the maternal type.'

'How long has Jenny been with them?' I asked. Though Gus never liked to talk about Ray and Pauline, I'd heard about the Heirs of Akasha. Everyone in Sturford had.

'About a month,' he told me.

'Have you had any contact with her?'

'Not directly. She stayed with a friend in London before she joined up and the friend, bless her, was worried enough to get in touch with us. God only knows what Jen thinks she's playing at. If you ask me, it's just a wind-up, but Hat is determined to get her back. She's been on at me all the time, so of course I said I'd give it a try, but the fact is I'm only here for a week and this is the only slot I've got free in my entire schedule. So I thought, what about her good old Uncle Gus? I'm sure he'd be delighted to help out for a change.'

Gus stared at him incredulously. 'You expect me to go and track Jenny down and show her the error of her ways?'

'Well, put it like that and it does seem a bit far-fetched, but you stand a better chance than I do. The last time Jen listened to anything I told her, she still had a brace on her teeth. I reckon if I went near the place she'd sign up for life membership just to spite me. And you never know, Gus. She might listen to you. After all, you're family and families need to help each other out when the going gets tough, don't you agree?'

Gus asked, 'Did Harriet ask you to come?'

'Christ, no. And I'd rather she didn't hear about this, either. This is strictly between you and me. Hat's still a bit touchy on the subject of her little brother. She'd go ballistic if she knew I'd come to see you. Not that she doesn't want to see you, but I think she wants you to make the first move. There's no guarantee you'd get much encouragement, though. She's always been a bit of a female spider, that one, but of course she'd got worse since she was ill.'

'Harriet's ill?' I asked. 'It's not serious, I hope.'

'Bad enough,' he said quietly, and suddenly I knew he was being sincere. 'The poor old girl first got cancer about three years ago. She had all the treatment and for a few months she was fine, but now it's back again. The quacks are full of plans but Hat won't play any more. Can't say I blame her, though it's hard not to be able to do anything at all.' His eyes filled with tears. 'She wants to do it her way, like the song. Typical Hat. But now they're talking months, not years.'

'But that's terrible!' Horrified, I turned to see how Gus had taken this news of his sister's illness. He'd just put the milk away and was standing by the fridge, cradling his mug of tea in his hands. He was staring at a patch of floor just in front of his feet and he was smiling. For a moment I was even more appalled – how could he take this news so calmly? – but then I realised he must have known all along. Jenny must have told him when she came, but he hadn't bothered to pass the information on to me. Ian, his narrow eyes flicking back and forth between us, was piecing this together at the same time. I felt humiliated by my public ignorance, but why should I be surprised? When had Gus ever confided in me the matters that affected him most deeply?

'Poor Harriet,' he said quietly. 'I didn't realise it was as bad as all that.'

'Jen must have down-played it all. Typical. Of course, it doesn't look good, her running off and leaving her ma all alone just when she needs her. That's why I'm counting on you, Gus, to make the girl see some sense. Hat wants her home.'

'I don't suppose Jenny would listen to me any more than to you. Why the hell has she joined Ray's group?' He was thoughtful for a moment, as we both silently supplied the answer. I remembered her anguished, sleepless face that last morning we'd seen her: if we wouldn't tell her straight, she'd go and find Raymond, the man whose name had been liked with her father's death. A stupid thing to do. Or maybe it was just desperate.

Gus must have been thinking along the same lines,

because he said, without much conviction, 'I shouldn't worry about it, if I were you. From what I saw of Jenny she's headstrong but she's not stupid. She's only gone along to that group because she was curious about Tucker. She'll get bored with it when she's seen enough, and then she'll quit.'

'If she can, Gus. If she can. You know what those groups are like once they get their claws into you. Leaving's not that easy, I'm afraid. I've looked them up on the Net and it doesn't make pretty reading.'

'She'll sort it out for herself. Just give her time.'

'That's why I'm here: time is what we don't have. Hat's getting worse every day. And obviously the worry over Jenny doesn't help. Hat's pining for her, that's part of the problem. And if you want to know what I think, I think she's pining for her home, too. She far too proud to admit it, but she wants to be back in this country, with her family. She often talks about this place, you know. All the happy times you had here together.'

'Does she really?'

Ian had missed the scepticism in Gus's voice. 'Oh yes, talks about it all the time. Happiest days of her life. I think what she'd like best is to come back here, be among her family again. In this house. She's often said this is where she really belongs.'

Gus didn't respond; he was gazing at Ian as though he only half believed him.

I said, 'Do you know where Jenny is? The Heirs have centres in more than one country, don't they?'

'That's right. UK, Spain and Mexico. We have reason to believe she's still in this country, but of course they could move her if they got suspicious. That's another reason why it's best for me not to get involved directly. Don't want her going to ground, if you know what I mean. The last time she got in touch with Mike she was still in Cornwall.'

'Who is Mike?' I asked.

'Our investments man.' Ian was cheerful again. Sick wives and straying children were foreign territory but investments was a topic he was at home with. 'Like I said, Jen's never wanted for anything and I brought her up like my own child, so she came into quite a bit of money when she was twenty-one and there's more tied up in trusts. Obviously your friend Tucker is keen to get his grubby paws on it. The stupid girl's been trying to get the funds released so she can hand it over to the group and become a full member a.s.a.p. Mike's a good mate of mine and he's been delaying all he can, but legally the money's hers and he'll have to release it soon. I hate to think of all that lovely money going to a bunch of fruitcakes.'

Gus promised he'd consider how he could help and they exchanged phone numbers. When Ian still showed no sign of leaving an hour later, Gus told him that we were due to go out that evening, otherwise Ian would of course have been more than welcome to join us at Grays. I backed him up by glancing at my watch and saying I ought to go and change.

Gus stood beside me on the gravel outside the house and we waved together as he drove off in his hired BMW. In his rear-view mirror, we must have looked the picture of a happy couple. It was odd, I thought, that our first solidarity in weeks had come from a shared lie. As soon as the car was out of sight, Gus moved away from me and said bitterly, 'He wants to dump her.'

'Jenny?'

'No, Harriet. He's tired of being lumbered with a sick wife and he wants to pack her off back to the old country for her family to care for. He knows Jenny won't listen to me any more than she does to him – that was just an excuse to come down here. And that's why he doesn't want Harriet to know. What a creep. Christ, she always had an odd choice in men, but that one is the worst of the lot. "*Hat*" – how does she stand him?'

And with that he retreated, as always, to his studio.

I've never been all that good at doing nothing. If there's a problem, I'll pitch in and find a way to get it sorted, or at least have a damn good try. That's how I came to be involved in my dad's business while I was still at school. Come to think of it, that's probably the reason I was running it still. Right now, my life had got snarled up in a whole tangle of problems, most of them other people's, but they were affecting me, all the same.

If I'd thought Gus was remote before Ian's visit, he got worse afterwards. He actively pushed me away. I got the impression that if I'd told him I'd had enough and was leaving, he'd have helped me pack my bags. Luckily, I've got a stubborn streak and didn't plan to give up on him so easily. I tried to be sympathetic – after all, it's grim being told your sister only has months to live, even if you haven't seen each other in years, and on top of that he'd just seen three years' work destroyed – but when my sympathy was rebuffed, I tried to find another way round the problem.

Jenny was the key to it. All the problems between me and Gus had begun when she turned up, but I didn't feel so angry with her any more. After meeting Ian, I felt sorry for her. His sympathy for Harriet had been genuine enough, but there'd been no hint of tenderness when he spoke about his daughter. He might have lavished trust funds and material goods on Jenny, but it was hard to imagine he'd ever been loving. Maybe that was why she'd invested such hopes in the meeting with her uncle, and reacted so hysterically when it seemed to be going wrong. Poor Jenny, she must be one of those unfortunate people whose efforts to improve their situation only make matters worse, like throwing herself into the arms of the Heirs of Akasha when her reunion with her uncle went sour.

Still, of the three it was Harriet, whom I'd never even met, that my heart went out to. Bad enough to be ill, but to be alienated from your only child and unable to reach her, that made it tragic.

'Brian,' I asked one afternoon, when we were at Gander Hill marking out the ground for the landscape team to start work the next day, 'how much do you know about the Heirs of Akasha?'

He shot me a look. 'Not much. Why do you ask?'

I told him briefly about Ian's visit and what he'd said about Jenny's involvement with the group. 'Gus thinks she joined because she was curious about Raymond Tucker. Ian wants Gus to go and rescue her.'

'Does he now? And what makes him so sure she wants rescuing?'

'It's for her mother, mostly. She's really ill.' I told him the little I knew about Harriet's illness. 'Can you imagine how Jenny would feel if Harriet died before they were reconciled?'

'Gutted, obviously, but isn't that her decision?'

'Not if she's being brainwashed.'

'I'd like to see anyone try to brainwash Jenny,' and he smiled. It was a smile of genuine admiration and I wondered if during that weekend they'd spent together, the weekend that Brian still hadn't told me about, Jenny had made more of an impression on him than I imagined. He said firmly, 'That girl's well able to look after herself. What about this boulder? Can we make a feature of it, do you think? Or does it have to be moved?'

'Why not try it on its other side? Here, I'll give you a hand.' Between us, we shoved and pushed to get it in the right place. 'It might inspire them to put in a rockery,' I said. The only time, these days, that all my worries seemed bearable was when I was working alongside Brian.

When it was in position he said, 'You've got that look about you, Carol. What are you planning?'

'I thought I should find out a bit more about the group first. Maybe go to one of their public meetings.'

He looked doubtful. 'If I was you, I'd stay out of it. You don't know Jenny and you've no idea what goes on in that family.'

'It's my family too, remember. And I can't see the harm in just going to a meeting. I've looked the Heirs of Akasha up on the Net and it's all mad stuff about the end of the world and Atlantis. It can't be good for Jenny to be mixed up in all of that.'

'It won't do her any harm.'

'You don't believe that rubbish, do you?'

'Of course not, but I don't believe in any religions. It's just fairy stories. But that doesn't mean I want to go and drag people out of the churches and the mosques and tell them how wrong they are. If it makes them happy, that's fine by me. There, how's that?' He planted his foot firmly on the boulder, in the pose of a mountaineer who's just reached the summit, and turned to me with a grin.

I noticed then that Brian was changing. His face had grown harder, leaner, over the past months. No longer the lad who'd worked for my father since leaving school and then lavished his unspoken puppy love on me for years, but a man, purposeful and confident and, it struck me now, surprisingly good-looking.

Chapter 6

Summer had been late to arrive but by mid-August it was making up for lost time. In London the Underground was stifling; after half an hour in a hot, smelly train I emerged feeling sick and sweaty. As I walked along the litter-strewn street my heart was thumping and I was tempted to go into a café and have a cooling drink before launching into the unknown. It had been difficult to find a way of making contact with the Heirs of Akasha: if mass recruitment was what they wanted, they had a lot to learn. A couple of days before, I'd found a notice on the Internet about a public meeting in Ealing. Even though it was such short notice it was too good an opportunity to miss, but I hadn't the slightest idea what to expect. I remembered all the rumours about weird cults using brainwashing and turning people into zombies. I began to examine the others walking down the street in the same direction and to wonder if they were also going to the meeting.

Big mistake. The street was full of truly miserable-looking people. There's nothing like a failing marriage to make you acutely sensitive to the unhappiness of others. Ahead of me an overweight boy with greasy hair was trudging down the street on his own while a gaggle of lads about his age larked about outside a newsagent's. I saw the wistful way the fat boy glanced across at them before looking back at his feet and plodding on. His loneliness hurt.

Don't be stupid, I told myself. You can't do anything for him, but you might be able to help Harriet and her family.

Added to which was the hope that by helping them I might do something to sort my own problems out. There had to be a solution to all this misery – and anyway, I was curious.

I crossed the road to walk in the shade, past a couple of DIY shops and tacky furniture depots. Where the row of shops petered out I found the house I was looking for: a red-brick semi with only a narrow alleyway separating it from the house next door. A dusty hydrangea with flowers like pink candyfloss took up almost the whole of the front garden.

The door was open and a handwritten note taped to the glass read: '*Heirs of Akasha: first floor*'. I hesitated. A headache was beginning to nag. Behind me the garden gate creaked and an elderly man brushed past the hydrangea to join me on the threshold.

'Is this the place for the meeting?' he asked.

'Yes.'

We went in together.

The house had been divided into two flats. The stairway was shabby and the white paint on the banisters had long ago gone grey with a thick layer of London grime. From the first floor came the murmur of voices.

At the top of the stairs a large woman in her sixties with hennaed hair and a brown silk shirt darkly blotched with sweat was registering arrivals.

'Hello, my name is Maureen.' Her amber necklace bounced on her bosom as she spoke. 'Just sign your name here . . . and your address. That's splendid. Necessary for the records. And if you'd just write your name on this badge and pin it where it can be seen . . . brilliant. Now we all know who's who. Do go in and make yourself comfortable. Find a chair and . . . Good evening' (this to the elderly man, who had climbed the stairs slowly behind me). 'My name is Maureen. Just sign your name here . . .'

Her welcome brought back a vivid memory of children's parties and I half expected her to give me a balloon. Resisting the urge to rip off my badge and run back down the stairs I went through the open door.

I don't know what I'd been expecting – the para-phernalia for a black mass, probably; at the very least some incense and mystic symbols – but it certainly wasn't this ordinary living room full of ordinary-looking people. No signs of occult strangeness anywhere. The walls were an unexciting magnolia and the furniture had been pushed to the sides to make room for a circle of assorted chairs.

About a dozen people were already seated. As I sat down on a green plastic garden chair and shifted it a few inches back from the circle, I looked round at them quickly. Apart from a couple of Japanese girls on my right who were chattering quietly to each other, everyone seemed to have come alone, like me. My unhappiness sensor was working overtime. The anxious anticipation and embarrassment were so potent you could almost taste them.

From the street outside came the roar of traffic. A fan was whirring on a low table in front of the mantelpiece. It was very hot.

I glanced down at my badge. It was covered in strange squiggles of green and gold and underneath the space where I'd printed my name there was written in phony Celtic script the single word 'Quester'. I felt as though just by wearing it I'd declared my approval of the group. I had hoped to remain a detached observer and slip away before things got heavy, but obviously it wasn't going to be that simple. There was worse to come.

Eight more people came into the room, looked around awkwardly, then found themselves an empty chair and sat down. Several, like me, shifted a little way back from the circle as they did so. Hardly anyone spoke and most people avoided making eye contact.

Then we heard a female voice downstairs say briskly, 'It's gone seven. We might as well begin.' There were light footsteps on the stairs and two women came into the room and closed the door behind them.

They couldn't have been more different. The older one must have been about fifty. She was short and dumpy, with squashed-looking features and brown hair in neat curls like an old-fashioned perm. She looked practical and down-to-earth, the kind of person who instantly gets heaped with responsibility and does all the work, complaining only occasionally.

The other woman was about my age. She was tall and regal, her skin the colour of caramel, her black hair tightly curled and spangled with beads. She had high Asiatic cheekbones and eyes like dark almonds and she walked with flowing grace. Both women wore long robes of watery blue silk: on the older woman they were lumpy and shapeless as an old dressing gown, but on the other they were robes of state.

The Questers sat up straighter in anticipation as the women took their positions with a rustle of cool silk in front of two chairs placed like thrones before the fireplace. The older woman was carrying a large board. She lifted the fan on to the floor and placed the board on the table, displaying a computer-enhanced photograph of Raymond Tucker. He looked a good deal older than he'd done in

Gus's *Gone to Atlantis* portrait, even though someone had been busy with an airbrush. His head and shoulders were surrounded by a sunburst of golden light with a vivid rainbow arching above. His deep black eyes gazed out of the portrait with a knowing smile. I wondered if this made anyone else want to giggle.

The tall, beautiful woman sat down on her high-backed chair and stared up at the ceiling while the older woman looked around the circle and began to speak. 'Good evening, Questers. My name is Palu and together with my colleague Serafa we'll give you a brief introduction to the Heirs of Akasha.' She had a flat voice with a strong Midlands accent. 'First of all Serafa will explain the background to our movement, then there'll be an opportunity for each of you to say a bit about yourself. We're especially interested to hear what each Quester can offer our group in terms of skill and experience. Then I'll cover some of the practical questions you may have about our work, after which there'll be a brief question-and-answer session. Then there'll be a short break for tea and biscuits while Serafa and I decide on each person's status category within the group. We should be finished about nine if anyone is worried about late trains. Right, over to you, Serafa.'

My palms were sweating. It had never occurred to me that I'd have to speak. How was I going to convince them I was a genuine Quester? And if I succeeded, would that mean being hounded for months to join their crazy group?

As Serafa was about to start there was a commotion by the door. She sat down again with a frown of irritation. A late arrival was squeezing past Maureen, who'd placed her chair in front of the door. She bounced up at once to allow him to come in, then tiptoed round the back of the circle to guide the newcomer to one of the few remaining chairs, a rickety-looking pine ladderback. The young man gestured his thanks and sat down.

There was a ripple of interest among the group. The latecomer must have been about thirty; he had a clean-cut, handsome face with eyes of clearest blue and a shock of fair hair which flopped engagingly over his forehead. Most of the other men in the room looked like misfits, but he had the air of a man completely at home in the world, not seeking a way to escape it. In fact, he looked as though he'd stepped out of the pages of a catalogue, confident and well-dressed. I've never been attracted by that kind of immaculate appearance, but he certainly was good-looking. He was seated across the circle from me. His cool blue eyes met mine for an instant and narrowed slightly, as though he recognised that, like him, I didn't belong in this group of weirdos. I looked away quickly.

Serafa waited until all was quiet again before she rose from her seat and stood, imperious and beautiful, before us. She looked slowly at each person in the room, and then said slowly, 'Pay attention, all of you. The countdown has begun. We are passing through the nightmare of our world. Mankind has no weapons to avert the catastrophe that approaches.' She paused, allowing her words to sink in. Her voice was low and melodious, more like a chant than a normal speaking voice. In spite of the doom of her message, there was no urgency in her delivery, which paradoxically only made her words more chilling. She went on, 'The signs are all around us. Listen to the radio, watch the evening news: everywhere there is disaster. Misguided scientists call it global warming, but they mistake the symptoms for the disease. Our beautiful planet is rising in revolt against mankind: tidal waves and floods, earthquakes and hurricanes, all on a scale never before seen on Earth, bush fires raging out of control and the ice-caps melting. Every year there are new diseases, new plagues and pestilences to torment mankind. Soon these so-called natural disasters will be so common they will not even make the news. Everyone can see the results of Earth's sickness, but few can see the underlying cause. Why are even the cleverest scientists blind to the truth? Because they are locked into a pseudo-rational model of the universe. They refuse to acknowledge that our planet is a living, breathing organism and that these catastrophes are Earth's attempts to rid herself of the parasites – those teeming, endlessly multiplying parasites called men and women – that are destroying her. Soon Earth must resort to her final weapon to rid herself of this human infestation.'

Serafa paused again. Everyone was absolutely still. Her delivery compelled attention.

'Imagine,' she continued coolly, 'that our planet is like a huge bear whose coat has become full of lice and fleas. What can this poor creature do to rid herself of the vermin tormenting her? First she scratches and shakes. This is the stage of earthquakes and tornadoes through which we are now passing. But it is not enough. There is only one way for the bear to cleanse herself, just as there is only one sure way for Earth to be free of her human destroyers.'

A smile lifted the corners of her mouth. She seemed to contemplate the imminent destruction of mankind with remarkable equanimity.

She reached down to the table for a glass of water. She took a sip, raised the glass in a gesture like a salutation, then put it down. 'Water,' she said simply. 'Ever since the first life form struggled from the oceans, water has been a symbol of purity, cleansing and rebirth. So it is now. The only way our beautiful bear can get free of the parasites attacking her is to plunge herself in a deep pool of crystal water and remain submerged until the last flea, the last louse, the last burrowing tick, has been drowned for ever. The same with our Earth. The time of great cleansing draws near, the time of cataclysm and upheaval when the magnetic poles will be reversed and the whole planet will be covered with the waters of purification. Even the highest mountain peak, even Mount Everest itself. Imagine it: fish swimming through the streets of London; seaweed floating round the top of the Empire State Building; dolphins and whales playing above the sands of the Sahara Desert. Mankind and womankind will be wiped from the face of the earth. All utterly gone.'

This is mad, I thought, but in spite of myself I felt fear trickle down my spine. I looked around to see how the other Questers were responding. Across from me a woman with huge circles round her eyes ran the tip of her tongue over dry lips. Beside her a nervous-looking youth was nodding so vigorously his glasses kept slipping down his nose. The two Japanese girls were mesmerised. And an elderly woman swathed in batik drapery who had come to sit beside me just before the meeting began was listening with rapt attention. Even the latecomer, the blond young man with his neat jacket and polished shoes, even he was watching closely, his eyes locked on Serafa's face. It was easy to see that most of those present were desperate to believe.

I hadn't given much thought to the group's philosophy; I'd been too busy trying to find out how they operated and where I could see them in action. None of the material I'd found on the Internet had made much sense, apart from the anguished warnings of one or two people who'd had bad experiences with them. All this end-of-the-world stuff was pretty much what one would expect from a lunatic cult, and I was looking forward to laughing about it later with Gus or Brian, just as soon as I was back in the world of normal people. Even so, it was easy to see how someone vulnerable like Jenny might be convinced by Serafa. She spoke with such certainty; far from trying to convince us, it was as if she was doing us all a huge favour by deigning to speak to us.

The silence, as we all sat and contemplated our approaching doom, was profound. After a few moments Serafa said, 'Some of you may be wondering how I know this. The answer is simple. The Sacred Knowledge has been preserved by a chosen handful of Initiates since the beginning of time. The history of civilisation stretches back much further than most people realise. Ten thousand years before the first Egyptian pyramid was built, the survivors of an earlier empire spread out into every corner of the world. The sacred flame has been kept alive throughout time by a select band of keepers of the truth. They have been known by many names, some of which may be familiar to you, such as the Heirs of Akasha. Always, in the hidden corners of the world, their descendants, the Acolytes of Ra have maintained the Eternal Truth.'

She stepped sideways so we could contemplate the portrait of Raymond Tucker. Again I felt that urge to giggle. Were we really supposed to believe that Gus's old friend was an Acolyte of Ra? Or that Ealing qualified as one of the hidden corners of the world? I shifted in my seat and coughed as my eyes filled with tears of laughter. Serafa looked at me thoughtfully for a moment before continuing, 'Those of you who progress further along the Path of Akasha – if any of you do – will learn more when you are ready. For now it is enough that you know that we have entered the final hours of this cycle. The clock that has been ticking for three and a half thousand years will strike on the 23rd of December, 2012. Everything has been foreseen.'

There was another long silence. She seemed to have grown taller as she spoke, and her expression was serene, triumphant. From the road outside the roar of traffic continued, the pulse of a universe hurtling blindly towards destruction. Serafa's gaze lingered on the face of the young man who had arrived late. He was seated with his arms folded, feet planted firmly on the floor. He couldn't meet her gaze for long and shifted slightly, glancing down towards his shoes. Once again, Serafa contemplated each Quester in turn. When her eyes fell on my face, the laughter that had been bubbling up inside me was killed at once. My mouth went dry, as though she was able to read my mind and knew I was an impostor. Don't be stupid, I told myself. These people are all crazy.

Serafa smiled a knowing smile. 'Does this sound crazy?' she asked. I shivered. She went on, 'Everyone knows that when Noah, who was a Keeper of the Sacred Knowledge, told mankind a terrible flood was coming, he was mocked. It was what he expected. It is what we expect now. Many hear our message but their inner ears remain closed to the Truth. We must work hard to open our eyes and ears to truth, the real truth, the great truth that cannot be understood by the five senses we share with animals. It is only by meditation that we learn to tune into the supersensory realities that will save us. At our centres we have workshops to develop these abilities, but the great majority of people do not understand our work. Their folly will set the seal on their destruction when the time comes. As in the days of Noah the Adept, only a few will be spared, just a handful of seeds to carry the hope of new life into the next cycle. Is there anyone in this room tonight who will have the resources and the dedication to carry human life forward into the great era to come?'

This time, when she stopped, the atmosphere was electric. Even the hum of traffic had dimmed to a distant blur. Despite the open windows it felt stuffy and airless. My head was swimming and for one strange and hallucinatory moment I thought: she's right. I'd better join up before it's too late. Then I pinched myself and I wondered if one of the group's tricks was to tamper with the oxygen supply so as to make Questers more receptive.

Having delivered her final question Serafa glided down on to her chair, like a tall blue bird coming down to roost. Palu stood up. Her face, now that I looked closely, was vaguely familiar.

'Thank you, Serafa.' Her voice was flat and uninspiring. There was a sudden flurry of movement as people emerged from their semi-trance: feet scuffed on the wooden floor and chair legs scraped. 'Now, before I outline some of our work, there will be a chance for each of you to say a few words about yourself, what you are looking for and what you have to offer. We'll start on my left and go round clockwise. Right then' – she leaned forward and peered at the badge of a young man with a shaved head – 'Troy. You can start.'

Troy looked panic-stricken.

'Age?'

'Twenty-three.'

A man seated just outside the circle picked up a note pad. He had wispy grey hair pulled back into a raggedy ponytail and he wore a coarse white caftan shirt. He began to write.

'Your profession?' asked Palu.

'Engineer.' Palu and the scribe looked at him with new interest. Troy grew bolder. 'I graduated two years ago and I've been in my present job ever since. My speciality is traffic flow. I've made a special study of synchronised lights.' He was beginning to warm to his theme, but Palu had lost interest.

She interrupted him curtly. 'Hopes?'

'I . . . I was looking . . .'

I wished there was some way of helping him through his ordeal. He looked so forlorn, as though what he was really looking for was friends and a family, a purpose in life, something to believe in.

Palu stared at him, her eyes hard. 'Well, Troy?'

'I want to travel,' he said finally.

It looked as though the scribe put a cross next to his name.

The two Japanese girls were next, but their answers were so quiet no one could hear them except perhaps Palu and the scribe, and they didn't seem all that interested. Then it was the turn of the batik-swathed woman next to me. She said her name was Fiona and she was forty-two, which I estimated was a lie by at least ten years. She was a bit vague about her professional skills, saying only that she had extensive experience in the arts and had once kept chickens and goats. Palu and the scribe looked unimpressed, but Fiona waxed lyrical when asked what she was looking for. She said a recent tarot reading had told her that a massive life change was on the horizon and a week later her elderly mother, whom she had looked after for fifteen years, had died and the same day a friend had told her about the Heirs of Akasha. She'd had a series of dreams which, when interpreted, made it obvious that she was destined to survive the great cataclysm.

And then it was my turn.

'Name?'

'Carol Brewster.' I had decided right away to give my maiden name and a fictitious address, in case anything got back to Raymond Tucker that might connect me with his old friend Gus. I'd given Gus only a sketchy idea of what I was up to, but knowing his aversion for anything connected with the old Grays Orchard group I didn't want to risk an overlap.

'Age?'

'Thirty-four.'

'Your work?' Palu glanced at her watch, a man's Rolex.

'I'm a builder.'

There was a buzz of interest. The three Heirs examined me closely, even Serafa, who since she finished her talk had been staring dreamily at the ceiling.

'You work for a building firm?' asked Palu.

'I run one. With a partner. It's going pretty well at present.'

'And how would you describe your role in the firm? Do you do any of the hands-on stuff?'

'Yes, of course. I keep track of all the finances and the strategy decisions. I'm working on a barn conversion right now, but I help my partner with the modern stuff, too.'

'So you'd be able to supervise construction work?' It was Serafa who asked. It was the first time she had even looked at one of the Questers since this part of the session began, let alone talked to one. It's ridiculous, I know, but I was flattered.

'Of course,' I told her. 'It's what I do every day. Depending on the scale,' I added swiftly. 'We've never tackled anything more ambitious than a five-bedroomed house.'

The scribe was writing rapidly.

'And your hopes from the group?' Palu asked.

This was the bit I'd been dreading. I had debated making up an elaborate tale of past-life experience or of premonition, but had decided it was safest to stick as close as possible to the truth. I said, 'I suppose I was just curious. I'd heard about the Heirs of Atlantis – I mean, Akasha – and I wanted to find out more. That's all, really.'

I dug my nails into the palms of my hands. How stupid of me to get the name of the group wrong. There was an awkward silence. The air was sour with the smell of anxious sweat. The prospect of being exposed as a fraud in front of the gullible Questers was not appealing. Outside, London life was continuing as normal, but already this weird group felt like a world apart, with its own rules and standards.

Palu was examining me, her pudgy features compressed into a frown; she seemed unable to make up her mind. The scribe had stopped writing. Serafa, an enigmatic smile on her face, spread her hand out in a fan and examined her nails. I held my breath.

The silence had become unbearable. I said, 'I've been interested for months, but it just never felt like the right time until now.'

At last Palu nodded her approval and the scribe made a mark next to my name. Now it was the turn of the man on my left, who described himself as a 'Sage'. I began to relax. The Sage wanted to know why Akasha didn't take environmental issues more seriously; he pointed out that their newsletter wasn't even printed on recycled paper. Palu said tartly it was far too late to be bothering with the environment since Earth was preparing her own solution and nothing humankind did was going to avert the coming catastrophe.

'Look at it this way,' suggested Serafa in her low, melodious voice. 'Imagine a vehicle, a huge lorry, for instance, a ten-ton truck. This lorry is hurtling down a steep hill. Its brakes are broken and it is about to smash into a sheer cliff-face at one hundred miles an hour. What does it matter to the driver if the lorry is running on ordinary fuel or unleaded?'

She settled back into her seat with a little smile of satisfaction. First the nit-infested bear, now a lorry without brakes; it was obvious Serafa liked to explain their philosophy with metaphors. I wasn't about to point out that a ten-ton truck would actually be running on diesel.

Palu moved on to the next woman, who said her name was Grisel and that she'd been burned as a witch in a previous life. This unfortunate experience had apparently resulted in giving her healing powers in her present life. She seemed to expect the group to be impressed, but Palu simply nodded and moved on quickly. She was eager to be finished. As each person stammered out their details, the

accumulated weight of so many confused and lonely lives
was overwhelming. I felt as though I was absorbing their
pain like blotting paper. I wondered how Palu and Serafa
could bear the strain of so many desperate hopes, but they
didn't look at all bowed by it. Perhaps the meditation
helped or perhaps they simply didn't care.

Soon it was the turn of the young man who had arrived
late. When he was asked his name he answered too quietly
and had to repeat it.

'Matthew Smith,' he said, too loudly this time. His cool
blue eyes held Palu's gaze with a touch of defiance and a
small muscle moved high in his cheek.

Serafa frowned. She glanced over the scribe's shoulder
and murmured in his ear. He stopped writing and
examined Matthew Smith.

'Your profession?' asked Palu.

'I'm a marine engineer,' he said firmly. That should go
down well, I thought, but the scribe didn't write anything
on his pad.

'Who do you work for?'

'I'm freelance so I go anywhere the work takes me.
Recently I've been under contract for one of the North Sea
rigs.'

Now all three members of the group were watching him
closely and the scribe had laid down his pen.

'Where did you study, Mr Smith?' asked Serafa.

He hesitated. His eyes narrowed. Maybe he was
wondering why he alone was being addressed by his
surname. I felt a prickle of anxiety. Why were they singling
him out in this way?

'London University,' he said, lifting his chin slightly.

'Which college?'

Another hesitation, then, 'King's,' he said.

There was another long silence. The air crackled with
tension. I thought maybe they suspected him of lying about

his qualifications in order to be more attractive as a potential member of the group.

At length Palu said quietly, 'It's Tim Fairchild, isn't it?'

'I said my name was Matthew Smith.'

'There's no point lying, Mr Fairchild. Your photograph is on our files.'

He flushed a deep scarlet. 'So? What does a name matter?'

'Mr Fairchild, we must ask you to leave at once.'

He folded his arms and planted his feet more firmly on the floor. 'This is a public meeting. I've as much right to be here as anybody.'

'Please go, Mr Fairchild.'

'Why? What have I done wrong? I've as much right to learn about your group as all the rest of them. I'm staying to the end.'

'No, Mr Fairchild. We must insist you go. Now. You're here under false pretences and hostile agents are not permitted to attend our meetings. Please leave at once.'

'You can't make me.'

'We'd rather not have to, but—'

'You're frightened of me, aren't you?' He looked around, disgust on his handsome face. 'You're afraid I'll tell this bunch of suckers what you're really up to. All this crap about global warming and the end of the world, that's just a way of hooking them in. Play on people's fears, that's what you like to do. Get them in your power. If this bunch knew the truth, they'd be out of here faster than you can say "fake".'

'That's enough!' Serafa raised her hand.

'Enough? You must be joking. I've only just begun.'

Then I noticed Palu glance towards the door and nod slightly. A man and a woman who'd been seated next to Maureen, stood up without making a sound and began circling round the back of the chairs towards Tim

Fairchild. They were an ugly couple. The man was big and blubbery, his beer gut spilling over his trousers, but the woman looked tougher. She had cropped grey hair, a tight black vest showing muscly arms, and a mass of vicious silver jewellery. I realised with horror that Tim hadn't noticed them.

'Christ,' he said with contempt, 'I don't know how you've got the nerve to sit there and spout all that nonsense about meditation and supersensory perceptions. That's not what you're about. You destroy people, that's what you do, you break up families and steal children away from their parents. You're twisted and evil and all you really want is power.' He looked round wildly at the Questers. 'Listen, you bunch of idiots, don't fall for it. Get out while you can. Don't let them brainwash you. Oh, I know they make it sound harmless, but it's not. They're dangerous. They'll destroy your life like they destroyed mine. They'll rip your family apart and leave you with nothing. They—'

He caught sight of my stricken face. The man and woman had halted behind him. Tim's head jerked round. He must have seen a flash of movement as the woman lunged forward. He tried to duck away but she gripped his wrist and wrenched it up behind his back. He flung himself sideways and his chair clattered to the floor. At that moment the blubbery man pounced with surprising speed. One hand caught hold of Tim's jacket collar while the other grabbed his left arm. Tim made heroic efforts to free himself, but the man yanked his head and neck forward just as the woman stuck her booted foot in front of him, throwing him off balance. With a yell of outrage he fell forward. His head was on a level with the woman's chest and his polished shoes were scrabbling for purchase as they dragged him across the wooden floor. Maureen, looking anxious and hot, had stood up to open the door. The

Questers watched in horrified silence, but everyone was too stunned to react.

'You bastards!' roared Tim, his blond hair tumbling over his eyes and his cheeks scarlet with rage. 'You bastards, how dare you do this to me! Let go of me, I tell you. You can't do this. Where's my son? What have you done with him? Where are you hiding him, you perverts? Psychos, I'll get him back. Let me *go*!'

His captors had bundled him as far as the door. He was still fighting, and by now they were both running with sweat and grunting loudly. But their combined strength was too much for him. Every time he tried to set his feet on the floor he was shoved off balance again. There was spittle and blood in the corner of his mouth and his shirt was ripped just below the collar. To my eyes, with his tousled hair and rumpled clothes, he looked ten times more attractive than before.

'Stop it, you scum. Let me go. You're all mad, you can't do this, I won't let you keep them, I'll find them. I'll—'

Elbows banged on the doorposts as they dragged him on to the landing. Despairingly, Tim yelled, '*Give me back my SON!*'

All we could see was the fleshy back of the fat man as he shunted Tim out of sight. What happened on the stairs none of us could see, but we heard loud grunts and the thud of bodies being slammed against the wall, stumbling feet and then a final roar of pain and desperation, 'Stop it, you bastards, you're breaking my arm. *Let me GO!*'

A loud bang echoed through the building as the front door closed, then there was silence. There was the sour taste of nausea in my throat. I couldn't believe we'd all just sat there and done nothing, but everything had happened so quickly and been so unexpected. I put my hand to my mouth. The other Questers looked equally shaken. Only Palu and Serafa were unruffled.

Serafa rubbed the tips of her fingers together, as though wiping off something gritty. Palu picked up the fallen chair and removed it from the circle, then indicated that the two people who had been sitting on either side of Tim should move their chairs to close up the gap.

She gave us a reassuring smile as she sat down again. 'Sorry about that, folks,' she said calmly, 'We've been expecting Tim Fairchild for some time. He's a nasty piece of work.'

I was horrified. He hadn't looked a nasty piece of work, far from it. He looked like an ordinary decent man who'd been driven to desperate measures. One or two people shifted uncomfortably but no one spoke. At last I could bear it no longer. I said, 'But what about his child? He sounded desperate.'

Palu looked at me coldly. 'We never discuss personal matters connected with members of our organisation. Our work is based on trust. Anyone who wishes to go now is free to do so. It is very difficult to join our organisation, but simplicity itself to leave.'

Give me back my son! What about a child? I thought. What choices do they have?

We heard the front door open and close again, then footsteps on the stairs, and the two bouncers resumed their positions, indicating with a brief nod that their job was done. In the street outside the roar of traffic drowned out all other noise.

Palu leaned forward to read the name of the elderly man who had followed me into the house. His seat was next to Tim's and he'd had to take avoiding action so as not to be hit during the 'incident'; he looked particularly shaken.

'Lionel,' Palu said briskly. 'Can you give us your details, please, Lionel.'

Gradually the tension eased. Lionel told her at some length that he was a pensioner but had worked for nearly

fifty years as a gentleman's outfitter. He thought he might
be able to help with some of the group's ceremonial
costumes, though he admitted humbly that he wouldn't be
much use after the great cataclysm, if indeed he lived to see
it. He explained he'd given the matter extensive thought
and was prepared to be left behind when the time came, so
long as he could be part of their community until then.

Palu looked thoughtful. 'And your hopes?' she asked.

'I'd like to have company. You know, be among friends
as I get older,' he said, his pale eyes blinking hopefully.
Then he added, 'My son and his wife went to live in
Canada and my sister's in a home.' It was all I could do not
to put my arms round him and take him back with me to
Grays.

'Right, then,' said Palu when the last of the Questers had
spoken, 'now it's my turn to tell you a bit more about our
Atlantic centres and after that we can break for tea and
biscuits. Serafa and I will be available later to answer your
questions.'

The meeting continued. I was only half listening. I was
still haunted by Tim Fairchild's agonised cry and I
wondered what lay behind his tragic story. He was
desperate to find his son, who must still be very young, so
presumably his wife or ex-partner had joined the group
against his wishes. Palu was talking in her flat voice about
their centre in Cornwall and the different status Questers
were given and what that meant, but as I had no intention
of ever setting foot in one of their places I didn't bother to
take it in. It was hard to believe that Jenny, vulnerable
though she was, had been duped by all this nonsense.

At last Palu announced that it was time to break for tea.
She said she and Serafa would go next door because they
had to assign the status of each person present, but when
they returned there'd be an opportunity for informal
questions.

The two women left the room and everyone began to relax, but warily, like a class of schoolchildren when the teacher's been unexpectedly called away. I decided to leave now: I didn't want their tea and biscuits and I certainly didn't want to know my status, but then I noticed Lionel looking around hopefully for someone to talk to; his neighbours had mysteriously melted away. I crossed the room, sat down beside him and said, 'Well, what did you make of that?'

He was so happy to chat that it was impossible to get away before Palu and Serafa came back. Meanwhile the two heavies had been recast as waiters. Supervised by Maureen, they handed round trays of tea and biscuits.

'Careful,' I said to the nervous-looking young man, who was sipping his tea, 'it might be drugged.'

The hot tea had made his glasses steam up. He blinked with surprise and didn't even smile.

I decided I'd had enough. Putting down my cup and saucer, I stood up and moved towards the door. Maureen, who was sporting a couple of new patches of sweat on the front of her shirt, intercepted me. 'Are you looking for the loo?'

'No, I'm leaving.'

'Oh.' She looked crestfallen. 'What about your status?' She followed me on to the landing. 'Oh, look, here's Palu now. I'm sure she'll give you your envelope.'

'No, really—'

But already she was telling Palu that I had to leave early. Palu gave me a searching glance, then flipped through a stack of brown envelopes until she came to the one with my name on it. As she handed it to me she said briskly, 'Maybe we'll see you in Cornwall.'

'Well . . .'

She didn't wait for my reply. She and Serafa went into the main room and Maureen followed them and closed the door. I heard the shuffle of chairs as the group resumed their seats and then Palu's voice saying, 'I expect you're all eager to know what status you've been given.'

Stuffing the brown envelope in my bag, I fled.

Chapter 7

I crossed the road and looked back at the house. Here on the street people were walking aimlessly, enjoying the last of the day's sun, while behind that upstairs window people were discussing the Acolytes of Ra and the end of the world. The unreality of it all made my head swim.

I turned and walked quickly towards the Underground.

A man's voice rang out behind me. 'Carol?'

I turned to see Tim Fairchild hurrying out of a café. There was an ugly bruise on his face and his shirt was grubby and torn.

He said, 'I thought I recognised you. It's Carol Brewster, isn't it?'

I nodded. 'Are you all right?'

'There are no bones broken, if that's what you mean – no thanks to those two gorillas. Did you leave early?'

'I'd had enough. They're all mad in there.'

His expression relaxed a little. 'I thought you looked too bright to fall for it. Are you in a hurry?' He glanced anxiously at the house. 'The thing is, I don't want them to see me. I've got to talk to them, but I'll have to take them by surprise. If they know I'm here they'll run a mile. We can keep an eye on the place from in here – will you join me?'

'Of course.' After what he'd been through I could hardly refuse and besides, as always, I was curious.

The café was ideal from a strategic point of view, but that was its only merit. It was stuffy and smelled of old grease; the mineral water I asked for arrived in a glass with smears of lipstick on the rim and when I pointed this out to the waiter he replaced it with a bad grace. Tim had taken a table near the window and throughout our conversation he kept glancing at the door across the road. With his floppy blond hair and regular features he would have had film-star good looks, except that anxiety had scored deep lines between his brows and the skin just below his left eye was puffy and bruised.

He glanced at me warily. 'Do you mind me asking why you went to that meeting?' he asked.

'Curiosity, I suppose.'

'You're not a journalist?'

'No. I'm a builder, like I said.'

'What did you make of it all?'

'It was crazy.' Now that I'd left the oppressive atmosphere of the group I didn't like to admit to those moments when Serafa's words and the way she seemed to know exactly what I was thinking had made fear crawl down my spine. 'It's a wonder anyone falls for that stuff.'

'Don't underestimate them,' he warned. 'They may look like a bunch of amateurs but they're brilliant manipulators. A lot of their followers are professional people you'd expect to have more sense. You'd be amazed how many people want to be told what to think and how to live their lives. It's all very beautiful and lovey-dovey until they get you hooked.'

'Is that what's happened to your wife?'

He looked away quickly. 'My wife is dead.'

'Oh, I'm so sorry. But you said they had your son so I assumed . . .'

'He's called Davy,' he said, and there was a catch in his voice. 'He's only six. Do you want to see a photograph?'

Without waiting for my reply he took a leather wallet from his breast pocket and pulled out a photograph which had been handled so much that the edges and corners were rough. 'That's my boy.'

'He's beautiful.' And he was, too. He had his father's blond hair and blue eyes and a smile of heart-wrenching innocence. It was appalling to think of the child being separated from his only remaining parent.

'I don't understand,' I said. 'If his mother is dead then you're his guardian.'

'Of course I am, technically, but it's not as simple as that. Hang on a minute.' His body was rigid with tension. 'They're starting to come out.'

I twisted round to look back at the house. The Sage was the first to emerge; maybe his concern over environmental issues made him critical of the group's methods. Then came Grisel, the reincarnated witch, then the two Japanese girls. One by one they all brushed past the pink hydrangea and walked down the street. A few had cars parked nearby but most, like me, were heading towards the Tube. The last to appear was Lionel, the retired gentlemen's outfitter, closely followed by Maureen, who seemed to be having trouble getting rid of him. Finally he set off down the road, the happy expression he'd had while chatting to her slowly fading to apathy. I imagined him returning to his lonely flat, maybe a budgie for company, or an aged cat.

'Look,' I said, 'there's that old man who was sitting next to you. Let's see if he wants to join us.'

I'd risen only a couple of inches from my seat when Tim

gripped my wrist, snapping my arm back on to the table. 'Don't move. They mustn't know I'm here. Their car's at the end of the street and—' He looked at me and released my hand. 'Sorry,' he said, smiling his apology. It was the first time I'd seen him smile and his face was briefly lit up by a boyish charm, before his attention returned to the activity across the street. 'Look,' he told me.

The two bouncers were coming out. They exchanged a few words with Maureen, then crossed the road and walked briskly along the pavement and past the café. Tim shrank back, but he needn't have bothered. The blubbery man and the mean-looking woman were deep in conversation as they hurried past without a second glance.

'Come *on*,' Tim muttered, staring hard at the front door over the road, 'come on, you bitches, what are you waiting for?' He seemed to have forgotten I was there. He shifted in his seat. 'Why don't they come out? I wonder . . .'

'What are you going to do?'

'They have to talk to me. I have to make them see sense—*no*!' He sprang to his feet. 'Damn them!'

He nearly knocked our table over in his dash for the door. After that, things happened very fast. Palu and Serafa came out of the house and stepped quickly past the hydrangea and on to the pavement. As they did so a dark green saloon car driven by the skinny woman with all the heavy silvery jewellery, the fat man sitting next to her, sped down the street and screeched to a halt in front of the house. Tim was dodging through the traffic to intercept them. Palu had walked round the back of the car to get in behind the driver. Her face went blank with shock as Tim hurtled towards the car. She wrenched open the door and, in her haste, she tripped on the hem of her long blue robes and fell forwards on to the seat. For a moment all that was visible was her large blue rump and her sandalled feet. Then she scrambled round to grab the door handle and pull it shut before Tim reached her. I saw her mouth moving; she was shouting to the driver. The car started to move away while she was still trying to close her door. Tim lunged forward to catch hold of the outside handle. There was a struggle and the car door swung wide, pulling Palu half out, but she wouldn't let go. Then the movement of the car gave her the advantage. The door began to close while Tim ran alongside, still hanging on to the handle, screaming to the driver to stop.

'Oh God.' I was out on the pavement and watching helplessly. 'Stop! Why don't you stop? He'll be killed.'

The car gathered speed. Tim clung on to the handle, but his arm was at full stretch and he was dragged along. For one stomach-churning moment I thought his hand was trapped, he couldn't let go and would be dragged to his death; but then he let out a yell of rage that could be heard above the roar of the traffic and fell backwards, flinging his arms up in despair as the car sped away, down the street and out of sight.

Tim was so badly shaken by that final encounter with the Heirs of Akasha that I'd have needed a heart of stone to abandon him then. Besides, I've always had a soft spot for a man in distress and Tim was in utter despair. He must have pinned all his hopes on this evening's meeting and all he'd achieved were a couple of vicious bruises and total defeat.

After we'd paid up at the café we walked without direction until it was dark. Tim was full of pent-up energy, the frustration of having come face to face with his enemy and getting nowhere.

'Those two bitches run the show,' he told me bitterly as we walked through a park that smelt of warm grass where some boys were kicking a football around. 'Tucker's just a figurehead these days. Apparently he took some kind of vow of silence and hasn't spoken in years. The women use sex to control him. They let him take his pick of all the girls in the group. It's sick, sick, *sick* and my Davy's in the middle of it. God, I miss him so much!'

It wasn't until I'd finally persuaded him to stop at a pub somewhere near Shepherd's Bush that the full story came out. At a table beside ours a trio of girls nudged each other and appraised Tim with interest while he ordered our drinks at the bar. They'd been talking about work and boyfriends in low, confidential voices, but their mood changed as soon as he came to join me carrying two pint glasses and a packet of sandwiches. Now they were talking for his benefit, loud stories of daring exploits and sexual adventure. I could have told them to save their breath. They might have been a trio of grannies swapping knitting patterns for all the attention Tim paid them. Given the story he had to tell, that was hardly surprising.

'If you'd met me a year ago,' he began with a rueful smile, 'you'd have thought I had it all: a fantastic wife, a beautiful child, and at last I was getting the breaks I deserved at work. We were still living in a flat that was too small, but we were planning on moving this year. My father was headmaster of the prep school he owned, and he was coming up to retirement. He was always incredibly generous. When he sold the school he planned to make over some of the money to me and Lucy so we could at last get a decent place for Davy to grow up. It seemed as if all our dreams were coming true.'

His blue eyes shone with remembered happiness as he spoke. At the table next to us, the girl with red corkscrew curls said, with a sidelong glance at Tim, 'Flat on my back I was, arse over tip like a bloody turtle, and he just walks on and shouts back, "What's keeping you, then?" ' She howled with laughter and the others joined in.

Tim carried on, 'I remember our wedding anniversary,

just over a year ago. We drove up to Kettering to spend the day with my parents. We had some children's tapes for the car, but most of the way up we were singing. Davy had just learned "What Shall We Do with the Drunken Sailor?" and we were making up verses to amuse him, stupid stuff like "Hang him in the cupboard and make him suffer", and "Tie him to a chair until he's sorry", and Davy was lapping it up. It was a fantastic day; everything was perfect and as we drove home in the evening I remember saying to Lucy, thank God we took some pictures because we'd always have a perfect day to look back on. I've never had that film developed. I've still got it, but I expect it's spoiled by now. I couldn't bear to see those pictures.'

His hand was clenched into a fist on the table. The girls beside us were telling tampon jokes, but he never heard them.

He drew in a deep breath and said, 'My wife drowned on October 24th last year. It was an accident. No one knows quite how it happened. My parents had come down to London for the weekend to look after Davy so Lucy and I could have a couple of nights on our own. We went to the Black Mountains. I blame myself, of course I do. I'm a fast walker and I'd got impatient having to slow down for Lucy all the time. We'd walked from our hotel to a pub to have lunch, but on the way back I said I was going to do a different route, and go over the mountain while she went back along the valley track, beside the river. The last time I saw her, she was waving to me as I set off up the mountain. Her face was radiant, so beautiful and happy, and I nearly turned back. I didn't want to be away from her, not even for a couple of hours. Oh, God—' He broke off.

I said, 'You don't have to tell me, if it's too painful.'

'No. It's in my head all the time. In my head and my heart. I live it over and over, every minute of the day. I knew as soon as I got back that something was wrong but I couldn't get those idiots at the hotel to realise how serious it was. They kept trying to reassure me but I knew something had happened. They didn't start a proper search until it was almost dark and by then it was too late. It was probably too late by the time I got back to the hotel, anyway. Lucy couldn't swim very well and the current where she must have slipped is treacherous, even for a strong swimmer. But they didn't find her body till the next afternoon. My father had come from London that morning, leaving Davy with my mother. He said it would be too upsetting for the child to be there and he'd be better off out of it. Now, of course, I wish Davy and I had gone through it all together, because afterwards, when the funeral and the inquest and all the rest of it was over, I couldn't face him. My parents kept telling me how happy Davy was with them and that he was fitting into life at the school and getting spoiled rotten by all the boys and was going to be the littlest shepherd in the nativity play. And I thought, we'll start again after Christmas. I was like a zombie. I wasn't fit company for a child.'

'You mustn't blame yourself,' I said.

'No.' His blue eyes softened with gratitude. 'But it's hard, you know. Not to, sometimes.' He blinked and smiled, as though he'd just remembered he had an audience for his story, which must be playing on an unceasing loop in his mind. I wanted to put my arm round his shoulders and hold him to ease the pain. Just the thought of it triggered a small but distinct throb of desire under my ribs. My loveless summer seemed to be making me susceptible, for the first time since I had met Gus, to the attractions of other men.

I asked, 'Did Davy stay with your parents?'

'Yes. After Christmas I had to go on a course. Then I arranged for someone to come in mornings and evenings while I was at work, to give Davy breakfast and take him to school and pick him up in the afternoon, but she broke her leg; it seemed as if all my efforts to get us back together were jinxed. I went up to see him every weekend, and he really did seem happy with my parents. I wondered if it was selfish of me to want to take him away from the loving security of the school. Then, before I knew it, Easter had come. We'd agreed that in the holidays, while I was working, Davy would visit my parents anyway.

'The day after Easter Monday, my father had a coronary. He was showing some prospective parents round the school and just collapsed in the art block. He was dead before they got him to hospital. I couldn't take it in at first. Coming so soon after what happened to Lucy, well, I have to say it hit me pretty hard. Now on top of everything I had my mother to think of. She'd always depended on my father absolutely. He made all the decisions, ran the school and took care of her as well. He was very charismatic. There were so many at his funeral that the service had to be relayed on loud speakers to all the people who couldn't fit in the church. It was incredibly moving to realise how many people's lives he had touched. After the funeral I sat down and talked it through with my mother. The school was being sold anyway. With some of that money we planned to buy a decent place near my work so she and Davy could come and live with me. Our poor family, what was left of it – but at least we'd be together.'

He leaned back in his chair and stared into space. The girls at the next table stopped talking at the same time. They must have realised, at last, that Tim wasn't exactly open to suggestions this evening. When he resumed his story, they spoke in low, murmuring tones, half listening to his words.

'That was when Raymond Tucker and his crew muscled

in.' He sighed. 'God, how they must have worked on her. Mind you, they've had plenty of practice. Little old ladies with lots of money and no one to protect them have been their speciality from the word go. Apparently Tucker and Pauline worked as minicab drivers in the beginning; his trick was to build up an old lady's trust, then spin her a line about how he was really an Acolyte of Ra, and bingo, one or two of the poor dears actually fell for it and left their money to him. He's never looked back. My guess is he saw my father's obituary in the paper and decided to see what he could get out of my mother. A letter of condolence, the offer of a visit – God, it makes me sick to think of it. I always knew she was gullible, but even so . . . I don't think she'd have fallen for it if she hadn't known him way back.'

A tremor of something like recognition touched the back of my neck, but before I was able to work out why, Tim continued, 'Those bastards worked on Davy, too. That's the most disgusting part, the way they turned my own son against me. I noticed he was acting strangely and didn't seem so pleased to see me when I went up on Friday nights, but to be honest I put it down to all the traumas the poor little chap's had to endure. First his mother, then his grandfather. He must have been wondering who was going to be next. I told myself it would all work out once we were all together in our own home. I'd found a house and put in an offer.

'Then, on the very day my mother got her hands on the money from the sale of the school, I got a message to say she and Davy had joined a group called the Heirs of Akasha and wouldn't be coming to live with me after all. I couldn't believe it. I thought it must be some kind of sick joke. I mean, I'd never even heard of the Heirs of Akasha. And why would she do a thing like that? All I could think was that the loss of my father had driven her over the edge. There'd been no signs before – in fact she seemed to be coping remarkably well – but now I can see that was all part of the way she was losing touch with reality. I did everything I could to contact her, but kept coming up against a brick wall. They wouldn't let me near her. They won't even allow her to use a telephone. This evening was my last hope. I thought I could go on one of their introductory weekends, get into the place and find a way to contact her. If I could only talk to her, just for half an hour, I know I'd be able to persuade her to see sense. She's not a wicked woman, just deeply unhappy and confused. They've brainwashed her and now I've lost everything.'

The girls on the next table were packing up and getting ready to leave. I gazed at Tim thoughtfully. A man with such good looks is often the son of an equally beautiful woman. I asked, 'What's your mother's name?'

'Fairchild. Same as mine.'

'And her Christian name?'

He looked surprised. 'Katherine,' he said. I felt a twinge of disappointment, but then he added, 'But she's always called Katie.'

I drew in a sharp breath. 'And did she and Raymond Tucker know each other because they had both lived at a house called Grays Orchard?'

His eyes darkened. 'How do you know? Are you one of them?'

'The Heirs of Akasha? Of course not. But I live at Grays Orchard. Gus Ridley is my husband. He painted those pictures of your mother.'

'I don't understand. That's such an amazing coincidence.'

I explained, 'Not really. It wasn't just curiosity that made me go to the meeting this evening. Gus's niece has joined their cult as well. Same connection: her mother used to know Tucker at Grays Orchard. In fact, there were rumours at the time that Tucker killed Jenny's father: he

was a member of the group too and his name was Andrew.
I think Jenny probably got in touch with them in the first
place because she wanted to meet Tucker and find out
what kind of man he is, but I guess once they get their
claws into someone they're reluctant to let go. Like your
mother, Jenny has money, which must make her a more
attractive proposition.'

Tim was catching up fast. 'The Grays Orchard group.
I've seen some of your husband's paintings.'

'Your mother was very beautiful,' I said. I was busy
making some mental adjustments of my own. Throughout
Tim's story about his wife's tragic death and how his
mother had fallen under the spell of the Heirs, I'd formed
a mental picture of a dowdy little old lady, all grey hair and
gloom, but the name Katie instantly conjured up an image
of a sensuous youth. *Being Katie*, the most famous portrait
of her, showed her sprawled naked across a double bed
(the bed Gus and I still used), her limbs spangled pink and
gold with sunlight, her sex displayed. When it was first
shown, it had caused outrage, but now it was hailed as one
of the twentieth century's most tender portrayals of erotic
love. Katie, the great love of Gus's youth; maybe, though I
hated to think it, the great love of his life. And for the last
three hours I'd been in the company of her son. I said, 'Gus
painted some amazing pictures of her.'

'Yes.' He smiled ruefully. 'They're pretty frank. My
mother used to pretend they were nothing to do with her
and you can see why. It didn't go too well with her being a
respectable headmaster's wife, and you can imagine how
the boys would have exploited those paintings.' In spite of
his smile, his eyes were troubled. I could imagine it might
have been difficult for him too, if he was still a child the
first time he saw how another man had looked at his
mother.

For a little while we pieced together the connections that

had brought us both to the upstairs room in Ealing and the Heirs of Akasha.

'Palu was one of them, too,' said Tim. 'Her real name was Pauline and she was in with Tucker from the beginning. It was her family's minicab firm she and Tucker worked for when they were persuading rich old ladies to leave them money. They're married, though now she has to share Tucker with that other woman, Serafa, who arrived on the scene about five years ago. There is a rumour that the two women are lesbians and now that Tucker is impotent he gets his kicks from watching the two of them having sex. It makes me sick just to think of my boy mixed up with all that filth.'

'But can't the police do anything to help? I mean, you're Davy's father. It can't be legal for your mother to take him away from you like that.'

'Of course it isn't, and if I have to get the law involved I will, but I've been anxious to avoid that. Poor Davy's suffered enough disruption already. Can you imagine what it would do to him to be torn away from his grandmother by strangers? How could we build up a relationship of loving trust after a start like that? In spite of all her mistakes, my mother's the only security he's got, right now. Besides, she needs help as much as he does. If I get Davy out, what about her? I owe it to my father to get her away from them, too, and I could do it, I know I could, if I could just talk to her.'

'There must be some way to make contact.'

Tim was looking at me thoughtfully. 'Are you planning to follow this up?' he asked. 'Are you going to track down your husband's niece?'

'How can I do that?'

'By going on one of their courses. It would be easy for you. They don't suspect you yet and that way you'd be helping your husband's family as well as me.'

'You?'

'Sure. Once you were on the inside you could contact my mother, maybe persuade her to meet me somewhere. If only I could talk to her, half an hour would be enough. It would make all the difference.'

'I don't think—'

He leaned forward eagerly. 'Have you got your status category? That's crucial.'

I'd forgotten all about the brown envelope Maureen had stuffed in my bag just before I left. When I'd dug it out I found a single sheet of paper with my name on it and the words, 'Category B. Introductory Quester weekend £30. Full week Questers' retreat £75.'

'Is that good or bad?' I asked.

Tim let out a long breath. 'B, that's brilliant. You being a builder must have really impressed them. Or did you make that up?'

'No. I told you. I'm a partner in a building firm.'

'Fantastic. They really want you along, that's why they've given you such cheap rates. That makes it all so much easier. Category B's about as good as it gets. You have to be a doctor or a rocket scientist to make it to A.'

'Or a marine engineer?'

He grimaced. 'That was a stupid mistake – trying too hard as usual – but I think they'd already recognised me; they must have my photograph on file.'

'What's so special about marine engineers?'

'It's all part of their mad preparations for the great flood – what they call the Watershed. They claim they're trying to find ways to maintain life during long periods when the world will be totally covered by water, but my hunch is it's just another way to get money out of gullible people like my mother and your husband's niece. All the proceeds from the sale of Dad's school have vanished, by the way. A whole lifetime's work gone for nothing. But I don't care about that. I don't care about anything, so long as I get Davy back again.'

'It's so terrible. I wish there was something I could do to help.'

'But there is.' He leaned forward in his chair, his blue eyes fixed on my face. I've never seen a gaze of such intensity. 'You will help me, won't you, Carol? Just when I thought I'd run out of options, you come along and there's hope again. You could go on a Quester retreat; it's only a week.' He must have seen my appalled expression because he said quickly, 'But even if you just went on one of their weekend courses it would be a start. Their English base is in Cornwall. They'd never let me near the place, but they'd welcome you. And once you were there, you could find out such a lot. You could make enquiries about Davy and my mother. If you were lucky, you'd be able to talk to them – and to Jenny as well.'

It didn't take me long to reach my decision. 'I wish I could help you, Tim, but it's simply not possible. For one thing, I don't suppose I could achieve much and for another . . .'

'Yes? What is it, Carol? Are you scared of them?'

I ran my finger round the rim of my glass before replying, 'Yes. Maybe I am.'

'There's no reason to be ashamed of that. The Heirs of Akasha can be a pretty scary bunch. I should know: I've got the scars to prove it, and that was done at a public meeting. I imagine they get really heavy on their own patch. But you don't have to worry about that. I'd make sure you were never really on your own. I'd find a place to stay nearby so we could keep in contact with mobile phones. And it would only be for a couple of days.'

I hated to let him down but 'Sorry, Tim. It's just not on.' I'd seen enough of the Heirs of Akasha in action to be absolutely certain I wanted nothing more to do with them.

Chapter 8

It led to a row the next day, the first real row Gus and I'd ever had. We'd had arguments in the past, raised voices and angry silences, but this was the real thing.

It started with my naive belief that if I told him about the meeting with the Heirs of Akasha, it might start to bridge the gulf between us.

'You'll never guess who I met yesterday,' I said when I got home from work. 'Tim Fairchild, your old friend Katie's son.'

'What?' Gus had been slicing tomatoes on a chopping board, a half-drunk bottle of beer on the counter top in front of him. He paused, the blade of his knife hanging over the ripe flesh. 'You saw who?'

'Tim Fairchild. He was at that crazy meeting I went to.' Instantly I knew it was a mistake to tell him, knew it by the way his neck and shoulders tensed with anger and his eyes narrowed. But it was too late to retreat and, anyway, I was fed up with being discreet and sensitive to his secretive troubles and getting nothing in return. And I wasn't yet ready to settle for a marriage that relied on silence and lies to survive. So I ploughed on and told him about Palu and Serafa and how Tim had been thrown out. And then I told him about Katie and the death of her husband and how she, like Jenny, had fallen under the spell of Tucker's group. I made my account brief, because I could see it wasn't working out, but by the time I'd finished Gus had worked himself into a towering rage. He roared that I had no business sneaking off behind his back, that I was an interfering bitch and should stay out of other people's lives. It was a side of him I'd never seen before, cruel and unyielding and out for vengeance, but what horrified me most was that he didn't care a damn about the tragedy that had destroyed Katie's family.

'They can rot in hell for all I care,' he stormed. 'Can't I get it into your thick skull that I'm not interested in any of them? Just leave it!'

But I wasn't going to leave it. I told him he was selfish and uncaring and he told me not to meddle in stuff I didn't understand. I told him he should stop trying to shut his life into separate compartments and he told me not to be jealous of people I'd never even met. He told me I was pathetic and I told him he was a bastard. I can't remember which of us was the first to point that if either of us had known what the other was like we'd never have married in the first place, but from there it was a short step to telling each other we were free to leave.

There was a moment when we stood face to face, so pumped up with hurt and anger it needed a real fight – actual physical contact – to resolve it. I was on the point of hitting him and I sometimes wonder what would have happened if I had, but I didn't, so the rage just hung between us and festered.

I said, 'What's wrong with you, Gus? Why are you doing this to us?'

And he laughed and said, 'You're the one who's wrecking everything, Carol,' and stormed out.

From the oven came the sizzle of meat burning. Mechanically I went to get it out: lamb cutlets I'd covered in rosemary and garlic and lemon, a special summery supper. I tipped the lot in the dustbin and went out. There's nothing more miserable than the remnants of a meal that's been prepared in happiness, then finished in solitary rage and misery.

I drove around for an hour or so, before coming back to Grays Orchard in the twilight. I was angry and hurting and restless. There was no sweet reconciliation after our row, just a gradual return to uneasy truce. I wanted to get away from the place for a while, so I could think things over, but I couldn't think of anywhere to go.

The men always said it needed a woman's touch, which was probably just their way of saying the task was beneath them. Whatever the reason, the final house-cleaning before the purchaser moved in was always left to me and Norma, Brian's mother. This morning we had to do the final clean on Sam Piper's house at Gander Hill. My heart sank when I saw how much Artex and paint had been spattered on the floor, but Norma relished the job. Brian had promised to come along and give us a hand when he could get away. It wasn't something he usually did, but recently he'd taken to turning up at odd times to help out. 'You're looking peaky,' he'd said a couple of days before. 'Man trouble?'

I'd hesitated. With Brian, more than anyone else, I'd always wanted to give the impression my marriage was rock solid, but I told him about my visit to the Heirs of Akasha meeting, and gave him a watered-down version of Gus's response. I don't think he was fooled for a moment, but all he said was 'Let me know any time you want to take the longer view. I hate to see the way you've lost all your sparkle the last few weeks.'

He didn't say any more, but then he didn't need to. Brian knew me better than Gus ever would: it was the reason we were so close and it was the reason I'd never contemplate life without him. Better the unpredictable Gus than a future that was secure and totally without surprises.

I was never sure how much Norma knew about how things stood between me and Brian. We'd always got along pretty well. She must have guessed his feelings, but she was far too tactful to comment. Norma had borne the brunt of so much negative gossip during the years when Brian's father, Jack, was making his drunken one-man stand against bourgeois morality that she had an aversion to gossip. In fact, one of the things I most admired about Norma was that she never said a word against anyone.

She was sturdy and strongly built, like Brian, and he'd inherited his gingery hair from her, too, though hers was fading to grey. She was a good worker. Our practice was to go through the rooms together and we were side by side on our hands and knees scraping paint and Artex off the floor. Talk always flows more freely when you're working together and inevitably, given my present obsession, our conversation turned to the Grays Orchard group – though to my surprise it was Norma who brought the subject up.

'Brian says that niece of Gus's has joined Raymond Tucker's cult,' she said, chipping away at a particularly large dollop of Artex. 'You ought to get her away from there before she comes to any harm.'

'I wish I could. Did Brian tell you I'd been to one of their meetings?'

She looked at me with disbelief and I told her about the Heirs of Akasha and Tim's rough treatment. 'That doesn't surprise me,' she said eventually. 'Tucker was rotten through and through.'

'Did you know him?'

'Well enough,' she said. 'Oh, he could be charming when

the mood took him, but he gave me the creeps. He had those kind of weird dark eyes that just seem to swallow you up. Did you know he used to practise hypnosis on people? Offered to give me a go once but I said, "No, thank you very much." Even then, I could see right through him. Hypnosis, indeed! That's how he trapped all those poor old dears into leaving him their money, I shouldn't wonder. It's a pity he wasn't locked up when the police had the chance.'

'What, because of the murder?'

'That's right. It was obvious he'd done it, not that poor lad from the fair. Look at the way he went abroad as soon as the police dropped the case – and to Spain, too. Funny that there just happened to be no extradition treaty in those days. Costa del Crime and all that.'

I could understand that Norma resented Raymond getting away, as she saw it, with murder, but there was a personal edge to her animosity which puzzled me. I asked, 'Did you know Katie, too? What was she like?'

'The pretty one? Oh, she was all right. The best of a bad bunch – not including Gus, of course. She had lovely manners, very ladylike but not at all stuck up. I got to know her quite well, because her little boy was the same age as Brian, near enough, and I used to mind him for her sometimes.'

'Tim?' I asked in amazement. 'Was he at Grays Orchard too?'

'Only now and then. He lived with his dad mostly, but he used to visit sometimes. A dear little fellow he was and never a moment's trouble. Mind you, he used to run wild at Grays. There was no routine in that house at all. It wasn't a suitable place for a child and after a while his dad had to put a stop to his visits. I don't blame him, I'd have done the same, but you could see Katie missed him to death. Right, that's this room done. Do you want to hoover or go on and do the kitchen?'

'I don't mind,' I said vaguely. I was stunned by this new information. So Katie was already married, and had a small child as well, when she went to live with Gus at Grays Orchard. It was further proof of my humiliating ignorance concerning Gus's life before he met me.

When Brian arrived, we were sitting outside in the sun and Norma had just uncapped a thermos of tea. We teased him about his impeccable timing. Then I said, 'We've been talking about Raymond Tucker and the Heirs of Akasha. Your mum thinks I should go and rescue Jenny.'

'Are you sure she wants rescuing?' asked Brian, his ginger hair a bright halo in the sunshine.

'She would if she knew what was good for her,' said Norma emphatically. 'And she was a nice enough girl, considering what she had for a mother.'

I turned to Norma in surprise. 'Didn't you like Harriet?'

Norma snorted, as though even the possibility of liking such a person was ridiculous. 'That woman,' she said, 'was the lowest of the low.'

'You sound as if you hate her.'

'I don't hate anyone. It's not in my nature. I feel sorry for her, that's what. I wouldn't want to have to live with her guilty conscience. She was the reason it all went wrong. Tucker got the blame, but it was really her doing. That woman preyed on men, she was wicked, a real nymphomaniac. They couldn't resist her. It was bound to end in violence, sooner or later. I'm only surprised they lasted so long. That place was a sewer.'

'Hey, Mum, steady on,' protested Brian, embarrassed. Norma gave him a look.

I asked, 'Do you think that's why Andrew was killed? Because Raymond and he had been fighting over Harriet – *if* Raymond did kill Andrew?'

'Of course it was. And she's the one who made them all lie about it afterwards. The facts speak for themselves, don't they? I mean, does it make any sense for a woman not to identify the man who attacked her? It wasn't like he was wearing a mask or anything. No one gets that close in broad daylight and then can't pick the man out at an identity parade.'

I agreed that it did seem weird. Norma went on, 'My guess is she just couldn't be bothered with the identity parade. She only ever thought of her own pleasures. I was glad to see the back of her. Australia's welcome to her – that's where they used to ship all the rejects isn't it? She should be right at home.'

'Mum—'

But Norma was past reason. Her face had flushed to a dull purple. I'd never seen her so agitated before. 'She was probably thrilled with all the upset. I bet the evil bitch got a kick out of seeing two men fight over her. It makes me sick. Pity she wasn't the one to end up with a knife in her guts. If you want my opinion, she's the one who ought to have been on trial for Forester's death. Tucker may have had the knife in his hand, but if there's any justice in this world she'll suffer for it one day.'

I was amazed. Norma was beside herself with bitterness. I remembered what Gus had said about Brian's father hanging round Grays Orchard and making a nuisance of himself: it was easy to imagine how Norma, whom no one could ever have described as glamorous, must have hated his fascination with the young bohemians. As she hated them now in memory. Flecks of spittle appeared at the corners of her mouth.

Brian shifted uncomfortably in his chair and said, 'Easy does it, Mum.'

She glared at him. 'I speak as I find,' she said, her voice like flint.

I said, 'Harriet's not having an easy time right now. Her husband came to see us and apparently she's really ill. She's got cancer. He said the doctors are talking about months, not years.'

'Is that true?' Norma turned to me. She was frowning, her natural sympathy for someone in distress battling with the longing for vengeance. Then she said, 'Illness is a strange business. I've heard stuff on the radio about how the mind affects the body.'

'What do you mean?' I asked.

'Sometimes people's bodies turn on them because of their bad actions in the past. They get eaten away inside.'

'Mum, that's witchdoctor stuff,' said Brian firmly. And then, 'I don't know about you two, but I've got a house to clean up.'

Later, when Norma had gone home and Brian and I were packing up, I said, 'I've never seen your mother like that before. Why's she still so angry about it all?'

He looked at me as though I was missing an obvious clue, then he sighed and said, 'You can't blame her. The Grays Orchard murder was a turning point for her and Dad. He'd always been a heavy drinker, but it only became a real problem after Forester died. It pretty well destroyed him, and their marriage too.'

'I don't see the connection.'

'Don't you remember, Carol? Gus mentioned it the night Jenny turned up at your place. Dad used to go up to Grays a lot and he was one of the prime suspects.'

I stared at him. His green eyes were flecked with gold and he was smiling, but it was a hurt smile. Brian had grown up knowing his father was the town drunk and a one-time murder suspect as well. Given the way adult gossip translates into playground bullying, I could imagine where his qualities of endurance and strength had been forged. We'd worked together for years, but there were sides to him I'd never bothered to find out about. I knew instinctively he was holding something back, though whether it was his family or me he wanted to protect I couldn't tell.

I said, 'I thought those interviews were just routine.'

'One might have been. Dad was interviewed five times. And when the whole business was over and Harriet had disappeared to Australia and Gus was in New York and Tucker had gone to Spain, it was Mum and Dad who had to stick it out in Sturford. Mud sticks, Carol.'

Mud sticks. I should know the truth of that one because mud was sticking to me right now. I felt bogged down in a hopeless mess which had begun when I was still a child. Worst of all, that mess was the reason my marriage was crumbling round me. I couldn't talk to Gus, but I had to act, do something. I remembered the terrible silences of my parents' marriage. 'Least said, soonest mended' had always been my father's motto, and I believed him until the day I found him sitting at the kitchen table weeping with that note in his hand, and all my mother's possessions packed up and gone.

The problems had begun with Jenny, and they'd got worse when Gus heard I'd been in touch with Katie's son. Maybe it was already too late to patch things up with Gus, though I wasn't about to give up on that one, but my ignorance tormented me, the sense that my life was being knocked off course by a mystery I had no way of unravelling. Jenny and Katie had both headed off to the Heirs of Akasha. Was that where the answers lay?

I said, 'Brian, can you manage on your own for a few days? I thought I might go away for the weekend.'

'Good idea. I was going to tell you to take a holiday soon, anyway. Where are you planning to go?'

'Somewhere by the sea would be nice. I thought perhaps Cornwall.'

Chapter 9

Tim and I travelled down to Cornwall on the same train but we were in separate carriages and avoided all contact. I passed him a couple of times when I went along to the buffet car; he'd bought a paperback at Paddington, but even after nearly four hours on the train he'd hardly read a single page. Each time I saw him he was gazing out of the window, his forehead creased by that painful frown. My heart went out to him: I knew his suitcase was weighed down with presents for Davy.

It was early September before I'd been able to book a place on one of the group's introductory weekends and the delay was frustrating. Gus and I were existing in the same house like two strangers. I took to staying late at work – anything to put off going back to Grays, which no longer felt like home. Also, when the office was empty I could get in touch with Tim and make the necessary arrangements for the weekend. Since Gus wasn't to know my destination, I thought of letting Brian into the secret, but in the end I decided not to. Instead I gave Tim Brian's name and phone number in case of an emergency. Just what might constitute an emergency I didn't like to think, but having seen the strong-arm tactics the group had employed during a public meeting in the middle of London, I didn't want to take any chances.

At the memory, there was a fluttery feeling of nerves just below my ribs. I touched my mobile phone, which was tucked into the pocket of my linen jacket: it was going to be my only contact with the real world. I touched it a lot during that long journey.

I got out at Redruth. Tim had planned every stage of the weekend in meticulous detail, and he was going on to the next stop, where a hired car would be waiting for him. As the train moved off I caught sight of him looking at me through the train window. For a moment I felt over-whelmed by his hopes. Then I squared my shoulders, picked up my suitcase and marched firmly out of the station. I had a lot at stake this weekend, too.

The taxi drivers were leaning against their cars, chatting to each other in the warm September sun.

'The Atlantic Castle,' I said, adding the name of the village near the hotel.

The taxi driver rolled his eyes. 'Been there before, have you?' he asked, putting my suitcase in the boot.

'It's my first time.'

'You're in for fun and games, then.' His voice had a Cornish lilt to it.

'Why do you say that?' I got into the passenger seat as he eased his girth behind the steering wheel.

'Not that I've got anything against them, mind you. Live and let live, and they pay their way, same as the rest. But you know what they say, Cornwall is like a Christmas stocking, all the nuts get shaken down into the toe.' He laughed cheerfully at his own joke. I got the feeling he'd told it many times before.

All the nuts . . . it was not reassuring.

The light changed as we got closer to the hotel; it was brighter, more luminous. When I remarked on this, the driver said, 'It's having the sea all round that does it. Reflected light. That's why you get so many painters round here.' He chuckled and added, 'And nuts.'

We were driving through narrow lanes with steep banks on either side. The driver explained they were called hedges, but that Cornish hedges weren't really hedges at all, they were walls with plants growing over them, but I wasn't really listening. I was struggling against increasing panic. Supposing the Heirs of Akasha guessed I wasn't a genuine Quester? And supposing they turned on me the way they'd turned on Tim? What if they didn't like me spying on them and decided to silence me?

Any time I felt like chickening out, I had only to remember the expression on Gus's face when I was preparing to leave that morning and I was instantly determined to see this through. For once his mask had slipped: there'd been relief that I was leaving, if only for a few days, so he'd have a respite from the strain of our hopeless marriage; but there'd been fear as well. Why fear? Was he afraid I wouldn't come back? But most of all there was despair, that everything we'd built together was falling apart and he was powerless to prevent it. If he'd spoken one word of encouragement, I'd have stayed, but he didn't.

Well, he might have given up, but I hadn't. Not yet.

'Getting cold feet?' asked the driver.

I grinned. 'Are you a mind-reader?'

'No, I leave that to this lot. There it is now.'

The roof of the Atlantic Castle Hotel was visible from half a mile away. Set on the edge of a valley with steep cliffs rising up on either side and the sea beyond, it looked like any large Victorian seaside hotel. However, as soon as I'd paid the driver, picked up my suitcase and gone into the lobby, I realised that inside it was very, very different.

For one thing, it was so busy. There were half a dozen people gathered round the reception desk, poring over lists; another group was clustered round the notice board; two people were running down the stairs with surfboards under their arms and from every room came the chatter of animated voices. I'd never been to boarding school, but if I had I'm sure arriving on the first day of term would have felt just like this.

I joined the group at the reception desk and eventually a harassed-looking woman found my name on one of her lists. 'Ah yes, Carol Brewster. Here you are. Introductory weekend retreat, Category B. Sorry it's such a scrum this afternoon but we've got two courses starting at once. I told management there'd be chaos, but no one ever listens. You're in Room 11 in the Nirvana wing with Elaine. She'll be your Chosen Guide for the weekend. Elaine!' she called piercingly over the hubbub, and a woman detached herself from the group round the notice board.

She walked over, smiling warmly. 'Hi, there,' she said. 'You must be Carol. I'm Elaine. I'll show you to our room.'

'We're sharing?' I'd been counting on a private room so I could keep in touch with Tim. 'I don't mind paying the extra for a room to myself.'

Elaine didn't look the least bit offended by my reluctance to share a room with her, but then she didn't look as if she was easily offended. She was about twenty, with a moon-shaped face and lanky brown hair. 'Private rooms aren't allowed, I'm afraid,' she said cheerfully as we set off up the stairs. 'You see, communal living is a key element in the programme and the Questers have to be accompanied by a Chosen Guide at all times. Pilgrims and Seekers all live in dormitories – well, here we call them long houses like the North American Indians do – so being just two to a room is a major concession, because Questers aren't used to sharing.'

She led the way down a long passage, through a connecting door and into a modern annex. Each time we met someone Elaine greeted them with the same bland 'Hi there.'

'Do you know everyone here?' I asked eventually.

'That depends what you mean,' she told me. 'We're all here for a single purpose, to seek enlightenment and make a bridge beyond the Watershed. So everyone here is my brother or sister. Hi there.' Another person was emerging from one of the rooms.

'Does that include me?' I asked with a smile.

'Oh, you most of all. After all, I'm your Chosen Guide while you're here. If there are any questions you want to ask, fire away.'

I thought for a while. 'How many people are here?'

'It's hard to keep track. There must be at least two dozen in the different groups that are starting today, and about thirty on longer courses. Then there are all the Pilgrims and Seekers, say another fifty or sixty of us. And that's just in the main building. I guess if you add in all the people in the New House and the Farm, it must be nearly two hundred altogether.'

I was beginning to think finding Katie and Jenny might be harder than I'd expected. 'How do you keep track of everyone?'

She looked puzzled. 'Well, I don't,' she said. 'Not personally. I'm just a First-level Pilgrim.'

'What does that mean?'

'Kitchen and household duties mostly. You're the first Quester I've had. I hope you don't ask too many difficult questions.' She grinned, showing her pink gums. 'Here we are, Room eleven.' She opened the door to a spartan room with two iron bedsteads and a small washbasin. 'You choose the bed you want.'

'Don't you usually sleep here?'

'Oh no, I've only moved in for the weekend, to look after you. Normally I'm in the Valhalla women's long house. That's in the old west wing.'

'I'll take the bed by the window.'

'Fine.' She plumped herself down on the other bed, then sprang up again. 'Oh, I nearly forgot. Here's your timetable for the weekend. The things with stars next to them are recommended for Second-level Questers.'

'Is that what I am?'

'Yes.'

'What about First Level?'

'That's going to a public meeting. I expect you'd like ten minutes to sort yourself out. Tea's in the dining room between four and five, so there's half an hour left. I'll wait for you down there.'

'Thanks. Oh, Elaine, I do have one question. Is there anyone here called Katie?' I hadn't meant to ask about her directly but Elaine seemed harmless enough, and if there were two hundred people here I could easily go the whole weekend without bumping into her. It would be too risky to ask about Jenny at the same time: I'd have to leave that till later.

Her face lit up. 'Katie? Do you know her?'

'No, but an old friend of hers asked me to look her out. He said she'd joined the group a few months ago.'

'Longer than that. Katie's one of my best mates. She's been on an AquaRetreat for the past month, but she finished yesterday. I expect she's in the dining room. I'll introduce you.'

'Thanks.' I hadn't expected it to be so easy. I was so relieved it didn't occur to me to wonder why Katie, who must be nearly fifty, had joined up with the youthful Elaine.

'Anything else you want to know, just ask.' And with a

cheery grin, Elaine shut the door behind her.

So far, so good. In ten minutes I was going to be introduced to Katie. In my role of earnest Quester it should be easy enough to get talking to her. If I got the feeling she was having second thoughts about joining the group, I could find a way to help her leave. If, as seemed more likely, she'd been brainwashed at a time when grief had made her vulnerable, my plan was to lure her off the premises with me, even if it was only for a walk along the coastal path. After that, it was up to Tim. He was adamant that if he could talk to her face to face he'd have no problems persuading her to go home again with Davy: he said she'd always been easily persuaded, that's what had made her such easy pickings in the first place.

Suddenly, I was excited. I realised that, ever since Gus's and my trip to Bath, Katie had been on my mind. Until then I'd been secure enough not to bother much with the woman he'd loved when he was painting his most famous pictures. Now, however, it was different. Now I was curious.

Jenny was more of a problem. Clearly, she needed help, too, but I'd have to be careful how I made contact with her. For one thing, she was the only person likely to question my motives and to link me to Gus Ridley. I'd have to give her an explanation that stayed as close as possible to the facts: that Gus and I hadn't been getting along too well; that I'd heard about Raymond's group and thought it sounded interesting so I'd decided to give a weekend workshop a try. I had a hunch she'd try to avoid me. She was hardly going to welcome a reminder of what she'd done to Gus, and she'd expect me to be furious with her.

One thing at a time, I told myself: first Katie, then Jenny.

Since privacy was at a premium at the Atlantic Castle, I decided to make the most of this opportunity and phone Tim right away: he'd be pleased to know Katie was still in

Cornwall. I pulled the mobile out of my pocket and turned it on.

No signal.

I pressed all the buttons, checked the batteries, tried again. Still no signal. Unease shivered through me. What was the problem? It had been working perfectly when I spoke to Tim on the way to Paddington that morning. Had it broken? Or did the group employ sophisticated jamming devices to make sure both residents and guests were cut off from the outside world?

I went to the window and looked out. The sun had vanished behind a high bank of cloud. Beyond the sloping lawns and the evergreen hedge along the boundary, the sea looked cold and threatening, as though a storm was brewing. I tried my phone one last time, but without success, then made my way back down the long corridor, out of the Nirvana annex and into the main part of the building. A low roar of voices guided me to the dining room.

Four long tables stretched the length of the room. There must have been well over a hundred people there. Tea was obviously an informal meal and everyone was tucking in with hearty appetites. I hesitated for a few moments in the doorway, scanning the sea of people for a familiar face, then saw Elaine waving vigorously to me from the table nearest the window. I waved back and threaded my way through the crowded room to join her. She was surrounded by a group of about her own age, twenty or so, and they all greeted me warmly.

'This is Carol, everyone. This is her first Quester weekend.'

A chorus of 'Hi, Carol', and Elaine said, 'I won't bother telling you everyone's name because you'll only forget. But they're all One LPs like me – that's First-level Pilgrims – and they can help you any way you like.'

'Thanks.'

'Oh yeah,' said Elaine. 'I nearly forgot. And this is Katie.'

I felt a leap of excitement, then my heart sank. The girl sitting next to me was far too young. She had dark hair and buck teeth. I cursed myself for my stupidity: of course among so many people there was sure to be more than one Katie.

'Hi, Carol,' said the wrong Katie, 'Elaine says you know a friend of mine.'

'Sorry,' I said. 'The Katie I'm looking for is more than twice your age.'

The wrong Katie pulled a face. 'I thought it was a mistake. I never had any friends until I came here.' Everyone laughed and said of course she had loads of friends and Elaine gave her a warm hug, but actually the wrong Katie did look socially inept. I wondered how much of this upbeat friendliness was for my benefit.

'Tea?' Elaine poured me a large mug. 'And these are laver bread scones. Laver bread is one of our staples. You get used to it after a while.'

The wrong Katie pulled a face. 'I don't,' she said.

Elaine started to explain about the group's efforts to eat as much as possible from the sea 'so we're adapted when the time comes'. She said, 'Last week they had another go at seaweed tea – ugh, it was disgusting.'

'Not as bad as the first lot,' said a bronzed lad with massive shoulders and spacey eyes.

To my relief the liquid I was drinking tasted perfectly normal. I said, 'Is there a ban on mobile phones here? Mine won't work.'

They laughed. 'It's the cliff. Sometimes you can get a signal if you go up on the cliff path. North is better than south.'

'It's an electronic shadow,' explained the spacey youth.

'Damn,' I said. 'I promised I'd phone someone today.'

'Don't worry,' said Elaine. 'There's a public phone in the hall. There's always a queue a mile long but I'll pull Quester Guide status and you can jump the queue. If we go along now there'll be time for you to make your call before the Induction Session.'

'The what?'

'Induction. It's the first thing on your programme.'

'Oh yes, of course.' Guiltily I pulled the timetable out of my pocket. I wasn't going to be a very convincing Second-level Quester if I didn't even bother to check the timetable. The sheet of paper Elaine had given me was alarmingly full and none of it, apart from Induction at five o'clock on Friday, made much sense. I forced myself to say brightly, 'Wow, this looks fascinating.'

There was a chorus of agreement.

'Life-changing,' said the wrong Katie.

'You'll have a great time,' said the youth.

'I know,' said Elaine. 'I'm nearly as excited as you are.'

Suddenly I got the feeling all this was being orchestrated to convince me what a great place this was. Pinning what I hoped was a look of mindless enthusiasm on my face I said, 'I can hardly wait to start.'

'We'd better get a move on, then,' said Elaine, 'especially if you want to make that phone call.'

'It's not that urgent.' I didn't want to talk to Tim in the middle of a crowded hall with Elaine listening to every word, but she was adamant.

'Come on,' she said, 'if you've finished your tea. There's just time.'

There were about half a dozen people waiting to use the solitary phone in the hall but Elaine must have been itching to exert her new authority as Quester Guide. 'Second-level Quester needs to make urgent phone call!' she trumpeted and they made way for me without a murmur. I dialled Tim's mobile.

'Carol?' The eagerness in his voice was painful.

'Hello, Mother!' I shouted, and I was rewarded with a startled 'What?'

'Hello, Mother, can you hear me?' Silence. 'It's Carol. I've arrived safely. No need to worry about me. I can't talk long now because there's others waiting to use the phone. But I just wanted you to know that mobiles don't work here apparently. Mother.'

'*What?*'

'It's something to do with being in the shadow of the cliff,' I said brightly. 'I know, it's a bit technical for me, too, but there's no point ringing that other number I gave you. I'll be in touch again when I can.'

'What? Wait, don't hang up. Carol, listen.'

I pressed the receiver close to my ear, hoping no one could hear the urgent masculine voice of my 'mother'.

'What is it, Mother? I can't talk long.'

'Phone again tonight,' insisted Tim. 'I'll think of something. I'll work out a code.'

People were beginning to look at me strangely. I said, 'Okay, don't worry about it. I'll try to phone again later to make sure you're all right.'

I put the phone down firmly before Tim had a chance to reply. 'My mother,' I explained to the circle of watchful faces. 'She's rather deaf.'

'Oh, poor thing,' said Elaine. 'Come along then, Induction's in the Clock Hall. We don't want to be stuck at the back.'

'Certainly not,' I said, though stuck at the back sounded fine to me. I followed Elaine out through a side door and across a wide lawn to what looked like a converted barn about a hundred metres from the main building. As usual, everyone we passed was treated to the same jolly 'Hi there.'

As we entered the large doors at the side of the building, Elaine stepped aside and turned to see my reaction. She was gratified by my amazement. 'Terrific, isn't it?' she beamed.

'It's . . . amazing.'

The whole of the opposite wall had been covered by an enormous mural in breathtaking colours of intense jewel brightness: glowing emerald green, vibrant turquoise, deep magenta and crimson, all linked with gold, the brightest gold I'd ever seen. At first I couldn't make sense of it: the patterning and detail were too intricate. Then I realised that what I was looking at were two enormous wheels, the left-hand one considerably larger than the right, and each wheel was divided into segments. The two wheels just touched each other, their cogs meshing like the parts of an enormous machine. Every inch of space within and around the wheels was covered with a riot of design: animals and birds, strange-looking men with feathered headdresses, huge serpents and fish and extraordinary squirls which might have been hieroglyphs but were unlike anything I'd seen before. And then, to my astonishment, I realised it wasn't a mural at all, or at least most of it wasn't. It was a vast structure and there was a smaller wheel, connected to the two larger ones, and every piece was free-moving.

'What on earth is it?' I asked.

'That's the Akashic Clock,' Elaine told me with delight. 'There's one at each of our centres. Lowell makes them. He's an absolute genius and Alana has a whole team to help with the decoration.'

'But what's going on?' I asked.

Elaine looked at me blankly. Suddenly I panicked. Oh God, had I given myself away already? As a dedicated Quester, should I have known all about it? I said quickly, 'I mean, I've read about the Akashic Clock, but I've never seen one close to before. It's far more complicated than I expected.'

That seemed to satisfy her. She explained, 'Well, as you

SURFACE TENSION • 133

know, it's based on the Mayan calendar and their short and long clocks. But Lowell has adapted it to fit our modern Western chronology and he's made it so that glass tube on the right fills up with sand, just a few grains each day, like an egg timer but much slower. As it fills up we know how much of the countdown is left.'

That word again. 'Countdown?'

'Yes,' she said lightly. 'You know, till the end of the world.'

I shivered. For a while I'd been lulled into thinking this wasn't so very different from an ordinary hotel after all: then the casual way Elaine mentioned the end of the world reminded me of the lunacy at the heart of this place.

The hall was filling with people, most of them in pairs like us, each Quester accompanied by their Guide. As I took my seat near the front beside Elaine I wondered if her role was really to answer my questions and help out, or whether she had a more sinister purpose. Like spying.

While we waited for the Induction to begin, the contrast between normal and crazy continued: from outside came the sounds and smells of an ordinary summer evening by the sea – waves breaking in the distance, holidaymakers calling to each other across the garden, gulls wheeling and crying – but here we were solemnly sitting in rows waiting to be told about the end of the world.

I asked Elaine, 'Will there be any time for doing ordinary things this weekend? Like swimming or going for a walk?'

'It's absolutely up to you what you do with your time,' Elaine assured me, but in a way that was not convincing. 'If we go for a walk after Induction you can try your mobile from higher up. Most sorts work on the clifftop.'

'Yes, I might do that. But you needn't come with me. I don't want to be a nuisance.'

'No fear of that. If I wasn't looking after you I'd be back on kitchen duties.'

My heart sank. Shaking her off was going to be difficult. And I was still no nearer to making contact with Katie or Jenny.

'Tell me about the other centres,' I said. 'Are there more in this country?'

She shook her head. 'There's a new one in Mexico, but the biggest is in Spain. That's where it all began. It's a wonderful story. Palu came over from Spain and gave us a talk all about it in the summer. I wish you'd heard her, she was really inspiring.'

'Is she here now?'

'I don't think so.' Elaine looked vague. 'The Inner Circle come and go quite a lot. In fact there's a rumour, and I wasn't going to mention it until I knew for sure because I'd hate you to be disappointed, but someone who works at the New House said Ra himself had come over and might even lead an AquaMed workshop on Sunday.' She squeezed my arm in excitement. 'Can you imagine? AquaMed with Ra on your very first weekend!'

I tried to look suitably thrilled, and in fact I was curious at the prospect of seeing the man whom Gus had known as Raymond Tucker, even though I didn't hold out much hope of questioning him. A man who was regarded as a semi-divine being by his gullible followers wasn't likely to want to talk about his misspent youth at Grays Orchard, especially if he'd taken a vow of silence.

I said, 'Is there any way of finding out where people are?'

'Oh, you mean your friend Katie. Well, I suppose Bronwen must have a list somewhere. She's in charge of residency and transfers. You could always ask her.'

'Is it easy to travel between the centres?'

'In theory it is, but in practice it's not always that simple. They have to keep a balance, so of course once we've taken the Loyalty Oath we're sent wherever our skills are most needed. And then we have to earn points. I'm hoping to get a few this weekend, looking after you. My boyfriend's on construction duty in Spain and I'd really like to join him.'

Loyalty oaths, points . . . it was beginning to sound horribly complicated.

'Supposing I wanted to go to Spain?'

'Oh, there'd be no problem for you, so long as you paid and you were still a Quester. Oh good, it's Amber leading the Induction.'

A tiny woman with golden hair plaited into loops around her ears made her way to the front of the auditorium and a hush fell on the fifty or so people in the audience. She stood behind a podium which was shaped like a leaping dolphin.

'Good evening, Questers and Quester Guides.' Her voice was thin and high, tinkling like wind chimes. 'Welcome to the Atlantis Castle.' I thought I had misheard but she smiled and said, 'That's right. Atlantis. To the outside world it's got a "c" but now we can use its true name. The Heirs of Akasha are also the Heirs to the Kingdom of Atlantis, and this weekend will give you a brief taste of our life and our beliefs. It will also' – she smiled in a falsely disarming way – 'give us a chance to get to know you better and to find out how – and more importantly *if* – you can help us. Many will hear the call but few will be chosen when the final hour comes. We must all do our work in a spirit of trust. Even I cannot tell if I'll be one of the lucky ones when the final hour strikes,' and she looked meaningfully at the glass tube which was, I noticed with relief, only about ten per cent full of sand. 'None of us does. But we can all do our best to be prepared, physically, socially, intellectually and spiritually. These four strands run through everything that has been arranged for you this weekend.'

She held up the timetable. 'You will notice that each item is marked by either a P for physical, an S for social, an I for intellectual or a Sp for spiritual. We recommend that you aim for a balanced programme, choosing at least one from each category.'

She then started to go through the timetable. Elaine nudged me and I pulled the folded sheet of paper out dutifully and pretended to ponder with rapt attention the competing merits of a lecture entitled 'Atlantis: the Scientific Evidence Reviewed', and another talk on 'Super-sensory Perception in Interpreting the Akashic Record'. She warned us about the dangers of trying to assimilate too much too soon, which I didn't think was likely to be my problem. In fact, if there was some way of discovering for sure that neither Jenny nor Katie were in residence I might even try to leave early. Though I was intrigued by the prospect of seeing Ra who was once Raymond, the idea of a whole weekend with the relentlessly cheerful Elaine clamped to my side like a baby monkey was not appealing.

While Amber talked us through the events available during the weekend, my attention wandered. I tried to work out a plausible story to tell Bronwen-in-charge-of-residence when I went to find out where the others were. I had a feeling the higher-ranking members of the group might be more suspicious than Elaine.

The talk continued. After about ten minutes I realised it was happening again, that strange sensation I had had during the meeting at Ealing. Even though I knew it was all quite mad, Amber's talk was starting to make a weird kind of sense. One moment she was telling us not to take the hotel's towels to the beach, and the next she was going on about using Spirit Guides to reach a place of higher understanding and how we could learn to interpret something she called the Sacred Language for All Time. It didn't come as much of a surprise to learn that Ra the Acolyte was the only person with a complete grasp of this secret language, leaving everyone else dependent on him for knowledge of what was written in the Akashic Record.

SURFACE TENSION • 137

Suddenly I had a great pang of nostalgia for the days when I used to take Gus home the latest slogans from the Elim chapel outside Sturford: '*Give your worries to Jesus: He'll be up all night anyway.*' If only we'd been getting on the way we used to, how I could have made him laugh telling him about this weird place and its even weirder residents. But then, if we'd been getting on like we used to, I wouldn't be here.

'Whatever else you do this weekend,' Amber said, 'I strongly recommend that all Second-level Questers take part in tomorrow afternoon's Compatibility Assessment.' I looked dutifully at my timetable. Two o'clock. And there was an S next to it for Social. 'This is a chance for us to take a good look at each of you and see what your potential strengths are as members of a team. Anyone wishing to move on to the next stage will have to have done at least three Compatibility Assessments, so it's best to get one under your belt right away.'

'What's that about?' I whispered to Elaine.

'Oh, it's loads of fun,' she whispered back, adding not very helpfully, 'You'll love it.'

'And finally,' said Amber, 'we trust and believe that all Questers have joined us today in a spirit of genuine exploration. Naturally, you will have doubts and questions, but if anyone has come here this weekend under false pretences we strongly advise you, for your own sake, to leave at once.'

Was I imagining it, or was she looking directly at me as she spoke?

'Why's she so suspicious?' I asked Elaine.

'Sometimes newspaper people try to infiltrate our centres. And there's been trouble with people who call themselves cult-busters. We had a couple of them in the spring.'

'What happened to them?'

'Oh, the Inner Circle sussed them out. They always suss out fakes. I think they know from the Akashic Record, or maybe it's because of their auras. Just as well, really.'

I touched my mobile anxiously, then remembered it was useless here.

'Then what?' I asked.

Elaine looked vague. 'I don't know exactly. But they won't be back here in a hurry, that's for sure.'

Amber was winding up. 'It's a lovely evening,' she said. 'Please relax and enjoy yourselves before supper. As you go out you'll be given a fact sheet which covers all the points I've raised. And your Chosen Guide will be able to answer any questions you may have.'

There was a clatter of chairs as everyone stood up and began moving towards the door. Outside the sun had broken through again and the air smelled salty and sweet.

'Let's walk down to the beach,' I said to Elaine.

'Sure. Don't forget your fact sheet.'

I reached out automatically to the middle-aged woman who was standing in the doorway with a fixed social smile pinned to her face. 'So glad you enjoyed the talk. Do have a fact sheet,' she said in a clipped, upper-class voice to each person as they left the building.

'Thanks,' I said.

Then I stopped. I was looking into a pair of intensely blue, very beautiful eyes and my heart skipped a beat. The resemblance to Tim was uncanny.

It was the real Katie.

Chapter 10

That night, as I lay sleepless in the spartan room I shared with Elaine (who snored), the wind grew stronger. The window rattled in its frame and beyond the lawns and the evergreen hedge the waves boomed against the rocks.

My brain refused to shut down. I thought about Gus, alone at Grays – was he missing me, or was he glad I'd gone? – and about Tim, who was probably sleepless too. I could imagine him waiting in an agony of suspense in the small guest house three miles away. We'd talked again on the public phone after the evening session – or rather, once I'd told my 'mother' the old friend was here but we hadn't managed to chat yet, he'd done all the talking. He gave me detailed instructions for future contact and listed the places he'd be able to get to without being intercepted by the group's security.

I also thought about Jenny. I hadn't seen her yet, though during the evening session, which was an illustrated talk about the group's centres in Mexico and Spain, I'd seen a slide of someone standing in the middle of an Andalucian vegetable patch. She might possibly have been Jenny, but the slide was out of focus making it impossible to say for sure.

But most of all, as I lay sleepless and listened to the wind and the waves, I thought about Katie.

She was still beautiful, no doubt about it. She had the finely chiselled bone structure that seems to improve with age; clear blue eyes which she had passed on to her son, and an air of grace, impossible to pin down. Maybe it was the supreme confidence of the beautiful, the serenity of people whose path through life has been smoothed in advance by their aura of charm.

I know what it is to turn heads. I've seen people's eyes light up when I come into a room, but whatever I've got, Katie had it in spades.

Gone for ever was my mental image of a dowdy little old lady, adrift and friendless in a harsh world. Katie was as far from being a female equivalent of Lionel, the retired gentlemen's outfitter, as possible. Nor did she have anything in common with the weirdos and losers who'd gathered at Ealing. What on earth was she doing here?

Now I was genuinely curious to find out. Even without Tim's burning need to be reunited with his son, I wanted to talk to her and discover what had drawn her to the group.

That first evening, I didn't have a chance. She handed me her sheet of paper, her serene gaze met mine for an instant, then she turned to the person behind me. 'So glad you enjoyed the talk. Do have a fact sheet.'

I moved out into the salty evening air.

'I think that was her,' I said to Elaine. 'Katie, the friend I was talking about.'

'Really?' Elaine was impressed. 'She lives at the New House with the Inner Circle. Her name is Lumina now. There's half an hour before supper. Shall we go down to the beach?'

For the rest of that first evening, in between trying to act like a genuine Second-level Quester, I kept a look-out for Katie, but she didn't appear at supper, nor at the slide show that followed. Elaine explained she spent most of her time at the New House: the hotel was for visitors like me and for Pilgrims and First-level Seekers.

I was still wondering how to make sure our paths crossed again when I fell asleep. A gentle rain had started to fall.

It was still raining the next morning, which was appropriate because the first session was entitled 'Surviving the Flood' (P: physical) and was about the experiments the group was carrying out to create structures in which groups of people could survive for a long time living on the sea bed. 'Noah built his ark,' explained a bearded boffin called Dr Protus, 'but such a structure on the surface of the water would be reduced to matchsticks in the mighty cataclysm caused by the switch in the earth's magnetic poles. The sea bed alone will be a haven of relative calm beneath the tides and storms at the Watershed. Therefore the only chance of survival for those who wish to carry life forward into the next era will be life underwater.' He showed us computerised graphics of people living in what looked like enormous underwater bubbles. Then he got sidetracked into a lot of technical detail about wave energy and the lessons to be learned from the Mir space station. And all the time the rain fell steadily against the windows of the lecture hall and sand trickled slowly into the glass tube at the side of the Akashic Clock.

It continued to rain during our second session, which was an introduction to meditation. My memory of it is somewhat hazy because the combined effect of a sleepless night, the rain drumming on the window and the gentle voice of our meditation guide telling us to tighten and relax each muscle in our body in turn while imagining our outbreath flowing through a point between our eyebrows as we lay in rows on the soft floor of the meditation room was definitely soporific and I was awoken suddenly by the sound of my own bubbling breath.

'Poor you,' Elaine commiserated as we ate lunch. 'Looks like it's going to stay wet for Compatibility Assessment.'

'Don't you have to shadow me on that one, too?'

'No, you're on your own this afternoon. It's their chance to see how you operate under pressure, so Chosen Guides would be in the way. I'll meet you at tea and you can tell me how you got on.'

'Maybe I'll give it a miss. It's not compulsory.'

Elaine looked worried. 'It's not *exactly* compulsory, but I'm supposed to encourage you to do it. There aren't that many opportunities for Compatibility Assessment and you don't want a bottleneck later on, do you?'

I was about to say I was prepared to risk it when I caught sight of a woman sitting at the table next to ours. Her eyes were fixed on my face, as though she was appraising me. It was the woman who'd thrown Tim out of the public meeting. She was still wearing a lot of silver jewellery, this time with a tight-fitting zipped black top. When our eyes met, she didn't look away at once. There was a little smile on her face, but it wasn't a friendly smile. Very deliberately, she gathered up her lunch things and carried them to the side of the room to be stacked. She was letting me know I was being watched.

'Who's that?' I asked Elaine.

'Karnak. She's deputy head of security.'

Had Karnak guessed I wasn't a genuine Quester? It was hard to see how I'd given myself away, but Elaine was certain they could always sniff out impostors. It seemed foolish to draw attention to myself by refusing a session as crucial as Compatibility Assessment.

I said nonchalantly, 'I guess I'll give it a shot, then.'

'Good.' Elaine grinned. 'I'd have been in trouble otherwise.'

Our timetables informed us we had to meet for Compatibility Assessment at the utility area at the back of the hotel. There we were divided into five groups of eight and each group was assigned to a team leader. Ours was a woman built like a small tank, with a hennaed crewcut and an uncompromising expression. She told us her name but it was unpronounceable and she suggested we call her Bill. She'd arrived pushing a wheelchair which she now sat in, explaining that for the duration of the exercise we were to assume she was paralysed from the waist down. She then counted us all again and said crossly that we were one team member short and we'd have to wait.

It was still raining steadily. We stood in the shelter of an open-sided log shed. Water cascaded off the roof and, even though we were under cover, the air was saturated with moisture and the temperature had plummeted. Apart from Bill, who was encased from head to toe in waterproofs, none of us was dressed for the weather. I was wearing practically everything I'd packed and still I was cold.

The other groups had all set off into the rain. Bill looked at her watch. 'Five minutes and we'll start anyway.'

I was stamping my feet to keep warm. 'I thought Cornwall was supposed to be sunny,' I said.

Bill flashed me a quick smile. 'Whoever told you that was lying. Ah, here we are.'

A well-wrapped figure was stepping carefully through the puddles. 'Sorree-ee. Am I late?' My heart skipped with excitement. It was Katie.

'For God's sake, Lumina,' said Bill crossly. 'Can't you ever be on time?'

'It simply was not my fault,' Katie began.

But Bill interrupted her. 'For God's sake, don't bother explaining. We'll waste even longer. Now, if a couple of you hefty lads would give me a push, we'll head for the pass.'

We all trooped out into the rain and down the drive, which led away from the sea towards the road. When we'd almost reached the perimeter hedge we struck off to the right, across an open field. I was trying to find a way to fall in with Katie, but a gangling man called Herman was determined to monopolise my attention.

'All this stuff is so mind-bending,' he told me. 'I mean, the writing's been on the wall for years. Why can't people wake up and see what's happening?'

Katie was ahead of me, chatting with Bill and generally getting in the way of the two young men who were manoeuvring the wheelchair across the field. Unlike the rest of us, she was perfectly dressed for the occasion: she wore neat brown hiking boots with flecked socks, stretch cord trousers and a smart waxed jacket. At her neck was a silk scarf, and a snug sheepskin hat was pulled down over her ears. Everyone else trudged gloomily through the rain, but she had a jaunty spring in her stride and seemed to be enjoying herself.

At the far end of the field we joined a cinder track that ran parallel with the road about half a mile from the sea. When the track started to wind steeply up hill, one of the chair-pushers turned to Herman and told him it was time he took a turn.

'But I've got a bad back,' Herman protested.

'Tough,' said the chairperson, whose name was Ryan. 'All that laver bread's upset my stomach. I need to find a bush.'

Herman gave in with a bad grace. Freed from his attention, I was able to fall in beside Katie as we crossed the brow of the next hill.

'Hi there,' I said, assuming Elaine's method of address was the correct one. 'I'm Carol.'

'Hello, Carol.' She smiled at me kindly and I felt a tingle of excitement. 'I'm Ka—' Frowning, she corrected herself. 'I'm Lumina.'

'Have you done a Compatibility Assessment before?'

'Oh yes, they're riveting.'

'What's the form?'

'That depends. We have to work as a team and make something or solve a problem. It's tremendously character-building.'

I looked at her sharply to see if she was being ironic, but she seemed sincere. 'Does your character need building?' I asked lightly.

'Oh, well, every little helps, I suppose.'

'What did you do last time?'

'The challenge was to make a boat out of oil drums,' she said, in her fluting, schoolgirl voice. 'I suppose you'd call it a raft, really. But the barrels kept floating off and no one could steer it and then it sank. We were all absolutely soaked. Two of the boys started punching each other and one woman nearly drowned. Our team leader said we were the worst group he'd ever had to work with.' She said this as though it were a compliment.

'Sounds grim,' I said.

'Oh well,' she flashed me a smile. 'That's compatibility for you.'

I didn't know how to reply to this, so I said, 'Lumina's an unusual name.'

'Yes, isn't it? I used to be called Katie but when we take the Oath of Loyalty Raymond – I mean Ra – gives us our Akashic name. Apparently it's been sitting there on the good old record all this time but no one ever knew how to read it properly until he came along. Lumina means light, apparently. In Akashic.'

'Is Akashic a language?'

'Well, yes, I suppose it must be, otherwise how could Ra read it? Actually, I don't know if he really does read it. I think maybe it's more of an interpretation. Ra's always been frightfully intuitive.'

Katie had a confiding, intimate way of talking, even to me, someone she'd met only a few moments before. Already I'd forgotten all the reasons why I was supposed to be talking to her, in the simple enjoyment of her company. She was one of those rare people, I realised, who radiates uncomplicated pleasure.

'I didn't know Akashic was a language,' I said. 'I thought it was a clock.'

'Well, it's a bit of both, I suppose.' She thought for a while, then said triumphantly, 'You know, like speaking English and having English summer time as well.'

'The clock looks very complicated. I don't really understand how it works.'

'Oh, it's very simple once you get the hang of it.'

'Can you explain?'

'Of course. You see, there's a long clock and then there's a short clock.' She paused for a moment, uncertain how to go on, then continued in a confidential tone, 'Actually, when you look at them it's obvious they're both round, but that's not the point. They each tell the time, but in a different way, and when you add them together you know when the world is going to end. Then you have to remember that every now and then you have a vague year just to keep everything in balance.' She threw up her hands in a gesture of delight. 'You don't need to tell *me* about vague years. I've had so many of those in the past I must be perfectly balanced by now.'

I burst out laughing. It was quite obvious Katie hadn't got a clue about the intricacies of the Akashic clock, any more than I had, but her ignorance didn't worry her in the least.

'Did Ra invent the clock as well?'

'Oh no, it was someone called Maya.'

John, an American walking in front of us, turned round with a puzzled look on his face. 'But Lumina, the Maya were an ancient South American people,' he said. 'The Akashic clock is based on their method of reckoning time.'

'That's what I said,' said Katie.

'But I thought—'

'Obviously,' said Katie, 'it's frightfully important to know when the world is going to end, but apart from that the Akashic clock does have its drawbacks. For one thing, it's huge, which makes it terribly inconvenient. Those poor people must have been so relieved when we turned up and gave them a proper clock. And watches. Just think of it.'

'Relieved?' John was astonished. 'But, Lumina, whole civilisations were wiped out when the Europeans invaded South America. The destruction of the Mayan sacred texts was the worst act of cultural vandalism of all time.'

'Oh yes, I do agree,' said Katie earnestly. 'I never throw books away, just too precious. Though I do sometimes give old paperbacks to charity shops. I expect the Europeans couldn't make head or tail of all those squiggles. It would have been different if they'd had proper writing. Still,' she added inconsequentially, 'thank heavens for salsa.'

I smiled, forgetting I was cold and wet and my shoes had been ruined by the mud. The imagined Katie had been a looming figure in my inner world all through my marriage and there'd always been an air of tragic mystery surrounding her: she was the beautiful muse who'd been the great love of Gus's life, loved and then lost. Now I was having to revise all my opinions: I'd never met anyone less suited to being a tragic heroine. Still, it was easy to understand why Tim felt so protective towards her: after only five minutes in her company I was beginning to feel protective too.

'Here we are,' announced Bill. 'Don't push me any further or you'll pitch me into the ravine.'

We had reached a patch of headland covered in heather and low shrubs. Just ahead of us was a steep-sided gully with a stream bubbling over stones about twenty metres below. Someone had already laid several rounded lengths of wood in a neat pile beside a coil of rope and half a dozen pulleys.

'Right then, you lucky Questers,' said Bill, 'your job is to get me across to the other side, preferably in one piece. Get it wrong and I'll most likely break my neck.'

There was a moment's silence, then Katie said brightly, 'Well, this *is* going to be interesting.' She went over to the pile of equipment and spun a wheel on one of the pulleys. 'All in proper working order, I'm glad to see.'

Ryan frowned. 'I think—' he began, and we all looked at him expectantly. He shook his head. 'Excuse me. Bloody laver bread.' And he set off in search of a discreet outcrop of rock.

Jim and Herman stepped over to the pile. 'This looks fairly straightforward,' said Herman. 'We'll have to lay the poles across the ravine, attach the wheelchair underneath by means of the ropes and pulleys, and hey presto, you'll be across in no time, Bill.'

Bill smiled a sphinx-like smile. I said, 'The poles are too short to reach across. Your plan won't work.'

'Of course it will,' said Herman. 'Why would they give us short poles?'

I've seen enough roof joists put across enough half-built buildings to be a good judge of distance. 'They're shy about two metres,' I told him.

He gave me a pitying smile. 'I'll put one across. You'll see.'

'Be careful you don't end up dropping it in the ravine,' I said. 'Why not try a triangular structure? After all, they've given us several poles.'

'That's for extra strength. Look, I'll show you.' He went to lift one of the poles.

'Here,' said Katie, 'I can give you a hand.'

'That's all right.' Obviously Herman was determined to score top marks in Compatibility Assessment. 'I can manage better on my own.' He bent down to pick up one of the poles, struggling to lift it in the middle. 'All I have to do is lay this across at the narrowest point . . .'

He hoisted the pole on to his shoulder. Katie, still eager to help, went to hold the back end of the pole, but Herman turned towards me, swinging it out of her reach. 'Now we need to find the narrowest point of the gully,' he puffed and turned back the other way.

'Watch out!' I called, but it was too late. The rear of the pole swung round in a wide arc and clipped Katie on the head. She sat down in the heather with a little exclamation of surprise.

I ran over. 'Are you all right?'

Her blue eyes looked up at me from under the dripping brim of her hat. She looked puzzled. 'I think so,' she said, reaching her hand up. I grasped it and pulled her to her feet.

'Sorry about that,' said Herman, still staggering about by the edge of the gully with the pole on his shoulder as he tried to find the shortest gap.

Katie looked disoriented. 'That was a nasty crack,' I said. 'It's starting to swell already. Someone ought to look at it. I'll go back to the hotel if you like and get them to send a Land-Rover.'

'Oh no, I'm sure I can walk.'

'I'll walk with you, then.'

Bill was watching our exchange impassively. I turned to the others. 'I'm sorry to leave you in the middle of it all like this, but Katie needs looking after.'

'That's okay,' said John, who had gone to help Herman with the first pole. 'We can manage this just fine.'

'Come on, then.' I linked my arm through Katie's and she smiled at me gratefully. 'Let's get you back to the hotel.'

As we set off back the way we'd come I heard a shout and a crash and a volley of curses. I smiled. Herman and John had pitched the first pole into the gulley. One way and another, Compatibility Assessment was turning out better than expected.

We walked about a quarter of a mile arm in arm without talking much. She was still dazed. The rain was easing to a fine drizzle, but by now I was wet through and it didn't make much difference. Once we were out of sight of the others and on a high piece of ground I said, 'That laver bread's got to me now too. Do you mind waiting while I go behind that bush?'

'Take your time. It'll give me a chance to catch my breath.'

She sat down on a boulder while I went and crouched down behind a bush and pulled out my mobile phone. The signal came on.

'Tim?'

'Yes?' He'd heard the eagerness in my voice. Suddenly my heart was beating rapidly.

'I'm with Katie and we're walking back towards the hotel from the south. We're on the track just inside the boundary. I'll try and get her to walk on the road but you should be able to get across without being seen. Can you get here in ten minutes?'

'Give me fifteen,' he said. 'I'm heading out to my car.'

When I got back, Katie was still sitting on her boulder. She smiled up at me. 'Poor you – all that laver bread. Are you better now?'

'Yes, thanks, but we can rest here a bit longer if you like.'

'How sweet of you. But you're absolutely sodden and I

bet you're longing to get back in the dry. Actually, my head's fine now. This is a brilliant idea of yours, much better than watching all those big boys prancing around and doing their silly Tarzan thing. It was exactly the same with the raft. Men always get so bossy, don't they, and have to take charge. And you told them it was too short. Clever you.'

We were walking along the cinder track just inside the boundary wall. Beyond that was a narrow road. There were no cars.

I said, 'This is my first time on a Quester retreat. I didn't have a clue what it was going to be like.'

'I hope you're enjoying yourself.' She sounded like a hostess at a party. Or a headmaster's kindly wife with a timid new boy.

'I could have done without the wet feet,' I said. 'But everyone's been very friendly.'

'Oh *yes*,' she said with enthusiasm. 'That's exactly what I thought. It was an absolute revelation.'

'Have you been with the group long?'

She looked vague and put her hand to her forehead. 'About six months, I think. One loses track.'

'What made you join?'

'Oh, this and that.' She frowned. 'And anyway, Ra's an old friend.'

'Really? Didn't he have his portrait painted once by Gus Ridley?'

'Yes!' She turned to me in delight. 'Do you know it? *Gone to Atlantis* – such a clever picture. Almost as if Gus knew Raymond had special powers. Gus did portraits of me, too, not that I had any special powers.' She giggled.

'Then you must be *Being Katie*.'

'That's right. What a lot you know about Gus's work. That painting caused such a fuss. Needless to say, my poor husband hated it, but I always thought it was sweet, really.'

The cinder track had given way to a muddy quagmire. I extracted one ruined shoe from the squelch and said, 'God, look at this. Do you mind if we hop over the wall and walk on the road for a bit?'

She frowned. 'Oh no, I don't think that's a very good idea.'

'Why not?'

'Well, that's a public road and we're not supposed to leave the hotel grounds.' Suddenly she was anxious. 'They're terribly strict about that sort of thing. It really is much safer here.'

I thought she was referring to traffic. I said, 'It's not a very busy road. I've only seen one tractor all afternoon.'

'Still, I'd better not. I promised I wouldn't leave the grounds on my own.'

'But you're with me.'

'I know, but the rules are very clear. I have to be accompanied by two trusted guards at all times.'

'Oh, come on. No one will know and my shoes have practically disintegrated.'

'Oh yes, you look like a poor little drowned rat. And you're quite right. No one will be any the wiser.' Suddenly her face lit up at the prospect of escape.

We found a place on the perimeter hedge (which, as the taxi driver had explained, was actually a wall with plants growing over it) where some of the stones were exposed, giving us footholds so we could scramble over. We were both giggling like schoolgirls as we dropped down into the road. It was narrow, with just room for two cars to pass each other if they were careful, but there was no sign of a car, just the steady drip of the rain and the distant roar of the sea.

'This is better,' I said, looking down at my ruined shoes.

She kept hold of my hand and glanced round nervously. 'We've got to find a way to climb back before we get in sight of the house. You've no idea how cross they'd be if they knew.'

'There's sure to be a way through.'

I was beginning to feel cold. The rain had long since penetrated all my clothes and my spine was wet and chilled. And then, in the distance, I heard the hum of a car's engine.

Katie's eyes widened with fright. 'Can you hear something? Let's climb back now.'

'But this is so much easier,' I said. 'I know, let's sing to keep our spirits up.' I instantly began a loud marching rendition of 'It's a Long Way to Tipperary'. Katie hesitated for a moment, then cheered up and sang along in a high, clear voice.

All at once she stopped dead in her tracks. A small white car came racing round the corner in front of us. Tim was at the wheel.

'Oh, my heavens.' Katie stood immobilised.

The car jammed to a halt a few yards in front of us and Tim leaped out. 'Mother!' he shouted. 'Oh, Mother, thank God you're safe. I've got to talk to you.'

'Tim!' she took a step back. Her eyes were huge.

'Oh, Mother,' he said again, more quietly this time. He hesitated for an instant, then took a couple of steps towards her. He raised his hands but she caught hold of my arm and drew back. 'Oh Mother.' His voice was breaking on a sob. 'What have they done to you?'

She let go of me and stumbled towards him. He folded her in his arms. Above her shoulder, his blue eyes met mine and they were smiling. He eased her gently away and looked down at her. 'You've no idea how I've missed you.'

'And I've missed you too, but . . .'

'How's Davy?'

'He's fine. He had a cold last week but he's over it now. He's got a gap in his teeth.'

'Does he ask about me?'

'Well, a bit, I suppose. Sometimes.'

'I tried to contact you, but they never let me near. They returned all my letters. You didn't receive them, did you?'

'No, yes, well, they said it was better that way.' She sounded so confused it broke my heart. 'I just got upset.'

'Well, we've got luck on our side for once. Let's make the most of it. Let's go for a drive, somewhere we can talk.'

She drew back, frowning. 'Oh no, I mustn't. It's not allowed.'

'A little drive won't hurt. No one will know. I'm sure your friend won't tell.'

'But I promised them—'

'Five minutes. Just five minutes is all I ask.'

He put his hand around her waist and began leading her towards the car. She was dragging her feet.

'I don't know . . .' She turned towards me, as though I could solve her dilemma.

'Is this your son?' I asked. 'There's no harm in talking, is there? And I promise I won't tell anyone.'

'But they'll find out, I know they will.'

'Please, Mother. I'll bring you straight back.' He was steering her gently towards the car, one arm round her shoulders and the other hand holding open the passenger door.

Her eyes were round with panic. 'But . . .'

I was so mesmerised by the drama between mother and son that I didn't hear the second car until it was right beside me. The gleaming bumper of an all-terrain vehicle stopped only inches from my legs and I leaped to the side of the road as two men jumped out and raced over the wet tarmac to Tim's car. One of them grabbed Katie by the shoulders and the second threw himself at Tim, wrenching his arms up behind his back and slamming him face down on the bonnet of his car. It all happened with such ruthless

professionalism that neither he nor Katie had a chance to
defend themselves.

'Lumina,' a man's voice ordered from inside the second
car, 'don't say a word. Get in at once.'

'But . . .' Katie twisted round in a panic, horrified by the
sight of her son struggling helplessly against the brute who
had crushed his face against the car.

'Don't go!' yelled Tim. 'Mother, don't listen to them.
Don't leave me. Where's Davy? Where's my son? Let them
go!'

'Quiet, you!' And Tim roared with pain as his attacker
twisted his arm up between his shoulder blades.

'Don't hurt him,' Katie begged, her face streaming with
tears as she was led towards the car. 'Please don't hurt
him.'

'Get a move on, Lumina,' said the voice. 'Let's get away
from here.'

Katie had time for a final, stricken look at her son before
she was bundled into the waiting car and the door
slammed shut behind her.

Tim was still struggling. 'You *bastard*!' he yelled. 'Let
me go, let me speak to her!'

But it was too late. The dark car with the tinted windows
purred away in the direction of the hotel.

There was an eerie silence. I examined the stranger. His
head shaved, he looked like a seasoned fighter. Just in time
I remembered I was supposed to be a neutral observer, and
I said coldly, 'Let that man go at once.'

He laughed and straightened up, pushing Tim roughly
away. 'With pleasure, miss. Delighted to see the back of
him.' He had a deep, menacing voice. 'Off you go, then,
and don't bother coming back neither. We all thought
you'd learned your bleeding lesson by now.'

Suddenly, I felt sick, the acid taste of bile rising in my
throat. It was hard to believe that someone could be

abducted from a public road in the middle of the afternoon right under our noses and we'd been powerless to prevent it.

The man walked over to me. That was the moment when I felt afraid for myself for the first time. He said, 'Let's get you back to the hotel, miss. Are you all right? Shame you had to get mixed up in all that, what with you being a Quester and all.'

Tim had put his elbows on the roof of the car and was holding his head in misery. I ached to go and comfort him, but for now the charade had to continue.

'Thanks,' I said. The man fell into step beside me and we set off down the road towards the hotel, leaving Tim alone on the empty road. 'What on earth was all that about?'

'No need to worry about him, miss.'

I knew I shouldn't say anything, but I couldn't help it. 'Did you have to be so violent?'

He laughed. 'That was nothing. Anyway, I don't make the decisions round here. I just do what I'm told.'

'What about Lumina? What happens to her now?'

'Oh, she'll be taken care of, same as always. Let me give you a word of advice. You don't want to go asking too many questions round here, not if you know what's good for you.'

Since all I could think of were questions, we walked the rest of the way in silence. When we reached the hotel I hesitated. Supposing someone in the group had guessed my connection with Tim? Did that mean I was going to be taken care of too?

'Come along, miss. What are you stopping for?'

With one last glance at the open road, I followed him inside.

Chapter 11

When I'd changed out of my wet clothes I went down to the dining room, but there was no sign of either Katie or Elaine. I hadn't expected to see Katie, but Elaine's absence was worrying. Had she got into trouble because of me?

At about ten to five my Compatibility Assessment team turned up. Every single one of them looked cold, wet and dispirited: their monosyllabic answers to my questions confirmed that their attempts to get Bill across the ravine had ended in failure.

With no Elaine to chivvy me into attendance I decided to skip the early evening session, a lecture on 'Tools for the Age of Aquarius: Enlightenment and Supersensory Perception'. I'd have a hot bath instead. I was sickened by that afternoon's events and I needed a breathing space before I could carry on pretending to be a gullible Quester.

In the privacy of the warm tub, I thought over what had happened. Until now, I'd assumed the reports of brainwashing and members being held against their will were exaggerated. But now I'd seen for myself how the group operated. Tim had told me his mother was easily influenced: she'd been no match for their combination of strong-arm tactics and manipulation. It looked as though Tim would have to resort to the courts to get his son back after all.

But what about Jenny? Had they exploited her anger and confusion to turn her into a docile member of their group?

I finally joined up with Elaine at supper. She was subdued and avoided giving a clear answer when I asked her where she'd been. Nor, in spite of her earlier enthusiasm, did she show much interest in hearing about our disastrous Compatibility Assessment.

'Don't you want to know what happened?'

'You left early,' she said dully. 'So nothing happened.'

'Who told you that?' No reply. I persisted, 'Did they tell you about what happened afterwards, too?'

Elaine stared at her plate and didn't answer. I gave her an edited description of our meeting with 'a man who seemed to be Lumina's son' but she wasn't very interested. I said, 'Do you know why they were so violent? I mean, the man said he was her son, and all he wanted was to talk to her, but they never gave him a chance. It was almost as if they wanted an excuse to rough him up.'

'I dunno. Maybe it was better that way,' she said listlessly.

'Why? What's the harm in talking?'

'The Inner Circle only want what's best for us.' She repeated it like a mantra.

I was about to challenge this ridiculous statement, but then I saw a large tear ooze out from under her eyelid and dribble down her cheek.

'Elaine, what is it? What's the matter?'

'I'm fine, really. Let's go along to the evening session. It should be good.'

My instinct was to drag her back to the safety of our room and insist she tell me what was bothering her. I was sick of standing by and doing nothing while the Heirs of Akasha reduced their followers to frightened zombies, but I knew I must not show my hand too soon or there'd never be another chance to talk to Katie or Jenny. So I checked my timetable to see what the evening's session was: 'The Akashic Record, A Musical Odyssey'. There was nothing for it but to play the game like a good little Quester.

The musical odyssey turned out to be a glorified talent show by residents, with lots of singing and dancing, strange tableaux and mimes, most with an underwater theme. If I'd seen it the previous evening I'd probably have enjoyed myself, because several of the performers were gifted and the whole show was remarkably professional, but after what I'd seen that afternoon and with Elaine cowed and uncommunicative beside me, it struck me as a smokescreen to mask the truth.

Afterwards, as we were filing out of the lecture hall, Elaine was called over to the side of the room by one of the stewards. It was impossible to hear what was said, but Elaine looked more and more downcast; then she turned and accompanied the steward out by one of the side doors, without so much as a backward glance or a word of explanation.

A couple of the people from Compatibility Assessment asked me if I wanted to go to the bar with them for a drink, but I was sick of the charade and decided to go straight back to my room in the Nirvana wing and wait for Elaine.

She didn't come.

It was getting dark. The rain had stopped but huge clouds were still blocking out the sun and the twilight was chill and foreboding. I longed to hear Tim's voice and thought of going out to the high point on the cliff and phoning him, but there was no point and it would only risk arousing the suspicions of Security.

By now, Elaine's continued absence was making me uneasy. I sat by the window and watched the sea turn dark purple, then black, and all the colour drain from the sky. At last, just as I was about to switch on the light, the door of my room opened.

'Elaine, where've you been? I was wor—' I broke off. It wasn't Elaine who was entering my room with sponge bag and towel over her arm.

It was the grey-haired woman who'd been staring at me in the dining room that morning. Karnak, deputy head of security.

'Where's Elaine?' I asked.

'She's been transferred.'

'Why?'

'The reasons do not concern you. I shall be your Chosen Guide for the remainder of your stay.' She had a harsh, unattractive voice and she was watching me closely.

I said, 'Is Elaine in some kind of trouble?'

'What makes you ask that?'

I smothered my anger as best I could. 'Elaine said she'd be my Chosen Guide for the whole weekend and now you say she's been transferred. Also, she seemed to be upset at supper. Is she all right?'

'She is being taken care of.'

The words sent a chill through me.

'Is it because of what happened today?' Karnak didn't answer, only stared at me. I said, 'Is she in trouble because of me?'

'Why do you ask, Carol? Have you done anything that might have got her into trouble?'

'No, damn it, but I want to know why she's gone.'

'Sounds to me,' she said quietly, 'as if you've got a guilty conscience.'

So that was why Karnak had been sent to be my minder: the Inner Circle had sent her here to suss me out, just as Elaine had said. My heart was pounding against my ribs.

Karnak sat down on the bed. She pulled a couple of heavy silver necklaces over her head and laid them on the bedside locker.

'Well?' she asked. 'Anything you want to tell me?'

'Of course not,' I said angrily. 'I left the Compatibility Assessment session because Lumina had been hit on the head and I thought she needed medical attention.'

'That must have been very convenient for you.'

'What do you mean?' She didn't answer, only stared at me. I said, 'I was looking forward to CA. It wasn't my fault that idiot swung the pole round and nearly knocked her out. And she was in no state to walk back on her own. How is she now? Has she seen a doctor?'

Karnak was removing several rings, heavy as knuckledusters. 'Lumina is fine,' she said in that rasping voice. 'She is being taken care of.'

Those words again. I shivered. What did it really mean?

'Can I see her tomorrow and make sure she's all right?'

'Why should she not be all right?'

'She was upset. That man said he was her son and he wanted to talk to her. Then she was taken away from him by force and bundled into that car.'

'You exaggerate. A decision was made to protect her.' Karnak spoke calmly.

'To protect her?' I was almost choking with anger. 'From her own son?'

'We are her family now. That man is no longer a part of her life. You must try to put him out of your mind.'

'Is that what you're telling Lumina to do?'

'Lumina has taken the Oath of Loyalty. She knows the rules.'

She had removed the last of her silver jewellery, a heavy

armlet shaped like a coiled serpent. She unzipped her black ribbed top and took it off carefully. Underneath she wore only a skimpy black singlet. Even though she must have been in her late fifties, she had the muscled arms of someone who works out daily, not an ounce of surplus fat anywhere.

She turned and looked at me directly. There was a toughness to her, a masculinity, that made the prospect of spending a night in the room with her particularly uncomfortable.

'Do you know Tim Fairchild?' she asked.

'Of course not.'

'Then how do you know his name?'

'He was at the meeting I attended in Ealing. When you threw him out, remember?'

'He was an impostor.' She paused, then said with clear emphasis, 'The Heirs of Akasha do not tolerate impostors.'

'So I've seen.'

'I repeat,' she was looking at me steadily, 'we do not tolerate impostors.'

'So?' I asked. 'Are you accusing me of being one?'

'Not yet. But we've had our suspicions about you, Carol, from the beginning. Let me warn you that unless you're a genuine Quester you'd be well advised to leave here and not come back.'

'That sounds like a threat.'

'Why don't we call it a warning?'

I turned away as she pulled the singlet over her head and stepped out of her pants. She put on an oversized black T-shirt and got into bed.

'Sleep well, Carol Brewster,' she told me.

But I didn't. Apart from anything else, I missed the burbling sound of Elaine's snores.

The next morning Karnak went out of her way to be friendly. Either she had decided I was not a security threat after all or else she had perfected the good cop/bad cop routine all on her own. Whatever the reason, I found her efforts to be friendly more creepy than her former tough image.

'I see you've got a taxi booked for the one o'clock train,' she said as we sat with the others at the long table and sipped our glasses of water – all that was permitted for Sunday breakfast. If I'd known starvation was going to be part of their tactics I'd have packed some fruit in my bag. 'So you've got plenty of time. This morning's session will be special.'

I checked my timetable: AquaMed 9–11. I remembered what Elaine had told me and said, 'Why? Is Ra going to take part?'

To my satisfaction she looked disappointed that I knew already. 'He may do. His appearances are never scheduled in advance.'

'Was he the man in the car yesterday afternoon when Lumina was taken away?'

She fixed me with an intense stare. 'We never discuss the movements of the Inner Circle.'

'Why not? What's so special about them?'

She said, 'You're asking a great many questions all of a sudden.'

'Isn't that what being a Quester is all about? I want to find out as much as I can about this organisation, so I can decide whether to go on with it or not.'

She considered this for a bit, then, her voice falsely gentle, she said, 'You're still asking questions with your intellect, Carol. It is the great error of modern Western civilisation. Modern man glorifies the brain while our other faculties waste away from lack of use. If you are sincere in your desire to follow the Akashic Path, you must stop placing so much reliance on the rational mind and listen instead to your heart and your instinct. Above all, you must develop your spiritual sense.'

Several arguments sprang into my over-developed Western mind, but I had sense enough not to voice them. It might suit Karnak to act the friendly Chosen Guide right now, but she could flip back to being the ruthless deputy head of security at any moment. I said meekly, 'I suppose I've still got a lot to learn.'

She smiled. 'No more than any other Quester. You'll be more in tune with the Akashic ethos after AquaMed.'

The weird thing was that, in spite of all my hostility to anything the group could offer, her forecast was almost correct. If it had been stripped of all the mumbo-jumbo and had formed a part of, for instance, a therapeutic weekend at a health farm, AquaMed would have been one of the most luxurious experiences of my life.

Around eight thirty Karnak and I, together with all the other Questers and their Guides, went down to the basement of the hotel. There was a strong smell of chlorine and antiseptic and gentle New Age music was playing over the loudspeakers.

'I didn't know there was an indoor pool,' I said.

She smiled an all-knowing smile. 'Wait and see.'

In the changing room we put our clothes into piles and put on swimsuits. There were disposable paper swimsuits, one size fits all, for those who hadn't brought their own. Luckily I had. Karnak and most of the other Guides stepped naked into the showers. Like most of the other Questers, I kept my swimsuit on.

Karnak watched me as I showered. Once again her gaze made me uncomfortable, not because I was being observed as a possible impostor but because she was enjoying the sight of my nearly naked body. I realised there were all sorts of hazards at the Akashic group which life in Sturford had not prepared me for.

As I stepped out of the communal shower, she handed

me what I thought was a giant brown towel, but which turned out to be a floor-length robe with deep pockets and an enormous hood.

'Sort of like being a bathtime monk,' said one of my fellow Questers as she was handed hers, and we both laughed. Our Guides, who were wearing similar robes of pale aquamarine, were not amused.

'Follow me,' said Karnak.

To my disappointment she led us not to a swimming pool but into a large, bare room with a blue curtain drawn across one end and a circle of tiny stools set out on the wooden floor. Questers were invited to sit on the stools, if they found them more comfortable; the Guides sat on the floor, either in the lotus position or cross-legged. In the middle of the circle there was a shallow glass bowl filled with water.

When we were all in position a man in a saffron-coloured robe drew the blinds down on the windows. For a moment we were in absolute darkness. Then there was the flare of a match and Karnak leaned forward and lit a candle in the centre of the glass bowl.

'Breathe deeply,' came a man's deep voice from somewhere behind me. 'Let your gaze focus on the candle flame. Let all thought flow from your mind. Be at peace.'

Far from being at peace, I was intensely aware of Karnak beside me. Her lithe body was absolutely still inside her robe. All her attention was fixed on the candle flame. But still she was aware of me, I knew it. For a brief moment I had the crazy notion that she could read my mind, that she knew I regarded all this as nonsense and that the last thing I was going to do while in the power of a bunch of ruthless crazies was empty my mind of all thought. Was that how they had trapped Katie, so she was too terrified even to talk to her own son? Was that what had turned poor harmless Elaine into a tearful zombie? And what about Jenny? The last time I'd seen her she'd been frantic with rage and misery and more in need of peace than anyone I'd ever seen. Had she abdicated responsibility for herself in return for the phoney comforts of soft music and a candle flame flickering in a bowl of water?

While these thoughts burned in my mind I sat like a good little Quester, breathed deeply when I was told to and kept my gaze fixed on the candle.

After a while I became aware of shuffling movement. The people on the other side of the circle, both Questers and Guides, were standing up and padding slowly out of the room. I felt a tingle of anxiety. Where were they going?

'Do not let yourself be distracted,' said the voice. 'There is only the flame. Surrender your thoughts to the flame. Let worries fall away. Breathe in . . . deeper . . . now out . . . slowly . . . more . . .'

It was getting hard to keep track of time. It was also difficult to remain angry. The music and the gentle breaking of the waves beyond the window was very soothing. Or maybe the waves were part of the tape, like the music. Or maybe the music was coming from outside, like the sea. It was difficult to know which.

The candle flame, as I watched it, divided into two, then three, then melted back into one.

After a while – I've no idea how long – there was a murmur of movement and the empty places on the opposite side of the circle were filled again. There was a faint smell of salt and chlorine.

Karnak stood up. She bent down and touched me on the shoulder, signalling me to follow her. I stood up and instantly felt light-headed; it must have been all the deep breathing. Karnak smiled and put her hand out to steady me, but I shook her off.

We joined a small procession of robed figures, blue and brown side by side like Noah's animals, filing out of the room through a pair of arched doors I hadn't noticed when we came in. There was a short, dimly lit passageway, then another pair of arched doors opening on to the most beautiful swimming pool I had ever seen in my life.

It was circular, with a domed roof of blue glass like a perfect summer sky. The walls were made of a translucent material which glowed like warm firelight, apricot and gold. Under my bare feet the floor was cool marble and the pool was marble, too. My builder's eye noted that every last detail had been executed by skilled craftsmen with no concern for cost.

When we were all standing in a circle around the edge of the pool, the Guides slipped off their robes and instructed us to follow suit. Then we stepped down the shallow steps into the water. It was salty and buoyant, the temperature of a warm bath.

We stood in the water, which came almost to my armpits. The disembodied voice that had guided our breathing in the other room told us to close our eyes. Once again we were instructed to breathe slowly and deeply. Now, as well as the gentle music being played over the loudspeakers, there was the soft bubbling of the water, little currents being jetted over our skin.

'Lean back,' said the voice. 'Stretch out your arms. Let the water be your support.'

I found myself doing as I was told. The warm air was wonderfully seductive. Then I tensed, opened my eyes again. Karnak had her hand on my shoulder. She smiled, gesturing me to relax. She was putting a contoured float under my neck. Then she moved down and placed another under my waist and a third under my ankles. I didn't like her touching me, but then, as she moved away and reached for her own set of floats from the side of the pool, I realised that someone had thought this through properly. Held up by the floats and with my whole body except my face and toes just below the surface of the water, I felt weightless, safer than I'd have thought possible, at one with the water. I didn't even mind when Karnak took my left hand and the Guide on the other side of me took my right. It all felt completely natural and good.

Careful, a small voice inside my head was trying to warn me, this is how they trap you. Look at Katie, look at Elaine. But I pushed the anxiety away. In three hours I'd be on the train and heading back to the real world: all I was doing now was experiencing some of what had seduced people more vulnerable than me. Besides, I felt pampered for the first time in months. Where was the harm in that?

The disembodied voice was telling us to do odd things with our breathing. Sometimes deep breaths, sometimes rapid and shallow. Then, as I was gazing up into the blue dome of the ceiling, it seemed as if the sky was revolving above us. I realised it must be a trick of moving lights, but it was more fun to flow with the illusion of a revolving heaven.

I was sorry when it stopped. Even more sorry when Karnak gently removed the three sets of floats and motioned me to follow her out of the pool. I felt a childish rage at being deprived of a pleasure so intense and so fundamental.

Reluctantly I wrapped myself in my brown robe and padded along with the others back to the first hall, where the candle still flickered in the gloom.

The stools had been rearranged in our absence. The semicircle of people who had gone to the pool before us were in their same position, but we formed two further semicircles behind them so that everyone was facing the wall of blue curtains. You had to be impressed by the way this session was organised; each stage flowed seamlessly into the next. It gave me the sense of being a cog in a well-oiled machine and that in itself was disturbing. Obviously this session was the bait which would lure us deeper into the way of Akasha. I pinched myself under my robes and forced myself to picture Katie, Tim and Elaine. There was no way I intended falling prey to the stage-managed manipulation of a bunch of loonies. Good: I was angry again.

The music grew louder, drowning out the voice that had been guiding our meditation. I could hear people singing. It was impossible to tell if they were recorded or somewhere outside the room. Karnak leaned forward and blew out the candle, engulfing the room in darkness. Only the image of the flame still burned brightly on my retina.

Suddenly a cacophony of sound filled the air: soaring voices, drums and strange, resonant wind instruments. The edge of my robes lifted as a cool breeze blew through the room. Then the dark blue curtains whooshed sideways and the whole space in front of us was a wall of blinding light.

As my eyes adjusted to the brightness I saw that we were looking up at a stage. The backdrop consisted of the most extraordinary mural I'd ever seen: a circle of moons and strange landscapes linked together by intricate designs of hieroglyphs which in turn were intertwined with writhing human figures. Four musicians stood on the stage: two had hand drums, the third played a strange instrument which looked like an enormous violin with only two strings, while the last was blowing into an enormous bamboo with a tube attached to it which emitted a constant booming. In the centre of the stage stood an empty throne shaped like a scallop shell. The singing was louder than ever: the singers must be in the wings.

The atmosphere was electric. All around me Questers and Guides, light-headed from hunger, the strange breathing techniques and the timeless bliss of floating in the pool, were looking towards the stage like a bunch of children waiting for Santa Claus. As the music grew deafening I felt myself being sucked into a flood of hysteria, and to stop myself getting swept away I pinched my arms until tears sprang to my eyes.

Six women dressed in pale yellow robes and singing their strange harmonies walked slowly on to the stage, followed by six men. They grouped themselves round the empty throne and stared at some point above and beyond us. They were singing, always singing, the music repetitive and hypnotic. In spite of all my efforts to remain detached, my heart was thumping wildly and my mouth was dry. Around me the Guides and Questers had joined in the music and were swaying to the rhythms. They seemed to have fallen into a collective trance.

Just when I thought my head was going to burst with the noise and the effort of keeping myself detached from the madness around me, a white-robed figure appeared from the right-hand side of the stage. He was carrying a stick, or a wand. Behind him came a second man with a long beard like an Old Testament prophet's, then a child, also in white robes. I blinked and looked more carefully. The child had fair hair and the kind of angelic face that could be either male or female, but I recognised him at once: Davy. Tim's son. He was holding what looked like a glass ball, carrying it with intense concentration. Obviously the effort of not dropping it and not tripping over his robes was taking all his attention. Behind him, looking proud and happy in her white robes, came Katie.

From all around me there was the sound of an indrawn breath and then a single word: 'Ra!'

His robes were gold. They shone in the bright light. He walked, slowly and deliberately, to the centre of the stage, turned and faced us for a moment, then sat down on the shell-like throne.

Behind me, a woman was sobbing.

It was suddenly very quiet. Ra reached out his hands and smiled down at us like a kindly father. The bearded man spoke, but in words that were incomprehensible. It didn't sound like a foreign language; it sounded like gobbledygook.

Then Ra gestured silently and his spokesperson said, 'Be at peace. Come, receive the blessing of Ra.'

What followed was like a parody of the communion service. Two ushers in saffron robes organised the first three Questers, who went up the shallow steps to the stage one by one and knelt down on a low padded stool in front of the throne. The man standing behind Ra murmured a few words, then Ra nodded and touched the first one lightly on the head. The Quester stood up again, looking dazed, and was guided back to his seat. The second Quester, whom I recognised as Grisel, the reincarnated witch, broke down in tears as soon as she knelt in front of him. I saw Ryan the laver-bread victim walk up looking distinctly uncomfortable and then walk away again with the same expression of mindless radiance I could see on the faces of all the Heirs ranged about Ra's throne.

I won't do it, I thought. No one can make me go through that pantomime. I'll refuse.

Several Questers were sobbing and being comforted by their Guides.

I felt a light touch on my shoulder. I stood up automatically. There was the tingling of pins and needles in my left calf and foot. Karnak led me to the steps at the side of the stage and I took my position behind Herman. Nerves fluttered in my empty stomach as he walked slowly up the steps and crossed the stage to kneel in front of Ra. Now there was nothing to shield me from the madness.

It was my turn. The usher touched my arm gently, urging me forwards. My legs felt clumsy and strange as I mounted the stage. At the top step my foot caught in the hem of my robe and I stumbled. Someone reached forward to steady me. It was Elaine: her face radiant with an idiot happiness. I shrank away from her.

Then I was kneeling on the footstool in front of Ra. Close up I could see his robes were woven with gold thread, shimmering and iridescent as a dragonfly's wing. He reached out and held his hand over my head. Even though he didn't actually touch me, I felt a jolt of energy blast through me and all the tiny hairs on my neck and shoulders tingled. Startled, I looked up.

He was smiling and his eyes were staring straight into mine. I've never seen eyes like those before. They were so deep and so dark I felt as though I might be swallowed up in their black depths and never recover. Dangerous eyes, hypnotic eyes, infinitely seductive eyes.

I felt sick with dread. This was the man most people thought had murdered Andrew Forester. This was the man who had gone to live in Spain to escape his accusers, the man who had conned old ladies into leaving him their money, the man whose strange cult destroyed families. Gazing into those extraordinary, bottomless, impenetrable eyes it was only too easy to believe all the terrible things I'd heard about Raymond Tucker, known to his followers as Ra.

But for a fraction of a second – and I swear it was no more than that – it would have been just as easy to believe he was in touch with worlds beyond my comprehension. And that was most frightening of all.

Chapter 12

The journey back to London was the strangest of my life. I'd been repelled by the Heirs of Akasha, but I'd been immersed in their fantastical world for forty-eight hours and it had affected me more than I realised.

For several hours after the AquaMed session I felt weightless, as though I was walking on a cushion of air a few centimetres above the ground. The world was more vivid than I'd ever known it, as if mufflers covering my eyes and ears and nose had been removed and I could see and hear and smell my surroundings distinctly for the very first time, like emerging from a fog. As the train passed along the coast a shaft of sunlight pierced the bank of clouds, casting a spear of light across the sea; the sight was so intense it brought tears to my eyes. I stared in disbelief at my fellow passengers, who were too bogged down in their magazines and their boredom to register the magic all around them.

Ra, Ra, Ra: the noise of the train blurred with the remembered chant until I fell into a weird sleep, filled with shifting lights and anxiety over objects mislaid, waking only as we pulled into Paddington.

The euphoria was wearing off. My head ached and there was a sour taste in my mouth, as if I had a hangover, when I stumbled off the train. My mobile phone rang the moment my feet touched the platform.

'Carol, we have to talk.'

'Tim? I've just arrived at Paddington.'

'I know. I can see you.' Automatically, I looked around for him, but he said, 'Not here. Someone from the Group may be watching you.'

Suddenly I was very wide awake indeed. Somewhere out of sight, Tim was observing my every move and he probably wasn't the only one. I felt vulnerable as a target in the sights of a sniper.

He said, 'Take a taxi and meet me at the café opposite Green Park Tube station in half an hour. I'll make sure I get there before you to check no one is following.'

'Okay,' I said. 'See you in half an hour.'

I decided to walk across Hyde Park. Maybe fresh air and exercise would revive me. Now that my earlier elation had vanished I was left with a cold shame, as though during the previous forty-eight hours I had said and done things I was embarrassed even to think about. It didn't matter that I'd only gone on the weekend in order to help other people: whatever the reason, I'd still been a part of the craziness. It had touched me and changed me and left me with this feeling of dislocation.

I walked slowly across the park, pausing every now and then to sit on the grass or a bench when my bag became heavy. There'd been no rain in London for weeks and the park was full of people enjoying the fine Sunday evening. Children were crowding round the ice-cream stalls; people were jogging, skateboarding, playing football and throwing sticks for their dogs. To begin with, I kept looking round to see if I was being followed, but by the time I reached Piccadilly, where the amateur painters were taking their pictures down from the railings, my paranoia had faded. This whole scene was too normal: none of these people looked as if they'd even heard of the Heirs of Akasha or the Secret Language of All Ages. They were all far too sensible to waste a moment of their precious time worrying about the date when the earth's magnetic poles would switch round and the great Watershed would drown civilisation. Already the past couple of days were beginning to seem as though I'd been watching a bad film and had just left the auditorium to find it was still light outside.

Tim had chosen his position carefully. There were a couple of tables between him and the window, so he wasn't visible from the street, but he had a clear view of anyone who entered or left the café.

'What can I get you?' he asked.

I watched him as he walked to the counter to order my mineral water. The two waitresses switched instantly from polite-service mode to big smiles while they served him, and no wonder. With his light tan and his earnest expression, Tim was handsome enough to brighten anyone's evening. While he was waiting, he turned to check the entrance, then glanced at me. His face creased into a smile as our eyes met and this time I felt a definite kick of attraction in the pit of my stomach. I relaxed into my chair. I'd expected this debriefing to be hard work: I calculated that Tim was sure to be devastated by his abortive meeting with Katie and by ending up no closer to a reunion with his son, but to my surprise he seemed quite cheerful. Either he was a brilliant actor or he had something up his sleeve.

He returned to the table with our drinks and we both began talking at once.

'I'm so sorry it didn't work out—'

'I want to thank you—'

We laughed.

'No, I insist. Me first,' said Tim, 'because you have absolutely no reason to be sorry about anything. I couldn't believe it when you phoned and said you'd managed to get my mother away from those maniacs. And then when I saw the two of you walking along the road together as if it was the most natural thing in the world – well, it was brilliant. How did you manage it?'

'Just my usual combination of luck and low cunning.' He looked intrigued so I told him about our failed Compatibility Session and how his mother had been hit on the head. 'It wasn't a bad blow, thank heavens, but we both saw it as a way to bunk off the rest of Compatibility. For entirely different reasons. It would have worked out fine if that car hadn't come along when it did. I never expected them to catch up with us so quickly.'

His face darkened. 'Don't underestimate their security. You were probably followed from the moment you left the group.'

It was a chilling thought, because if that was the case they must have also known about my secret phone call to Tim. Was that why Karnak had replaced Elaine as my Chosen Guide that evening? I glanced around at the anonymous faces in the café. Were we being watched even now? Was that sly-looking man with the Sunday paper held too close to his eyes eavesdropping on our conversation?

Tim looked from me to the man and shook his head. 'He was here before we came,' he said. 'And he's a regular. Don't worry, Carol, I'm thorough. I checked this place out last week.'

I sighed with relief. 'Thank God for that. I'm losing track of what's real and what's fantasy.'

'You're disoriented because you've been exposed to their crazy world. That's how they operate. They gradually erode all your values and replace them with their looking-glass madness. If you feel this weird after only a weekend, imagine what six weeks would do to you, let alone six months, and you'll have some idea what we're up against. How did you get on with my mother?'

'She's great.' Just thinking about Katie made me smile with affection, and Tim's expression softened as he saw how I'd fallen under her spell. 'I didn't spend long with her, but it was enough to see how special she is. I feel as if I've known her for ages. Right from the start she treated me like an old friend.'

Tim smiled. 'She's like that with everyone. Though I'm sure she did like you – who wouldn't?' The compliment was delivered with just the right trace of hesitation, which made it doubly attractive. Clearly Tim Fairchild had inherited a generous dollop of his mother's charm. He went on, 'Her openness is very endearing, but it does have its drawbacks. She's so kind and generous that she doesn't understand how unscrupulous other people can be. It makes her far too trusting, almost like a child. We've always had to protect her from being exploited: if she'd had her way half the parents at the school wouldn't have paid any fees. But I hadn't realised how much my father sheltered her until all this blew up.'

'I didn't get the impression she was unhappy,' I said, thinking this might ease his mind, 'except when she met you. It's as though she's blocked all her old life out of her mind.'

'Or someone else has blocked it out for her.' He pressed the tips of his fingers between his eyebrows. 'Poor Mum, she doesn't stand a chance.' He was silent for a moment, before saying thoughtfully, 'But even if she was unhappy, you wouldn't have known. She's always been brilliant at hiding her feelings. It's a lonely life, being a headmaster's wife, all that isolation without any of the satisfaction of the job. She learned to put on a brave face, no matter what.'

The thought of Katie having to put on a brave face made me feel suddenly empty. I said, 'I saw her again this morning and she looked fine, but maybe that was just an act too. She was taking part in some kind of weird Akashic ceremony.'

'What's that?'

I gave him a brief description of AquaMed and Ra's appearance on the stage, but I missed out the more extreme elements, partly for Tim's sake – it would have been terrible for him to imagine his mother forming part of a mad crowd chanting 'Ra, Ra!' and sobbing with emotion – but I was protecting myself, too. I still felt irrationally ashamed of having taken part.

'Also,' I said at the end, 'I'm pretty sure your son was there.'

'Davy? You saw Davy?'

'It looked like him.'

Tim pulled out the worn photograph from his jacket pocket and thrust it under my nose.

'Yes, that's him all right. He was on the stage with Katie.' Tim's expression was unbearable, so I added, 'He looked as though he was having a good time. You know how little children love to dress up and feel important. I don't suppose he had the first idea of what was going on.

'God, how low can you get. Poor Davy, he's such an innocent.'

'He probably thought it was just a game, like being in a school play. Once he's back with you, he'll soon forget about it.'

'Only if we get him back quickly. What was it Ignatius Loyola said? Give me a child until he's seven and he's mine for life. They're brainwashing him, Carol. They're corrupting my son, and the longer he stays with them the harder it's going to be to get the poison out of his soul. I can't let those psychos take him over, I can't.'

'Children are very flexible,' I said, 'and he's only six.'

'*Only* six!' Tim exclaimed in disbelief. 'That's the most important age of all. It affects your life for ever.'

I'd been doing some quick calculations. 'Why six, in particular?'

He looked at his hands and frowned as he said, 'It's crucial. You're old enough to know what's going on but your mind is still flexible. After that it's too late to save them.'

I said gently, 'You must have been about six when your mother lived at Grays Orchard. How much do you remember about that?'

'I remember missing her,' he said. He folded his arms and looked me straight in the eyes. 'Wondering why she'd left us, and when she was coming home again. *If* she was coming home.'

'Do you remember a boy called Brian? He would have been about the same age as you.'

He smiled. 'Don't forget, I lived in a boys' school. There must have been half a dozen Brians over the years.'

'No, this Brian was at Grays. Apparently you used to play with him there.'

'What are you talking about? I've never been to Grays in my life. When Mum left us, my grandparents moved in to help. My father would never let any child in his care be exposed to a bunch of druggy drop-outs, let alone his only son.'

'But this woman I know in Sturford remembers looking after you sometimes.'

'She must have muddled me with another child,' said Tim firmly, though it seemed to me more likely that he'd blocked out the memories because they were too painful.

He insisted, 'I'd hardly have forgotten if I'd seen my own mother. I do remember the day she came home again. She must have been gone for over a year and I was afraid I wouldn't recognise her, when suddenly she came back without any warning. I remember creeping downstairs and listening outside my father's study door while they talked. My father was amazing about it. He took her back without a word of reproach and they never spoke about it again. No one else was allowed to mention it, either. It was as if she'd never gone. That was the kind of man he was, you see. Sometimes I think she's taken Davy in some crazy attempt to make good the years she lost with me.'

'But that's terrible. It means you lose both ways.'

'Only for a while. Don't forget, I'm going to get them back.'

'So what will you do now? Will you go through the courts? Surely the police would help you get him back.'

He leaned back in his chair. 'Not yet. The law is such a crude instrument for getting what you want, and people always end up getting hurt. The Heirs have centres abroad. If they smuggle Davy and my mother out to Mexico or Spain, the whole process will take years. By the time I got him back he'd be a stranger and they would have taught him to hate me. Sometimes I'm afraid it's already too late.'

'Oh, no, he's still so young. And I can't imagine Katie would let Davy hate his own father.'

He shook his head. 'You still don't realise what a group like that can do to people, do you? And anyway, even if I got Davy back through the courts, what about my mother? It's vital to rescue her too. She and Davy are so close; it would be cruel to separate them after all they've been through. And I owe it to my father not to leave her there. In some ways she's as much of a child as Davy is – you've seen what she's like. I couldn't live with myself if I abandoned her to those maniacs.'

'That doesn't leave you many choices, then, does it? Where do you go from here?'

'I don't know,' he said simply, laying both his hands on the table in front of him. 'But I'm not beaten yet.' He contemplated his fingers and smiled, or at least tried to, and his attempt at bravery was almost more than I could bear. 'Don't worry, Carol. I'll think of something. I have to.'

Instinctively I reached out and put my hand over his. 'I wish I'd been more help.'

'You were tremendous,' he said generously, and our eyes met. His hand curled around and gripped mine. A shiver of energy ran up my arm. It was months since I'd felt so close to anyone and the shock of it was a revelation. And all with the touch of one hand on another. Tim said gently, 'Maybe we can go on helping each other, if you like. After all, you still want to trace your husband's niece.'

My husband. At the mention of Gus, I withdrew my hand from his grasp and regretted it at once. Instantly that simple gesture of friendship had been overlaid with something far more complex. Tim noticed it too and faint colour touched his cheeks.

It was time for me to go. 'Keep in touch,' I said as I stood up. 'I'd like to hear how you get on.'

'I'll keep you posted. Maybe the next time we meet I'll have Mother and Davy with me.'

His attempt at optimism was heroic, given the scale of the opposition.

I thought that was the end of it. My weekend in Cornwall had been interesting, but I hadn't achieved anything significant. I never intended going to the Atlantic Castle Hotel again. It was time to get on with my own concerns.

I stayed Sunday night at a friend's house in London and went straight to work from the station on Monday morning, so I didn't get home till the evening. Gus met me with a guarded welcome. He'd prepared one of my favourite of his New York meals, eggplant parmegiano with Caesar salad and a bottle of excellent wine. Over supper we carefully avoided any topic that might lead to difficulties.

While I was away, Gus had also moved back into our bed. I didn't comment when I saw him already lying there after I came in from the bathroom, but once I had switched off the light there was a rustle of sheets as he took me in his arms and began to kiss me gently.

I was confused. How dare he make love without a word of explanation or apology for all the pain of the summer months? But my instincts were all forgiving. I responded to his touch and my anger evaporated. There was sweet relief, then pleasure, the intense pleasure that he could give like no one else. Touch and gesture had always been Gus's preferred way of resolving problems. 'Words can lie,' he had said once. 'This is more honest.'

I had believed him at the time, in the way that I believed such a lot of what he told me, because he was older and more experienced and knew the world, whereas I had lived my whole life in Sturford and only knew about building houses. But later I couldn't help wondering if he was right. Love-making had brought down the barriers between us and I wanted to tell him about my Cornish weekend. Not telling felt like a secret, as though now it was me keeping him at arm's length. Most of all, I wanted him to know I'd met Katie; maybe at last we'd find a way to talk about the past.

'Gus?'

'Mm?'

I hesitated. His thumb brushed a strand of hair from my forehead. He dropped a light kiss on my bare shoulder. Don't be daft, I told myself. Why risk spoiling the first good moment there's been between us in months?

'It's great to be home,' I said.

'Mm.' It was a smiling 'Mm'.

I was glad I hadn't said anything about Katie.

The following morning, when I went to pick up the post, a textured envelope in a soft shade of greeny-grey slipped from the pile and fell on the mat. I picked it up. It would be wrong to say I recognised the handwriting, because I'd never seen it before, but I guessed at once, even before I saw the Australian stamp, that it was from Harriet.

Gus's name and address were written in a bold round hand. I put the letters in their usual place on the hall table, Harriet's on the top. I stared at it. I felt sorry for her, but all the same my instinct was to destroy the letter. All our troubles had begun with Jenny's arrival and now, just as we were starting to get close again, this had to arrive. Was it going to be spoiled again?

I picked up the letter gingerly, using my fingers like tongs. Maybe letter bombs feel like this against the skin. I hesitated, then laid it back on the pile, out of temptation.

Gus was coming down the stairs, his hand on the curving banister.

'There's a letter for you,' I said.

His eyes met mine and he smiled. It was one of the old Gus smiles, the kind that made something sing out with happiness inside me.

'Mrs Ridley, have I told you yet how stunning you look this morning?'

He moved forward to kiss me, but then he glanced down at the grey envelope and the smile froze on his lips. He picked the envelope up and stalked past me, down the corridor and into the kitchen.

I sorted through the rest of the post and then, when a decent interval had elapsed, I followed. He was standing by the kitchen window, gazing out towards his studio, the envelope unopened in his hand. At the sound of my approach, he shifted, jolted from his reverie, and dropped the envelope, still unopened, into the bin.

'Was that from Harriet?' I asked.

He didn't answer, didn't even look at me.

'Has she had any news of Jenny?'

'Who?'

It was impossible to know if he had heard my question. His face was like stone.

'Jenny,' I repeated.

Slowly he turned and his gaze focused on my face. He frowned slightly, as though surprised to see me there. 'Jenny?' he asked, and then, 'Oh yes, her. I don't know. It's not important.' Slowly he was forcing himself back into the present. He said, 'Never mind about them. It's nothing to do with us.' He managed a smile. 'What about you? Do you have to rush straight out to work or can I fix you breakfast first? Scrambled eggs? Pancakes? French toast? Grits?'

'No, thanks.'

'What did they feed you at that place in Cornwall?'

'Laver-bread toast,' I said without thinking.

'Really? I thought that was Welsh.'

'It was a very eccentric hotel,' I told him.

'It must have been.' He turned away, not wanting to hear any more. 'You'll have to tell me about it some time. Now, breakfast.'

'Sorry, no time.'

'Oh, that's a shame.'

But I could tell he was relieved.

As I drove away from Grays I contemplated the changed landscape of my marriage. Gus was setting out clear markers: we were to be loving but within definite limits. He was perfectly happy not to know where I'd been for the weekend because that meant I'd have no rights regarding the secrets he wanted to keep. The more separate we were, the better it was going to work.

It wasn't what I'd ever expected in a marriage. I'd hoped for a partnership where we could share everything, but maybe that was naive and Gus's way was better in the real world.

Compromise: was that what reality meant?

Chapter 13

Over the next few days, it was hard to settle. The work at Shorters Barn was nearly finished and it was just a question of decorating and cleaning up. All the big decisions had been made. While I was laying paving stones or mixing limewash, my mind kept wandering back to the Heirs of Akasha. I wondered about the sessions I had missed. What exactly was supersensory perception, and how did the Akashic clock work? Was there any evidence for the civilisation of Atlantis? And how had Raymond and Pauline transformed themselves from a couple of ordinary people living in a sort-of commune into the leaders of a cult with centres in Spain, Mexico and Cornwall? Did they believe all that stuff themselves, or were they just spinning a line to extort money from gullible losers? Were they mad or bad or a bit of both?

I thought it would be easy to put it all behind me, but it wasn't. I couldn't help wishing I could sneak back for a quick half-hour in the AquaMed pool. I savoured the memory of the warm water bubbling round my body, the miraculous feeling of weightlessness as I was suspended from the floats and the powerful combination of sensuous and spiritual. I wondered if the whole thing had been designed to trigger some latent womb-memory – certainly I would have given a lot to experience that level of bliss again. Sometimes I thought I'd even put up with the nonsense that followed if it meant I could recapture the state of heightened perception I'd known for a few hours afterwards. Every leaf and cloud and glitter of light had been so intense I'd wanted to gasp with astonishment. Now, as I looked out of the window while the September rain came down it felt as if someone had put a pair of badly focused, dirty glasses over my eyes: my surroundings were muddy and dull and I wanted the colours back.

I told myself firmly I'd been conned by nothing more than a clever marketing ploy: I'd forget about it all soon enough.

And then, when I'd been home for less than a week, there were two phone calls that changed everything.

The first came on Sunday morning, about nine thirty. Gus and I were just finishing breakfast. These days we did a good impersonation of a happily married couple, so long as I didn't overstep the mark. He'd made French toast and fresh orange juice and a large pot of coffee. Later that day the local scouts were due to come and pick some of the early apples to sell for charity. It was a long time since Grays Orchard had been a commercial venture, but in the six years I'd been there I'd tried to make sure the apples didn't go entirely to waste. This would be the second season we'd used the Sturford scout troop and I wanted to make sure we had learned the lessons of last year. Gus and I were discussing this when the phone rang.

Gus grinned. 'That must be Grey Wolf or Lone Alsatian or whatever scout leaders call themselves these days.' He tilted his chair back and picked the phone off the hook.

'Yes?' His eyes smiled across the table at me, but as soon as he heard the voice at the other end of the line his face darkened. He straightened his chair and frowned unseeing at his empty plate.

It was a woman's voice, mellow and firm. She spoke rapidly. I thought I heard the word 'Jenny' but it was impossible to be sure. When she stopped, Gus's face was like thunder.

'Well?' She had raised her voice and as it became shriller, I could hear what she was saying. 'What's wrong with you, Gus? Is that so much to ask?'

The receiver was clenched in his fist like a weapon. He said, 'Stop it. Get someone else to do your dirty work for you. I'm not playing.'

Before he banged the receiver back in its cradle I heard what sounded like a howl of rage or despair. Then silence.

I felt sick. Harriet was dying. Her daughter had abandoned her and she was appealing to her only other relative for support, and he had cut her off without even the courtesy of a kind word. What was wrong with him? How could he be so heartless?

I stood up swiftly and began clearing away the breakfast dishes. Gus's cruelty to his sister was nothing to do with me, but all the same I was so angry my hands were shaking.

After a while, Gus came and stood behind me; he wrapped his arms round my waist and slanted his cheek against my hair.

I tensed. 'That was Harriet, wasn't it?'

He sighed, but didn't answer.

'Why won't you even talk to her?' I demanded. 'Christ, Gus, she's your sister and she's really ill. Surely it won't hurt you just to *talk* to her?'

His hands tightened around my waist. He said, 'Aren't you happy with me, Carol?'

'Yes, but I don't see—'

'Then leave it alone. Don't risk everything now.'

'But—'

'Don't spoil it, Carol. Just trust me. Please.'

The second call came that afternoon, soon after the last of the scouts had departed, slightly green around the gills from eating so many unripe apples. This time I answered, as Gus had gone back to do some more work on one of his spiral paintings.

I picked up the phone. 'Hello?'

'Carol? This is Tim.'

To my surprise I felt a jolt of genuine pleasure at the sound of his voice. A vivid image came into my mind of him in the café near Green Park. He'd been wearing an open-necked shirt and his face had been tanned by the sun.

'Tim, how are you?'

'Much better. Things are definitely looking up.' I'd never heard him sound so buoyant.

'You've seen Katie?'

'Not yet, but I will. Good news. I've made contact with a fifth column in the group.'

'That's brilliant. Who is it?'

'I'm hardly going to tell you that, am I? But this person couldn't be better placed and they're keen to give me all the information I need to get Mum and Davy away from there.'

'Why?'

'That's not important. Look, it's all to do with internal politics. I don't think they're very happy with children being forced away from their fathers, either. It's too complicated to explain, and, anyway, the less you know the better.'

'I can't see what difference it makes,' I said naively. 'It's not as though I'm going to see any of them again.'

Silence at the end of the phone. A suspicion formed in my mind.

190 • JOANNA HINES

'Tim, I hope you don't think—' I began.

'The point is, my informant is one hundred per cent reliable.'

'Tim,' I said firmly, 'I'm really glad for you, but there's no way I'm going back to Cornwall.'

'Of course not,' he said smoothly. 'Besides, Katie's not there any more so there wouldn't be any point. She's been transferred to Spain.'

'Oh no! I'm so sorry. That's what you were dreading, isn't it?'

'Yes, but only because I didn't understand how it could work to my advantage. It's going to make everything much easier. For a start, the security at their Spanish centre is much less strict, so even though the legal system is a problem, it should be much easier for me to talk to Katie away from the group. Once I've done that, I know I can make her see sense.'

'Tim, that's wonderful. When are you going?'

'Just as soon as I can persuade someone to come with me and operate from inside.'

'I thought you had a fifth column.'

'There's a limit to what anyone in the group can do without arousing the suspicions of security. This person doesn't want to leave so they have to be very careful not to be found out. I need the help of a stranger to the group, someone like a Quester.'

'So long as it isn't me.'

'You haven't heard my plan yet.'

'I don't want to. Sorry, Tim, but there's no way I'm going through all that again.'

He was silent for a moment, then said politely, 'Of course. I wouldn't dream of trying to get you to do anything you didn't want.'

'I'm delighted to hear it.'

Another pause. This time, a distinctly cunning pause.

Then he said, 'She's there too, you know.'

'Who is?'

'That girl you were asking about, Jenny Sayer. Didn't you say she's Gus's niece?'

'Jenny's in Spain?'

'She's been there for a couple of months, so my informant tells me. She's due to take the Oath of Loyalty at the end of October. That's when she gets to sign over all her worldly wealth to the group. Apparently she's quite an heiress – did you know that? After the Oath of Loyalty it becomes much harder for people to leave the group.'

'But that's terrible. Her mother is dying and she's desperate to make contact.'

'Well, she can forget all about that once the girl's a full-blown Pilgrim. She'll have the devil's own job to get Jenny free of them then.'

For a moment, I was almost tempted. Then I pulled myself together. 'It's ridiculous. You don't seriously expect me to go all the way to Spain, do you?'

'Why not? They say Andalucia is great this time of year. Plenty of blue sky and sunshine. As it happens there's a fortnight Quester retreat starting in a couple of weeks. My contact says they've had a cancellation and they can make sure it's held open for you. Your building skills are a great attraction, apparently.'

'Well, I hate to disappoint them, but they'll have to manage without. I can't just take off like that.'

Disbelieving silence.

'I do have a life, you know, Tim. Like a job and a husband.'

The silence deepened.

'Honestly, Tim, I'd love to help you, really I would, but it's just not possible.'

The silence ended with a sigh. 'Okay, but you can't blame me for trying. You know what's at stake. When are you coming up to London again? We could meet for lunch and talk it over some more. You'll discover how persuasive I am.'

'Tim, I think I know that already.'

It was a seed planted in my mind. I thought it would wither away and die, but instead it flourished. I was fizzing with restlessness. All my life I've tried to make the people round me happy and now I was surrounded by people who were deeply unhappy, not just Tim and Harriet, but Jenny and Katie and Gus as well. I seemed to be the only person with the freedom to unravel the pain.

I told myself there was no way I was going to visit the Heirs of Akasha again, but actually I was intrigued by the idea. That trip to Cornwall had been the first time in my life I'd travelled anywhere alone. When I was a child I went with my parents, then I went with friends, more recently with Gus. Even though the Heirs of Akasha were weird and scary, that weekend had been so different from the rest of my life it made me realise how bogged down I'd become. Gus had been my ticket to adventure and travel, yet here I was, still in Sturford, still doing the job I'd always done. It was tempting to explore some more. Even the danger was part of the attraction, like skydiving or climbing a mountain.

Tim phoned again. As usual, he'd worked out a detailed plan. He'd fly ahead and meet me at the airport. It would look as though I was travelling alone, but in reality he'd shadow me every step of the way. There was nothing for me to worry about.

I wasn't convinced. His solutions didn't touch my real fears regarding the group. I'd seen how ruthless they were with anyone who threatened their security. The thought of being in a strange country hundreds of miles from home when Karnak denounced me as an impostor and set her heavies to 'take care' of me was not appealing.

But my worst fears, the ones I hardly admitted even to myself, were more subtle. I was afraid of falling under their spell. After all, when I visited the Atlantic Castle I thought I'd remained a cynical onlooker throughout, and there'd been no shortage of incidents to reinforce my scepticism: I'd seen Katie practically kidnapped on a public road, and I'd seen Elaine chastened and subdued, then radiant with mindless joy the following morning. When I came face to face with Raymond Tucker I'd seen him for what he was, a dangerous and evil man.

Yet in spite of all that, some dark magic from the place had rubbed off on me. I hadn't been hooked, far from it, but I'd seen how easy that would have been, if I'd been a weaker or less informed person. If two days had been that powerful, what would a whole fortnight be like?

Tim wasn't going to understand this. To him they were the people who had destroyed his family. He'd never heard their siren songs, so he did what he could to assuage my fears, but he only knew the half of them.

'I'll be close by the whole time,' he told me. 'There are no cliffs to block the signals there. You'll be perfectly safe, I promise.'

'Too right,' I said. 'For the simple reason I'm not going.'

Still, I never closed the door completely, because I had come to enjoy our phone calls. Tim was charming and persuasive and in an odd way it felt like an old-fashioned courtship. He was wearing down my defences – at least, he was trying to.

'Is your passport up to date?' he asked one morning, soon after I got into work. 'Only one more week till lift-off.'

'Tim, you know I'm not going.'

'We'll see about that. There's a flight from Gatwick early afternoon and there's a few seats still free. By the way, it's twenty-two degrees in Málaga today, just about perfect. You'll love Spain.'

'Tim, don't be such a bully.'

I'd used the word lightly, but there was an awkward silence. After a bit he said in a low voice, 'This isn't a game, Carol. My little boy is a hostage out there and I have to get him back before they destroy his mind. If you won't help me, I don't know what I'm going to do.'

'Okay,' I promised. 'I'll think about it. Final answer tomorrow.'

That night, not for the first time, I dreamed of floods and giant clocks and a child drowning in heavy seas while I stood on the shore, the water lapping round my ankles, and did nothing. I woke with the knowledge that my inertia was contributing to the misery of an innocent child. I went downstairs and stood by the phone for several minutes, fighting the urge to call him and say I'd come.

Instead, I set off for work. When I dropped in at the yard office, Brian was already there. He was the person I needed to talk to: if anyone could persuade me not to tangle with the Heirs of Akasha again, it was Brian.

I said, 'Do we have time for the longer view?'

Brian's freckled face broke into a grin. 'I was wondering when you'd ask. You've been moping around here as if you carried the weight of the world on your shoulders.'

'Maybe I do. Supposing I told you the world was coming to an end in December 2012?'

He looked at me hard. 'I'd say you'd been working too much and ought to have a holiday.'

'Ah, but you see, that's just the problem. It all depends on the kind of holiday.'

We drove in the lorry to Gander Hill, where Sam Piper had moved in and the second house was almost ready for cleaning. We chose the third house, where the external work was nearly finished. Brian was held up briefly by a query about the siting of power points and I went ahead of him to the front bedroom and looked across the late-summer landscape of harvested fields towards the orchards at Grays. The house looked placid and secretive, set among the rows of trees: it still surprised me to think of it as my home.

I heard Brian's steady footsteps on the stairs.

'Sorry to be slow,' he said. 'What's up?'

'Do you remember that group Raymond Tucker started? The Heirs of Akasha?' He nodded. I said, 'Someone's trying to persuade me to spend a fortnight at their centre in Spain.'

Brian's ginger eyebrows bristled with indignation. 'I hope you told that daft someone to get lost.'

'Not exactly. You see, I've already spent a weekend at their Cornish retreat. They were the strangest two days of my life.'

It takes a lot to surprise Brian. The thought of me becoming a follower of Ra the Acolyte seemed to be doing the trick nicely. He let out his breath slowly. 'What the hell are you up to, Carol?'

'It's a bit complicated.'

'You don't say.'

I told him most of it. I didn't bother to tell him about Harriet's recent attempts to get in touch with Gus, mainly because I didn't like to tell him about Gus's treatment of his poor sister. But I told him about Tim and Katie, the Akashic Clock and Compatibility Assessment, about Karnak and the Questers. He listened with growing amazement.

'What a bunch of loony buggers' was his final verdict. 'No wonder your friend Tim's in a state.'

'He's much happier now he's got someone working with him from the inside. He thinks it will be much easier to get access to them both. There's a vacancy on a two-week course starting next Friday.'

'The bloody nerve of it!' said Brian angrily. 'How dare

he try to make you put yourself in danger on his account?'

'He promises it won't be dangerous. He'll be staying nearby and we can keep in touch every day by phone.'

'Fan-bloody-tastic. And exactly what does he intend doing when things turn nasty?'

'They won't.'

'Says who? You've told me what you've seen them do, and that's probably just the tip of the iceberg. Supposing they decide it's your turn to be "taken care of", as they so quaintly put it? What's he going to do then? Ride in on his white horse and rescue you all by himself? Wake up, Carol. What chance will he have against a hundred nutters who think the world's going to end in ten years? It's all very well for him, he'll be safe on the outside. You'd be the one taking all the flak.'

'He'd go himself but he can't. They all know who he is.'

'That's his problem, not yours.'

'It's Harriet's problem as well. Did you know Jenny was at their centre in Spain?'

'Why the hell should I know what Jenny gets up to?'

'You spent some time together in the spring. I just thought . . .'

He shook his head. 'Carol, that was five months ago,' he said. 'Doesn't mean she has to tell me what she's up to now. I don't think you need to worry about Jenny. She's wild but she's not stupid. She'll see through all that malarkey soon enough.'

'She hasn't got long. Her mother's dying and Tim says Jenny's going to take the Oath of Loyalty in October. Apparently that's when she signs over all her worldly goods and promises to do exactly what they tell her for ever and ever.'

Brian shrugged. 'Doesn't sound like my idea of fun, but if that's what she wants to do, it's up to her. I got the impression she was itching to get rid of her heiress status anyway; she said it was a burden.' He grinned. 'Come to think of it, maybe you should scrub that bit about her not being stupid.'

But I wasn't in the mood for jokes. I said, 'It doesn't matter how bright Jenny is since she's obviously unbalanced. After all—' I broke off, remembering that the destruction of the pictures had to remain a secret, even from Brian. 'The poor girl's just the kind of lame duck they love to get their claws into. Can you imagine how terrible it will be for Jenny if her mother dies before they can be reconciled?'

Brian was thoughtful. I was furious with myself for being so tactless: when his own father had died, an unredeemed drunk, Brian had hardly been on speaking terms with him. I was about to apologise, but he said quietly, 'Carol, you can't solve everyone's problems for them.'

'Does that mean I can't even try to help anyone at all?' Too late, I realised my discussion with Brian had had the opposite effect from the one I'd been hoping for. When I talked to Tim, I listed all the reasons for not going to Spain. Faced with Brian's opposition I'd spent the last ten minutes talking myself into helping Tim after all. I said, 'It's no good, Brian, I can't just stand back and do nothing.'

'Why the hell not? Sometimes that's exactly what you have to do. Besides, you've already done what you could. No matter how badly your friend Tim is hurting, he has no right to make you do any more. Promise me, you won't go to Spain. It's downright dangerous.'

'You're right,' I agreed.

Brian smiled, not noticing that I'd made no promises at all.

Chapter 14

I must be mad, I thought, as my plane took off from Gatwick. Definitely insane, I told myself as we flew up through the clouds. I ought to be locked up. But in spite of everything it felt good to be taking action at last. Whatever happened, at least I wouldn't be able to accuse myself of not having tried.

My mobile phone sounded within minutes of landing at Málaga. It was Tim, his voice clipped with tension.

'Carol, your hired car is waiting for you by the bus stop outside. Go out through the main doors and turn right. I'll be watching, but don't look for me. I'll be following in a white car and I'll give you instructions all the way. You won't be on your own for a minute, I promise.'

'Thanks.'

'Good luck.'

The moment I settled in the car and had fired up the engine, all my anxiety fell away and a sense of adventure took over. I intended to put Gus and Grays Orchard and my life in England behind me for a while: it was too painful

to dwell on it, anyway. I'd told Gus I was going to stay
with friends in the South of France. I'd been half hoping
he'd challenge my transparent lie, but of course he didn't.
After all, this was how he wanted things to be between us:
polite and civilised but no questions asked. Maybe the next
fortnight would give me the clues I needed to get our old
closeness back: there was no harm in being optimistic.

Above me, the Andalucían sky was purest blue and the
afternoon air was the temperature of a perfect summer's
day. All the tasks that had seemed so daunting when I
contemplated them in Sturford – travelling alone, driving
on the right, negotiating foreign roads – were perfectly
straightforward now that I was actually doing them.

Which was a cheat, really, because I wasn't alone: Tim
was following in a Fiat identical to mine and making
contact at regular intervals. After a while I found myself
wishing we'd agreed on radio silence. Just because I was a
woman on a mission it didn't mean I couldn't enjoy the
novelty of it all. His seriousness was an unwelcome
reminder that he had much more riding on this fortnight
than I did.

Beeeep. Tim's earnest voice over the mobile: 'Watch
your speed here, Carol. We rejoin the motorway in a
couple of miles. Keep a look-out for the sign.'

'Okay. Wow, just look at all this development, Tim! Do
you realise this whole coastline is a builder's paradise?
Brian and I could make a bomb out here.'

'Don't get distracted, Carol. The road divides up ahead.
It's important we get to Tarifa before dark.'

'Don't worry, I'm watching.' It was easy to forgive his
nagging because he was the one with everything at stake
here, not me.

Our plan was to spend the night at Tarifa, right at the
south-west corner of Spain, just past Gibraltar. This was
where Tim would be lying low while I went on to the

group's headquarters, which were some way north of there about five miles inland from the Costa del Luz. The Heirs of Akasha had offered to send a car to the airport to meet me, and Tim had advised me to go along with their plans so as not to arouse their suspicion, but I told them I preferred to find my own way. Obviously they thought this was odd, but there was no way I was going to be stuck in Akashic HQ with no means of escape. Besides, I had a secret fantasy which involved whisking Jenny, Katie and Davy away under cover of darkness in my car.

Once I'd convinced Tim of my need for separate transport, we decided it was best if I phoned them in the evening and told them I'd been delayed and had decided to make an impromptu stop-over in Tarifa. That way Tim and I would have a chance to look over one or two locations where we could meet away from ever-watchful eyes. We might even find a spot to which I could entice Katie so she and Tim would at last have a chance to talk to each other.

All in all, I felt more optimistic than I'd done in weeks. But my cheerfulness clearly irritated Tim: I suppose it made him worry I wasn't taking all this seriously enough, so I did my best to sound suitably low-key when I spoke to him.

After skirting the edge of what looked like one long coastal building site we drove past Gibraltar on our left. It was a massive industrial complex, with huge docks and not a Barbary ape in sight. Across the narrow strip of ocean beyond Gibraltar was the purple outline of the North African coast.

'Look at that,' I burst out the next time Tim phoned. 'I never realised Morocco was so close. And look, it's all hilly.'

'Those "hills" are the Rif mountains.'

'They're so beautiful. I wasn't expecting that.'

'We should get to Tarifa in about twenty minutes' was his only comment.

My excitement grew. The mountains of Morocco were

shadowed mysterious purple in the evening light. Our own road began to ascend steeply: suddenly all the hillsides were covered in massive wind turbines, a whole army of them marching down the barren slopes towards the sea.

At Tarifa Tim had booked us into separate hotels. 'Turn left here,' the instructions continued over the mobile phone. 'That's yours up ahead on the left. There's parking right outside.' As I pulled into the kerb, Tim drove slowly past, without a glance in my direction. He looked strained, as though he hadn't slept much since his arrival.

I checked in and the receptionist showed me to my room. It had been painted in lurid colours and there were bad pictures of women in flamenco costume on the walls. I drew back the curtains. Outside there was a castle, lit bronze by the dying sun, a harbour and beyond all that the sea and the mulberry-coloured mountains of Morocco.

It was a shame our plan didn't include two nights in this place. I dug the Heirs of Akasha's Spanish number out of my bag and phoned their centre.

A woman's voice answered. 'Hello? El Cortijo Tartessus.'

'Hi, this is Carol Brewster. Look, the journey from the airport has taken much longer than I expected. I'm going to spend tonight in a hotel.'

'That's a pity. Where are you?'

'I'm in a place called Tarifa.'

'We're less than forty minutes from there. Are you sure you don't want to come straight here? It would have saved you a lot of trouble if our car had picked you up from the airport with the others.'

'I know, but it's too late now. And anyway, this looks an interesting town. I might snoop around a bit in the morning. But I'll be with you by midday.'

'That means you'll miss the morning session, but it's up to you.'

Her voice had cooled by the time I hung up. Clearly it was hard for any of the poor deluded Heirs of Akasha to imagine why anyone would prefer sightseeing over preparations for the end of the world.

I leaned out of the window, fascinated by the roofscape of domes and chimneys and tall palms, by the rich brew of noise rising up from the street below and the magical sunset of purple and gold. Yesterday, my last evening with Gus, had been a misery of false cheerfulness; tomorrow I had to play the part of a dedicated Quester: this felt like my last night of freedom, the only moment of real holiday in the whole fortnight. I intended to make the most of it.

During the two days he'd already spent in Tarifa, Tim had identified a restaurant where we could meet in privacy: it was down a narrow back street a little distance from the main part of town. When I arrived I saw to my delight that there were a dozen or so tables set outside and already some people were eating there. It seemed so incredible to be sitting outside in only a light jacket in the middle of October that I was all for joining them, but Tim insisted we go inside.

'It's too risky out there,' he said as we settled at a table right at the back of the restaurant, by the door to the kitchen. 'Someone from the centre might see us. There's no point exposing you to unnecessary danger.'

I glanced round swiftly. Determined to enjoy my single evening of freedom, I turned my attention firmly to the menu. Tim had ordered a bottle of red wine. It was full-flavoured and mellow and by the time I'd drunk two glasses, which didn't take long, I was much more relaxed.

Tim had hardly touched his. He was wearing a crisp white shirt and a light jacket and his hair was brushed into absolute obedience, but his eyes were shadowed with fatigue and I wished there was some way to help him relax.

'Easy does it, Carol,' he said, observing my no-doubt flushed face. 'You're going to need a cool head.'

'Yes, but not until tomorrow. Tonight you can keep a cool head for both of us.' I poured myself another glass. 'Let's order a second bottle.'

He leaned back in his chair and regarded me thoughtfully. A pulse was beating just below his left eye. He said quietly, 'Don't underestimate them, Carol.'

'Who?'

'Them. The Heirs of Akasha. The group.' He paused, then added, 'Our enemy.'

'Oh, no need to worry about that. I know what they're like.'

'Do you? What happened in Cornwall was child's play. We neither of us really know what they're capable of.'

I took another swig of wine and stared meaningfully at the empty bottle. 'Well, I'm going to find out soon enough. I don't intend worrying about it now.'

He leaned forward suddenly and laid his hand over mine, gripping it tightly. His blue eyes were locked on my face. He said, 'Carol, it's no good. I can't let you go through with this.'

I stared at him in amazement. 'Don't be daft, Tim. You've spent the last month twisting my arm to make me come here. You can't go getting cold feet now.'

He hadn't let go of my hand. I was glad; he had a comfortable hand, warm and dry and exerting just the right amount of pressure. He'd spruced himself up for the evening and I had to resist the urge to reach over and muss up his hair.

He said in a low voice, 'I'm serious, Carol. I'd never forgive myself if anything happened to you.'

'Well, that's all right, because nothing will happen to me. Those crazies will think I'm just another eager Quester. And if anything does go wrong I'll have the mobile and my own car. Don't worry, Tim. We've got it all planned.'

'God, I hope you're right.' To my regret he released my

hand as the waiter arrived with some complimentary plates of tapas and asked us for our orders. I couldn't decide between squid and aubergines and ended up asking for a small plate of each, but Tim just laid down the menu with a sigh and said he'd have an omelette. The waiter retreated to the kitchen.

I said, 'Don't worry about me, Tim. You've no idea how stubborn I am and I certainly haven't come all this way just to chicken out now.'

He was not so easily roused from his sombre mood. 'Still, if you change your mind . . .'

'I won't.'

'Okay, but you must promise you'll leave the instant there's any danger.'

'Of course I will. I'm not completely stupid.' I began helping myself to tapas, suddenly realising how long it had been since my dolls' house meal on the plane. Tim watched me. He was still brooding. Eventually his anxiety must have got through to me because I said, 'What's bothering you, Tim? Is it something to do with your fifth column?'

'On the contrary, they managed to check through your file. Apparently there was a security query against your name when you were in Cornwall, but that's been deleted now, which must mean they've decided to trust you.'

'Good. It might help if you told me who the fifth column was, just in case.'

'There's no point. They were transferred back to Cornwall a few days ago.'

'Oh no! That means I'll be alone there.' I searched his eyes. 'When did you learn they were moving?'

'Yesterday. I know, I should have told you—'

'Yes,' I said coldly. 'You should have done.'

'You can still pull out if you want to. The whole thing is too dangerous. You've seen them in action twice, so you know how unscrupulous they can be.'

'Quite sure there's nothing else?'

'It's just a feeling.' He shifted uncomfortably. 'Maybe it's this place. I don't like it here. In England I know how the system operates. It's different here. I found out this morning there are at least three different sets of police. How are we supposed to know who to contact if things get heavy?'

'We'll just have to make sure they don't, then, won't we?'

'God, I wish I spoke Spanish. I thought they'd all have learned English, but hardly anyone speaks it.'

I smiled. 'Anything else?'

He glared at me. 'Yes, damn it, there is. I care about you, Carol.'

'Oh.' I cast around for a light-hearted or flippant reply, but the words died in my throat. There was no doubting his sincerity. I began vaguely, 'Well, you mustn't—' but he interrupted.

'I know I twisted your arm to get you here, but now I wish I hadn't. While I was in England, I was so desperate I would have sacrificed anyone without a second thought. But now you're actually here I realise I had no right to drag you into this. It's not fair to ask you to run risks for me. I'll have to find some other way.'

'Stop torturing yourself, Tim. No one forced me to come here and I certainly don't intend to turn back now. It's not just Davy, remember. I've got my own reasons for being here too.'

'But surely—'

'Listen, if your mother walked in here right now with Davy and said they'd left the group for good and all, I'd still go.'

'Because of your husband's niece? You'd run the risk just for her?'

'It's a bit more selfish than that. I can't explain because

I don't fully understand it myself, but Jenny triggered something when she turned up at our house in the spring. Ever since then there's been a barrier between me and Gus. I don't think he wants it and I know I don't, but neither of us can shift it.'

'So?' demanded Tim. 'What does that have to do with the group?'

'Maybe nothing at all. But I think it's all connected. Something to do with the time when they all lived at Grays.'

'What does your husband say?'

'He won't talk about it. Maybe someone else will. There are three of the original bunch at the centre now. Maybe one of them can tell me something. I don't intend to give up on Gus just yet.'

'Give up? Is it as bad as that?'

I nodded. Suddenly there was a lump in my throat. 'It's about as bad as it gets,' I croaked.

'I'm sorry.'

I shrugged. 'Thanks.'

'Would it help to talk about it?'

His question was so proper, like a well-meaning counsellor, that without thinking I burst out laughing. Tim flushed with annoyance and I realised I'd hurt his feelings, so I said quickly, 'It's really kind of you Tim, but no, thanks. The last thing I want to do right now is talk about my husband.' As soon as I'd said it, and saw the way his eyebrows twitched upwards in a question, I realised this statement was open to misinterpretation, too, so I added hastily, 'I just want to relax a bit. After all, this is the only proper holiday I'm having. Tomorrow I've got to switch into Quester mode and be on guard all the time. Tonight I just don't want to bother.'

'I understand.' He grinned. 'What a time for me to start having cold feet.'

'On a lovely warm evening like this?'

'You're right. Stupid of me. Let's enjoy ourselves. Waiter, another bottle of wine.'

The rest of the evening passed without a hitch. Tim was funny and entertaining. He hardly mentioned Davy or his mother, which considering he'd thought of nothing else for weeks must have taken a huge effort of will. Instead he told me about his work with a finance company and his real passion, which was hiking. It soon became obvious that when he talked about hiking he was actually describing an activity closer to mountaineering than my idea of a hike. And he was interested in me, too. I found myself opening up and talking about my mother and how I'd had to support my dad when she walked out on us, and how I'd given up my plans for a career to stay behind and help.

Tim regarded me thoughtfully. He said, 'Gus Ridley must be quite a bit older than you.'

'Fifteen years. And yes, I know what you're thinking. My father had died the year before and part of Gus's attraction was as a father figure – at least, that's what everyone assumes. Who knows? Maybe they're right. I can think of worse reasons for marrying.'

Tim frowned. 'That's not what I meant. I was wondering if marrying him didn't seem like a way of getting out and finding a new kind of life.'

I didn't answer right away. He was right, of course, though over the years I'd conveniently forgotten some of the details. Grays Orchard had still been on the market when Gus asked me to marry him. We'd been planning to spend time in New York or Rome or wherever the mood took us and decide later where we wanted to make our base. And then, just before the ceremony, Gus said would I mind very much if we stayed put for a bit. Grays had been working its magic and he'd started some of the best work he'd done in years. Of course, I agreed. That was six years ago.

That evening, sitting with Tim in the restaurant and enjoying the thrill of not knowing what the next two weeks would bring, I wondered if part of my reason for being there was straightforward hunger for change.

When the meal was over and it was time to return to our hotels, I was half sorry we had to leave the restaurant at separate times and go in opposite directions. It was the not quite perfect end to an almost perfect evening.

Chapter 15

By the time I reached El Cortijo Tartessus around noon the following day, my hangover had almost gone. It wasn't hard to find the centre because there were no other properties for miles around. High wrought-iron gates marked the entrance. Each gatepost was topped by a stone statue of a rough-looking character wearing a lion's skin and carrying a club. By now I knew enough about the mythology of the group to recognise Hercules; the ancient name for the Strait of Gibraltar was the Pillars of Hercules, beyond which lay the fabled civilisation of Atlantis. Presumably this was intended as a sign that I was entering sacred territory. A more modern touch was the CCTV camera poised just below the foot of the left-hand Hercules.

When I got out of the car to press the entry buzzer I noticed the gates were decorated with an intricate pattern of birds and fish, reminding me of the Akashic clock in Cornwall. A disembodied voice asked me my name and then the gates swung open and I drove into the compound.

On either side of the gate there was a high fence that followed the undulation of the hillside as far as the eye could see. Tim had said security was laxer here than in Cornwall, but the fence would not have been out of place in a prison camp. What was it for? To keep trespassers out? Or to keep reluctant Questers and Pilgrims trapped inside?

The narrow track led for about half a mile before the first building came into sight. The landscape was parched and brown after the long Andalucían summer: far in the distance, between two bare hills, a small strip of iridescent sea was visible and in the clear blue air above me three or four huge birds were circling slowly. Soaring slowly with their massive wings outspread, they looked like eagles.

If this was the main house, it was smaller than I'd expected, more like a guest house than a hotel. Then I noticed several smaller buildings scattered among the trees on either side and a track twisting away along the curve of the hillside. But apart from an elderly donkey drowsing in the shade of a plum tree, there was no sign of life.

I parked and went in. The hall was cool and airy, with a red tiled floor and a broad staircase leading up to a first-floor gallery with doors opening from it. I was reminded suddenly of Grays Orchard and sliding down the banisters on my first visit there with Gus. Pulling myself together I approached the reception desk, where a woman was staring at a computer screen.

She looked up. 'Carol Brewster? We've been expecting you.' She was in her twenties, tall and heavy-looking with dark hair scraped back from her face and a stolid expression. She regarded me critically. 'You've missed your group's Induction session. There's only another ten minutes to run. You'll have to get some of the other members to fill you in. It's a pity you didn't arrange to be picked up at the airport with the others.'

'I was on a different flight,' I said. 'Is it okay to leave my car at the front?'

'I suppose so,' she answered dully. 'We can return it to the car-hire firm for you, if you like. There'll be no time for you to use it and it'll save you a lot of money.'

'That's okay. I might want to do some sightseeing.'

The look she gave me implied I'd made an indecent suggestion; she shook her head. 'You'll find your days are very full.'

'Oh good.' Time to establish my Quester credentials. 'I can hardly wait to start.'

She sighed. 'I suppose I'd better show you your villa. My name is Intara, by the way. You're in Hesperides Two. Lunch will be served on the terrace at one thirty.'

She glanced at a small screen on the wall above her which showed a snowy image of the entrance gates, then sighed again and emerged from behind the desk. Without offering to help with my bags, she led me back out through the front door and along a path round the side of the building past the kitchens: the sound of pots banging and laughter and a delicious scent of herby cooking wafted out on the warm air. A little further along, on a vine-covered terrace, two men in baggy swimming trunks were setting places at long trestle tables.

I tried to sound enthusiastic. 'Lunch outside in October. What a treat!'

'It's too hot in the summer,' she said.

We walked in silence for a while, then she glanced at me with sudden shyness and said, 'When you get your timetable you might be interested to know that I'm giving the talk on Thursday night.'

'Really?' It was hard to sound interested because I'd caught sight of a group of people working in a vast vegetable patch on our right. One of them, even at this distance, looked strikingly like Jenny Sayer. 'What's it on?' I asked politely.

212 • J O A N N A H I N E S

'The *Book of Thoth*.'

I glanced at her quickly to see if she was joking but she was in deadly earnest. I said, 'I've never heard of it.'

'That's so typical,' she said with another sigh, as if my ignorance was symptomatic of all the ills of the modern age. 'People just don't realise its significance.'

'Can I get hold of a copy?'

'Oh no, it hasn't existed for over fifteen hundred years. But lots of the ancient texts refer to it. I've spent the last six years piecing together the evidence and filling in some of the gaps by tuning into the astral plane. I think I've got most of it now. It provides the most vivid evidence we have about Atlantis.'

'Fascinating,' I said automatically, though by now I was hardly listening. The girl who looked like Jenny was acting in an extremely Jenny-ish way: having a furious row with an older woman who wore white cotton overalls and an enormous straw hat.

'Is that by any chance Jenny Sayer?'

Intara followed the direction of my gaze, then pursed her lips with disapproval. 'Yes, do you know her? She thinks she's going to take the Oath of Loyalty at the end of this month, but quite frankly she's nowhere near ready.'

As if to prove the truth of this statement, Jenny flung down her fork, stomped off across the vegetable patch, and disappeared behind a stone wall.

'What happens if she isn't ready? Is the ceremony delayed?'

'That's not for me to decide. Here we are. These are the Hesperides.' We had reached a group of three stone bungalows, each with a shady porch and a terrace open to the sun. We were just in time to see Jenny, wearing grubby shorts and a T-shirt, march up the steps and into one of the others.

Seeing an opportunity to meet Jenny away from the

prying eyes of the Heirs' security system, I was eager to shake off my guide. It meant promising not to miss her talk on the *Book of Thoth* and then pretending to be suffering from the laver bread syndrome. In this case I blamed the airline food. Intara sighed again, as though it was only what she had expected, and plodded back towards the main building.

'Jenny, are you alone?'

'Christ, what are you doing here?'

'Same as you, probably.'

She was sitting on the edge of one of the six beds in her villa. She had been looking thoroughly fed up when I tapped on the open door and stepped quietly inside, and the sight of me did nothing to cheer her up. If anything, she looked even more dismayed.

'Are you one of the new batch of Quester?' she asked.

'I'm doing the two-week retreat. I should have arrived yesterday but the drive from the airport took ages so I stayed last night in Tarifa.'

'Oh.' She flung herself down on the bed and crossed her arms behind her head. She was tanned and healthy, but there were dark circles ringing her eyes and she looked no happier than she had done in the spring. 'So?' she asked. 'What do you think?'

'It's too early to say; I've only just arrived.'

She frowned. 'I wouldn't have thought this was your scene.'

'That's what I'm here to find out. What's it like?'

'God, what a question.' She turned her face away. 'You'll have to work that one out for yourself.'

'What about you? Have you found what you were looking for?'

She turned back to glare at me. 'What makes you think I was looking for anything?'

'Isn't that why everyone is here?'

She didn't answer. I guessed she was afraid I'd mention her destruction of Gus's pictures. I said, 'Look, Jenny, I'm not here to talk about what happened at Grays.'

'Suit yourself.' She stared at me a bit longer, then said in a hoarse voice, 'Has someone put you up to this?'

'What do you mean?'

'Did my mum ask you to come here?'

'I've never spoken to your mother.'

'What about Gus, then?'

'He doesn't even know where I am.'

She smiled for the first time, but it was a bitter smile. 'Have you two split up, then? Have you left him?'

'Certainly not. I just wanted to get away on my own for a bit, see what this place has to offer.'

'Good luck to you.'

'What's that supposed to mean?'

Her face sank back into its sulky look. 'You'll find out soon enough.'

I took a deep breath and said, 'Okay. All I wanted to say was that while we're here we both have the right to leave our past behind us. I've registered here in my maiden name: Brewster. No one knows I'm Gus Ridley's wife and I'd like it to stay that way. After all, he and Ra used to be friends and I don't want anyone to think I expect different treatment.'

'No worries. I won't tell anyone.'

'Thanks,' I said. 'I'd better go and unpack.'

'Okay.' I turned to go. Just as I was moving towards the door she said, 'How's Gus getting on with his painting?'

I froze, then turned slowly back to face her. Was she being deliberately provocative? I said with cold fury, 'He didn't paint at all for a while, but he's started again now.'

She returned my gaze steadily. 'Are you sure Gus didn't put you up to this?'

'Quite sure. He wouldn't have wanted me to come.'

'That's what you say,' she muttered grumpily, then rolled over on her side to face the wall.

I didn't see her again until the evening, by which time I'd been given a tour of the estate – or at least some of it, because the whole place was huge and people used golf buggies for getting to some of the remoter areas. I had also met my fellow Questers-on-retreat who were, as I'd expected, a mixed bunch. One or two had been on the first weekend in Cornwall and we greeted each other like old friends. The ratio of out-and-out losers was lower than on previous occasions and I felt a pang of sympathy for the luckless few who'd been weeded out already; even so, there were several in our group who would normally have triggered my unhappiness sensors, except that they didn't seem to be as active as usual, mainly because the whole atmosphere of the place was relentlessly upbeat and all the other Third-level Questers – which was what I'd become – were full of hope at what the coming fortnight would provide.

Although not on the timetable, sexual adventure seemed to be as much a part of the equation as spiritual enlightenment. Already a runty-looking man with a wispy grey ponytail had paired off with a buxom forty-year-old called Marcia, and the two unattached young women had been snapped up by programme leaders, who made no bones about the criteria they'd employed. And Herman, who'd tagged along beside me during our Compatibility Assessment and seemed to think we were practically an item, was approached during our first lunch on the vine-covered terrace by a woman called Pam. She looked him up and down with an approving eye and asked him if he'd like to help her fix the shutters in the Women Pilgrims' Long House. He agreed happily and loped off after her through the trees, not appearing again until the evening meal by which time he looked relaxed and extremely content.

In best Sturford curtain-twitching style, my immediate reaction was disapproval. All the clichés about cults and sexual exploitation were being confirmed with a vengeance, but alongside my disapproval there was another emotion which felt uncomfortably close to envy. For one thing, everyone was so open about what they were up to – often quite literally. They had to be: as everyone except the Inner Circle lived either in long houses or dormitories, there was no bedroom privacy to retreat to, so people made love whenever and wherever they got the chance. That first afternoon I was startled, as my tour of the estate took us past a high evergreen hedge beside the Lunar Potager where Jenny had been working that morning, to hear energetic grunting and gasping coming from the other side, and even more surprised when my guide merely grinned and said cheerfully, 'We'd better leave Solon's Terrace until later.'

A little way into that first tour I realised I was being shown only a fraction of the premises, just as in Cornwall I'd never seen the New House or the farm. This time my tour encompassed only the main administration building where the reception desk was, which was called Lyonesse, and a handful of villas and long houses and workshops nearby. There was a further cluster of houses about half a mile away, which I was told was high-security and off limits to Questers. And when I asked about the enormous aircraft-hangar-like doors which seemed to lead straight into the hillside itself, my guide told me firmly that they were top-security and only a chosen few were allowed to enter.

'Science and technology departments,' he said. 'Only Inner Circle and the Priests of Science can go in.'

'The Priests of Science?'

'Yes,' he explained earnestly. He was a soft-spoken Scandinavian with enormous biceps and delicate glasses. 'You see, mainstream Western culture in the Doomed Outside has made the mistake of trying to separate science from the Divine. Our belief is that science is merely the manifestation of Divine order, so it is essential that scientists should also be people of heightened spirituality. As well as practical experimentation, such people must have heightened powers of supersensory perception so they can tune into the harmonies of the universe. It's the only way forward.' He grinned at me with shy enthusiasm. 'There's real cutting-edge stuff going on behind those doors, believe me.'

It was odd how quickly I slid back into the same conversations and concerns that had dominated my Quester weekend in Cornwall. Here once again there was endless talk of the Akashic record and supersensory perception and the woeful blindness of the human race as it hurtled towards the catastrophe they called the Watershed. After a short while it all began to seem perfectly normal. I reminded myself of that walk across Hyde Park and all those ordinary people engaged in ordinary Sunday-evening activities like roller blading and eating ice cream, but already, from the distorted perspective of Tartessus they seemed far away and naive.

When supper was over, I was making my way to a talk on *Channelling Your Personal Angel*, which seemed the sort of thing an enthusiastic Third-level Quester ought to be doing, when a familiar voice called out behind me, 'Carol! Are you free?'

It was Jenny. She had changed out of her grubby shorts and T-shirt into a flowered cotton dress and her hair was brushed and shining. More remarkable still, her scowl had been replaced by smiling friendliness.

'I was just off to the channelling talk,' I said.

'Well, if that's what you want to do . . . But my friend's offered to do a rune reading. Would you like to give it a try?'

I had no idea what a rune reading was, but I said quickly, 'Sure. It sounds interesting.'

Jenny grinned and linked her arm through mine. 'It's Elaine. I expect you remember her from the Atlantic Castle. She rooms with me in Hes One. We should have the place to ourselves for at least an hour. I thought you might want to give them a try.'

The temperature had dropped dramatically as soon as the sun had sunk over the distant sea and I was cold in spite of my sweater as we followed the path back to the Hesperides. The temperature inside was not much higher than outside: Elaine was sitting cross-legged on one of the low beds. Her round face lit up when I went in.

'Hi there, Carol.'

I grinned. How could I have expected any other greeting. I answered in kind, 'Elaine, hi there. It's great to see you again. And you finally made it over here to be with your boyfriend.'

She pulled a face. 'Except he's not my boyfriend any more, the cheating bastard. But that's okay, we've worked it through. Apparently I double-crossed him in a past life, so now we're quits. But it's really exciting because I'm scheduled to take the Oath of Loyalty at the end of the month.'

I looked cautiously at Jenny. 'What exactly does the Oath of Loyalty entail?'

'Let's not start on all that now,' said Jenny impatiently. 'We can get the runes read before the others get back from Lyonesse if we start now. Are you ready, Elaine?'

'Sure. I've got them right here.'

'Do I have to do anything special?' I asked.

'Just make yourself comfortable opposite me. You can

sit in the lotus position if you like but cross-legged is fine, too. Now, I want you to take this bag of runes in your hands and hold it close to your chest. Close your eyes. Breathe deeply. Try to make your mind go blank . . . That's great.'

When I opened my eyes again Jenny had switched off the light and lit a single candle which she'd placed on the window-sill so its delicate flame was reflected on the glass. Otherwise the room was in darkness. Jenny settled herself in a lotus posture on the next bed and observed us with a smile of cat-like satisfaction.

A tingling in my spine warned me that I was being set up.

Elaine took the bag of runes from my hands with exaggerated reverence and loosened the drawstring. She scattered the runes on the white blanket between us. I'd never seen runes before: they're not part of a country builder's stock-in-trade. They looked like a cross between small pebbles and ordinary dice, except each one was covered in strange marks and squiggles. Elaine hooked her lank hair behind her ears and peered down at them thoughtfully.

'Oh dear,' she said in a low voice. 'I'm so sorry, Carol. This isn't looking good at all.'

'What is it?' Jenny demanded sharply. 'What can you see?'

I looked from one to the other and my earlier suspicions were confirmed. 'How about a tall dark handsome stranger?' I asked. 'Or maybe a win on the lottery?'

'Oh no.' Elaine's brow was deeply furrowed. 'There's conflict ahead. Someone's really got it in for you, Carol. They're giving you a really hard time. Looks like violence. Then there's a long journey. It's very dark.'

'Yeah, the sun's gone down,' I said lightly. 'And I am going back to England at the end of next week.'

'This is serious, Carol,' said Elaine sombrely. 'This rune

configuration is really weird. I've never seen anything like it. I don't like to give advice, but if I was you . . .'

'You think I should leave? What a surprise. Or maybe you'd like me to leave, and this is your way of dropping the hint?'

'No, I'm serious, Carol, honestly I am.'

Just then, the door burst open and a woman blasted in like a whirlwind. I'd noticed her in the dining room at supper. She was painfully thin, with raven-black hair and enormous features. Right now she looked ready to kill.

'You bitch! What are you doing with my runes?'

Elaine stared at her, slack-jawed with horror. She was too appalled to move, and it was Jenny who slid off the next bed and gathered the runes back into their pouch.

'We only borrowed them, Anya,' she said. 'It's no big deal.'

She offered the pouch back to the newcomer, who snatched it with bony fingers.

'You idiot!' She was spitting with rage. 'You pathetic little moron! Have you got any idea what you're playing with here? You've corrupted them with your phoney energy. It'll take me weeks to get their full power back.'

'Oh, don't be such a drama queen,' said Jenny with contempt. 'We were only mucking about.'

I thought Anya was going to explode with rage. She clutched the bag of runes in her fist like a weapon, ready to smash it against Jenny's skull.

'You stupid, stupid girl! I've a good mind to teach you—'

Elaine had broken out of her trance. 'God, Anya, I'm so sorry. I wasn't thinking. I . . .' She uncrossed her legs and scrambled off the bed. 'I'd better go. I'm supposed to be helping clear up. I'm really sorry, Anya. I never thought . . .' Still jabbering apologies, she scuttled out of the room.

Jenny tilted her chin defiantly, there was no way she was

going to be cowed like Elaine. 'Don't get your knickers in a twist, Anya. You make all that prophecy stuff up all the time. I've watched you doing it. You're just a phoney.'

Anya became very still. All the colour drained from her face. She said quietly, 'Do you really think that?'

'Of course I do. Everyone thinks so.'

'Do they indeed? Well then, why don't we give it a go right now and find out?' She clasped the bag of runes to her bony chest and inhaled deeply. 'The stones are angry. I can feel their heat. They are ready to speak out. They want to be heard.'

'Oh, give it a rest, Anya. That's all crap.'

Anya moved across the room and smoothed the blanket in front of Jenny. Then she glanced at me. 'Your friend,' she asked, 'does she also think the stones are crap?'

'Sure she does; she's not stupid,' said Jenny and I didn't contradict her. I was curious to see how this played out.

'Very well. We'll see what message they have for us.' With a movement like someone stirring an enormous pot, Anya passed the bag of runes in front of my face. I tilted backwards automatically. Jenny, who'd been expecting the gesture, did not flinch.

Anya bared her teeth, looked at each of us in turn, then cast the runes on the taut white bedspread in front of Jenny. She examined them hungrily, like a hunter, then her face darkened.

'Well?' said Jenny, curious in spite of herself. 'Tell us what you see then.'

Anya was frowning. Her rage had vanished. She gathered the runes up swiftly and put them back in their pouch. 'I should not have asked them in anger,' she said. 'It was a mistake.'

'Go on, tell us what they said.'

'The anger was in them. It is better not.'

'Jesus, Anya!' exclaimed Jenny. 'You can't cop out now.'

'Yes, go on, what did you see?' In spite of my scepticism I was uneasy. Just as I'd known beforehand that Elaine was faking, now I was equally sure that Anya, crazy though it seemed, believed utterly in whatever it was the stones said.

She turned to look at me and her eyes were no longer angry, only wary. She said, 'Who are you?'

'Carol Brewster. I'm a Third-level Quester.'

'You should not have come here,' she said.

'Hah!' Jenny was triumphant. 'I knew it.'

'Why not?' I asked.

'Do you really want to know?'

'Yes.' For once Jenny and I spoke with one voice.

'Okay, then I will tell you what I saw. There is danger ahead for both of you. Carol, you are the cause. There's a small space, like a cupboard. Or a coffin. You are both there. I see fire and smoke. The danger is for both of you. And it is right here.'

Chapter 16

We were bringing down the energy of the moon. At least, that's what they said we were doing. What it looked like to me, the most sceptical of Questers, was a bunch of freaks in long robes standing around in a pseudo-Greek temple banging drums and chanting.

Or that's what one half of me thought. The other half, the half that would have been quite tempted to be brainwashed if I hadn't known about the seamy side of the Heirs of Akasha, was thinking how beautiful it all was.

Cool night had fallen over the barren hills of El Cortijo Tartessus. The crescent moon, delicate as a fine scratch in the blackness, hung beside a single star. There must have been over a hundred of us gathered in the Temple of Tartessus, which was a collection of pale columns and arches, with slabs of white stone beneath our feet. Far away, a shimmer in the dark was the ocean.

Everyone was dressed in long robes, their colour as always depending on rank. I was once more clad in the brown robes of a Quester. There were blue-robed Pilgrims, pale-green Seekers and cream Acolytes. This ceremony was performed each month on the day of the new moon, but tonight, I'd been told, was a specially auspicious occasion because it was the last Invoking before the Oath of Loyalty ceremony in two weeks' time.

Instead of supper that evening, there had been an hour-long meditation for the whole community in the Hall of Atlantis. As in Cornwall, there was a massive Akashic clock all along one wall, though to my eye this one looked cruder. Probably the lessons learned in constructing this one had been incorporated in the design of the later one. Ra and the other members of the Inner Circle, including Katie, were present for this meditation. All of them, including Ra/Raymond, wore white robes trimmed with gold, denoting their status, but there was none of the theatrical frenzy I'd witnessed in Cornwall. In fact this was all fairly casual, but missing supper, combined with an hour of the weird breathing techniques in the meditation session, left me feeling light-headed by the time we filed out into the Andalucían night.

Then the chanting began, and the singing. Sometimes it felt outlandish and strange, at other times it felt oddly familiar, like a campfire sing-along. Mostly we stood in a huge circle, but every now and then a few people would break off and weave in and out of the tall columns, or sway up to the raised dais where the Inner Circle were also singing and swaying. A bowl of fire burned in a ring of water in the centre of the dance, but apart from that there was no lighting.

Faces were oddly lit by the flames, making them appear ghoulish against the night. Every now and then I glanced across at Ra, who was surrounded by the women of the Inner Circle, Palu, Serafa and Katie, and I thought how sinister it all was. The next moment a member of the community would beam up at me from under a blue or brown hood and the whole thing seemed harmless.

There was a great deal of hugging. Apparently it was the effect of the new moon's fragile energies: people were brimming over with goodwill for each other. And who knows, maybe there was something in it, because at some stage in the Lunar Invoking a blue-clad Pilgrim stumbled up to me in the darkness and said, 'Sorry about the runes, Carol. It was only meant to be a joke.' And Elaine's round face beamed at me apologetically from under her voluminous hood.

'That's okay,' I said without hesitation, for which I was treated to a lunar-inspired hug.

It was even more surprising to discover a little later that the Pilgrim singing away lustily beside me was Jenny. It would have taken more energies than any moon could organise to get Jenny to apologise, but she did turn to me with a wary smile and squeeze my hand, which, I thought, was the closest she'd ever get to saying sorry. I smiled back: there'd be time enough to take her to task once she was free of the group.

She and Elaine and all the other Pilgrims due to take the Oath of Loyalty at the full moon wore enormous gold sashes over one shoulder. They reminded me of the coloured bands we used to wear at school to show which sports team we belonged to.

As the ceremony was reaching its climax, a stooped Quester in a long brown robe manoeuvred his way through the crowds to stand beside me.

'Isn't this amazing?' he asked.

It was Lionel. His thick glasses were orange in the fire-light, making him look like some exotic frog; he was radiant.

'I've never seen anything like it,' I said, truthfully enough, over the din.

'I'm moving on to First-level Pilgrim next month,' he confided. 'How about you?'

226 • J OANNA H INES

'No, I'm just here on a fortnight's Quester retreat. You know, still trying to make up my mind.' I couldn't help wondering why the group had accepted Lionel, since he didn't strike me as being the kind of recruit they were looking for. I asked, 'Does that mean you can stay here for ever, then?'

'Oh yes,' he replied eagerly. 'I've been accepted as a PP, a Paying Parasite. That means I make over all my assets to the group and in return I can live here for the rest of my life – or until the Watershed, whichever comes first.'

'But suppose you change your mind? What happens if you want to leave?'

He stared at me blankly, muttered something inaudible and swayed off to find someone who wouldn't spoil his happiness with awkward questions.

Strange and barbaric as the Lunar Invoking was, it proved to be a brilliant way to get an appetite. Once it was over we all trooped back to the main house where the long tables had been laid for a feast. There was paella and lamb stew, freshly baked bread and olives, fruit and cheese and as much wine as anyone wanted. The ceremony had left everyone with a euphoria that even affected the taste of the food. And the wine.

As well as making everyone extremely hungry, the moon's energies had also had a marked impact on their libido. Several couples slipped out of the hall during the meal, some- times taking a carafe of wine with them. I saw Elaine, rosy- cheeked and happy, sloping off with a dark-haired youth of about her age. Jethro, the Yorkshire-born Pilgrim in my work group, had taken to sitting next to me at meals. He glanced at his watch. He repeated the action on their return.

'Eight minutes,' he said. 'That's fast work, even for Dan.'

I smiled. 'No wonder Elaine looks dazed. It must have been over before it began.'

Jethro treated me to a lingering look. 'Want to give it a try?' he asked casually. 'I can guarantee you at least half an hour, all included.'

'Thanks for the offer, but I'm more of a dinner-and-flowers date myself.'

He grinned. Maybe he was even relieved. There were more women than men at El Cortijo Tartessus and sexually active heterosexual men were in constant demand, as Herman was discovering.

Afterwards, I wondered why I hadn't told him I was married. Maybe because I didn't feel all that married, not here. After only three days at the Centre, my life in Sturford was beginning to seem far away and irrelevant.

And that, disturbingly, included Gus.

I needed to make contact with the outside world. Tim and I had agreed that for security reasons I wouldn't phone him until there was something significant to report. I didn't want to phone Gus because I'd lied about this fortnight to him. He was under the impression I was staying with friends in the South of France. Actually, I was pretty sure he knew I was lying and had accepted it as part of the way things stood between us. Still, talking to him about fictitious friends on a fictitious holiday in a fictitious *gîte* was hardly going to make me feel connected with reality.

I took my mobile to a secluded corner of the estate and phoned Brian. Apart from Tim, he was the only person who knew where I was. With any luck he'd tell me about roofs and drains and after a bit I'd feel grounded again.

Above me, as I punched the familiar sequence of numbers on the phone, huge birds were circling slowly: not eagles, I now knew, but vultures. There was a flock of small birds in the meadow below me feeding on dried seed heads.

'Brian?'

'Carol, how's it going? Have they brainwashed you yet?

Have you signed your half of the business to them? And what about the end of the world? Is that still on schedule?'

I laughed. I knew Brian was anxious, and he'd been dead set against me coming here, but the sound of his sensible, sceptical voice made me feel instantly better. I told him a bit about the Lunar Invoking and the runes.

He was not impressed. 'Does Jenny really buy into all that nonsense?' he asked. 'Haven't you been able to talk any sense into her yet?'

'I'm choosing my moment carefully; you know how prickly she is. And I haven't spoken to Katie at all.'

'So what are you doing with yourself? You can't spend the whole day meditating and waiting for the world to end.'

'Guess what. They've got me building a chrysalis.'

'Isn't that best left to caterpillars?'

'A Tartessus chrysalis is a bit like a hermit's cell. There are quite a few of them about the place. It's where you go when you need to be on your own. Here it's called Solo Meditation, or SoMed for short.'

'I thought you said they were dead keen on communal living. How do they square that with shutting yourself away from everyone?'

'It's a yin and yang thing,' I said uncertainly. 'Everything has to have its opposite, or something like that. Jethro says that, in order to be able to experience communal living fully, each person has to have gone through Solo Meditation. It's good for the soul, I think. Like solitary confinement.'

'You're not thinking of giving it a go, are you, Carol?'

'Questers aren't allowed, even if they want to.'

'Good. Hurry up and come back. The business is doing fine, but your co-director misses you.'

After the call ended, I lay back on the warm ground and watched the five birds circling in the Andalucían blue. The days were beginning to blur one into another, and the urgency I'd arrived with was ebbing away. I really must make a proper effort to talk to Katie. I closed my eyes and slept.

I didn't meet Katie properly until the first week was nearly over. I'd managed to talk to Jenny a few times, usually at meals or in the lazy afternoons, but I was careful to keep the conversation casual: I had to build up her trust before I asked her about taking the Oath of Loyalty or getting in touch with Harriet, or she'd run a mile.

From time to time, as at the Lunar Invoking, I'd caught tantalising glimpses of the Inner Circle, but they mostly kept themselves apart from the lower ranks. It was very frustrating: I longed to sit down with Raymond and Pauline, as well as Katie, and ask them about their years at Grays Orchard. Ra's vow of silence was obviously going to be a problem, but he must have developed some way of communicating. I imagined long conversations in which they'd feed me with insights into Gus's strange behaviour, though it was hard to know how I'd raise the big question, the one that seemed to be the key to all the others: *Raymond – I mean Ra – was it you who killed Andrew Forester? Did the others have to cover up for you?*

I was anxious that time was slipping away and I was no nearer achieving any of my goals. After early meditation and breakfast, the mornings were spent with the chrysalis-building team. In the afternoons we were free to follow our own devices for an hour or two. Mid-afternoon and early evening were devoted to more meditation, compatibility groups and educational sessions on topics such as reading auras, divination with crystals and probable systems of government in Atlantis.

The system of government at Tartessus was definitely autocratic. On the fourth day of my stay Ra issued an edict through Palu and Serafa to say all locks were banned. The maintenance team spent a morning gouging them off lavatory and bathroom doors, and people who'd been keeping their valuables in lockable suitcases were no longer allowed to do so. This caused a good deal of ill feeling, though so far as I knew, everybody complied.

True to my promise, I went to the receptionist Intara's talk on the *Book of Thoth* which she gave, appropriately enough, in the Hall of Atlantis. The stage behind her was covered with artists' impressions of Atlantis in shimmering blues and greens. Intara was obviously immersed in her subject, but she spoke in a dull monotone and one or two of her audience had trouble keeping awake. She described a civilisation of great beauty and harmony at a time when humankind's rational sense was less well developed but intuition was paramount and people were able to communicate by means of telepathy. It was only in the final centuries of the era that evil made its presence felt in their world. The *Book of Thoth*, apparently, described the fall of Atlantis – or at least it would have done if all known copies hadn't been destroyed. Luckily for Intara, the Akashic Record filled in the gaps. I could see the usefulness of the Akashic Record: you could make up anything you wanted (the more outrageous the better), with none of the inconvenience of boring old rational proof; all you had to do was say you'd tuned into the Akashic Record using your supersensory perception. I wondered if Brian and I could try that next time the bank asked us for a financial forecast.

In the evenings there was a choice of more meditation, various study groups or simply relaxing, talking, drinking and making music. As there were a lot of talented musicians at the centre, this last was usually my choice.

The weirdest part was how quickly it stopped feeling weird and felt perfectly natural.

It was twelve thirty and our building work was over for the day. It had been a highly unsatisfactory morning because the cement mix kept turning out crumbly and unstable. It was obvious they'd been supplied with sea sand and the salt was spoiling the mix, but our team leader, Damon, who took his responsibility as team leader very seriously, refused to accept this and kept insisting we mix fresh loads, only to have to discard them. By noon the area round the half-built chrysalis was dotted with little mounds of rejected cement, like anaemic elephant droppings, and everyone was bad-tempered.

'Time for a group embrace?' suggested Jethro, looking round at all our sweaty, grimy faces. 'We need to draw some positive energies into this chrysalis or its karma is going to be a real mess.'

Damon said the chrysalis's karma could go stuff itself, and several other members of the team looked as though they'd cheerfully second his opinion. They declined the group embrace and ambled off towards their long houses and villas to get washed and changed before lunch.

'That's a shame,' Jethro said as he watched their retreating backs. 'It would have made them feel much better.' He turned to me with an engaging grin. 'How about a group embrace, just the two of us?'

His invitation was so direct it was almost tempting, but, 'Thanks all the same,' I began. I was interrupted by a piercing cry.

'Coo-ee! Carol! It's me, Ka—Oops, Lumina!'

I couldn't believe my luck. Dressed in flowing linen trousers and loose-fitting top, Katie was picking her way over the rugged ground towards me.

'Lumina, hi, it's great to see you.'

She looked from me to Jethro, her eyebrows raised slightly, then gave a little shrug as if to say, oh well, it's none of my business.

'What's this you're building?' she asked.

'It's a chrysalis,' said Jethro. 'For SoMed.'

'Oh, what a good idea.' Katie responded with her customary enthusiasm. 'You just can't get enough of meditation. SoMed, AquaMed or just ordinary old meditation; it always makes me feel better afterwards, just like after a really blissful facial or a mud bath.'

Jethro was looking perplexed. I assumed he hadn't spoken to Katie before. 'A facial?' he echoed incredulously.

'Mm. Absolutely.' Katie smiled at him kindly. 'Or one of those really wonderful sessions at the hairdresser's. But heigh-ho, that's all becoming a bit of a dim and distant memory these days, isn't it, Carol?'

'I'm only here for a fortnight, not a life sentence.'

'Hm. It is Carol, isn't it? I always remember a name. You were so helpful when I had that unpleasant accident during Compatibility and I never had the chance to thank you properly.'

'It was nothing.' I was relieved she didn't seem suspicious about our 'accidental' meeting with her son.

She said, 'I was wondering if you'd like to come and join us for lunch today.'

'I'd love to. I'll have to get washed and changed first.'

'Are you staying in one of the Hesperides? I'll walk with you.'

'Hes Two.'

'Good heavens! That's the *very* one I stayed in. What an amazing coincidence. And such a dear little villa, too. I was only there for two days, though, because of Davy.'

'Davy?' Just in time I remembered I wasn't supposed to know who he was.

'My grandson. You'll meet him at lunch.'

It was easy to see why the villa where Ra and the rest of the Inner Circle lived was off limits to most of the community. The level of luxury would have caused serious discontent, if not out-and-out mutiny. I'd never seen such a beautiful living space outside the pages of a glossy magazine.

From a distance, it didn't look all that big because of the way the architect had incorporated the contours of the hillside into the design, but the moment I stepped inside I realised it was enormous. From an inner courtyard came the musical splash of a fountain. All the rooms were huge, with marble floors, massive white leather sofas and white rugs and curtains. The walls, in contrast, were washed over with warm ochres and softest pink. A tray of drinks was laid on an antique sideboard, but there was no one about.

'I can guess where the boys are,' said Katie with a sigh of resignation. 'At the pool as usual.'

We walked through the house and emerged into bright sunlight. It was a shock to realise that 'the boys' was a reference not to Davy and his little friends, whoever they might be, but to Davy and Ra himself.

I had seen Ra the Initiate, medium for the Sacred Language of All the Ages and interpreter of the Akashic Record, in his formal robes of gold and in his workaday robes of white with gold edging. Now I saw him dressed in a pair of skimpy black swimming trunks, being pushed into the pool by a shrill-voiced little boy.

'Attack!' squealed Davy as he toppled Ra off balance. 'Back to Atlantis! Bam!'

Ra struck the water with a resounding splash and Davy tucked his knees in front of his chest and bombed in after him.

Katie told them both that lunch was due in a quarter of an hour. They hauled themselves out of the pool and dripped off to get showered and ready. 'Men,' said Katie. I didn't know what to say.

Lunch was served in the dappled shade of a terrace covered with about five different colours of bougainvillea. The air was filled with a scent that was delicate and exotic at the same time. We ate mouthwateringly tender squid with salads and fresh bread. The only note of austerity was that no wine was served, only water.

Ra sat at the head of the table. To my surprise, Intara was also present. Seeing her there with the members of the Inner Circle, I saw at once that she must be Palu's daughter. They had the same doughy features, though whereas Intara looked slow-witted Palu was obviously a good organiser and not at all stupid. It was a shame, I thought, that Intara didn't more closely resemble Ra, who must be her father.

I couldn't make him out at all. Still slightly damp from his swim, he was wearing a white cotton kurta. True to his vow of silence, he contributed nothing to the conversation, but each time anyone spoke they did so obliquely to him, as though he was the only audience that counted. It was his eyes that affected people, I decided: so dark they were almost black, and so dense and unblinking they were hypnotic. Only twice during the meal did his gaze fall for a few moments on me and each time I had the ridiculous notion that he knew all about me, even what I was thinking. To my annoyance I found myself blushing furiously, a thing I hardly ever do. The next moment Davy plucked at the sleeve of Ra's kurta and whispered to him and the two 'boys' dissolved in giggles.

Conversation was dominated by a young man and a middle-aged woman who were guests from the Centre in Mexico. Their names were Zostro and Agape, and they were technicians who were reporting to their opposite numbers at Tartessus on developments in their experiments in prolonged living in capsules on the sea bed. Palu asked them detailed technical questions: Katie graciously told them they were engaged on thrilling work and made helpful comments like 'Recycled air, now there's a challenge if ever there was one.'

Towards the end of the meal, Palu addressed me for the first time. 'Are you enjoying your stay here, Carol?'

'It's very interesting.'

'Intara tells me you've hired a car. Have you been able to get out and do any sightseeing?'

'Not yet. Intara was right when she said I'd be too busy.'

'Oh, but you ought to get out at least once. There are so many places near here worth visiting.'

'Can you suggest anywhere in particular?' I asked.

'Well, Ronda is always very popular and Cádiz is fascinating. You've seen Tarifa already.'

'I glimpsed it,' I said quickly. 'But there's a lot I missed. I thought I might go back again and see it properly. Take in the castle and the church.'

'What a good idea.' To my surprise Palu was all enthusiasm. 'Why don't you get someone to go with you? I'm always telling this lot they ought to get out more.' She paused, and then, as if the idea was just occurring to her, added, 'Why don't you take Katie? What do you think, Katie? You've hardly seen any of the sights around here, have you? I'm sure Carol wouldn't mind if you tagged along.'

I could hardly believe my luck. 'Do come,' I said. 'It would be much more fun going with someone else.'

A frown puckered her broad forehead. 'It's terribly kind of you to invite me, Carol, but I think I'd better not. Everything I need is right here.'

Palu smiled, a knowing little smile, and I realised the exchange had been orchestrated. Maybe even inviting me to lunch hadn't been Katie's idea originally. The whole episode had been designed to counteract any unfavourable impression I'd got in Cornwall. And now Palu had given Katie the opportunity to go to Tarifa with me and Katie had oh so conveniently turned it down. I was supposed to think Katie was free to come and go as she wished. There was no question of coercion; it was just that she preferred never to leave the group's land.

But I wasn't taken in, not for a moment.

Chapter 17

When I got back to the Hesperides there was a text message on my mobile: *Phone Victor. Urgent.* This was part of the code we'd worked out. The fact that Tim was using a pseudonym beginning with a letter so high in the alphabet meant it must be very urgent indeed.

I took the mobile to a deserted area of scrub some distance from any building and called Tim's number. His voice, when he answered, sounded oddly distorted.

'Tim, are you all right?'

'I s'pose so – Well, no, damn it, I'm not. It's okay, though, you mustn't worry. Everything's going to be just fine.'

'Tim, you're not making sense. Have you been drinking?'

'Y'know I never dring . . . never drink.'

Drugs, then? Or tranquillisers? But Tim would never admit to that. 'What's up?'

'I needed to hear your voice,' he said. 'How's it going?'

Wanting to hear my voice didn't justify such an urgent

message; maybe the strain of his solitary wait was getting to him. I said as cheerfully as I could, 'I've just had lunch with your mother and Davy.'

He let out a long sigh. 'How are they?'

I told him briefly about our lunch, and about my efforts to persuade Katie to come to Tarifa with me. He was disappointed by my failure, but I said, 'Don't worry, I'll keep trying, and I'll be in touch as soon as I've got anything to report.'

'No, Carol, don't hang up. Don't stop talking to me. I haven't spoken to anyone in days. I'm beginning to forget what my own voice sounds like. This waiting around, not doing anything, just waiting and waiting, it's driving me crazy. It's all right for you, you've got people around you, you're not melting away into nothing. When can you get them out of there?'

I reassured him as best I could, but he sounded like a man who's been banged up alone with his nightmares too long, so I said, 'Look, do you want me to come to Tarifa and see you? I can get away tomorrow afternoon. Then we can talk this through properly.'

'Make sure Katie comes too. I *must* talk to her. Just for an hour. That's not so much to ask, is it? Christ, she's my own mother . . .'

'I'll try, Tim, I promise, but don't raise your hopes too high. I'll get to your hotel about two. Will you be okay until then?'

'I suppose so. I'm relying on you, Carol. Don't let me down.'

'I'll try not to.'

As I suspected, I was given no opportunity to talk to Katie the next morning, let alone invite her to visit Tarifa with me. I'd just have to go on my own. But at lunchtime, when I was putting the car keys in my bag and heading out of my villa, Jenny appeared suddenly from the shadows.

'Where are you going?' she demanded.

'To Tarifa for the afternoon.'

'Tarifa?' Her face lit up. 'In that case I'm bloody well coming with you.'

After Cornwall I was constantly on the look-out to make sure we weren't being followed, but the roads were empty, so it would have been easy to spot a following car. We kept the conversation neutral. Jenny told me a bit about her work in the vegetable garden and the friends she'd made at Tartessus, but she was more interested in pointing out things she saw along the way, and she talked about the group without enthusiasm. I was curious, but I didn't want to get involved in deep discussions on our outward journey, because I was already worried about how to shake her off once we arrived. I reckoned the return journey would be the perfect opportunity to tackle her about her membership of the group. First, there was Tim to deal with.

It was early afternoon when we reached Tarifa: the cafés were emptying and a siesta-quiet was descending on the town. As soon as I had parked, to my relief Jenny said, 'I'm going to push off on my own for a bit. All that communal living gets you down after a while.'

'I can imagine.'

She gave me one of her odd looks and we agreed to meet in the café by the church at five o'clock. That gave us each three hours of freedom. She set off towards the beach. Over the house tops I could see a couple of kites waving and dancing in the air. Tarifa, I had learned, was closely associated with any sport that required strong winds. Jenny didn't look back once. I watched her thin, angular body as she walked briskly towards the sea. Suddenly she looked vulnerable and alone and my heart went out to her in spite of all the trouble she'd caused. She was due to take the Oath of Loyalty in two weeks, but she never acted as though she belonged with the Heirs of Akasha. Even there she was an oddball: it was hard to see why she'd give up everything for a place where she didn't fit in.

I turned briskly and walked into the centre of town. Right now Tim was the priority.

We'd arranged to meet in the bar on the ground floor of his hotel, a modern building near the central square. I saw him at once. He was seated at a table in a shadowy corner. His hair was combed and parted, but his shirt hung limply, a casualty no doubt of hand washing in his hotel bedroom. The clean-cut lines of his face were spiky with tension. I was careful not to look in his direction, but ordered a coffee and a glass of water and, once he had walked through the door that led towards the lift, I settled back in my chair to wait.

Ten minutes crawled by. At last the moment arrived for me to stand up, pay for my coffee and go out to the lift. It creaked up to the second floor. I went to room six and tapped three times on the door. It opened at once.

'Carol, thank God.'

His face was shining with expectation and he raised his hands slightly as though to put his arms round me. I thought of Jethro's words, 'a group embrace, just the two of us', and it didn't seem such a bad idea, but then I realised it wasn't me alone he'd hoped to see. He turned away and slumped into a chair by the window.

'No Katie.' His voice was hollow with disappointment.

'I told you it wasn't likely,' I said as I closed the door. 'They don't want her going anywhere, even though they pretend she's free to do what she wants.' And I described the little pantomime they'd laid on at lunch the previous day.

'Why didn't you insist?' He stood up and began pacing the tiny patch of floor beside the bed. 'Why did you just let it go at that?'

'There was no point making them suspicious.'

'Oh God, we're not getting anywhere,' he said bleakly. 'I know it's not your fault, Carol. It was always going to be tough. If I could just *talk* to the woman. That's all. Just talk to her and make her see sense for once in her life.' He flung himself down on the bed. 'It's no good, this is hopeless.'

I moved across to the window. The curtains had been drawn against the afternoon sun; I pulled one back slightly and peered out at rooftops and the arching fronds of palms.

'You mustn't give up, not yet,' I told him. 'Maybe this is all just terribly obvious, but why don't I simply tell Katie you're here? Surely she'd want to see you if she thought there was some way of doing it without getting into trouble. Palu has already played into our hands. She as good as suggested Katie come with me when I go sightseeing, so she can hardly change her tune after all, can she? Maybe we could even find a way for Davy to come as well.'

Tim raised his eyes and for a moment seemed almost hopeful, but then his habitual frown returned. 'Too risky,' he said. 'That bunch of crooks have done such a good job blackening my name she'd probably run a mile if she thought I was in the area. She's terrified of what I'll say because she doesn't want to face up to what a fool she's been. I mean, deep down she *does* want to see me, of course she does, but she's been brainwashed. She can't be trusted with such an important decision.'

'Then what choices do we have? I suppose I could always smuggle you into Tartessus in the back of my car, but you'd be running a huge risk. And if it failed we'd have lost everything. Besides, Katie isn't often on her own.'

'Oh God, this is driving me crazy.' He stood up and ran his fingers through his hair, mussing it up so it fell over his eyes, with the result that he looked ten times more attractive. He went on, 'All I do is sit around, day after day, waiting, just waiting for that damn phone to ring. Can you imagine what that's like? The greatest crisis of my whole life and I'm powerless. There's nothing I can do except wait. I'm going mad here, Carol.'

I peered down at the noisy street. Even though this was the quietest time of the day it was lively with tourists and locals going about their business. On the corner a man was shouting out the same phrase again and again, breaking off only when someone stopped to talk to him. I said cheerfully, 'I can think of worse places to kill time in.'

'You can, can you?' I turned, taken aback by the venom in his voice. In that moment he looked as though he hated me for being free to come and go and not being trapped in this stuffy bedroom waiting for a phone call that never came. 'Well, bully for you, because I can't. I hate this dump. The people here are all morons and the food is disgusting. Just listen to that idiot outside calling the same thing all the time.'

'What's he saying?'

'How should I know? He can bloody well shut up, that's all. I'm telling you, Carol, this place is driving me insane.' He dropped down on to the bed again and put his face in his hands. 'Oh God, I'm sorry. I didn't mean to get angry with you, Carol. You're all I've got. But I don't know how much more of this I can take.'

It's my Achilles heel, I know, but I've always been a pushover for a gentleman in distress. Tim was every inch the gentleman and right then he was definitely in distress. I sat down on the corner of the bed and took his hand. 'I wish there was more I could do,' I said gently. 'This must be such a nightmare for you.'

His tendons were raised ridges on his arms as he gripped my hand. He turned towards me and said, 'I keep telling myself to be positive, but it's hard, you know. All I do

every day is walk around this place, waiting for the phone
to ring and thinking about Davy having his brain
destroyed by those creeps. I never talk to anyone. I'm
beginning to feel as if I'm not real any more.'

'Oh, Tim.'

I must have leaned towards him. He pulled my hand and
pressed it tight to his chest, then raised it to his mouth and
kissed it. His lips were soft and warm against my skin. 'At
least you're real,' he breathed.

'Definitely.'

He was gripping my hand so hard it hurt. 'Don't make
fun of me, Carol. I can't stand being laughed at.' He
released my hand and put his palms on my shoulders and
said in a low voice, 'You must promise never to laugh at
me. Not ever. No matter what.'

'Of course not. Why would I?'

His arms went round my shoulders and he pulled me
towards him. He laid his cheek against the side of my head
and I felt a kick of sexual energy spark between us.
Actually, if I'm honest, that energy had been there since the
moment I entered his bedroom. I relaxed in his embrace.

'Tell me this is real,' he whispered, his breath stirring the
hair behind my ears.

'It's real all right.'

He shifted his head so his mouth brushed my cheek, then
sought out my lips. We kissed long and slow. He stopped,
drew back slightly and fumbled with the buttons of my
shirt. His hands were shaking. My own were quite steady
as I undid his shirt, but I was amazed by the strength of my
desire. It wasn't just that he was an extremely handsome
man and also a deeply troubled one, though that was
combination enough. But my chilly summer with Gus had
left me with a hunger to be held and loved, a longing for
the confirmation of desire.

It was a heady cocktail. Tim was tender, almost

questioning, as we explored each other's naked bodies, while the motor scooters buzzed up and down the street outside and the man on the pavement shouted his wares, whatever his wares were. When Tim tried to rush ahead I made him take his time: he'd been on his own too much over the past few days, and probably for weeks before that too, and he needed to be coaxed back into connecting properly with another person. He'd felt that he was going mad and this love-making must ground him in the here and now. And that way I'd have more pleasure, too.

After our long, exploratory caresses, the tempo changed abruptly. He pushed me over on to my back and entered me quickly. The next part was fast, almost brutal. He was like a man who's been hungry for too long and I was surprised by how erotic that was and I came quickly. When he'd climaxed he rolled on to his back with a groan. I propped myself on my elbow and leaned over to kiss him, but he turned his head away. Then he stood up and went to the shower. I could hear him cursing the inadequacies of the plumbing. A little later he emerged, a towel wrapped round his waist, and put his clothes on quickly, as though ashamed to let me see his nakedness now our love-making was done.

'Your turn in the shower,' he said.

'I'm in no hurry.'

'Doesn't it make you feel dirty?'

The way he said the word 'dirty' shocked me. 'Of course not,' I said at once. 'Do you?'

He didn't answer, but the way he slid me a look made me suddenly embarrassed.

'Tim, what is it? What's the matter?'

He stared at me for a moment, as if I was a complete stranger, then his eyes focused on me properly and he smiled. 'Sorry, I was miles away. And thanks, that was wonderful. You were great.' He hesitated only for a moment before he crossed the room and kissed me lightly on the forehead.

I was confused and disappointed, but while I was in the shower I told myself it was pointless to feel used. Hadn't I been using Tim too, as a way of feeling good again after my loveless summer with Gus?

It was uncomfortable to be reminded of Gus. It was even more uncomfortable to think that if he knew what had just happened he probably wouldn't mind at all. Hadn't he been trying to drive me away since the spring?

It was simpler to concentrate on practical problems, so when I'd showered and dressed I said, 'Listen, I've had an idea.'

Tim turned to me with interest.

'Why don't I tell Katie there's someone else on the outside who wants to see her? Does she have a close friend or a relative who might have come out here for a visit? Someone who wouldn't pose a threat but who she'd want to see?'

Tim had been combing his hair back into its neat, glossed down look, but he stopped, suddenly excited. 'That's a brilliant idea, Carol, you're a genius. Let me think . . . There's Aunt Tor, that's my father's sister Victoria – but she always travels with her husband, and he and my mother never got along, so that might not work. Who else? I know, Hilda Bissell. She was matron at Hollings for years – that was my father's school. She and Mother had their ups and downs but they were pretty close by the end. And she's older than Katie. Suppose we pretend she's terminally ill and wants to see Katie one last time before she dies. Mother could never refuse her then.'

The suggestion troubled me, since I had a superstitious feeling inventing a terminal illness was too close to Harriet's reality, but Tim was so excited he was unstoppable. 'You'll have to go back to Tartessus and tell her it's this most amazing coincidence, you got talking to this woman in a café in Tarifa and she asked you if you knew anything about the Heirs of Akasha. She told you a friend of hers was there and she was desperate to meet her because of her illness. She'd heard outsiders weren't welcome to visit. Did you know of a way she and Katie could meet up?'

It seemed to me that this scenario would be stretching credibility a bit far, but Tim said Katie would never notice if I played my part carefully and I had to agree. With anyone else there'd have been a problem, but Katie was so trusting . . . I remembered her amazement that I was staying in the same villa she'd been assigned on her arrival, despite the fact there were only three. Probability assessment was not Katie's strong point.

Tim told me everything he could remember about Hilda Bissell. 'The great thing about her,' he said eagerly, 'is that she adored Davy. She had no children of her own so she always made a fuss of me, and once Davy arrived on the scene she'd have moved in with Lucy and me permanently if she'd had the chance. Poor Lucy said it was like having two mothers-in-law. So you can tell Katie that Hilda is pining for a glimpse of Davy. If only there was a way of making sure Katie had her passport with her, we could just make a run for it.'

'Maybe she keeps it in her bag like I do.'

'Try and check, if you get the chance. I know, you need a passport to cash travellers' cheques, don't you? If Hilda had had her bag stolen and was strapped for cash, she could send an appeal via you and then Katie would have to bring her bag and—'

I cut off this flight of invention. 'No one uses travellers' cheques any more, Tim. They just get their money from a hole in the wall, same as in England.' It was nearly five o'clock. 'I've got to go.'

'Not yet. You only just got here.'

'I have to. I'm meeting Jenny at five.'

'So? There's lots of time. It doesn't matter if you're late. Stay here, Carol, please. Don't leave me.'

He was getting aroused again. His mouth closed over mine, but I turned away and extricated myself from his grasp.

'I really do have to go.'

He was breathing heavily and his blue eyes were very intense as he stared at me, but I no longer felt attracted to him, since I guessed he only wanted me as a shield against the horrors of solitude. He said, 'Stay with me. Hold me.'

'Another time. Not now.'

'Yes. Now.' For a strange moment I thought he was going to try and prevent me from leaving the room. He looked like a man teetering on the brink of breakdown because of the horrors he'd endured, and I was more than ever determined to see him reunited with his son.

I said firmly, 'Don't be daft. If I turn up at the café half an hour late and fresh from having sex with you, Jenny's hardly going to think I've spent a lonely afternoon sightseeing, is she? And she certainly won't think I've been chatting with a retired school matron called Hilda Bissell.'

'Well . . .'

'I'll come back soon, I promise. And next time, with any luck I'll have Katie with me.'

He ran his fingers through his hair, then stepped to one side and grinned. 'Okay, then. Don't forget. I'm relying on you, Carol.'

I ran quickly down the stairs and out into the bright sunlight. I was uneasy and anxious to get away from the hotel. I didn't want to reflect on what Tim and I had just said and done. The man whose repeated phrase had woven its way into our love-making was seated on an upturned box outside a shop selling pottery and tourist items. He'd said the same words so often they'd become a blur, like sellers of evening papers in London.

It looked as though he was selling lottery tickets. I wasn't sure why, but lottery tickets seemed appropriate.

Neither Jenny nor I spoke much for the first part of our drive back. Jenny was reticent when I asked how she'd got on, and predictably she showed not the slightest interest in my activities, so I didn't get to practise my story about Hilda Bissell. She sat scrunched into an unhappy ball near the passenger door, presumably to put as much distance between us as possible, and stared morosely out at the brown, barren landscape.

After a while she sighed and said, 'God, this is bleak.'

'Rugged,' I said, looking on the bright side.

'Yeah, like the far side of the bloody moon,' she said.

It was time we talked. I was still wondering how to draw her out when she said, 'God, this is awful, like going back to school after an exeat.'

'Did you go to boarding school?'

'You bet. Mummy packed me off as soon as she could. Eight years old.'

'I can't imagine it.'

'It was all right. Better than being stuck at home, anyway.'

'Really? You can't have been very happy at home, then,' I said tentatively.

'Mm.'

'Weren't you and your mum close?'

She slid me one of her odd looks, hurt and wary and calculating all at the same time. Then she said, 'Not really. We've never got on particularly. I mean, we're fond of each other and all that, of course we are, but we always wind each other up. It's probably because we're so much alike.'

Lord help us, I thought. Two Jennies. Their home must have been an emotional minefield. I felt sorry for Ian.

I said, 'Does she know where you are?'

'Sure. She always has her spies posted.'

'But you haven't contacted her directly since you joined the group?'

I was half expecting Jenny to bite my head off for being nosy, but all she said was 'Not properly.'

'You know she's ill, don't you?'

She twisted round in her corner of the car and glared at me. 'You said you hadn't spoken to her. Have you been lying to me, Carol?'

'No, I promise. I've never spoken to your mother in my life. Ian visited a while back.'

'What did he want?'

'He was concerned about you. Harriet didn't know about his visit but—'

'Typical bloody Ian. Always sneaking off behind her back.'

'He was only trying to help, poor man. He said your mother's really very ill. You know she's ill, don't you?'

Jenny glared at me, her eyes hard as flints. 'So?' she asked savagely.

'Ian seems to think she hasn't got long, maybe only months – but I expect you know all about that.'

'Yes, I do, as a matter of fact. And it's the oldest trick in the book. There's hardly a single member of Akasha who hasn't been summoned home by a relative who's suddenly contracted a highly convenient illness. I'm not falling for that old hoax.'

I thought guiltily about the fictitious Hilda Bissell and her terminal illness, but all I said was, 'I don't think this one's a hoax.'

'Yeah. Well. She was fine when I saw her. Very

convenient of her suddenly to go and get that much iller just when it suits her.'

'Jenny, that's not fair. I heard her on the phone to Gus and she sounded really desperate.'

Jenny flinched and turned her head away. 'Tough,' she said, but I thought I saw tears in her eyes.

After a while I said quietly, 'You pretend not to care, but I know you do deep down.'

'Bully for you.' For a while she sat hunched in her corner. Then she turned to me and said, 'You've got it all wrong, Carol. I don't care about Harriet, not any more. I used to, but that's all in the past. The Heirs of Akasha are all the family I need. They've been wonderful to me and I owe everything to them now.'

Her words sounded false, as though she was reading them off a cue card. I said, 'But what about poor Harriet? You can't just abandon her.'

'Why not? Try to understand that my mother belongs with the old life and I've turned my back on all that. At the next full moon I'll take the Oath of Loyalty and be given a new name. I don't know what it is yet but I know it will be something wonderful. They say it's like shedding an old skin you don't need any more. I'll be born again into my new life. It's sad about Harriet, of course it is, but what she's going through is just a trial of the body. She still has choices, but I can't make them for her. She could join the Heirs herself if she wanted and then she'd be reborn as a whole new person, same as I'm going to be. Who knows, her illness might even fall away from her.'

'That's a wicked thing to say,' I protested. 'They've no right to fill your head with that kind of dangerous nonsense. She needs to be where she can get proper medical treatment.'

'Is that why you came on this Quester retreat, Carol? So you could put the emotional screws on me to going back to Mum?'

'Don't flatter yourself, Jenny. I had plenty of my own reasons for coming here.'

'Oh yeah? I wonder what they were. I ought to expose you as an impostor. That might liven things up a bit. Do you know the system they have for taking care of impostors?'

'I'm telling you, Jenny, I'm not an impostor. I came on this retreat with an open mind, which is what being a Quester is all about, isn't it? But now I've had a chance to investigate it properly, yes, as a matter of fact I do think it's crazy. I can't believe you've swallowed all that nonsense about Atlantis and the world coming to an end.'

'Don't you? Well that shows how little you know, Carol.' Her eyes glittered with a fanatical light as she went on. 'You see, I know it's all true because I've seen it on the Akashic Record.'

'What?'

'It happens sometimes when you meditate. You can see things with your inner eye that aren't visible to ordinary people. It's fascinating.'

'I can't bear to hear you spouting all that stuff. And now, just because of some terrible mind games they've played on you, you're going to hand over all your money to the group and you'll never get it back.'

'Oh, now we're getting down to the nitty-gritty. I knew money'd come up in the end. That was what Ian was really bothered about, wasn't it?'

'He's concerned about you, that's all.'

'Money's all he cares about. God, I'll be so glad to let go of all that crap. I can't think of anything better than handing over responsibility for my life to people who actually care about me. And it means I can spend my time concentrating on spiritual things instead of being obsessed with money and status all the time like Ian and my mother.'

'The Inner Circle live pretty well,' I said. 'Nothing hairshirt about the way they carry on.'

'So? That doesn't bother me.'

We had reached the Pillars of Hercules. The two stone figures stared down disapprovingly at our argument. While we waited for the gates to open I said, 'Jenny, you're not stupid. Surely you can see you're making the most terrible mistake, maybe one you'll regret for the rest of your life. I can't bear to watch you destroy yourself like this.'

'So? It's my life, isn't it?'

'But why can't you just give Harriet a call? It would make such a difference. She's so unhappy.'

I eased the car forward and the gates swung shut behind us. Jenny turned to me, her eyes sparkling with laughter. 'You're such a sucker, Carol. You just don't get it, do you?'

Chapter 18

Katie was nervous.

'It's ages since I left Tartessus,' she exclaimed as the heavy gates swung shut behind us. 'This does feel like an adventure.' She was dressed for the outing in a pale lilac jacket and skirt, pearls at her ears and throat. Her fine blond hair was brushed away from her carefully made-up face.

'Hilda's so excited at the thought of seeing you again,' I said with enthusiasm.

'That's nice. Dear old Hilda.' She turned in her seat to get a last glimpse of the Pillars of Hercules, anxiety shadowing her face. It was terrible how quickly group members became dependent and lost their ability to function in the real world. I was checking behind me too, but my only worry was to make sure we weren't being followed. She turned back and asked nervously, 'Is it far to this Trafalgar Square place?'

'Only about half an hour. And it's called Cape Trafalgar – Cabo Trafalgar.' I'd explained before but Katie must have forgotten. I said, 'It's near where the battle was fought.'

'Yes, I know,' said Katie brightly. 'But I still think it's peculiar naming a sea battle after a London square.'

I glanced at her quickly to see if she was pulling my leg. She wasn't. 'I think you'll find it's the other way round,' I said. 'The square was named after the battle.'

'Yes, of course it was,' she agreed vaguely.

I changed the subject. 'Have you seen that man again?' I asked. 'The one we met in Cornwall?'

She didn't answer right away, but unfastened the clasp on her bag and thumbed through the contents – handkerchief, compact, purse – then pulled out a pair of dark glasses and put them on. She turned to me with a smile and said, 'I wish I'd brought a present for Hilda. Vincent and I always used to pick her up something when we went to Scotland, shortbread or a scarf or something like that. Poor Hilda wasn't much of a one for holidays. I think she always had to make do with some doomish old aunt in Torquay.'

'Then obviously she's making up for lost time,' I said. I wondered why she avoided talking about Tim. It must be so painful for her, being separated from him. I tried again. 'Didn't that man call you Mother?'

She was staring straight ahead of her. 'Tim,' she said simply.

'And he's your son?'

She nodded, then reached into her bag and pulled out a handkerchief to blow her nose.

'Do you have any other children?'

She shook her head. 'Wanted to but . . . two miscarriages. Only Tim.'

'You must miss him dreadfully. Don't you want to see him sometimes?'

Now the tears spilled out from under her dark glasses.

Still looking straight ahead of her, she said woodenly, 'I'm Lumina now. I don't need my old family any more.' She spoke as if she was reciting a lesson she'd been taught, just like Jenny, repeating the same moronic phrases. 'He's part of the old life. Davy and I have a new future to look forward to now.'

She sounded so stoical and so misguided it almost broke my heart. I pressed my foot harder on the accelerator and thought how happy she was going to be when she was reunited with Tim. Every now and then, when we were on a straight stretch of road, I checked the rear-view mirror. Not much longer now.

We'd been told that Cape Trafalgar was one of the well-known beauty spots in the area. Apparently it was famous as a place from which to view the setting sun. We'd timed our visit for about four o'clock, so if Katie and 'Hilda' found they had a lot to discuss, I might end up catching one of those famous sunsets.

We reached the coast and drove through a small town, hardly more than an overgrown village. To my relief there was a signpost for Cabo Trafalgar. We drove through an area of dunes and reed beds.

Katie grew agitated. 'What a peculiar place for Hilda to choose,' she said. 'There's not even a café here.'

'Look, that must be it over there. You can see the lighthouse.'

In winter, or on stormy evenings, this must be a desolate place. A thin road stretched out to a wild bank of sand dunes where the lighthouse stood all alone. A single car was parked at the end of the road, near to the dunes. I drove slowly along and halted about twenty feet behind it.

'That must be her,' I said.

Katie peered doubtfully at Tim's hired car. 'Hilda always drives a Metro,' she said.

'Let's go and see, shall we?'

We got out and walked along the white road. The dunes were busy with chirruping birds, but otherwise the silence was profound. As we drew level with the car the driver's door swung open and Tim stepped out. He'd taken every care with his appearance, hair parted and flattened in obedience, clothes ironed to within an inch of their life, shoes gleaming with polish.

Katie stopped dead in her tracks and let out a little cry. 'Oh, my heavens, what have you done with Hilda?' she exclaimed.

'There's no Hilda,' said Tim quietly. 'She was my idea. Sorry about the lies, Mother, but I had to see you.'

Katie turned to me with something like panic on her face. 'You said it was Hilda.'

'She's not coming,' I told her. 'I've never met Hilda in my life and certainly not in Tarifa. We made that up so you and Tim could have a chance to talk. It seemed like the only way to get you away from El Cortijo.'

Katie was looking more and more bewildered. She said to Tim, 'Have you two met before?'

Tim smiled. I knew him well enough by now to detect the signs of acute tension: the pulse that moved just below his left eye and the tremor of his hands. He said gently, 'Yes, we've been planning this for weeks. Don't be angry with us, Mother, please. Carol knows how desperate I've been to see you and Davy again. How is my Davy?'

'Davy?' Katie was still in shock.

'Don't tell me his name's been changed as well.'

'Oh no . . . he's . . . he's well. Davy is.'

'You must have a lot to say to each other,' I said, since my presence was obviously acting as a brake on their reunion. 'I'll leave you in peace for a bit. We've plenty of time. I told them we'd be late back.'

Katie turned to me, her eyes wide with alarm. 'I'll stay with you, Carol,' she said. 'You might get lost on your own.'

'Oh, Mother, for pity's sake. You can't run away from me now!' Tim's voice broke on a sob. He must have been as horrified as I was by the fact Katie was afraid to spend time with her own son. 'Mother, please, I'm begging you. Just a little while. You can't leave me here, not after I've come all this way to see you.'

'We-ell . . .'

'Surely it won't do any harm to talk.'

She was wavering. He held out his arms. Katie took a tentative step towards him. He put his arms round her and held her tightly.

No longer a go-between, I had become an interloper. I walked quickly away.

I turned and saw them go side by side up the path that led over the crest of the dunes towards the sea, then I set off in the opposite direction, heading north past the lighthouse. It was gone four o'clock. We hadn't said anything about timing, but I calculated they'd want at least an hour together. Tim would be desperate for news of his son, and, in spite of his confidence, persuading Katie to leave the group was hardly going to be achieved in minutes.

The air was soft as a caress. The beach below the dunes was busy with sea birds, but otherwise the area was deserted. From time to time I heard a car puttering slowly down the narrow road to the lighthouse, but no one stayed long, just long enough to stretch their legs, walk a little way towards the lighthouse and glimpse the sea, then back to their car and on to the next town, the next hotel, the next meal. *We saw Cape Trafalgar. It's right by where Nelson had his great victory.* Or, if you were Katie, the place that had been mysteriously named after a London square.

I found a spot among the dunes where I could lean back in the warm sand and look out over the ever-changing ocean. It was intensely satisfying to know that Katie and

Tim had been reunited thanks to my efforts. With any luck my next task would be to arrange Katie and Davy's escape from the Centre, which meant it was about time I concentrated on Jenny. There were only five days left of my Quester course, and as the day of my departure drew nearer I felt less anxious about being unmasked as an impostor, in spite of Jenny's threats. I could always say I'd come on the retreat with an open mind and it wasn't my fault if I was not impressed by what I'd found. No one was going to find out about my alliance with Tim unless Katie told them, and why would she do that?

I wandered back down to the cars and waited for a bit, then glanced at my watch. It was gone five o'clock. I was growing curious about how they'd got on. I walked slowly up the path into the dunes.

The sun was directly ahead of me, an orange ball suspended above the horizon. I scanned the huge beach. Far off to the south I could make out two figures walking slowly towards me. They separated, then moved closer again. I waved, but they didn't respond. A small breeze had sprung up, so I tucked myself down behind a bluff of sea grass and stretched out in the warmth. It was luxurious to be basking in the October sunshine. I thought of grey autumnal days in Sturford, bonfires and mist and the chill rising from the hollows. Here was a different season and I intended to make the most of it.

Tim and his mother were certainly taking their time. Maybe they were already planning how she'd be able to escape from the Heirs of Akasha. It was all very satisfying.

I drifted for a moment. When I came to, I heard a voice the other side of the bluff. It was a man's voice, low and insistent. Tim. He seemed to be giving instructions. My first thought was that he was telling her how to get away.

Then, as the sound came closer and I made out the words, a chill of disbelief spread through me.

258 • JOANNA HINES

'No, Mother. You can't have him, because you're not fit and you never have been. Look at the way Father always had to do everything for you. You've fucked up your whole life, and everybody else's too, just like you're fucking up now. You'll never change.'

'But this time it's different, Tim,' Katie protested, 'because I'm not on my own any more. I've got friends now.'

'Those people aren't your friends, they're exploiting you, same as people always do. Face it, Mother, you've never had any friends. Why would anyone want to be friends with you?'

'They like me, I know they do. And they love Davy.' There was a pleading note in her voice. 'He's so happy Tim. If you could only see him. You know you're welcome to visit at any time, if you just agree to their conditions. If only you'd give it a try.'

'Never!' exclaimed Tim savagely. 'I will see him, oh yes I will, but on my terms. There's no way I'm going to visit my own son among a bunch of crazies, so you can forget all about that idea. You're such a stupid bitch, you've got it all wrong, same as always.'

I was on the point of scrambling to my feet and interrupting them, but I held back. What I was hearing didn't make sense. Tim was the wronged father, the devoted son who wanted to rescue his mother from the clutches of her evil friends. I'd believed that for so long that I couldn't believe what my ears were telling me. And so I listened and waited for them to fit back into the roles I'd assigned them.

Katie was doing her best to defend herself. She said, 'It's not the way you say it is. You're putting me down, just like your father always did, but I've got friends now who value me. I'm not giving them up. Not this time.'

There was a long silence. I wanted to know what was

going on but didn't dare risk being seen. The next time Tim spoke, his voice was gentler. He said quietly, 'Do you know, Mother, I almost feel sorry for you. You fucked up with me and now you're fucking up all over again with Davy, only this time you won't succeed. I won't let you. But you can't help yourself, can you? You simply have no idea how much pain you cause. For years and years I blamed you for abandoning me the way you did—'

'But Tim, it wasn't like that. I took you with me, but your father—'

'Shut up and listen to me, will you? My father was a fine man and I won't hear a word against him. If I've made mistakes sometimes, it's all been your fault. And now you're doing it all over again. My God, how can you be so evil?'

'Tim, no, please . . .'

I should have stopped them. I should have, but I was so horrified and fascinated that I couldn't move.

A shift had taken place between them. Tim's voice was softer. 'Come home with me, Mother. We're a family. I need you, Mummy, can't you understand that? I can't bear it without you any more. Oh God!' His voice was muffled, as though he was crying or had buried his face against her shoulder.

'Oh, Tim, I'm so sorry. But I can't leave them, not now. They're my family. I want them to be yours, too. Just try it. You'd be so happy. Just like I am. For the first time in my life I'm happy.'

'Happy?' Tim snarled. 'You selfish bitch, how can you say you're happy when you're ruining my life? We'll see about *happy* when I get Davy back. Because you know I'll win in the end. The solicitors say I only have to snap my fingers, snap, like that, and the police will come to your door and they'll tear him away from you, and dear God, unless you help me now you'll suffer for it then.'

'Tim, no.' Katie's voice was constricted with pain.

'Yes. So that gives you a choice: bring Davy back yourself or the law moves in and gets him for me. Either way, I win: he's mine and there's nothing you or your psycho friends can do to stop me. But if you play it my way I might just consent to let you cook for us and clean, and if you're very good you'll still be able to see Davy sometimes, when I let you. But I'll decide, do you understand? So which is it to be, eh? Are you going to join my team, or do you want to lose Davy for ever?'

'No . . . keep . . . Davy . . .'

I leaped to my feet. So this was what Tim meant when he said his mother was easily persuaded. This was what he'd meant when he said he only needed an hour to make her change her mind.

They were below me on the shore, further away than I'd imagined. Their voices had carried on the quiet evening air. Tim had his back to me. His left hand was buried in Katie's hair, yanking her head back so she was forced to look up into his face. Her sandals dangled from her hand.

'What did you say?' he demanded and he jabbed a punch into her ribs. She gasped and dropped her sandals. He repeated, 'What did you say? Tell me, bitch. Say yes.' And he jabbed his fist into her chest again. For a moment I thought I was going to be sick.

Katie caught sight of me. Her expression didn't change but she said, 'All right. I agree. I'll do what you want.'

I opened my mouth to yell at Tim to leave her alone, but Katie frowned and shook her head slightly. Then she called out in a voice that was bright and social, 'Carol, there you are.'

I had been slithering down the bank towards them, but I stopped at once. Tim spun round and for a split second I caught a glimpse of a red-faced thug, then he, like Katie, switched back into his public guise.

'Carol!' The bastard actually sounded pleased to see me.

The moment he turned away from her, Katie took a step backwards and, still looking straight at me, put her finger to her lips. 'My heavens,' she exclaimed, 'just look at the time. Here we've been chattering away like a couple of birds on a perch, and poor Carol must be sick of waiting for us.'

There was nothing for it but to follow her lead. Maybe she knew that was her best chance of getting away safely. I was still so shocked I didn't feel as if I knew anything any more. I said feebly, 'Don't worry about me. I had a great walk.' My hands were balled into fists.

'Oh good,' said Katie. 'How nice for you.'

Tim slicked back his hair and his face lit up in a blameless smile. 'Which way did you go?'

I gestured vaguely behind the lighthouse and said, 'Over there. It's beautiful. Sorry to interrupt, both of you, but we ought to be making tracks.'

'Oh dear,' said Katie, 'but all good things come to an end.'

She moved towards me, but Tim caught her by the arm. She stopped, her eyes wide with fear, and he stooped to pick up her sandals. 'You're not thinking of going back barefoot, are you, Mother?'

'Of course not. Silly old me.'

'Shall I help you with these, Mother?' he asked, his voice smooth as silk.

'Oh, would you, dear? That's very kind.'

He knelt down, took her slender foot in his hands and slid on the sandal. The whole performance was grotesque. All the time Katie smiled that bright, brittle smile. I wanted to push him away from her and run with her all the way back to the car.

'We're going back to Tartessus,' I said.

'Yes, it is rather late,' said Katie.

262 • JOANNA HINES

I saw the way Tim's hand closed round her ankle. Katie stood absolutely frozen. Tim looked up, his eyes all innocence, and said smoothly, 'You won't forget what we just agreed, will you, Mother?'

'I won't forget.'

'Next time you'll bring Davy. And the passports.'

'Yes, dear.'

I was about to protest but Katie gestured behind Tim's head, counselling silence.

'You're sure you won't forget?' he insisted.

'Quite sure.'

He released her ankle and stood up. Katie moved over to join me and I slipped my arm through hers. My heart was pounding as we all walked over the bluff to the waiting cars.

'Remember,' said Tim, 'Carol has a mobile phone so you can contact me that way. We'll speak again this evening to confirm the arrangements.'

'Yes, dear.'

'Tomorrow, then? Same time, same place?'

'Yes, dear.'

I was so angry I could hardly breathe, but the pressure of Katie's hand warned me not to speak. You bastard, I thought. *You evil bastard.*

We reached the car. It was almost a disappointment that Tim remained so quiet and calm. Part of me longed for him to repeat his performance so I could show him there was one woman present who knew how to fight back.

The sun was going down in a blaze of fiery red and gold, the famous sunset of Cape Trafalgar, but I hardly noticed it.

'Goodbye, Mother. See you tomorrow. And this time, no mistakes, remember.'

Katie made no protest when Tim put his arms round her,

though she flinched as her rib cage was pressed against his chest; then he released her and she ducked down swiftly into the car.

'Goodbye, Tim. Until tomorrow.'

She even managed a bright little smile of farewell. My hands were shaking so much that I scrunched the gears as I did a three-point turn and we bumped away down the narrow road towards the hills and Tartessus.

Where safety lay.

We drove in silence. After about ten minutes there was a toot from the car behind. I glanced in the rear-view mirror and saw Tim indicating to take the road that led to Tarifa, while we were heading inland and north. I raised my hand in farewell, but beside me Katie sat still as stone.

Only when I was sure we had the road to ourselves again, did I speak.

'Katie . . .' She didn't seem to find it odd that I used her real name. 'Katie, I heard what Tim was saying to you on the beach. I saw him hit you. I'm so sorry. It's all my fault.'

She didn't answer. As soon as we got into the car she had slipped on her dark glasses and behind them her eyes were unreadable. Her profile was delicate and fine; I could imagine how beautiful she had been and how Gus must have loved her. I was silent for a while, giving her time, but still she didn't speak, just sat staring straight ahead, holding her handbag upright in her lap.

I said again, 'Look, I know I'm to blame for this and I'm sorry, so terribly sorry. I thought I could help. You see, I met Tim at this introductory meeting in London and he seemed so lost and unhappy. He told me you'd been brainwashed by the group and he was desperate about losing his son, so I agreed to try and set up a meeting. He said that if he could only talk to you for half an hour you'd leave the group and then everyone would be happy again.

I never imagined he was so cruel. Jesus, why did you stop me from saying anything back there?'

'No one must ever know,' she said quietly. 'That was always the family rule.' She was speaking almost to herself. 'No matter how bad things were, we always put on a good show. That was very important to Vincent.'

'Your husband?'

She nodded. 'Vincent had very high standards. He had to have – he was a headmaster – but at home . . . he was a very strict man. Tim takes after him.' She shuddered. 'Vincent always made me pay for it later if he thought I'd been disloyal. The trouble was, half the time I didn't know what I'd done wrong. It could be such a little thing that sparked him off.'

'Your husband was a bully?'

'One shouldn't speak ill of the dead,' she said.

'Did Vincent hit you?'

'Oh yes.' She spoke almost lightly, as though it was only to be expected. 'Not all that often, but the trouble was I never knew when it was coming.' She crossed her arms. 'He was always careful to make sure it wouldn't show. Tim's learned that lesson well. Vincent said I provoked him, and I believed him for years, but Serafa says it was his fault. I think maybe she's right, you know.'

'Of course she is. Oh, Katie, if only I'd known. Didn't you ever tell anyone?'

She turned to me with an odd little smile. 'Only once. That's the funny part. The only person I ever confided in, and that was years ago, was Hilda Bissell. Vincent respected her, so I thought she'd be able to make him stop. But she just went on about what a brilliant man he was and what a lot of responsibility he had, and of course she was right, in a way. She said if I just stopped thinking about myself all the time and learned to help him more he wouldn't get so frustrated and turn on me. Actually, I think she was a bit in love with him herself. Vincent could be very charming when he wanted to be, just like Tim. That's why I wanted to see her today, so she'd know I was happy at last, that I wasn't ashamed of myself any more.' Her voice broke as she ended, 'That's the only reason I came.'

'And walked straight into a trap. I'm so sorry.' She didn't answer, just threw me a little smile of reassurance. I knew it was the sort of question you're not supposed to ask, but I had to anyway. I've never been able to understand why any woman would stay with a violent man. It just doesn't make sense. 'Why did you put up with it?' I asked. 'Why didn't you just leave?'

'Well, I did once.' She fingered the clasp of her bag. 'I went to live with some friends who had a house in the country. Tim came with me. He was about four years old and he loved it there. He was such a dear little boy – oh dear.' Her voice was wobbling.

I said, 'Was that when you went to live at Grays Orchard?'

She was so absorbed in her memories that she didn't notice that I knew the names of the house. She just nodded and said, 'That's right. Grays Orchard. It was a lovely place and we were really happy there, but then Vincent came with his parents and they took Tim away. They told me I wasn't fit and . . .'

'And you believed them?'

She nodded miserably. 'They were so powerful, you've no idea.' If Tim's tactics today had been anything to go by, I had a very good idea indeed. She said, 'If Gus or any of the others had been around, I might have been able to keep him, but they tricked me, and I lost Tim. It was terrible. I had to go back eventually. I couldn't just leave him there, poor little boy.'

'Tim can't remember Grays Orchard at all,' I said.

Katie sighed. 'Sometimes it's the happy memories that

are unbearable,' she said which struck me as one of the saddest things I'd ever heard. A great wave of sympathy for Tim, the child who'd had to forget all the happy times at Grays Orchard, swept over me.

After a while I said, 'Grays Orchard is where I live now.'

'Really?'

'Yes, Gus Ridley is my husband.'

She didn't answer right away. I assumed she was still so shaken by everything that had just happened that she hadn't taken it in, but eventually she said, 'Gus Ridley. How strange. It's such a coincidence, I can't really understand it. And Grays Orchard. How I loved that house.'

'It's not really a coincidence,' I said. 'I'm here because of Gus's old friend Raymond Tucker, same as you.'

'I suppose so,' she said vaguely. 'Dear Gus, does he still do his nice paintings?' In spite of everything that had happened, I couldn't help smiling. She made his painting sound like a hobby, like stamp collecting.

'He's had a bad time recently. All his paintings were destroyed in the spring by . . . by an intruder.'

'Oh, I am sorry. How dreadful for him. There's always been trouble with intruders at Grays. I suppose it's because it's so isolated. Are we nearly back at Tartessus yet?'

'About ten minutes more.'

This was the chance I'd been waiting for, though after what Katie had been through that afternoon, and all because of me, it felt shabby to be pumping her for information now. Still, I might never get another chance. I said, 'What do you remember about that time at Grays Orchard? Did you get on well with the rest of the group?'

'Yes, it was a wonderfully happy time. Even that last summer, when the sun never stopped shining and Gus's paintings just got darker and darker and everyone was so restless, I was even happy then. I think after what I'd been used to – but of course, I missed Davy all the time.'

'Tim,' I corrected her.

'Yes. Tim. Silly me.'

'Andrew Forester's murder was the reason it collapsed, wasn't it?'

'I suppose so.' Katie pulled out her powder compact and peered at her reflection in the mirror. 'Everything just sort of fell apart after that.'

'A lot of people locally thought it was someone in the group who killed Forester, not an intruder at all. Some people say it was Ra – Raymond Tucker as he was then.'

'Such nonsense.' Katie snapped her handbag shut and folded her hands over the clasp again. 'People do say the silliest things. Ray's always been the gentlest person in the world – in any world. Did you know he can talk to the Ancients? It's quite fascinating to think of the conversations they must have.'

'But if it wasn't him—'

'Let's not talk about the murder,' she said firmly. 'It spoils my memories of those happy days.'

I couldn't insist, not after what I'd put her through, even though I was itching with curiosity. I said, 'And you're happy again now, with the Heirs of Akasha. God, I can't believe I nearly made you lose all that.'

'Yes, and Davy's happy, too, which is the most important thing. If only I could get Tim to join us too, but he never will. That was what I was really hoping for, when I went to live with them. I thought Tim would follow us and we could all be happy. You must have a terrible impression of him after today, but he wasn't always like that, you know. He changed when his father died. It was as though Tim stopped being Tim and became his father. The only difference was that instead of Vincent bullying me and Tim, it was Tim bullying me and Davy. And he was so cruel. I never thought there was anything worse than

Vincent's beatings, but sometimes it seemed as if Tim revelled in finding new ways to be cruel. Davy's always been terrified of the dark and so Tim used to shut him in a cupboard for hours, just for the silliest little thing. And tying him to his chair for hours if he misbehaved at table. Then punishing him again if his bladder gave out. And I thought it was never going to end. Then Ray got in touch and invited me to visit them, so I did. He and Palu were wonderful. They arranged everything, all the finances and the legal side of things. And Serafa has been an absolute life-saver.'

'Then I came along.'

'Don't blame yourself, Carol. Tim can be very persuasive, just like his father. That was why everyone admired and respected him so much. Vincent never lifted a finger to any of the boys in the school. People always remarked on how gentle he was, the gentle gentleman. I made sure no one ever knew what happened behind doors at the headmaster's lodge. Everyone thought I was just the fluffy wife he'd got saddled with and that he was an absolute hero for letting me home again after Gus. If only they'd known.'

'And all the time you were the hero.'

'That's what Serafa keeps telling me. She says I must learn to value myself again. But sometimes it's hard to know where to start.'

We had reached the high gates to Tartessus. Unusually, they were wide open and the two stone Hercules were staring down at a couple of men from maintenance who were working on the control box. As we drove in I said, 'Well, at least you're safe again now. You don't have to see Tim ever again.'

It wasn't comforting at all. Her voice was trembly as she said, 'But I do, that's the worst part of it. I see him every day in Davy. I know Tim's behaved badly, but he's not a monster, really he isn't. Deep down he's just a lost little boy, like he always was. Oh Carol, he was such an angelic child, just like Davy is now, so sweet and loving and I always wanted to take care of him and protect him and I couldn't. Of course, going to live at Grays was a terrible mistake and Vincent and his mother never let me forget that, so I've been trying to make it up to him ever since. And now it feels as though I'm ruining his life all over again. He's still my son, no matter what he's done.'

We drew up in front of the Inner Circle's villa and now, at last, at the memory of Tim the child, the tears began spilling down Katie's cheeks. 'He's under such pressure,' she sobbed, 'and I blame myself. If I'd been able to care for him properly he wouldn't be so mixed up now.'

'Oh, Katie.' At last I understood why the Inner Circle had been so ruthless about keeping Tim Fairchild away from his mother and son. It wasn't just the bullying that made him so dangerous; it was the appeal of a lost little boy who'd grown into a scheming and manipulative adult, who'd go to any lengths to get what he wanted.

I said, 'He's not mixed up, Katie. He's a bully and a liar.'

'He's not all bad,' she said. 'And most men are bullies underneath.'

'I don't believe that.'

She took off her dark glasses and dabbed her eyes, then turned a penetrating look on me. 'No? But aren't you running away from Gus?'

'Of course not.'

'Has he been violent to you yet?'

'No!' I was genuinely shocked. 'Gus would never be violent.'

Katie didn't answer.

I said, 'Katie, are you telling me Gus used to hit you?'

'Not me, no.' Her eyes misty, as though she was looking far into the past, she said dreamily, 'Hitting her and crying . . .'

I shuddered. 'Who, Katie? Who was he hitting?'

She blinked and turned towards me. 'I don't want to talk about it.' She fiddled with the clasp of her bag, then said firmly, 'Please, Carol, let's not dwell on the past.' She pulled out her compact and examined her face in the tiny mirror, repairing the damage with practised skill. 'You see, bad things happen but then we have to move on. I want to move on now. I stood up to Tim today, didn't I? Maybe I've learned so much from being with the Heirs that I'd be able to deal with it differently if he tried to bully me again.'

'Katie, no. Don't risk it.' My anxiety at what she might do swept aside all thoughts of Gus and his unknown victim. 'Tim's too dangerous for you.'

'Yes, maybe. Oh, I don't know. I'll talk to Serafa and Ra – they'll help me see straight again.'

My heart sank. There was no way I could ask her not to tell the Inner Circle that I'd double-crossed her and exposed her to danger, but I dreaded their reaction.

'Okay,' I said. 'If you think that's going to help.' Whatever the Inner Circle did, it would be no more than I deserved, I thought grimly as I followed her up the wide steps to their villa.

But that wasn't much of a comfort.

Chapter 19

As Katie and I went into the Villa Omega, I was still so gutted by what I'd seen and so stunned by Katie's apparent reference to Gus's violence that I had no time to work out how to explain my role in the afternoon's events. Which was just as well because, whatever I told them, it was going to look bad. It made me sick to think of how I'd been fooled by Tim: all that sympathy squandered on a sadistic liar. And not just sympathy: I'd found him attractive, attractive enough to have sex with him. How could I have got it so wrong?

Several members of the Inner Circle were in the main living room. If I'd had any illusions that they spent every moment of their free time communing with the departed spirits of Atlantis or plotting how to get money from gullible Questers, what I saw would have soon put me right. Serafa was stretched out on one of the enormous white leather sofas while Palu, perched on the end, painted her toenails a vibrant orange. Davy was sprawled on his stomach on a rug in front of the fire, and opposite him Ra sat motionless in the lotus position. He wasn't meditating, though, not if the chequers board between him and Davy was a clue.

Davy looked up and said to Katie, 'I'm winning, Grandma. Ra's won three games in a row but I'll win this one.'

Ra raised his eyebrows and hopped one of his counters over five of Davy's, then smiled.

'Oh, no!' Davy looked dashed. 'Four nil to you.' But he brightened again and said, 'One more game? Best of five?'

Serafa laughed lazily. 'That won't help you much, and anyway, you've had three "one more" games already.' Still smiling, she looked across at Katie. 'You okay, Lumina? How was your friend Hilda?'

'Well . . .' Katie began.

My heart sank. It would have made more sense to see Katie safely back to Tartessus and then make my getaway, rather than being revealed as an impostor, and, worse, someone who had exposed her to real danger.

But I had reckoned without Katie.

She said crisply, 'Dear old Hilda, she hasn't changed at all. Still meddling in my private life. I should have guessed. She didn't really want to see me at all; it was just a trick to get me to see Tim.'

'What?' Serafa's eyes darkened; she sat up and swung her elegant feet to the floor. 'You've seen him?'

Ra and Davy had stopped setting out the chequers and were listening intently.

'That's right,' said Katie. 'It was a trap, and like a fool I walked straight into it.'

'Lumina, that's terrible.' Serafa crossed the room and put her arms round her. 'Are you okay?'

'No, she isn't.' I spoke for the first time. 'Tim was saying hideous things, and then he hit her.'

Serafa turned to me with surprise. 'You were there?'

'I saw the last part.'

'And you didn't stop him?'

'Oh, Carol was wonderful,' said Katie swiftly. 'I don't know what I've have done without her.' She extricated herself from Serafa's embrace and took my hand. 'I can't begin to thank you, Carol, for everything you've done today.'

I mumbled something incoherent. I had no idea why Katie was lying to protect me, but I was grateful. How I had underestimated her. Years of covering up for her violent and oh-so-respectable husband had turned her into the most efficient liar I'd ever met.

Davy had wriggled across the carpet and settled on Ra's lap. Ra patted his shoulder and regarded Katie thoughtfully. Then, for a couple of moments only, his extraordinary eyes lighted on me and I felt it again, that certainty that he knew the inmost secrets of my heart.

Palu said, 'Lucky you didn't take a certain person with you or we'd have really been in trouble.'

Ra patted Davy's shoulder again.

I said, 'He made her promise to go back tomorrow and take another person with her.'

Ra nodded. Davy said, 'Who?' and Katie said, 'Never you mind, sweetheart.' She even managed a smile, though her hand, which was still grasping mine, was trembling. This performance was for Davy's benefit, I was sure, and it was costing her dear.

Ra must have realised, too, because he stood up abruptly, tipping the child off his lap and took him by the hand. Palu said, 'Say good night to everyone, Davy, and go with Ra. It's your bedtime. Maybe we can persuade Tris to tell you a story.'

Davy began to protest loudly but Serafa, seeing that a distressed small boy was more than Katie could handle, shooed him out of the room. Still complaining, but only for form's sake, Davy was led away by Ra.

'Okay,' said Palu, as soon as they had gone, 'tell us what happened.'

Serafa said, 'You needn't if you don't want to. Are you badly hurt, honey? Shall I get you some crisis drops? Or we could do a healing. Or a pujah meditation.'

'I'm all right,' said Katie. 'Just a bit shaken.'

'Why not try all those things?' I suggested. 'The bastard was using some serious emotional blackmail to make her promise to see him again. And then by way of thanks he used his fists.'

Serafa drew Katie down beside her on one of the enormous sofas. Palu, seated opposite, watched them closely. When Serafa put her arms round her, Katie flinched. Very gently Serafa pulled up her cotton top to reveal ugly bruising all round her ribs. I groaned. Why hadn't Katie cried out? Why hadn't I intervened sooner?

'Jesus!' Serafa spoke through clenched teeth. 'He's going to pay for this.'

Katie pulled her top down, ashamed that we'd seen injuries.

'You don't ever have to see him again,' said Palu.

'I know.' Katie leaned back against Serafa's shoulder with a sigh. 'I know.'

I said, 'So you won't go and see him tomorrow, in spite of your promise?'

'Oh, no.'

It was said easily, just a little bit too easily. Now that I knew what a practised liar Katie was, I didn't intend to underestimate her again. In the car she had been so distressed at the thought of the poor little boy lost tucked away inside the monster, she'd even deluded herself she'd be a match for him in future, and now I had no idea whether this was just another clever performance to throw us all off the scent.

I could think of only one way to make absolutely sure

Katie didn't keep her promise to Tim, and after all the misery I'd caused her, it seemed the least I could do.

I said, 'Listen, I'll go to Cape Trafalgar tomorrow in your place. I'll tell him you're not coming and why. It'll give me great pleasure to tell that bastard exactly what I think of him.'

'Don't be insane.' Serafa was outraged. 'Do you have any idea how dangerous that man can be?'

'I think I got a pretty good idea today, yes.'

'That?' she asked scornfully. 'That was nothing.'

'It was bad enough. And he wouldn't dare to attack me. I'm well able to take care of myself.'

Serafa laughed. 'You little innocent! Why do you think we've gone to such lengths to keep him away from our group? We're not talking about someone who gets busy with his fists from time to time. That man is powered by dark forces, he—'

'Don't!' Katie begged, her tears flowing again. 'Please don't say it!'

'I have to, honey, so Carol here knows what she's up against. Otherwise she'll go off and try to be heroic and she might end up like poor Lucy did.'

'But we don't know for sure,' Katie interrupted desperately. 'It's all just circumstantial evidence.'

'Circumstantial evidence is plenty for me as far as that creep is concerned,' said Serafa. 'I'm sorry, Lumina, I know he was your son in the old life, but that man was born with a dark soul. It's not your fault. It's his karma and he has to work it out for himself. He's nothing to do with you any more.'

'What are you talking about?' I was bewildered.

'Have you heard what happened to his wife?' asked Palu.

'Yes, she died in an accident.'

'That's right,' said Palu. 'She drowned. A tragic

accident, according to her death certificate. Only problem is, no one is quite sure if that's how it really was. His story was that they'd taken different routes home and she must have slipped and lost her footing. The first he knew was when she didn't turn up that evening.'

'People do drown,' whispered Katie miserably. 'Accidents happen.'

'Sure they do,' said Serafa. 'It just seems strange that the poor lady goes and drowns the very day before she was going to leave him. Her friends said it was his sadism to the kid that was the final straw. She wanted to find a place where Davy could be taken care of properly, before that psycho did any more damage to him, but somehow Tim found out. I'd call that more than a coincidence, given his track record.'

'That's right,' said Palu. 'So if you go telling him you think Lumina is better off with us after all, he's not going to like it one little bit.'

'So what can we do?' I asked.

Soft footsteps padded down the corridor and Ra came back into the room. He looked round at our anxious faces, then crossed the room and crouched down in front of Katie and took her hands in his. The silence was gradually filled with a deep, resonant sound which, I realised after a few moments, was humming. Ra closed his eyes and began rocking gently from side to side, then passed his hands rapidly back and forth in front of Katie's face. She was sitting upright, and very still. Finally Ra held both his hands over her head, about an inch away from her scalp. The room was deep in silence. At last his arms fell to his sides and he sat back on his heels.

Katie's mouth twitched into a smile. 'Thank you, Ra,' she said. 'That was very nice.'

Her drawing-room politeness in this weird situation made me want to laugh. But then I remembered her equal politeness when Tim helped her with her sandals on the beach and the laughter died inside me.

Ra was writing something on a piece of paper. He handed it to Serafa who read, 'Tim's dark energy has gone deep into your soul, Katie. At dawn Ra will gather all the Acolytes for a Sun Healing.'

'Excellent,' said Palu.

Ra turned his lamp-black eyes on me and raised his palms as though showing he had nothing to hide. Serafa said, 'He wants you to join us tomorrow, Carol. The evil one has also touched your soul with his negative force.'

I nodded, but didn't know what to say. Those weren't the words I'd have chosen, but as a statement of what had been going on recently they felt pretty close to the truth.

Katie said, with an attempt at her usual brightness. 'That'll be nice for you, Carol.'

'The Sun Healing is fine as far as it goes,' said Palu, 'but we need to take positive steps to keep Lumina and the boy safe. They can't stay here.'

'Oh no!' Katie wailed. 'Does that mean we have to move again?'

'Sorry, but Palu's right, honey,' said Serafa. 'As soon as that man knows you're not going to play along with his little game, you won't be safe here any more.'

'Oh dear, and just as we were getting settled again.'

'Are you sure it's okay to move them?' I asked. I thought of what Tim had told me about the fifth column being transferred, but I didn't see how I could warn the Inner Circle without giving away my own part in his schemes. I comforted myself with the thought that the fifth column might have been merely an invention, a way to manipulate me into going to Spain. I said, 'Surely Tim can't break in here – your security's much too good. What can he do?'

Serafa regarded me coolly, as if wondering how far I could be trusted. Then she said, 'Until now he's been

278 • Joanna Hines

hoping to get Lumina away from here as well as Davy.
When he realises that's impossible, he'll settle for just
Davy.'

'But how?'

'Through the courts, of course. It may take him time and
it may be messy, but he's got a good chance of winning in
the end.'

'Surely no judge is going to take Davy away from a place
where he's happy and make him live with a sadistic father?'

Serafa laughed bitterly. 'Oh no? Welcome to the real
world, Carol. That kind of thing happens all the time. And
in this case, who knows about the violence apart from us?
No one.'

'He doesn't wear his dark heart on his sleeve,' said Palu.
'He can put on a good show. I'd have thought you could
vouch for that, Carol. That first time, when we threw him
out of the meeting, can you honestly say you saw him as a
threat? Or as a victim?'

I didn't answer. I had been wondering if Palu and Serafa
remembered I'd been at that first meeting with Tim. What
else had they observed about me but not yet bothered to
mention?

'We have to be realistic,' said Serafa. 'If this comes to
court it's not going to look good for Lumina. Can you
imagine what fun the media would have with it? Tim sells
his story to the papers: handsome young father with a
respectable job in finance breaks down as he talks about
his little boy being brainwashed by a bunch of crazies. And
lo and behold, yes, we do dress in long robes and talk
about Atlantis. Is there any contest? Game, set and match
to Mr Fairchild, I do believe.'

'And that's only if they play by the rules,' said Palu. 'If
Tim's lawyers know their job they'll dig out the old
rumours about me and Ra. All those stories about that
incident in the old life and then all the lies about how we

got our first money. Lumina wouldn't stand a chance, and if it got really nasty the scandal could sweep us all away. Everything we've worked for all these years finished by one evil father. We have to hide Lumina and Davy away so the forces of dark aren't channelled through him to destroy our work.'

'Surely he's not that powerful?' I said.

'No? Who would you put your money on, the fine upstanding young headmaster's son or the loony granny who's fallen into the clutches of the Paki guru's mad cult?'

I looked at Ra to see how he was taking this unflattering description of himself, but he only smiled.

'We're going to have to act fast,' said Serafa. 'We've got less than twenty-four hours. Lumina, you must speak to the man and make him believe everything is going according to his plan. Meanwhile, we'll make the arrangements for your transfer.'

Ra gestured as though querying where they should go. He had crossed the room and crouched down to put away the chequers.

'Back to Cornwall?' suggested Katie hopefully.

'No,' said Palu, 'and Mexico is out of the question, too. Both places are far too well known. Look how quickly he tracked you here. It'll have to be one of our safe houses, or else a sister group. Secrecy is going to be your only safety for quite a while, Lumina. You and Davy will have to disappear.'

Those last words sent a chill through me. I thought of all the crimes that have been covered by the simple euphemism 'disappear'. I said, 'Don't you think you're overreacting?'

'No,' said Serafa, 'I don't. But there's only one way to find out and I don't intend to risk it.' She put her arm round Katie's shoulders. 'Don't worry, honey. I'll come with you wherever you go. We can still be together.'

Ra nodded. Palu said thoughtfully, 'is that wise, Serafa? Lumina and Davy are less likely to attract attention if they travel alone. With a discreet escort, of course.'

'Lumina needs someone with her,' said Serafa in a tone which indicated the subject was closed. 'I will go.'

'I can't get to sleep.'

No one had noticed Davy's reappearance. More than ever he looked like a small angel; his golden curls were tousled, his cheeks flushed, and he wore a home-made-looking nightshirt of white cotton that came to his knees. His small feet were bare.

He glanced round the room cautiously, to see how his interruption was being received and then, emboldened by the silence, he crossed the room and scrambled on to the sofa beside Katie. She put her arm round him and then winced as he bounced happily into the crook of her arm.

'Careful, there,' warned Serafa. 'Your Lumina's not feeling too well.'

Palu stood up and held out her hand. 'Come along with me, young man, and leave your gran in peace. She's had a busy day.' When Davy started to protest, Palu said firmly, 'No arguments. I'll make you a hot drink and then tell you a story. You'll be asleep before you know it, I promise.'

Davy slid reluctantly off the sofa and put his hand in Palu's outstretched one. She had the kind of manner that children know it's not worth arguing with, and Davy was no exception.

'While I'm in the kitchen I'll get Tris to send us up a tray of food,' she said. 'I don't suppose anyone feels much like a proper meal. And I'll contact Karnak, too. The sooner she's involved the better. We'll have to double all security measures until the danger's gone. I'll put Intara on reception – some of the new ones can be a bit slack.

Heaven knows what that man will do when he realises we've outwitted him again.'

'Palu's right,' said Serafa, when the older woman had led Davy away. 'We need to get Karnak over from Cornwall; she's the best we've got. And we need a breathing space. Maybe we should put the meeting back twenty-four hours. That would give us more time to make the arrangements for getting you out of here. How can you get in contact with him?'

'He's got a mobile phone,' I said, before Katie had a chance to answer.

'Excellent. Lumina, why don't you phone him now?'

'All right.' But in spite of her agreement, she didn't move.

'Do you have his number?'

'What?' asked Katie vaguely. 'Yes, I suppose he must have given it to me.' She was careful not to look at me. 'But . . . do I have to talk to him? It . . . it just makes it all so complicated again.'

'Why don't I call him for you?' I suggested. 'I'm sure I wrote his number down this afternoon. He won't think it's strange. After all, I was there while they were making the arrangements and I can always tell him it's too risky for Lumina to make the call herself.'

Serafa regarded me coolly, her long eyes filled with mistrust. 'Okay, just so long as you make the call right here,' she said. 'Where we can hear you.'

I was annoyed, but I tried to laugh it off. 'Why the precautions? Are you afraid I might be tempted to warn him? After what I saw him do today?'

But Serafa wouldn't budge. 'We can't take any chances on this one. Just make the call from here,' she said.

The first time I tried, his number was engaged. I prayed silently that he wasn't ringing me: the last thing I wanted was to have to parry his call under the watchful eyes of Serafa and Ra.

On the second attempt I got through. 'Hello? Is that Tim Fairchild?' I made my voice as formal as possible.

'Carol?' He sounded surprised.

'Listen, this is Carol Brewster – we met this afternoon at Cape Trafalgar. I've got a message for you from your mother.' There was a startled noise from the other end of the line. It sounded as though he was moving around in his hotel room, with the phone crooked under his chin. I wondered what he was doing. 'Are you at your hotel?'

'Just give me the message.'

'Your mother can't get to the phone herself right now, but she asked me to give you a message. She says the plan is fine, but she needs another twenty-four hours to make all the arrangements. She'll meet you as planned, but not tomorrow. The next day.'

'Is that it?'

'Yes.'

'Tell her that's fine by me.' He sounded tense, more keyed up than I'd ever known him. But he had accepted the change of plans without a murmur of protest, and that didn't feel right. I'd expected disappointment, anger and argument, not this bland acceptance.

I said, 'Are you sure?'

'Of course. Is that all?' he asked.

'Yes.'

'Then tell her I'll see her on Thursday.'

He hung up and I switched off my phone and put it back in my jacket pocket.

'What did he say?' asked Serafa.

'He said fine, see you Thursday. It doesn't feel right. I expected him to be disappointed, or to argue.'

'Oh, the poor boy,' said Katie, her eyes filling with tears. 'This whole business must be torture for him.'

Serafa said firmly, 'If so, it's his own fault. He didn't

have to take the path of violence. He could have chosen the ways of peace.'

'I thought it was all in his karma,' I said.

Serafa didn't deign to answer.

Palu returned and told us she'd already been in touch with Karnak, who'd come straight over from England in the morning. As luck would have it she'd been at a meeting in London and would get the first available flight. Then Tris arrived with a trolley laden with food and I realised I was ravenous. Katie picked at the food. Palu and Serafa discussed the merits of various places where Katie and Davy might be sent.

They were courteous to me, but not all that welcoming and Serafa, I was sure, was suspicious of my role in the day's events.

One way and another, I was not looking forward to meeting Karnak again.

Chapter 20

The moon was rising, touching the hillside with its eerie light, so there was not much need of the solar lamps beside the path. I was dazed as I walked slowly back towards the Hesperides after my second visit to the Villa. That afternoon, when I set off to Cape Trafalgar, I'd had a clear picture in my mind of the situation and what needed to be done. Now the waters had been stirred up and muddied and everything was uncertain, and I didn't know where I stood in the picture any more.

I told myself to stick to the facts: there could be no doubt that Tim had manipulated and betrayed me; he was a sadistic bully, who had driven Katie to seek refuge with her old friends at the Heirs of Akasha – but just because I'd been wrong about him, that didn't mean I'd been wrong about the group, too. Their ideas were still crazy. 'Out of the frying pan into the fire' sprang to mind as a description of the way Katie had dealt with her problems.

Besides, Palu's suggestion that Tim had caused his wife's death was not convincing. If he had, surely the police or someone would have been suspicious. People didn't go around bumping off their wives because they said they were leaving. Tim was a bully, but that didn't make him a murderer. It seemed more likely that Palu and Serafa had concocted this scenario to make it easier for Katie to give up on her son. I felt some sympathy for Katie's loyalty towards Tim: it was too easy just to call him a dark soul. Surely there were solutions that might be tried – anger management or therapy or something – before he was written off as hopeless.

Still, as I walked along the moonlit hillside and thought over all that had happened, the problems of Tim and Katie were eclipsed by worries nearer to my heart. There was a riddle I'd been avoiding for a long time, maybe since Jenny's first visit in the spring. It was to do with Andrew Forester's murder and Raymond Tucker and it was to do with Gus.

I think it was while I watched Katie wriggle and squirm to avoid facing the ugly truth about Tim that I realised it was time for me to confront my own deepest fears. We find so many excuses to avoid facing unpleasant truths about those we love, and in my way I had been just as protective of Gus as she was of Tim. But all the time the doubts had been nagging away at the back of my mind. I tried to think about it logically. All the people who knew Raymond agreed he was incapable of harming anyone, and the little I'd seen of him bore this out. Right now, I knew better than anyone how deceptive circumstances can be, but it did make him less likely as a suspect. Which meant that, if some of the Grays Orchard residents had covered up for the murderer with that story of an intruder, Andrew's killer must have been one of the others: Katie or Pauline or Harriet.

Or Gus.

It wasn't that I believed what Katie told me about Gus's

violent past; I assumed she'd made that up because it made Tim's bullying less horrific, but I had to face the possibility that Gus might have killed Andrew. Not that I believed he had. After all, I'd lived with Gus for six years; he was my husband, for heaven's sake. I knew him and I trusted him.

But I'd been wrong about so many things already that my confidence in my judgement was severely shaken. I stopped walking, horrified by the route my thoughts were taking. It was ridiculous. What possible motive could Gus have had for killing Andrew, one of his closest friends? Why would he destroy everything they'd worked so hard to build at Grays Orchard?

But then, if Gus had (accidentally, perhaps?) killed Andrew, much else was explained: that dark guilt which drove him to blacken and destroy all his subsequent paintings; his reluctance to see Harriet again; his dismay when Jenny burst into his life, reviving all that he'd spent a quarter of a century trying to forget. It was possible – not likely, you understand, but just possible – that Gus refused to talk about the Grays Orchard years because that final memory had poisoned all that went before.

An owl called in the darkness. I continued along the path. It may sound strange, but the idea that Gus had been harbouring this secret guilt throughout our time together made me feel, more than anything else, compassionate towards him. Just imagine how desperate he must have felt, all those years of secrecy and remorse. And it made it easier to deal with the way he'd been blocking me out since the spring: it wasn't just that the early attraction between us was wearing off, it was his dark secret that opened the chasm between us. He must have been eaten up inside. If only he'd been able to confide in me, I could have helped him come to terms with what had happened. There had to be a way to love him into forgiving himself.

But how could I even begin until he told me the truth?

I was back at the Hesperides. It was nearly eleven and the lights inside the villas were dim: at Tartessus the day began at six and most people were glad of early nights. I walked up the steps into my villa and my roommates greeted me sleepily. 'How was Cape Trafalgar?' 'Did Lumina meet her friend?' I parried their questions as best I could and then, realising there'd be no chance of sleep for me for a long time, I slung a light jacket over my shoulders and went out again.

I walked towards Solon's Terrace. A little distance from the Hesperides, it had one of the best views on the property and at night it was especially beautiful.

Someone else had had the same idea. I saw the glow of a cigarette end in the dark. I hesitated. Of all the crimes that could be committed at Tartessus, smoking was the most heinous. To be caught meant an instant summons to the Judgement Spiral and usually merited a punishment such as cleaning lavatories for a month or even being demoted from Acolyte to Pilgrim. So the secret smoker was not going to welcome my attention.

I was about to move away when the figure shifted slightly: a bony body hunched under a man's oversized jacket. Jenny. She must have bought the cigarettes in Tarifa. Was that why she'd been so eager to accompany me? She was taking a huge risk, because if she was caught she'd most likely lose her chance to take the Oath of Loyalty at the end of the month. After a few moments, curiosity drove me forward. Curiosity and an overwhelming urge to have a cigarette myself.

She was sitting on one of the shallow steps that led down from the terrace and overlooked the valley, and she looked round at my approach. From what I could see of her expression she didn't seem too alarmed at being apprehended, just the usual combination of sour grapes and gloom.

'Oh,' she said. 'It's you.'

'Can I take one?'

'Help yourself.' She indicated the packet on the stone beside her: it was almost full.

'Thanks. Do you mind if I join you?'

'Do what you want.'

I settled down beside her on the cool stone and looked out over the valleys and the hills towards the small patch of sea. There were a few lights, but not many, and the occasional fan from the headlights of a far-away car. But above our heads the sky was freckled with a million stars. I lit the cigarette and inhaled deeply.

Jenny tilted her head and looked at me quizzically. 'So you do have some vices. You know smoking's a hanging offence around here.'

'I'll risk it,' I said.

'Why? Feeling guilty because you landed Lumina in the shit?'

'How do you know about that?'

'Bush telegraph. A friend of mine's a helper at the Villa. If the Inner Circle want privacy, they'll have to do their own dirty work. It'll be all over the camp by tomorrow.'

'What did your friend tell you?'

'She said Lumina got tricked into meeting her psychotic son. The story is you were an innocent bystander, but I don't buy that myself. Knowing your love of sticking your nose into other people's business, I'd guess you were a key player. Right?'

I took a long drag on the cigarette, exhaled slowly and said, 'You'd be doing yourself a favour, Jenny, if you stopped being so hostile all the time. But don't worry, I'm not about to give you another lecture. I thought the Heirs exploited people.' As I spoke I realised I was using the past tense. Didn't I think so any more? The truth was that I didn't know, but after what I'd seen that evening I was prepared to give them the benefit of the doubt. 'Now I can see it's not so simple. I still think their philosophy is mad, but if this is where you want to make your home, that's up to you.'

'Am I supposed to be grateful?'

'Oh, for God's sake, Jenny. I'm only trying to help and I still think you should get in touch with your mother, because you'll regret it for the rest of your life if you don't. I just wanted to say I may have been wrong about the group, that's all.'

'Yeah, well, it doesn't matter. I'm out of here in a couple of days.'

'You're leaving?'

'Damn right I am.'

'But what about the Oath of Loyalty? I thought you were so excited about it.'

'That was just to wind you up. I was going to leave last week, but then you turned up and started trying to tell me how I had to live my life and I thought I'm damned if I'll let you take all the credit for rescuing me from the clutches of an evil cult, so I decided to grit it out a bit longer. I've cursed you up and down the past few days when I've been slogging away in their stupid lunar vegetable patch.'

I was astonished. What about the spiel she'd given me in the car that afternoon? Then I remembered her final words, and the way her eyes had danced with mischief. *You're such a sucker, Carol.* Well, she'd been righter than she knew.

I asked, 'Why the change of heart?'

'I never intended to stay here more than a month or two, and I've been here nearly six. It's been one of the best summers I've ever had so I don't regret it. And I got to talk to Ra and Palu about Andrew and all the Grays Orchard stuff, which is what I'd come for. They told me loads about him. They think I take after him a lot.'

290 • J<small>OANNA</small> H<small>INES</small>

'They know you're Harriet's daughter?'

'Sure. That was the reason they let me join, even though
I don't have any skills they're interested in. Probably the
reason they turned a blind eye when I acted up.
Apparently, Ra said I was the bait and all the others would
follow. He's got some weird idea that all the Grays
Orchard people will be reunited in time for his precious
Watershed. He was really excited when you showed up.
He thinks it means Gus will be next and then my mum.
And then the circle will be complete.'

'So he knows about me and Gus?'

'Sure he does. They're pretty well informed.' I suppose I
shouldn't have been surprised, but all the same it was an
odd sensation, like discovering someone's been watching
you when you thought you'd been on your own. She went
on, 'They may seem like they're off with the fairies, but
they know what's what. Especially Palu. They make sure
they know the important stuff. Ra's dead keen on getting
Gus and my mum here. And who knows, they might have
come looking for me by now if you hadn't volunteered to
do their dirty work for them.'

'I'd have thought you'd be relieved it wasn't Gus.'

'Why?' she asked plaintively. 'He's my uncle, isn't he?
He was worried about me, I know he was, but you had to
spoil it by interfering.'

I was trying to figure this out. 'You really wanted Gus to
come and have a showdown with you? Is that why you did
it?'

'Did what?'

She was staring at me blankly. I'd read about the mind's
amazing ability to dissociate itself from painful memories
and I wondered if she'd edited the events of that last
morning from her memory. I said slowly, 'When I saw you
driving away from Grays the last time, you were so upset
at what you'd done that you drove straight into the middle

of the traffic. I wanted to call the police, but Gus was determined to protect you.'

'From what? There's no law against driving when you're in a state of shock. And it wasn't anything *I'd* done that upset me.'

I was curious to know how much, if anything, she remembered of her frenzied attack on Gus's paintings. I said, 'So what did upset you?'

She shuddered. 'That creepy portrait, of course. I wondered why he wouldn't let me look while he was painting it. I just thought it was the kind of thing he always does.'

'Used to do,' I corrected her automatically.

'Yeah, like the ones he did of Mum watering lettuces and carrying flowers. But when he showed it me that morning – ugh – it made me want to throw up. It was disgusting, totally perverted. Ra and Palu said I shouldn't have taken it so personally, it was just his artistic interpretation. But at the time it really hit me.'

'So much that you had to destroy it?'

She turned to me in surprise. 'Why would I do that? It wasn't going to be my twisted mind on display for all the world to gawp at. Maybe Gus hadn't realised how kinky it was until he saw my reaction. I remember, he came and stood just behind me. He wanted to know what I thought of it and so I told him straight. Maybe I was a bit too straight, but I never thought he'd react like that.'

The temperature must have dropped because suddenly I was shivering. 'Like what?' I asked.

'The mad bastard attacked it, didn't he?' She was speaking in a low voice. 'He had a knife in his hand, one of those sharp, stumpy ones with an orange handle. He said something about critics never lying and then he stabbed the knife into the picture, right in the middle of my forehead, then dragged it down through the canvas, right through my body and that hideous flower. He wasn't laughing exactly; he was making this weird noise halfway between laughing and crying and I thought, "This man is losing it for sure. I'm out of here." I know it sounds over the top, but I was half afraid that when he'd finished with the picture he might start on me. He was acting like someone demented. I think he started on one of the other pictures before I'd gone, but I didn't stay to find out. God, if that's artistic bloody temperament, you can keep it.'

I didn't say a word, but reached for another of her cigarettes. If only I thought she was making this up too, but her story had the ring of truth. And I couldn't remember Gus himself saying it was Jenny. I had automatically assumed she had vandalised the pictures. But it could just as well have been Gus.

It was definitely possible.

Sitting there in the dark, smoking one of Jenny's disgusting cigarettes, I knew it had been Gus.

Finally I said, 'He didn't stop there. He destroyed them all. Every single one.'

'Did he? Christ, but I'm not really surprised. He must be insane.'

'Maybe.'

'I couldn't have stopped him, Carol. He was dangerous.'

I was shivering, but not with cold. Jenny put her arm round my shoulders. I had wanted to call the police, but Gus had refused. And he had sworn me to secrecy. I had thought it was Jenny he was protecting. Wrong again. The only person Gus had been protecting was himself.

How much else had I been wrong about?

I ground my cigarette butt on the stone and stared across the dark landscape to the distant sea. Tim's deception had made me furious, but this latest image of Gus destroying his own pictures and then allowing me to commiserate with him over Jenny's vandalism left me numb with shock.

What a creep, I thought. What a coward.

'Someone's late,' commented Jenny, shifting slightly and looking back towards the hills. Half a mile away the security light had snapped on at the Pillars of Hercules and in the midnight stillness the low hum of a car was audible. 'I wonder who it is.'

I wondered, too. The Heirs of Akasha kept early hours, and visitors in the middle of the night were a rarity. Suddenly, I was uneasy.

Jenny said, 'Someone must have caught the late flight to Málaga.'

It couldn't be Karnak already. Were they bringing reinforcements from somewhere nearby? The engine cut out just before the car reached the main reception building. The security light at the Pillars went out. Darkness and silence enveloped El Cortijo again.

Jenny yawned. 'I'm heading for bed,' she began. 'More bloody vegetables in the morning. It's—'

'Sssh.' I put my hand on her arm. She drew it away swiftly and was about to protest, but I pointed silently through the darkness to the path below. A figure was walking cautiously along the track. Someone who didn't know the path well. Someone in light trousers and jacket. Someone whose fair hair gleamed pale in the moonlight.

'Who?' breathed Jenny.

'Tim,' I said. 'Katie's psychotic son.'

'What's he doing here?'

'Someone must have tipped him off,' I said, cursing myself for my stupidity. Once I'd realised that he'd double-crossed me over Katie, I should have remembered the person who'd been helping him on the inside and who'd been oh-so-conveniently moved just before my arrival. 'He's come for Davy.'

'Who let him in?'

'I've no idea.' Frantically I flipped through all the

people at the Villa Omega to work out who'd betrayed them, but it could have been anyone. It could have been Tris from the kitchen or even – terrible thought – little Davy himself. I said, 'We've got to raise the alarm. He doesn't know the layout of this place. We can take a short cut through the Temple. If we run, we'll reach the Villa before him.'

'But—'

Already the pale figure had vanished behind a long hedge. I scrambled to my feet. 'For God's sake, Jenny, for once in your life stop arguing and bloody well help!'

Already I was heading up the hillside, following the narrow path that led along beside the lunar vegetable patch towards the Temple. After a few moments I heard Jenny padding swiftly behind me. We raced across the huge circle of the Temple, its white columns like ghostly figures in the moonlight, and sprinted the last hundred yards to the broad steps of the Villa Omega. All the windows were shuttered and dark.

I ran up the steps to the front door and turned the handle. It was locked from inside. I felt around for a bell or a knocker but without success.

'Hey!' I yelled, pounding the door with my fists. 'Hey! Let us in!'

The door opened at once. Palu, dumpy and unattractive in the blue robes that on her always looked like a shapeless dressing gown, peered out at us angrily. 'Quiet! Do you want to wake the whole house?'

'Yes,' I said. If I didn't know who to trust, the only safety lay in telling everyone. 'That's exactly what I want to do.'

Jenny came panting up the steps behind me. Before I could stop her, she blurted out, 'Palu, quick, alert the security. Lumina's son got in. He's trying to steal the boy.'

Palu gave me a sharp look. 'Why didn't you say so at once? Where is he?'

'He's coming along the main path from reception. We took a short cut, but he'll be here soon.'

Palu was thinking rapidly. She drew us both into the protective darkness of the hallway and shut the door quietly behind us. 'This is a full alert,' she said. 'I'll make sure Davy's hidden and send out a search party. You must find Ra. He's the only one who can activate Total Red security so they can't escape.'

'Where's his room?'

'Upstairs, but he isn't there. He's doing a vigil for tomorrow's Sun Healing. Do you know where the Omega chrysalis is?'

Before I could answer, Jenny said, 'I do, Carol. I'll show you.'

'Hurry,' said Palu, leading the way through the villa. 'I'll let you out the back.'

'What about Katie?'

'I'll wake her. She can hide with Davy until we've caught Fairchild. He's made a big mistake this time. Through this way.'

She opened a door on to a paved area at the rear of the villa. After the darkness of the house, the landscape was washed with moonlight, making it easy to find our way. 'Go round the pool on the right, then up the track and the Omega chrysalis is about fifty yards on the left. Tell Ra we have to go for Total Red. We can't take any chances with that man on the loose. Hurry!'

Jenny was already running up the hill as Palu closed the door. I didn't know if I could trust either of them, but I didn't relish the idea of coming face to face with Tim alone and in the dark. Tim, who by now had been told by his anonymous informer of all that I had and had not done, was sure to be out for revenge.

I took off up the hill after Jenny.

The Omega chrysalis looked from the outside and in the

dark exactly like the one I'd been working on this past week. There were no lights and the door was closed.

'I bet he's bloody sleeping, not meditating at all,' said Jenny in disgust. 'Hey, Ra, wake up! It's an emergency.' She pulled open the door and went inside. 'Ra, quick. You have to do the Red Alert or Total Red or whatever it's called. Lumina's son has—' She broke off. Then, more cautiously, 'Ra?'

I was about to follow her in but at the last minute I held back. I was waiting on the threshold as she swivelled round to face me and said in a puzzled voice, 'There's no one here.'

'We've been tricked.'

'Why would Palu send us to the wrong place?'

'Jesus,' I said.

Palu.

Just as I was about to turn round, a huge weight cannoned into my side, knocking me off balance. I reached out to grab the doorpost but something whacked me in the middle of my back. The force of the blow took my breath away and pitched me into the inky blackness of the chrysalis, hurling me against Jenny. I put out my hands to stop myself falling but clutched only air. As I crashed down against the hard floor I heard the door slam shut behind us, the metallic thud of a bolt shooting home.

Crunch of footsteps on the stony ground outside. It sounded like two people, but I was so stunned by my fall it was hard to be sure. There was a murmur of voices, then I heard Palu saying with quiet satisfaction, 'They'll be safe there till morning. I'll get the boy.' And the footsteps faded into silence.

'What the hell?' Jenny nearly stumbled over my legs in her hurry to get to the door. I could have told her not to bother.

'What's going on?' Suddenly her voice was childish and

dismayed. I struggled to my feet. There was a sharp pain in my left side.

'Palu's been working with Tim all along,' I told her. 'God, how could I have been so stupid? Now they've got rid of us until Davy's out of the way.'

'What are we going to do?' she demanded. 'How can we get out of here?'

The irony was lost on me right then. For the first time since we had met in the spring, Jenny had turned to me for help. She actually wanted my advice.

And for the first time since we'd met, I had absolutely none to offer.

Chapter 21

Jenny scrabbled at the door of the chrysalis for several minutes before she gave up and accepted defeat. Having spent the previous week building one, I could have told her right away that she was wasting her time. I knew our gaoler had dropped a heavy metal bolt in position on the outside of the door. Though they weren't often used, bolts were fitted as standard on all the chrysalises: very occasionally a solo meditator asked to be locked in so they couldn't cheat – or that's what we'd been told. Now I wondered if they'd had a more sinister dual purpose all along. These little huts were built to withstand the fierce summer sun, so the two windows were tiny; they might be just big enough for a cat to slip through, but not an adult human. The light stayed out, and we stayed in.

Jenny clutched my arm. 'Shout!' she ordered. 'Shout as loud as you can. Someone's got to hear us. We can't stay here all night.' She pounded the door with her fists. 'Help! Come and find us! Help, we've been locked in!'

I threw my weight against the door and shouted with

her, though I didn't hold out much hope. This chrysalis was a long way from the Villa Omega, which in turn was half a mile from the rest of the sleeping accommodation, with a broad hillside in between. But I shouted with her, because I couldn't think of anything else to do.

'Help, someone help! For God's sake, we're going to die in here! Come quickly! *He-elp!*'

Gradually I realised Jenny's cries were getting shrill with panic. 'Stop it,' I told her sharply. 'You're just getting hysterical and no one can hear us.'

She rounded on me. 'Fuck you, Carol! It's all your fault we're stuck in here. You had to poke your nose in, didn't you? You got me into this, you interfering *bitch*!' In the darkness I never saw the blow coming, only heard the rush of air as her fist swept down to strike my cheek. I put my hands up to protect myself and pushed her away.

'Don't be a bloody idiot, Jenny. I'm on your side, remember? Tim's crazy, and I think Palu's been working with him all along. She would have let him in anyway.'

'I hate you!' she yelled. 'Fucking – hate – you!' She was gasping, so choked with anger she was having trouble drawing breath. 'Your fault! Everything you did . . .'

My eyes were adjusting to the pitchy dark inside the chrysalis and this time when she raised her arm I was ready for her and caught hold of her wrist before she could hit me. 'Fuck – you – !' She broke off and took a sharp, painful breath. 'Oh – oh!'

'What is it?'

She twisted free of my grasp and stumbled away from me in the darkness. She banged against something and doubled over. 'Oh – God.' She spoke between whistling breaths. 'Need – my – fucking – inhaler.'

My heart sank. I reached out to put my arm round her but she shook me off angrily. 'Jenny, what's the matter?' I asked. 'Are you asthmatic?'

'Help me. Can't – breathe.'

'Listen to me,' I said firmly, 'you have to stay calm. Let's sit down here, there's a sort of bed. Is it easier if you lie down? No? Okay. Try to relax.' Even as I spoke, the words sounded hollow and ridiculous, but what other comfort was there? 'You're going to be all right. Just breathe slowly.'

'Need – my – inhaler.'

'It's not here, Jenny.' For the first time I felt real fear rising inside me. How was I supposed to help her? 'Please try not to panic. I'll think of something, but you have to stay calm.' I started to take long, deep breaths, as though by doing so I could breathe for her.

'Can't – breathe.'

'I know, I know. Don't worry, it's going to be all right.'

'No! Get – help.'

Her voice was turning into a strange growl and she gripped my arm so tightly my fingers were going numb. This was serious. It was no good telling her it was going to be all right. I didn't know much about asthma, but I did know it could be fatal, especially if it wasn't treated. There had to be a way to escape from the chrysalis; I couldn't just wait here and do nothing.

I went to the window and pushed it wide. 'Help! Somebody help us!'

The moonlit hillside was bathed in silence. I thought of all those people sleeping profoundly in their communal villas and long houses. Was there no one taking a midnight walk? No one sneaking off for a forbidden cigarette? No one out there who could hear my shout?

'*Help!*'

Behind me, hunched on the narrow bed, Jenny was struggling for every breath. It was hard to say which was worse, her painful, wheezing gulps for air or the terrible silences in between when I kept glancing round to check she was still conscious.

'*HELP!*'

I thought of Tim and Palu – surely once they realised how serious the situation was they'd let us out? – and I thought of Davy being woken in the night and carried down the path by his father. Even a child could raise the alarm. 'Jenny's ill! She can't breathe! *Somebody help us!*' But there was only a breeze rustling through dry leaves.

Okay, no one was going to help, so I had to find a way out of the chrysalis. I knew how sloppy the construction was on these huts. I rattled the windows in their frames, tore at the cement with my fingers, then tried the door. It was badly built, but not so badly that I could wrench it apart with my bare hands. I needed a lever, some kind of tool.

The windows let in hardly any light. I groped around in the darkness. Damn them for their spartan ways. There was just a narrow bed where Jenny was sitting, still gasping in panic and pain, and a small wicker locker, but nothing else. Nothing that could be used to dig or gouge or batter our way out.

'Shout.' Jenny gasped. 'Keep – shouting!'

I went back to the window and shouted louder than I'd ever shouted in my life before, a banshee shriek they must have been able to hear all the way to the coast, a shriek to raise the dead and surely . . .

Yes. It was the sound I'd been aching to hear: footsteps hurrying down the track towards us.

'Hurry! Jenny's ill. She needs help.' I was almost sobbing with relief as I turned to Jenny, still crouched and wheezing on the bed. 'Someone's coming,' I told her. 'You'll be okay now.'

She raised her head and the deathly face in Gus's portrait stared back at me. 'By – my – bed.'

'Your inhaler? Yes, I'll run as fast as I can. Don't worry.'

The footsteps were very close. Whoever it was must be going straight to unbolt the door.

'Quick,' I shouted. 'I have to get Jenny's inhaler. She can't breathe.' The footsteps came to a halt outside the door. I was frantic with impatience. 'Hurry, for God's sake!' I pressed my hands against the door. 'It's a metal latch,' I told our rescuer. 'All you have to do is lift it.'

A man's voice. 'You must be joking.' It was the one voice I never wanted to hear again.

Tim.

Why was he here? By now he ought to have got Davy and be heading through the Pillars of Hercules. Disappointment was dulling my brain. I fought to think clearly. I said, 'Tim, listen to me. The girl who's with me is asthmatic. She can't breathe. You have to let us out of here.'

'Tough,' he said quietly.

'Tim, please, this is serious.' I was trying to speak calmly, though my heart was pounding with fear. 'Jenny's ill. She needs her inhaler. You must let me out of here. I know you don't want anyone to get hurt. You just want us to stay out of your way while you get Davy. Well then,' I drew in a deep breath, then said, 'I won't stop you taking Davy, I promise.'

He grunted. It sounded as though he was stooped over and moving about on the other side of the door. What on earth was he doing? Why had he come back? 'You don't think I'm falling for that old trick, do you?' He spoke with lethal calm.

'For God's sake, it's not a trick. I promise you it's the truth. Look, come to the window and see for yourself.'

I couldn't make it out. He was moving around purposefully. I could hear the dry plants crackling under his shoes. What was he up to out there? I turned just in time to see his face appear briefly at the window. Moonlight glinted on his fair hair but his face was in shadow, blank as a mask. He wouldn't have been able to see anything inside the chrysalis, but Jenny's ragged breathing was all the proof he needed.

'Fakers,' he said tersely, and when I protested, he said, 'Ugh, it's cold in there. A fire will keep you warm.' And then he chuckled. I'd never heard Tim laugh before and the sound was more chilling than any outburst of rage. Whatever he was doing, he was enjoying himself thoroughly.

'Tim,' I said. 'Don't be crazy. We've got to help Jenny, she could die in here.'

'Good,' he said crisply. 'And you'll have to stay there and watch her, won't you? It's time someone taught you a lesson.' He was still moving around, stooping from time to time as if he'd dropped something.

Jenny's breathing was getting fainter. I said, 'Tim, for God's sake, you can take Davy, do what you want with your family. Only let us out of here!'

His eyes glinted in the moonlight as he straightened up and came to the window. His face was only inches from mine.

'No bargains,' he said quietly. 'You betrayed me, Carol. I thought you were on my side. I trusted you, but you went over to the enemy. Now you have to take your punishment.'

He moved away. On the ground beside the path I could just make out what looked like a pile of crumpled clothes. But then again, it might have been a child wrapped in a white sheet. Yes, there was a small foot sticking out from the bundle of cloth, but no movement.

I stared. 'What have you done with Davy?'

'Davy's mine,' said Tim with quiet satisfaction, as he continued to pull up bits of dry grass and scrubby bushes and toss them towards the chrysalis. 'I'm going to look after him now. He'll be safe with me. Those weirdos won't get their hands on him again, not ever.' He straightened up and his eyes locked on to mine. 'I'm warning you, I'd rather see Davy dead than let him fall into their clutches again.' He went back to his task.

For a few moments I was too horrified to speak. Where had Palu got to? Would she have helped him if she knew what he was really planning?

'Tim, don't do this. It's not worth it.'

He walked slowly over to the window and chucked the bundle of dry brush against the wall of the chrysalis. Then he looked at me and said, 'You're wrong. My only regret is that I can't stay behind and watch you suffer.'

'You bastard!'

'And anyway,' he added with an odd little smile, 'you're nothing but a slut.'

'You're insane! No one's going to let you keep Davy, not after this. Jesus, why did I ever believe you? Tim, you fucking bastard, let us *OUT*!'

He ignored me and rubbed his hands together lightly, as though brushing off bits of dirt, then took a box of matches from his jacket pocket and crouched down. He struck the match and held the flame to a wad of dry grass, then stood back and watched as the stalks crackled and burned.

He glanced up at me, satisfaction making his handsome face look boyish and untroubled, like an eager boy scout who's just made his first campfire and is waiting to be praised for his cleverness. He spoke to me just before he turned away. From his expression you'd have thought he was offering encouragement, but I couldn't hear because by then I was screaming for help louder than ever.

Under the tiny window the fire was burning merrily, and through the haze above the flames I saw Tim bend over and pick up his son, who hung limp and lifeless in his arms. My cheeks were pressed against the window frame as Tim walked slowly out of my line of vision.

Smoke was stinging my eyes. I fell back from the

window. Jenny was watching me from the bed. Her knees were drawn up in front of her chest and her face was lit by the wavering light of the fire. Her eyes were huge with fear. She opened her mouth, but whether to speak or gasp for breath I had no idea because no sound came out. She was struggling. As the first coils of smoke drifted through the open window she shrank back against the wall. As if that would help. Her mouth sagged and her pupils slid up under her lids. She was losing consciousness.

'Jenny,' I began, but the smoke was clogging my lungs and I choked.

I pulled the window shut and secured it tightly. Then I knelt on the bed, slid my hands under Jenny's armpits and dragged her off, laying her down on the floor by the door, where the smoke would be less dense. It was a narrow space, like a coffin. Wasn't that what the runes had predicted?

For a moment the hopelessness of it all overwhelmed me: how could I fight against what had been foreseen? In a blurred way I wondered if all this was written in the Akashic Record and therefore inescapable. Then my anger revived: Tim and those crazy runes weren't going to win, not that easily.

I shifted the bed into the middle of the room, then lifted the bedside locker and placed it in the centre of the bed. The mattress dipped in the middle and the cabinet rocked from side to side as I climbed on top of it and caught hold of the rafters to steady myself. Reaching up through the roof joists, I tried to dislodge the earthenware shingles that formed the roof. I pounded them with my fists and tore at them, but without success. I tried everything. Then I hit one on its lower edge and it bounced free. I slid it sideways, revealing a tiny sliver of night sky. After that, I worked quickly, punching the tiles upwards to dislodge them and send them hurtling down to smash on the ground below.

But now the hole in the roof was acting like a chimney, drawing the smoke up around my head, so I was working blind, hardly able to breathe, my eyes and nose streaming. At last, by feeling round with my hands, I calculated the space must be big enough to allow me to squeeze through. Using strength I've never had before or since, I took hold of the joists and hauled myself up through the narrow gap in the roof, then perched for a moment on the rim of the hole. There was smoke everywhere, and through the smoke I could see the brushwood burning, a funeral pyre blazing all round the chrysalis and sending out little snakes of bright flame to kindle the shrubs and grasses all around. A few minutes more and this whole hillside would be a sea of fire.

Jenny.

I slithered down the bumpy roof and dropped to the ground. I put my hands out to break my fall and my right hand smacked against a blazing patch of straw. The sleeve of my jacket was smouldering.

Barely pausing to beat at the flames, I sped round to the front of the building and shifted the heavy wooden bolt. The moment I pulled open the door a wall of smoke billowed up against my face, forcing me back. I took a deep breath, raised my forearm to protect my streaming eyes, and plunged in, almost tripping over Jenny's body in my haste. I caught hold of anything I could find, and dragged her out by one elbow and the waist of her jeans.

'Jenny,' I gasped, hauling her over the smouldering brush. 'It's going to be all right. Wake up. I'm going for help.'

There was no response. I stumbled with her as far as the relative safety of the rough track where there was nothing for the fire to catch, and all the time I was telling her to breathe, breathe normally, it was going to be all right, but she made no sound. Carrying her was too slow: I had to get help for her quickly, so I left her on a patch of stony ground.

I set off at a run towards the Villa Omega. Behind me, I heard the flames roaring through the chrysalis, its wooden door, the simple mattress and the wooden furniture all tinder-dry and burning fiercely. If we hadn't escaped . . . Don't even think about that. Run.

I was at the Villa Omega and beating on the door and windows as I went round the side. 'Fire! Wake up! Jenny needs help!'

A window opened as I got round to the front and Serafa put her head out. 'What is it? What's going on?'

'Tim has taken Davy. It's Palu, she's been helping him.' Behind Serafa, Katie let out a cry of despair. 'She locked us in the Omega chrysalis and then Tim came back and set fire to it. Jenny's on the path but she's unconscious. I'm going for her inhaler.'

Those last words were shouted over my shoulder as I sped away down the path, taking the short cut through the gardens and the Temple to the three villas of the Hesperides.

I raced up the steps into Jenny's villa and switched on the lights, shouting at everyone to wake up. Five sleepers grumbled and pulled the blankets over their heads. 'Where does Jenny keep her inhaler?' I yelled, crossing the room to the single unoccupied bed. 'She's passed out. The hillside's on fire.'

Suddenly everyone was wide awake. Elaine's round face peered up at me in bewilderment as they all scrambled out of bed and crowded round me, demanding to know what had happened.

'No time. Got to find her inhaler.'

'Here it is,' said a woman called Sue, who slept in the bed next to Jenny's. She was pulling on a pair of cotton trousers. 'Where is she? I'll come with you. I know some nursing.'

'I left her near the Omega chrysalis, but they should have got her down to the Villa by now.' I leaned forward to ease the searing pain in my chest, but when I put my hands on my knees it felt as though my palms had caught fire.

'What have you done to your hand?' Sue exclaimed. 'Look, stay here. You need help. I'll see to Jenny, but if it's a bad attack she'll need oxygen. Elaine can come with me. You follow.'

'But—'

'You'll only hold us up,' said Sue briskly. 'Come on, Elaine. Run.'

Following them to the door of the villa I could see a red glow spreading across the sky behind the curves of the hillside. Then I looked the other way, towards the Pillars of Hercules, where there were no lights at all. The gates must be closed. It was just possible Tim had left already, but it seemed more likely that carrying the child would have slowed him up. I remembered that when Palu had led Davy away to have his 'hot drink', she'd said she'd put Intara in charge of reception for the night – for extra security, she'd said. That must have been when she phoned Tim to warn him: I remembered that the first time I tried phoning him he'd been engaged. So Intara must be part of her mother's scheme to help Tim. Would they have been so eager to help him if they'd known his plans had included arson and murder?

Sue and Elaine had vanished. The others were milling around on the terrace, looking towards the soft glow on the horizon, waiting to be told what to do next.

I said, 'Wake everyone. They've got to get that fire under control.'

One girl asked, 'Are you going to help Jenny?'

I looked towards the fire. There wasn't anything more I could do for Jenny; Elaine and Sue must be halfway there by now. But if Tim hadn't left the grounds yet, there was still a slim chance of stopping him.

A cold fury was burning inside me. The bastard had nearly killed me. There was no knowing if Jenny was going to recover. Maybe it was already too late for her. And as for Davy, that lifeless shape wrapped in the white sheet . . . like a shroud. A shivery sweat covered my body.

I said, 'there's a psycho out there. It's Davy's father and he's trying to steal his child. He's got to be stopped.'

They looked at me as if I was mad, and I must have been a wild sight, with my face smoke-blackened and my hands burned.

'Warn everyone,' I said sharply. 'He started that fire to kill me and Jenny.'

There was no time to answer their clamour of questions. My right hand felt as if it was still burning and there was an agonising pain in my side, but as soon as I began running towards the main building the pain vanished. Behind me, I could hear bells ringing the alarm. There were lights going on in all the residential blocks as the Heirs of Akasha swarmed over the property like a nest of disturbed ants to fight the spreading fire.

Ahead of me, all was darkness.

As I rounded the corner I saw a single light shining in the main building and Tim's car parked near to mine. I slowed to a walk, so as not to make any noise, and crept closer to the car. Davy was lying on the back seat, still wrapped in a pale blanket. His eyes were closed and he appeared to be sleeping. Dear God, let him be sleeping . . . I felt in my pocket: I still had my car keys. If I could just transfer him to my own car, I could drive him back to the safety of the Villa Omega. Where was Tim?

Treading as lightly as I could, I moved across the gravel towards the open door. From inside came the sound of low voices. I tried not to make any noise but each time I gasped for air, my breath was harsh as a scream.

I crept closer, hunkering down in the shadows beside the open door.

Palu, her voice low and angry, said, 'Where've you been? You were supposed to follow me.'

Tim sounded pleased with himself. 'I had to go back to the chrysalis,' he said. 'I wanted to finish the job.'

'Have you got the boy?'

'Of course. He's in my car. Open the gates so we can get going.'

'Wait,' said Palu, her voice anxious. 'What about me? Carol must know I've been helping you.'

'That's your problem. Davy and I are leaving.'

'Wait, you can't just walk away like that. It's your fault she knows about me. If you'd waited until I told you it was safe to come in, she'd never have known a thing.'

'Never mind. Carol's not part of the picture any more.'

'Why not?'

Tim chuckled. 'Look.'

I flattened into the shadows as they crossed the room to look out through the open door. There was a faint glow of firelight beyond the lattice of trees.

'My God,' breathed Palu. 'What have you done?'

'Me? Nothing, that fire's a tragic accident.' He sounded so pleased with himself I knew he must be smiling and I wanted to smash the smug grin off his face. He said, 'No one will ever guess it was started deliberately. The chrysalis went up like a torch.'

'But what about Carol? And Jenny?' Palu's voice rose in panic. 'They'll be killed.'

'I know. Clever, isn't it? I said there was no need to worry about them.'

'But this is crazy! We have to get them out of there.'

'Sorry, but you're too late. About fifteen minutes too late is my guess. Don't look so worried, Palu. You and Intara will benefit from their death even more than I will.'

Palu said, 'Forget it, Tim, this was never part of the plan.' Her voice grew fainter, as if she was backing away from him. 'I only helped you because you said you wanted to get Davy away from here, but I'm not helping you any more. Not murder. I'm sounding the alarm.'

'No!' There was a loud grunt, the impact of two bodies colliding in rage. I drew away from the wall, stood up in the shadows beyond the pool of light and looked through the window. Tim had seized Palu by the arms and flung her down into a chair. She tried to rise but he punched her in the chest and she collapsed. She was white with shock.

'No!' Tim was standing over her. 'You stay right there. Listen, you dumb bitch, you can't betray me now. You're as deep in as I am. Just think about it for a minute: you're the one who shut them in the chrysalis. Who's going to believe you didn't start the fire too?'

'I never wanted anyone to get hurt.'

'It's too late for second thoughts. Just tell me which button to push,' demanded Tim. He had crossed to stand in front of the control panel, every now and then glancing up at the CCTV screen on the wall behind the desk. There was no picture, because the gates were in darkness.

And then, in the far corner of the room, I saw Intara. Her feet and hands were tightly bound and there was a scarf round her throat as if a gag had just been removed. What was going on? Was this all part of a plan to make it look as if she was Tim's victim, not his accomplice? Or had Palu been prepared to sacrifice her own daughter? Intara's heavy features were shiny with horror and disbelief and she kept looking back and forth from Tim to her mother, as though she was trying to work out what was going on.

'Mum?' she said. 'Mum, I'm frightened.'

Suddenly Palu seemed to reach a decision. She struggled to her feet and said, 'Okay, Tim, I'll let you out, but you'll have to take us with you.'

'Over my dead body,' said Tim.

'There's no choice. We can't stay here, not now.'

'That's your problem. Is it this switch?'

'No, don't touch it, that's the power switch. Listen, we'll only be with you for a little while. Just until we're clear of here. The button you want is on the left.'

I saw his hand move and he grinned. Then he glanced across at Palu, who had knelt down to untie the ropes round her daughter's ankles. 'What are you doing?' he demanded.

He watched in triumph as the screen showed the entry illuminated by the security light. Over by the Pillars of Hercules the gates were opening. His way out was clear.

Intara twisted round so Palu could untie her hands. 'We're coming with you,' said Palu.

'Not a chance,' he said coldly. 'You've done your bit. Now you can both rot in hell for all I care.'

He was striding towards the door. Palu moved fast. She'd been kneeling and there was no time for her to stand, but with a roar of rage she flung herself across the room and caught him round the knees, sending him crashing headlong on to the floor. He yelled, spun round and hit back savagely.

I didn't wait to see any more. They were making so much noise that this was the best chance I was going to get. I ran to the car and opened the back door. Davy did not stir, and dread made me hesitate. I leaned forward and touched his cheek with my finger tips. It was cool . . . but then he sighed and his soft lips rounded into a pout.

It was enough. 'Come along, Davy,' I said gently. 'Let's get you back home.'

I pulled him gently towards me. He mumbled in his drugged sleep. I put my arms round him to lift him clear. All I could think of was getting him into my car, then back to his grandmother and safety. From the Villa Omega and the Hesperides came the noise of alarm bells ringing, tractor engines firing up.

'Let's go.'

The next moment I was sprawled on the ground beside the car and my head felt as if it had split in two. I opened my eyes and saw Tim bundling the boy back into the car. 'Stop it!' I yelled. 'You can't take him!'

'Damn you!' Tim snarled. He kicked out, but I rolled away so the tip of his shoe only grazed my hip. I struggled to my feet and hurled myself at him, lashing out with my fists. He slammed the back door shut and spun round to fight me off, but before he had a chance I brought my knee up between his legs with all the strength I had left. He let out a howl of pain and doubled up, then hit me on the side of my head. For a crucial moment I lost consciousness. Then I was lying on the ground and his white car was driving away. Towards the open gates.

All I could think was that he mustn't escape. Hardly able to stand, and half blinded by the pain in my neck and shoulders, I staggered into the main hall. Palu was slumped on the floor in front of the desk and Intara, her wrists still tied, was crouched over her, saying over and over again, 'Mum, wake up. It's okay now. He's gone.'

' 'S'all right.' Palu's voice was slurred. 'Help me up.'

I was behind the desk. I'd watched from outside and had a good idea where the control was that operated the gates.

'What are you doing?' Intara was holding her mother, rocking her backwards and forwards, and made no move to intervene.

'He's not getting away,' I said, and pressed the button firmly. The picture on the screen was fuzzy, but as I watched it the gates swung closed.

'Yes!' I watched in triumph as two bright lights, the headlights of Tim's car, came to a halt in front of the gates. A figure jumped out and ran up to them.

314 • JOANNA HINES

'Why did you do that?' Intara asked stupidly. 'He's taking Davy. We don't want Davy here any more, do we, Mother? Mother, say something.'

Palu heaved herself to her feet. One side of her face was bruised and swollen and her words were mumbled. 'All right, Baby,' she said to Intara. ' 'S'going to be all right.' She struggled with the knots which tied Intara's wrists, then cursed quietly when her hands wouldn't do what she wanted.

As soon as Intara was free, Palu slumped back against the wall and slid down into a crouch. Her eyes were unfocused.

Intara lumbered over to where I was standing by the reception desk. 'Get away from those controls,' she ordered. 'We don't want them here any more. We have to get rid of them.'

Tim's voice came over the intercom. 'What the hell's going on?' he raged. 'Who shut the gates?'

'I did!' I yelled in triumph. 'You'll never get away from here. You're fucked, Tim!'

He let out a howl of rage.

Intara had the strength of an ox. I was looking at the screen, relishing the furious shouts of the snowy figure trapped behind the gates, so I never saw her pick up the fax machine and bring it crashing down against the back of my head. All I saw was the cool terracotta tiles as they whizzed towards me and Intara's feet in their heavy sandals. And, behind her head, the strange scribbled activity of the man on the screen.

'Mum,' Intara wailed, 'it won't open. I keep pressing the button and nothing happens. The gate's broken. What shall I do?'

'They must have overridden it at the Villa,' said Palu, her speech still blurred. 'The alarm's gone off, Total Red. That means everything shuts down. No one can get in or out.'

'So what can we do?' Intara was frantic.

'Get me out of here!' roared Tim.

'All right, don't panic,' said Palu. She tried to get up but her legs wouldn't hold her. 'He'll have to do it manually,' she said with a groan. 'Intara, tell him he'll have to do it manually.'

Intara repeated her mother's message. The CCTV showed a chalk man banging his fists on the gates. 'How?' he yelled. 'Tell me how!'

'There's a control box on the side,' said Palu. 'Ask him if he can see it. It's about five foot off the ground.' Intara did as she was told, and Tim shouted, 'Got it!'

'Good,' said Palu. 'There's a switch on the left. That controls the power. You have to disconnect that first. Move it to the up position.'

Intara started to repeat all this but Tim shouted, 'Okay, okay, I heard. The switch is already up.'

'Is it? That's odd. Okay, then.' Palu was frowning, as though it was a struggle to make her brain work properly. 'Ask him if he can see the knob next to it. Good. Now tell him to move that clockwise to three o'clock. Now he can open the gates manually.'

From where I'd fallen I could see the screen quite clearly. I watched as Tim went to the control box and opened it, then reached inside and moved his hand, then strode purposefully to the gate.

I tried to shout out, to get someone to go after him, to stop them, but my voice was only a whisper.

I was still watching as he raised his arm. Then there was a weird noise; it might have been a cry. He seemed to jump, but no, it was more than that. It was as though a great gust of wind had swept him off his feet and thrown him backwards out of sight. His body curved through the air in those last seconds in a manner that was almost balletic.

The screen showed no movement. And on the intercom there was only the hiss of static.

Chapter 22

Morning sunlight filtered in through the shuttered window. I lay in a narrow bed in a strange room and moved as little as possible. I'd lost track of all my different aches and pains, but I did know moving was agony. If I lay still, only the burns on my right hand were really painful, that and the raw feeling in my chest each time I drew breath.

It was quite a tally: minor burns, the effects of smoke inhalation, a couple of cracked ribs, a sprained ankle and some colourful bruising – not bad going for a single night's activity, though I'd been lucky to get off so lightly. Jenny had nearly died. If Sue hadn't had some medical experience and known exactly what to do, the consequences could have been fatal. As it was, the medics reckoned she'd be up and about in a couple of days.

Not so, Tim. His injuries were too serious to be treated at El Cortijo Tartessus and he'd been taken by ambulance to the hospital at Cádiz. At first he was not expected to survive, but now, on the morning after his near-fatal electrocution, they said his chances were fifty–fifty.

All this I learned from the healers who were looking after me. They told me Davy had only a rotten headache to show for the powerful sedative Palu had given him. They told me also that the fire had been extinguished just before dawn, though shifts of group members were still stationed all round the property in case it blazed up again. They told me not to worry about any of it.

I'd been taken to the Annex of Renewal, which apparently was the Akashic name for a medical centre. Quite sensibly, for a group who intended to survive the destruction of civilisation, they had more than their share of doctors and nurses, though of course they weren't called that. Nor did they employ any medical practice that I recognised, but their methods seemed effective and were definitely enjoyable. About mid-morning I was helped down the tiled corridor to a small, round pool, similar to the one in Cornwall but only a fraction of the size. The water was warm and buoyant and deliciously soothing. When the time came to get out I was wrapped in soft towels by two of the healers, Sue and an older woman called Imogen, and gently rubbed with herbal oils until my skin glowed. They put cream on my burned hand and mixed a pungent tonic for me to drink. A week ago I would probably have suspected them of poisoning me, but now I enjoyed their attention.

Back in my room again, I fell into a state halfway between drowsing and wakefulness, a twilight filled with fires and imaginary figures, so that when a woman with grey hair and lots of heavy silver jewellery pulled up a chair and sat down beside the bed it was some moments before I realised it really was Karnak, and not an image conjured out of nightmare.

'Carol?' she said. 'Can you talk?'

Yes, I could, but I'd rather not. I nodded.

'I need you to tell me exactly what happened, so I can make a full report.'

I laid my head back in the pillows and closed my eyes. Feverishly, I began to work out how much Karnak knew already, how much she would have guessed and what scope there was for lies. But then my woozy brain seized up with the complication of it all. In two days my stay at El Cortijo Tartessus would be up: what could they do to me in such a short time? Brainwashing? I almost laughed aloud. I didn't feel as if I had much of a brain left, washed or dirty.

When I had told Karnak, slowly and painfully, all the relevant events of the last few days – omitting the session with Tim in his hotel room, which I had no desire ever to be reminded of – she was silent for a few moments. At last she set down the notebook in which she had been writing rapidly, looked up at me and smiled. It was the first time I'd seen her smile and she suddenly looked much less predatory. She said, 'You acted bravely. Everyone was so busy with the fire that Tim would certainly have succeeded if you hadn't closed the gates. God knows what would have happened to the boy then.'

I said wearily, 'when I came here I wanted to help everyone. God, what a mess.'

'Don't worry. Jenny's going to be fine.'

'And Tim? He nearly died.'

She shrugged. 'A lot of people think it would have been better if he had. Still, Palu did the best she could.'

'But that was an accident,' I protested. Karnak raised a sceptical eyebrow. I insisted, 'I know it was. I was there and I saw what happened. She wasn't thinking straight and she got into a muddle over the switches.'

'If that's what you want to believe, don't let me stop you. But I've known Palu a long time and she doesn't make mistakes like that. Though maybe she's losing her judgement. She should never have helped Fairchild in the first place.'

'She was his fifth column, wasn't she?'

'You knew about that?'

'He told me someone had been helping from the inside, but he said they'd been transferred back to Cornwall before I got here. Why was she helping him?'

'To get rid of Katie.'

'Why? Was she jealous?'

'Of Davy, yes. She and Ra had originally planned their own child would take over when the time came.'

'Intara?'

'That's right, but it's been obvious for years she isn't up to it – obvious to everyone except Palu. Intara's only interested in her researches into the *Book of Thoth*, and her leadership qualities are zero. Davy is due to be given his Akashic name at the full moon, and Palu was afraid Ra would name him formally as his successor at the same time. For different reasons, she and Tim wanted the same thing. But she read him all wrong. You've every reason to be furious with her, but she was distraught when she realised Tim had tried to kill you and Jenny. The fact that she tried to remedy her mistake at the end will count in her favour.'

'What's going to happen to her and Intara now?'

'They are being taken care of,' said Karnak briskly.

That phrase again. When was the last time I'd heard it?

'What does being taken care of mean, exactly?'

'What it says. Palu has undergone a major trauma. She's done more than any single person to set this organisation on its feet, even more than Ra. For the first ten years she was the one who got it all going, raised money, checked out recruits, took care of all the details. Ra dreamed the dreams, but it was Palu who made them happen. Last night she was on the brink of abandoning everything she'd spent her whole life working for. Where did she think she could go? And as for Intara, she's never known any world but the Heirs. They didn't stand a chance. I expect Palu will be sent to one of our frontier settlements in Mexico. She's forfeited her place in the Inner Circle, maybe for ever. She and Intara must both begin again as First-level Pilgrims and work their way up like anyone else. It will be hard work, but we believe physical labour is the best way to work off spiritual toxins. They have a difficult road ahead of them, but we will help all we can. Does that satisfy you?'

Taken care of . . . I was being taken care of by the healers with their water therapy and their strange ointments. It felt fine, not sinister at all. Maybe it would be that way for Palu and Intara, too.

But still. 'They wanted to leave,' I said.

'That choice is always open to them, but I'll be surprised if they do. We're family, no matter what they've done, and we stick together through everything.'

When she had gone the healers brought me a light lunch of fruit and cheese and a glass of fresh grapejuice. After I'd picked at the food, I drifted once more into a troubled half sleep. The next time I saw a figure standing in the doorway, it was so incongruous I was sure it must be a dream: that frizz of ginger hair and that square, no-nonsense face belonged in the builders' yard at Sturford, not here.

'Brian?'

The dream figure moved across the room and sat down on the bed beside me. He took my left hand – the right was red and raw under its coating of cream – and held it firmly. Not a figment of my imagination after all.

'Brian, what on earth are you doing here? Who told you?'

In the whole of my life I'd never been more glad to see another human being. His hazel eyes warmed into a smile and he said, 'Let you out of my sight for a week and look what you get up to. Anyone would think you'd gone ten rounds with Mike Tyson.'

'It's not that bad. Maybe just one or two rounds.'

He was regarding me with a new kind of loving admiration. If I hadn't known the result would be agony, I'd have thrown myself into his arms. As it was, I leaned forward and brushed my cheek against his, realising as I did so that what I really wanted to do was kiss him.

Brian did not respond, only kept hold of my hand and said, 'They tell me you saved Jenny's life.'

'Really? Did they also mention that I was the one who got her into danger in the first place?'

He nodded. 'You stopped that maniac taking his son. That makes you number-one hero, as far as this bunch are concerned. They'll probably vote you chief witch at the next full moon.'

How I'd missed his earthy scepticism! I said, 'They don't have witches here, and anyway, I'm leaving in a couple of days. Just as soon as I'm fit to travel.'

Still, it was good to know my status was high among the Heirs. It's always nice to be appreciated, even if you know you've been acting like an idiot. Jenny's accusations still stung.

Sinking back into the pillows, my hand still in Brian's, I felt all the tension and stress of the previous weeks ebb away. I hadn't realised how anxious I'd been for – how long? The last two weeks? No, longer than that. All summer, ever since Jenny had burst into my life and my marriage had collapsed under the strain. A sense of well-being spread through me, in spite of my injuries, a contentment that had everything to do with the strong, familiar, well-loved face of the man sitting on the edge of my bed. In my enfeebled state I saw no reason why we need ever be apart again. The insight came with the force of a revelation.

I said, 'I still don't understand how come you're here.
Did they phone and tell you?' But even as I asked I knew
that was impossible. Brian must have caught the early-
morning flight and driven straight from Málaga, and to do
that he would have had to leave Sturford in the middle of
the night. 'Were you coming out anyway?'

'No, I was perfectly resigned to waiting the three days
until you came back.'

'Then I don't understand.'

'That makes two of us. I'm as surprised as you are.'

'Brian, just when did you start talking in riddles?'

'Probably when I discovered I was living in one.' He
shifted in his seat and grinned in a baffled sort of way.
'Okay, I'll try to explain, though I haven't got the first idea
myself. Last night everything was perfectly normal: I
watched the news, tidied the kitchen and went to bed. All
just as it should have been. Then I started going to sleep.
No worries, or at least no more than usual. I think I was
trying to work out the best time to put the third house on
the market. Then suddenly – wham! I was sitting bolt
upright in bed and I knew, as surely as I knew my own
name, that the woman I loved was in danger and I had to
come out here at once. So I dug out my passport and drove
to Gatwick.'

'Brian, that's incredible.'

'Tell me about it. When I got to Gatwick I decided to
phone here and find out what was going on. I expected to
get an earful for waking everyone up, instead of which
some stranger started babbling about fights and a fire and
ambulances and people nearly dying. Your name was
mentioned, and Jenny's. So I got on the first flight, and here
I am.'

The woman he loved . . . Happiness was a wash of warm
light all around me. 'Are you turning psychic on me? Since
when did you start having premonitions?'

He frowned. 'God only knows what you'd call it, but I've checked with the people here and the moment I knew I had to come was the exact moment you and Jenny were locked in that hut.'

'But that's amazing.'

'Yes,' he said simply. 'It is. Don't ask me to explain it. All I know is that it happened.' He frowned. 'It's probably something to do with electrical energy, or maybe it was just a one in a million coincidence or . . .'

'It doesn't matter why,' I said. 'I'm just glad you're here.'

Because the woman he loved was in danger . . . I guess sometimes it takes an almighty shock to make you recognise the truth that's been staring you in the face for years. Well, I'd wasted enough time already and I didn't intend wasting any more. 'Brian . . .'

He set my hand down on my lap and shifted away from me, then said quietly, 'I'm going to see her now.'

'Who?'

'Jenny.' There was a brief pause before he added, 'The woman who was in danger.'

It took me a little while to work out what he was saying and Brian was far too generous to spell it out, but all the same the truth was there, a warning in his eyes. I drew back. How quickly the balance of power can shift. Ever since I'd known Brian it had been the unwritten rule between us that he adored me, while I regarded him as no more than my trusted friend. And now suddenly I was the one on the outside.

I smiled. In that instant, all the might-have-beens of my life rushed past me and vanished into nothing. It was better that way. What had seemed like a moment of truth was probably just a by-product of shock.

I asked, 'How long have you known? About Jenny, I mean?'

He looked relieved. 'We've kept in touch all summer.

We hit it off straight away that weekend she came to Sturford, but we both assumed it would end there. She knew I was holding a torch for you and she was determined to come and join this bunch here. But then, when she started to get fed up with this place, she got into the habit of ringing me up whenever she got the chance. We just talked – about everything under the sun. She couldn't decide what to do when she left here so I tried to help her sort it out. The last time she phoned was from Tarifa a couple of days ago.'

'I drove her there.'

'I know. I'd told her to let me know if you were running too many risks. It was you I was concerned about, not her. Until last night, that is, when I woke up and knew I had to help her.'

'Does she know how you feel?'

'I haven't seen her yet. She's got a visitor right now so I'll have to wait my turn. She'll probably think I've gone raving mad – and maybe I have.'

He was joking, but his eyes were deadly serious. The events of the previous night must have rocked his world to its foundations. Brian, who believed in nothing unless he could touch it or build it or read the scientific evidence, had just travelled halfway across Europe on the strength of . . . what? A bad dream? A hallucination? Telepathy? It would have been extraordinary enough from anyone else, but coming from Brian, it was breathtaking.

I said, 'Why didn't you tell me you were in touch with Jenny?'

'I wanted to. It felt all wrong not telling you, but she made me promise. She didn't want Gus or her mother to know.'

I tried to imagine Brian and Jenny together. It was easier than I'd expected, and more painful, too. I said, 'You'd better go and see her now. End the suspense.'

'And you need some rest.' He hesitated, then said, 'Gus will be here this evening.'

'Gus?' I sat up very straight, ignoring my sore ribs and aching muscles. 'You've spoken to Gus?'

'I thought I ought to phone him from Gatwick once I'd found out what was going on. He said he was coming straight out.'

I was amazed at the speed of events. So now Gus was on his way, too. I remembered Jenny saying Ra wanted to get all the Grays Orchard group together again. Katie and Palu were here already. Gus was due to arrive at any time. That left only Harriet.

Brian stood up. 'I'll come and see you again later. Or tomorrow.'

'How long are you staying?'

'That depends. They've put me in some kind of barracks. Would you believe I'm sharing with sixteen others?'

'You must be in one of the men's long houses.'

'Next time I come to Spain I plan to have my own room with en suite bath,' he said ruefully, and I thought, yes, and Jenny there to share it with you. 'Still,' he went on, 'I'm glad they're looking after you properly.'

'Oh, I shall be fine.'

'I know you will, Carol.'

He grinned, then turned and went out. I knew that a whole stage of my life, the years of being secure in Brian's love but always belittling what he offered, was finished.

I didn't have any regrets, not really, but all the same, I was glad to be alone for a while.

But this was to be a day of visitors. By late afternoon I had dressed and tidied myself and was sitting on the verandah outside my room. I was reclining in a large wicker chair, watching the sun sink low over the curve of hills that framed the sea. There was an acrid smell in the air, the aftermath of fire. I was trying to make sense of everything that had happened and wondering what I was going to say to Gus, when there was a light tap on the glass behind me and Katie appeared through the french windows. I turned to welcome her, but shock silenced me. Her face was haggard; overnight she seemed to have turned into an old woman. She sank down on the chair beside mine and searched my face eagerly.

'Carol,' she breathed, 'thank God you're safe. They told me you'd been hurt, that you nearly died, but—' She caught sight of my hand, red and shiny with burns, and her face crumpled. 'It's true, then. Your poor hand. I can't believe it.'

'I'm all right now,' I said, trying to calm her. 'This will heal.'

'And was it . . .?' She stared at me, the question almost literally choking her. 'Did my son really . . .?' It was no good. She couldn't bring herself to ask.

And then, suddenly I understood. It wasn't just horror at Tim's injuries that was breaking her heart, it was the knowledge of what he had tried to do. I remembered how Katie had lied to keep me out of trouble just twenty-four hours before, and for a moment I was tempted to return the favour. But this was too important and, besides, I could tell from her eyes that she knew the truth already.

I said quietly, 'Palu shut me and Jenny in the chrysalis so we'd be out of the way, but yes, Tim knew we were there when he started the fire. He knew he was putting us at risk.'

'Oh, dear.' She crumpled, and for a few moments, it was all she could say. 'Oh dear, you see, I thought perhaps it was an accident. That he started the fire as a diversion and didn't know what Palu had done. I thought perhaps Serafa had exaggerated because . . . because she never liked him. But he did know you were there and you might have been . . .' She still couldn't say the word.

'How is he?' I asked.

'All they'll say is that he's out of danger, but they don't know more than that yet. I've been at the hospital all night. Serafa made me come back because Davy was getting anxious. I'm on my way back to the hospital now, but I had to see you first. If it wasn't for what you did, I'd have lost my Davy.'

'How much does he know?'

'It's hard to tell, because he's still confused from the sleeping pills Palu gave him. I want to thank you, Carol, because it feels as if you saved my life. If Tim had escaped with Davy, I don't know what I'd have done.'

'You're both safe now.'

'Yes.' But she was still shaking. 'You see, they told me that even if he survives he'll never really be himself again – and he looked so beautiful lying there, like he was when he was a child, like the man he might have been if he hadn't . . . and I was so sad, so terribly sad . . . I'm sorry. It's wrong to burden you. I'll leave you in peace. Oh!'

She had started moving towards the glass door, which led back into the bedroom, but blinded by tears she didn't see the figure standing in the doorway until she almost ran into him.

Apologising, Gus took a step backwards. He looked like a man who'd been woken in the middle of the night by a crazy phone call and who'd just travelled halfway across Europe without time even to pack a toothbrush. He looked like a man who'd suffered a series of shocks and thought there might be more in store. Katie pulled a handkerchief from her pocket and dabbed her eyes.

Gus frowned. 'Am I interrupting?' he asked, glancing briefly at Katie but addressing the question to me.

'No, no, I'm just leaving.' I was amazed by the speed of Katie's recovery. It must have taken years of practice. Her voice, which only moments before had sounded brokenhearted, was brightly social. I was even more astonished by the fact that she and Gus didn't seem to recognise each other.

Gus stood aside to let her pass. Katie smiled up at him and then turned and said, 'Bye for now, Carol. I hope you're feeling better soon. I'll try and stop by again tomorrow.'

It was only then, as she was leaving, that Gus frowned and said, 'Katie?'

'Yes?' She looked up at him. Then, 'Gus? What on earth are you doing here?'

'Visiting my wife.'

'Your . . .? Oh, of course. That's right. Carol did tell me and I'm such a bird-brain I went and forgot. Will you be here for long? Maybe we'll have a chance to see each other again and catch up. Talk about old times.'

Gus smiled. 'I hope so, Katie. It's been quite a while.'

'Hasn't it, though? Oh well, I'd better go. Bye, Carol.'

And that was it.

Somehow, I'd expected more. After all, during the Grays Orchard years Katie had been his muse, his great love, and now tragedy had brought them together again after all these years . . . and they had greeted each other with bland politeness. It was all wrong and I felt cheated.

Gus loomed over my chair. 'Are you all right, Carol? God, what a stupid question! Look at your hand. And they said the smoke . . . Christ, I'd like to get hold of the bastard who did this!'

'I'm going to be okay, Gus. I'm a bit sore but there's no permanent damage.' The sight of him, his concern and anger, made me feel inexplicably close to tears. I forced myself to remain calm, even to smile. If Katie could manage it, sure as hell I could, too. Suddenly there seemed to be too much of him: he filled the verandah as no one else had. I said, 'Gus, sit down, please. Have Katie's chair.'

He spun the chair round and sat down. He hadn't kissed me or touched me, and I was glad of that. He said, 'Christ, I've been so worried about you. When Brian phoned this morning, I came straight out. What's been going on?'

'It's hard to know where to start. I wanted to help Tim.'

'But why did you lie to me? Why did you come out here? You don't believe all their end-of-the-world Atlantis bullshit do you?'

'Of course not. I haven't gone soft in the head just yet. I thought I could help Tim. And there was Jenny as well.'

'Are you saying you lied to me and came out here and put yourself in danger, all because you wanted to help a couple of people you hardly know?'

'No.' I met his gaze levelly. 'No, that was part of it, but it wasn't everything. The main reason was that I wanted to meet the others.'

'What others?'

'Raymond and Pauline and Katie. Look, Gus, things started to go wrong between us when Jenny arrived on the scene. I knew there was something you weren't telling me, and I knew it was to do with the Grays Orchard group. Everything pointed to Andrew Forester's murder and those old rumours of a cover-up.' I paused, but he didn't offer any comment, so I carried on. 'I thought I could kill two birds with one stone: help Tim and Jenny, and maybe find a way to save my marriage at the same time.'

Gus hesitated. Then, 'And did you?' he asked.

'I don't know. I'm still waiting.'

He let out a long sigh and leaned back in his chair, gazing up towards the ceiling. Then he straightened up again, laid his hands on his knees and looked at me very directly. I sat very still. Slippery as an eel, always evasive, always the one pursued, but now, for the first time, Gus was facing me head on.

He said quietly, 'I've had lots of time to think since you left. I know I've been impossible, but it's different now. Jenny turning up out of the blue like that, I admit it gave me a shock, but that's over. When you come home, we'll be just like we always were, I promise.'

He smiled. He leaned towards me. So that was it. He thought all he had to do was turn the clock back and nothing would have changed. I said, 'No, Gus. You've lied to me too often.'

'Lied?'

'Yes, you let me think it was Jenny who destroyed the paintings when all the time it was you. You had no right to let her take the blame!'

'You think I don't know that? It nearly drove me out of my mind, having you feel sorry for me when all that time, if you'd known the truth, you'd have despised me, maybe even thought I was insane.'

'So? You should have risked it anyway. Damn it, I loved you, Gus!' Past tense. Loved, not love. Was that how it was now?

'I know, I know. God, you don't have to rub it in. I should have come out with the truth straight away, but you never even asked me. Right from the start you were so certain it was her. I was in shock and then it all carried on, like a dream, and I was watching it and couldn't intervene.'

'But it wasn't like that. You refused to talk to me about anything.'

'If you're saying I'm a coward, you're right. I always have been, only you never saw it before. You thought I was some kind of wounded hero and I'm not. I'm just an ordinary man who's fucked up badly with the one thing he really cares about. I knew you hadn't gone to France, but thought you'd found a lover. To my surprise I discovered that idea didn't appeal to me at all. I've missed you, Carol. The simple truth is, I need you. I know it's not fashionable to need people these days, but tough. I don't want to live the rest of my life knowing I threw away the most precious second chance a man was ever offered. I'm prepared to do whatever it takes.'

'You mean no more secrets? No more lies?'

He shifted uncomfortably in his chair, but met my gaze and said, 'Yes.'

'You'll tell me about the paintings?'

'Yes.'

'And about Andrew's death?'

He closed his eyes and his hands balled into fists in his lap, but at length he said in a low voice, 'Okay, then. Yes, that too.'

It made me feel like a skilled torturer. He was prepared to be honest, so I had to do the same. I said, 'You'll tell me even though it may be too late to save things between us?'

Pain shadowed his eyes. 'I hope to God it isn't. But yes, whatever happens now, I owe you the truth.'

Suddenly my eyes were brimming with tears. 'Oh Gus, why the hell did you have to leave it so long?'

'It was a promise I made. And silence becomes a habit it's hard to break.'

There was a rustle of noise behind us. Gus and I had been so locked in our dialogue that neither of us had heard the uneven tap-tap of her approach. We turned at the same moment, then I glanced quickly at Gus. His face was ashen with shock.

I felt as though I was floating into unreality, as though our conversation had conjured her out of the ether. She had changed a lot since the days when Gus used to paint her hoeing lettuces or carrying a long-necked white goose or with her arms heaped with flowers. Her brown hair was streaked with grey, there were bitter lines round her mouth and she leaned heavily on a metal stick, one of those with a support for the forearm and elbow. But she was handsome still, with a strong, vibrant face, and in spite of her stoop she held her head proudly.

It was the last remaining member of the Grays Orchard group: Harriet.

Chapter 23

'What the hell are you doing here?' demanded Gus.

'Same as you, I expect,' said Harriet with an enigmatic smile. 'As you know, I've been in England for a month. I decided it was time to track Jenny down. I've been talking to that neighbour of yours, Brian Dray; he's the only person Jenny's been in touch with all summer. He phoned from Gatwick last night, told me there'd been an accident. Luckily I was able to come out with him on the first flight.' She turned to me, her eyes guarded. 'You must be Carol. They tell me you saved Jenny's life, and for that I thank you from the bottom of my heart.'

'How is she?'

'Shaken. But she'll be herself again in a couple of days.'

It was Harriet's voice that was her real, enduring beauty. It was a rich contralto, the kind of voice you want to listen to for ever. For the first time I realised that portraits, being silent, inevitably miss the essentials. I thought of all the hours I'd spent poring over the copies of the Grays Orchard portraits, trying to decipher what they had to tell me, when a few spoken phrases would have said it all.

Harriet was leaning heavily on her stick. Gus still had not moved. I said, 'Gus, Harriet needs a chair.'

He was like a man emerging from a trance, but as he set a wicker chair down next to mine, I saw he was shaking. He resumed his seat but his eyes remained fixed on Harriet.

'Thank you, Gus,' she said. He didn't reply, only stared at her, and she put her hand up as a shield against his searchlight gaze. 'You look as if you've seen a ghost,' she said wryly. 'I may be ill, but I haven't yet been elevated to that state.'

'I'm sorry.' He lowered his eyes. Then he stood up abruptly and went to the window. His gaze kept returning to Harriet. 'It's just . . .'

'What? Have I changed so very much?' Harriet made a valiant attempt to keep the question light, but her pain was obvious.

'No,' said Gus in a low voice, 'no, that's the whole problem. You haven't really changed at all.'

Harriet sighed and was quiet for a few moments, then collected herself. She said, 'I overheard what you and Carol were talking about just now.' She paused. The atmosphere between them was so highly charged the air crackled with electricity. 'You never told her?'

'No.'

'And that's caused problems?'

'Yes.'

'And you were going to tell her now?'

'Yes. Look, Harry, I've got no choice.'

She raised her hand. 'God knows, Gus, I'm not here to stop you. But I am curious. Do you plan to tell her . . . everything?'

Gus still couldn't tear his eyes away from her face. There was no place for me in their dialogue, even though they were talking about me. Every ounce of their energy was concentrated on each other. 'I hadn't thought, but . . .' He glanced at me, then said, 'Yes, Harry. Everything.'

Harriet leaned her head against the back of her chair and closed her eyes. It was as though a shadow was passing from her face. 'Well, thank God for that,' she breathed. She turned to me and smiled. 'You see, Carol, I've been weighed down by it for so long, all I want now is to be free of it. The prospect of dying with only Gus knowing the truth is hideous.' She frowned. 'But we're being selfish. What about you? Are you sure you want to be burdened with our truth?'

Her question didn't make much sense. I'd been waiting so long, I didn't see how the truth could be burdensome. I said, 'Of course I am. Is that why you've been trying to get in touch with Gus?'

'Partly, I guess. But it was mostly because of Jenny. I thought Gus might be able to make her see sense. She doesn't listen to me. We've never had an easy relationship. I thought silence was best, but it creates its own problems.'

'But it's not too late,' I said. 'You can tell her now, same as Gus is going to tell me. You'll never be able to get close to each other until she knows the truth.'

'Oh, Carol, how easy you make it sound.' Harriet's mocking tone made me suddenly aware that I was closer in age to her daughter than to Gus and her. 'It's far too late for Jenny and me. I can't tell her, not ever. The most I can hope for is that she may end up knowing I've loved her the best I could, and that most of the time I tried to put her interests first.'

Harriet was being very pessimistic, I thought. In the way that you do, in order to prepare myself against shock, I was trying to anticipate what their secret could be. It must be to do with Andrew's death, probably that Gus had been responsible. Maybe it had been a quarrel that got out of control or else perhaps a hideous accident. In their panic that hot summer's afternoon, Harriet had agreed to help cover up for her brother and the crime had haunted both of them ever since. That would explain why they had broken all contact; it would explain why Jenny's arrival at Grays had had such a shattering impact on his carefully restructured world. She was the niece who had grown up fatherless because of him. Maybe she even looked like Andrew, which only made it worse.

That was a challenge I could cope with. Gus had told me he was a coward, not the wounded hero I made him out to be, but I wasn't about to give up on him because of a single tragic accident. If he told me the truth, there was no way I'd turn my back on him now.

Harriet regarded Gus thoughtfully. 'Are you going to tell her,' she asked, 'or shall I?'

'I don't know,' said Gus. 'Where do we begin?'

Harriet's brow wrinkled. 'Ah, that's a tough one. I've never known when it started. Was it that first day we went to Grays and that ridiculous little Mr Cheeryble was showing us round and then you shocked him by sliding down the banisters?'

Gus said in a mincing voice, '"Careful there, Mr Ridley. They've not been tested for woodworm." And then we sent him away and went out to the first orchard.'

Harriet's eyes were shining. 'Then you had your mystic vision.'

'Or thought I did. And we decided to stay on at Grays.'

'And invite our friends to join us.'

It looked as though they were about to slide into a glow of reminiscence about the early days of the commune, but I already knew about their first meeting because Gus had described it to me on the way back from Bath, so I interrupted. 'Isn't it more important to tell me about Andrew's death?'

Harriet looked startled, almost as though she had

forgotten I was present. Then she smiled and said, 'Yes, why not? That sounds like a properly Alice-in-Wonderlandish way to begin. One ought always to start at the end.'

'Quite right,' agreed Gus, his face lighting up in a smile. 'And then we can work our way back to the beginning.'

'That's the way, topsy-turvy as always.' Harriet was laughing.

I couldn't believe it. They were carrying on like a couple of children, as if the whole business of Andrew's death had been a joke. Worse still, they were excluding me from their conversation.

I said angrily, 'What's so funny about someone dying?'

The brief spell was broken. Harriet's eyes clouded and she said, 'You don't understand, Carol. You're still young enough to think people should laugh at what is funny and weep at sorrows. But in fact the opposite is true.'

'Yes,' Gus agreed. 'It's just because this is so serious that we have to make light of it.'

'If we didn't laugh,' said Harriet, 'we'd go mad.'

'She doesn't understand,' said Gus.

'How could she?' asked Harriet.

Before they could head off again into their private dialogue like some nightmarish double act, I said swiftly, 'There never was an intruder, was there?'

There was a pause, then, 'No,' said Gus.

I was stepping on to thin ice, each step fraught with danger. No intruder, but Harriet's bruising had been all too real. It didn't make sense. And then I remembered Katie's words as we were driving away from Cape Trafalgar: 'Hitting her, and weeping . . .' I took a deep breath and said, looking steadily at Gus, 'It was you, Gus, wasn't it? Katie saw you beating Harriet, hitting her and crying, but that was just to back up the story about the intruder.'

'Katie saw?' Harriet was appealing to Gus.

Another long silence before, 'Yes,' answered Gus. 'She confronted me with it that evening. I told her exactly what to say to back up our story. I made her promise never to tell anyone. I always knew she'd die before she betrayed our secret. Katie's middle name is loyalty.'

'You were crying,' said Harriet, her own eyes filling with tears. 'Do you think she knew all of it?'

Gus shrugged. 'I've no idea. There was no way I could ask her that.'

'Poor Katie.' Harriet was subdued. 'So she got sucked into the lies as well.'

'We all were.'

'Yes.'

They lapsed into silence. I was seething with impatience and said, 'Tell me about the day of the fair.'

Harriet looked across at Gus, but he said nothing, so she began quietly, 'It was hot, oh, so hot. I stayed behind. I meant to go, but at the last minute I told them I wasn't feeling well.'

'Because you were pregnant already, weren't you?' I asked. At last we seemed to be getting to the heart of the story. I turned to Gus. 'And you went with the others?'

'That's right,' he said. 'It was another sweltering day. I've never known Sturford Fair so crowded. All those red-faced people slurping candyfloss and carrying yellow teddy bears.' Now they were started I got the impression he was relishing the memory.

I said to Gus, 'Did you go back to Grays before the others?'

'Yes, I'd had enough. I was glad to get away. I came back across the fields. God, it was hot.' He ran his finger under his collar.

'Wasn't it? I'd made some lemonade,' Harriet continued in a dreamy voice. 'Real lemonade with proper lemons whizzed up and just a tiny scoop of sugar. God, how I craved all that citrus stuff in the first couple of months. Oranges, grapefruit, but lemons most of all. Sometimes I wonder if that's why poor Jenny turned out such a sour little puss. I've never touched lemonade since.'

She puckered the corners of her mouth, as though the acid flavour of the fresh lemons was stinging her still.

'First thing I noticed when I got back to Grays was the silence.' Gus took up the story. 'I went up the steps to the loft and you were sleeping there on the chaise longue.'

'Not the hammock?' I asked.

He looked surprised. 'The hammock? Oh no, Harriet was already in the studio when I got back. There was a big jug of lemonade on the floor. I was so thirsty, I remember drinking straight out of the jug. The whole room smelled delicious. Lemons and turps' – he was looking at Harriet – 'and your smell mingled in. Then you woke up.'

He fell silent. After a moment, Harriet said simply, 'Yes.'

Something in the finality of that single word sent a tremor of apprehension through my body. I said quickly, 'So then Andrew must have come back before the others, right?'

'Yes,' said Harriet again. She was watching Gus and her face was flushed. 'Shall we skip through to the end?'

'Carol wants to know about Andrew,' said Gus.

'She has every right to know.' Harriet sat up straighter in her chair and continued in a businesslike manner, 'Andrew came back and he picked a quarrel with Gus. They started to fight. Andrew would have beaten Gus to a pulp – he'd always had a vicious temper. I yelled at him to stop but he was like a maniac and he turned on me. I had to stop him somehow. I saw a knife on the table, the one Gus used for canvases. I must have picked it up, and he threw himself on me and the blade sliced into his chest. I remember his face, his look of surprise. I remember him walking around saying, "Look what you've done. Just look what you've fucking done," and I thought, this isn't real, it's not really happening. But then he just collapsed. One moment he was standing up, saying, "Look what you've fucking done!" and the next . . . he wasn't . . . he was lying on the floor.'

This was so different from the story I'd been expecting that it was a few moments before I asked, 'Are you telling me *you* killed Andrew?'

She nodded. 'Oh yes, I killed him all right. The police described it as a frenzied attack, so I suppose it must have been. At some stage the jug got knocked over, and there was lemonade everywhere, all mixed in with the blood. The soles of my shoes kept sticking to the floor. You've no idea how sticky a jug of spilled lemonade can be, especially when it's mixed with blood. That's what I remember most vividly: the way my feet kept sticking to the floor and the noise my feet made each time I moved, like pulling off a plaster.'

'I can't believe it,' I said stupidly, because I'd been so sure it was Gus. Was she making this up to protect him? For one hideous moment I wondered if they'd set up this whole meeting in order to feed me their version of the story. Was this some twisted act of generosity on the part of a dying woman?

She was looking at Gus. 'How did that sound?' she asked him. 'Do you think it would have convinced the police? Maybe I should have told them straight away. After all, I was pregnant. I could have pleaded wonky hormones. I might even have got off with probation. What do you think?'

Gus said slowly, 'Are you going to leave it there?'

'I was just wondering. It's a good story. I think the police would have bought it.'

'But what about motive?'

'Simple. I was defending you. Andrew was always getting into fights. He'd had a go at Ray in the pub just the week before. We could have thought up a motive. My brother was being attacked and I saw red. I got hysterical and lost control. That was near enough the truth.'

'Near enough?' I asked. 'You've made it all up.' I was no longer so confident that I wanted to know exactly what had taken place on that hot summer's afternoon in Gus's studio.

But Gus and Harriet ignored me again, looking only at each other. Harriet began in her dreamy, sing-song voice, 'Poor Andrew, he was certainly hot and bothered when he came back from the fair. He wanted to surprise us.'

'But he didn't like what he saw,' said Gus, 'and you can't really blame him.' He had moved closer and was now crouched down in front of us both. 'You see, Harriet and I were together on the chaise longue.'

'Yes,' said Harriet. 'We were naked.' She was smiling. 'Making love.'

'Stop it! You're making this up!'

Gus laughed, a hard, bitter laugh, stood up and walked away.

Harriet leaned towards me, so close we were almost touching. 'Listen, you fool,' she snarled, and her voice no longer sounded the least bit beautiful, 'you were the one who was so determined to learn the truth, so you can't back off now. I warned you. What were you expecting, for God's sake? Why do you think we've kept silent and lied all these years? Why do you think we've hated ourselves, hated our lives? Damn you, Gus and I have had to live with this for twenty-five years. All you have to do is listen.'

I rounded on her. 'Okay, I have listened. I know your sordid little secret, you don't have to spell it out. What do you want me to do now? Tell you it's all right? Tell you not to worry about it?'

'Shut up,' said Harriet. 'We're not finished yet.'

'There's more,' said Gus.

'No!' I stormed. 'I don't want to hear it.'

Gus said, 'Leave it Harry. Leave it there.'

Harriet looked up at him with scorn. 'Are you out of your mind, Gus? Is that really what you want? God, you always were a spineless little wimp. No wonder you fell apart when the group split up. I'm surprised you survived at all. Just as well you met up with little miss Nurse Cavell here and found someone to take care of you.'

'Shut *up*, Harry. You've always had a vicious line in half-truths. You don't know the first thing about me and Carol.'

She laughed bitterly. 'Don't I? Jenny's told me plenty already and the rest I can work out for myself. But don't worry, little brother, I have no plans to mess up your cosy little nest. After all, I'm only doing what nice Carol told me to do. Tell the truth, she said, it's always better out in the open, and she's right. Don't you understand anything, Gus? Right now I'm in what those jokers call remission, but it won't last. Next week, next month, within a year at any rate, it'll all be over. And before that I'm going to make sure there's someone else who bloody well knows the truth.'

'All right, all right,' said Gus, retreating from her rage. 'Tell her if you must.'

'No, you. She's your wife.'

'Christ! All right, then.' Gus turned to me with a sigh. 'It wasn't the first time,' he said.

The first time? I opened my mouth, but couldn't speak.

'No, it wasn't,' said Harriet sombrely. Then her mood changed again and she asked him, 'Do you remember the first time?'

'Of course I do,' said Gus. At once the two of them were away again, tossing the conversation back and forth, speaking as one. 'It was after Aunt Meg's funeral. You were wearing that ridiculous floppy hat.'

'At least it was black,' said Harriet. 'You didn't even have a tie.'

'And afterwards there were sandwiches and coffee at that grotty little pub. We were avoiding each other, because we both knew what was coming. We'd been fighting it so long and for once we were on our own, away from Grays, away from the others.'

'Away from all our chaperones,' said Harriet. 'You kept eating sandwiches.'

'And drinking horrible coffee. And talking to dreadful relatives I'd never set eyes on before. And then everyone else left and it was just you and me and some crumbly old verger. So we had to leave too. We went out to the car.'

'That funny old Morris Minor you had,' said Harriet.

'My district nurse's car. We drove away from the church, but we only got about half a mile. It's a wonder nobody spotted us, but we were past caring by then.'

'Past everything. A Morris Minor. My God.' She laughed, a deep, contented laugh, not bitter at all. 'Heaven and back in a thousand-c.c. tin helmet. Oh, Gus.'

There was a long silence. They had forgotten I was there. I was desperate to break the spell, but I felt sick and couldn't think of anything to say.

At length Harriet gave a sigh of infinite sadness and regret. She said, 'That was March. March '76. We'd been battling against the inevitable for months.'

Gus nodded. 'Literally fighting, most of the time. Do you remember? All those fights. I had to get my hands on you somehow, and you were evil with your fists.'

'Wasn't I?' Harriet grinned. 'Do you remember the time you picked me up and carried me out of the kitchen and hurled me halfway across the yard? I landed in a filthy great puddle.'

'Mud all over you,' said Gus. 'But you picked yourself up and came roaring back into the house and nearly scratched my eyes out.'

'God, I wanted to kill you.'

'I wanted to make love to you right then.'

'Well, anyway, it was worth waiting for.' Harriet smiled, subdued again, and they lapsed into silence. Watching them was like seeing waves gather and break on the shore: their emotions followed the same rhythms, flaring up suddenly, then dying back as quickly as they had begun. It was like being a spectator at a well-rehearsed routine, except that Gus and Harriet hadn't seen each other in nearly a quarter of a century; their rhythms and mutual harmonies were entirely instinctive and excluded everyone and everything around them, even now.

Especially me.

'Yes,' Gus echoed eventually, 'it was worth waiting for, even though we knew it had to end.'

'But we never imagined how . . .' Harriet was frowning, her euphoria evaporating again.

In the deep silence that followed, I asked, 'Did you kill Andrew because he'd found out your secret?'

A longer silence, then, 'Yes,' said Gus.

But Harriet said, 'It wasn't quite that simple.' She turned to me, her manner brisk and matter-of-fact, as it had been when she gave the first version of the murder. 'You see, Carol, sex between Andrew and me was always a disaster. And we were the generation that was supposed to have discovered endless, guilt-free, libidinous sex, so there was no way we could admit we had problems. Andrew blamed me, of course. He said he was fine with anyone else. The only trouble was, he didn't want anybody else, just me. Some men are like that: they can't have sex with the woman they really love, only if it's casual. I didn't understand that then, and nor did he. Anyway, in all the time we were together I don't suppose we made love more than a couple of dozen times.' She looked directly at me. 'So you see, Carol, when I became pregnant . . .'

'No.' I turned away, unable to meet her eyes.

'Yes.' She was relentless. 'I knew it might be Gus's child.' She went on swiftly, 'There was no way of knowing for sure then, at least no way that I could use, and I wouldn't, anyway. Jenny thinks Andrew was her father – end of story. And if I juggle the dates a bit, it's a possibility.'

'She does look like Andrew,' said Gus.

'Do you think so?' Harriet was smiling. 'I've never seen it myself. Besides, there were plenty of others. All that summer I was trying to break away from you. I didn't know what to do. I had to get free of the trap I was in. Sex with Andrew was a non-starter, so I made the most of any chance I got.'

Gus scowled. 'I never knew.'

'Of course you didn't. I wasn't entirely stupid.'

'Who?'

'Oh, I can't remember. Some dopey accountant. That Jack-the-lad builder who used to come up from the village sometimes and help out.' She paused for a moment and I shivered. The sun had sunk beyond the horizon and a chill breeze had sprung up, rustling through the bougainvillea. Harriet hadn't noticed. She went on lightly, 'And let's not forget the man who came to read the meter – no, no, that was just a joke. A very bad joke. I'm sorry.' Suddenly Harriet looked exhausted. Defeated and exhausted and like a woman who might indeed be close to death. 'My poor little Jenny. What do you think now, Carol? I can't ever tell her, can I?'

I had no answer for her. The silence grew.

At last Harriet drew in a deep breath and said, 'I had to kill him. It wasn't a frenzied attack. On the contrary, it was quite deliberate. If I was faced with the same situation, I expect I'd do the same again. You see, Carol, he threatened us. He was so angry he swore he'd tell everyone. Can you imagine how that would have blighted Jenny's life? It didn't matter about me and Gus, but I had to protect her. She mustn't ever know.'

'No,' I said. 'You can't ever tell her that.'

'There.' She smiled at Gus with quiet satisfaction. 'The oracle has spoken. There are times when the truth is best kept hidden after all. You're a lucky man, Gus. She's learning fast. Don't throw such good fortune away.'

I said coldly, 'Maybe he already has.'

At once she was anxious again. 'You were going to tell her, weren't you, Gus?' He nodded slowly. 'Thank God for that,' she said. 'I'd hate to think I'd fouled that up, too.' But, watching her, I had the impression she was past caring. She gathered up her last remnants of strength and said, 'I expect you two want to be alone. I'll go and see Jenny again.'

'Is she sleeping?' I asked.

'No, Brian is with her. What a remarkable man he is. Did he tell you how he knew he had to come out here?' Gus shook his head. 'He said it came to him as a revelation in the middle of the night that the woman he loved was in danger. Isn't that romantic? Did you know you had a rival, Gus?'

Gus nodded. 'Brian's been Carol's faithful swain for years. If she had any sense she'd have shacked up with him long ago.'

'But it wasn't me who was in danger of dying,' I said, 'it was Jenny. Brian is in love with Jenny.'

'Are you sure?' asked Gus. 'They hardly know each other.'

'They spent that weekend together in the spring and they've been in touch off and on ever since. Brian says they hit it off right from the start, but he still doesn't know how she feels about it.'

'Oh, she adores him,' said Harriet comfortably. 'At least, that's the impression I got just now. Hardly surprising. He's got a lot of his father's charm. You remember Jack, don't you, Gus? He used to—' She broke off, and her face was ashen with shock. 'Jack Dray. Brian is Jack Dray's son. Are you sure?'

'Of course I am,' I said.

Harriet was frowning. 'Dear God,' she murmured. Then she shook her head, as though shaking off an unwanted thought. 'No,' she said firmly, 'that's impossible. Quite impossible.'

She reached for her stick. Gus watched her in horror as she shuffled to her feet. This was one truth too hideous for any of us to put into words.

'I must go and see Jenny now,' she muttered. 'My poor baby.'

Slowly, painfully, and without a glance at either of us, she made her way back into the villa. Gus and I remained a little longer, but we avoided each other's eye, talked only about banalities and then he left, saying I must be tired, it had been a long day, we'd see each other again.

It was cold, but I wasn't ready to go back inside, not yet. I stayed on the verandah and watched the darkness spread up from the hollows and realised I'd got what I'd wanted all along. It didn't feel like much of an achievement, more like the beginning of a life sentence. Fool that I was, I'd walked blindly into their conspiracy of silence.

Chapter 24

During the night, clouds massed over the hills to the north of El Cortijo Tartessus and it rained heavily, dousing the last wisps of the fire. The next morning there was the sweet smell of damp earth in the air and a hint of autumnal chill.

That turned out to be my only meeting with Harriet. She collapsed later that day and was unable to leave her room at the Villa, where she was cared for by the senior healers until a way could be found of escorting her back to England. The journey to Spain and her meeting with Gus had exhausted her reserves, or maybe she had been holding on until this moment and now had no reason to hold on any longer. I don't know.

Gus was the first to leave; he stayed only till the following afternoon. We spoke to each other once more, but it was horribly painful for us both. He let me know that, if I wanted to come back to Grays Orchard, he thought we had a good chance of rebuilding our marriage. He tried to explain that his feelings for Harriet had been different from how he felt about anyone else, not love exactly, more like an inevitable joining of two halves. He didn't mention the sexual attraction, but he didn't need to: I'd felt its power between them. He said he was a different man now and there was no reason why what had taken place between him and Harriet should ever alter the love we had. He came as near pleading as a man like Gus can ever come, and I knew he meant every word.

I told him I needed time, that it had been a shock and it was too soon for me to make up my mind yet, but neither of us really believed that. It was just impossible for me to come straight out and say: 'It's over.'

Brian and Jenny left a day later. I'd been keeping to my room in the Annex of Renewal, to avoid having to meet them, but they came to see me anyway. Jenny was transformed. She'd been running away for months, hoping that either Harriet or Gus would come looking for her, and lo and behold, they'd both done precisely that. I remembered Harriet's hope that Jenny might know she'd loved her the best she could, and it looked as though she'd got her wish. Jenny told me with delight that Gus had invited her to stay at Grays Orchard any time she wanted. It wasn't hard to imagine what the invitation had cost him.

Jenny was happy because of Harriet and Gus, but most of all, I guessed, she was happy because of Brian. They looked so right together that I couldn't remember why I'd thought them an unlikely couple. If Jenny was changed, so was Brian. No longer Mr Second Best, he'd been transformed into Mr Right. For the time being at least, their love had made them a fine and handsome couple.

They wanted me to be happy for them and I tried to laugh and joke with them, but all the time my secret was weighing like a boulder in my chest. They redoubled their efforts to reach me: Jenny didn't quite apologise for her earlier hostility, but she threw in a remark about hoping we'd be friends in future. And Brian was at pains to reassure me that he'd always be there for me. My responses must have seemed frozen, because that was how I felt. Numb. Now I understood why Brian's mother had reserved her bitterest hatred for Harriet. All the time they were with me, Harriet's final words, 'Oh no, that's too terrible', hung in the air. Jenny and Brian were so happy together, but were they blindly following in Gus and Harriet's footsteps? There was no way I could warn them or haul them back from the horrors, but nor could I share their joy. As a refinement of the torture, they obviously thought my coolness was due to sour grapes. If only.

The secret Harriet and Gus had shared with me was like a moat, cutting me off from Jenny and Brian's happy ignorance. No matter how they chatted about future plans, I was stranded and unreachable, longing for them to go so the charade would be over.

And when they had gone, and I was left in solitude again, I realised that this was exactly how Gus must have been feeling ever since Jenny had turned up at Grays and why he'd pushed me away, but of course it was much too late.

While I was officially convalescent, the Heirs invited me to join in their activities, but during the first week or so I mostly stayed in my room. For once, I was enjoying being fussed over. It was a novel sensation which made me uncomfortable at times, but I must have been learning fast because I spun out my convalescence longer than was strictly necessary, putting off the time when I'd have to start making plans and picking up the threads of my life in England.

Time alone and time to think were, I discovered, a mixed blessing, especially during those first days when all my thoughts were painful ones. I went over and over what I'd learned from Harriet and Gus about that final summer. At last I understood why Gus's paintings had grown darker, why even the sunny ones were permeated by a growing sense of menace.

All through that spring and summer Gus had been in the grip of his obsessive love for Harriet. I'd always known there was something, but naively I'd assumed it was Katie he loved, Katie who was his muse. How wrong can you be? Poor Gus: his passion for Harriet had been as irresistible as it was doomed. If I hadn't been feeling so hollow inside – as though some core part of me had been cut out with a sharp knife – I'd have had ample reason for sympathy. I was gripped by a desperate sadness, but it wasn't for Gus. I was grieving for the loss of what we'd once shared, a love which would have survived in different circumstances but which now didn't stand a chance.

There was no going back. No matter what Gus said to distance himself from the events of '76 nothing was ever going to erase the fact that I'd seen the way he and Harriet had interacted. Closer than love. Closer than sex. If they'd been reared as brother and sister they could have enjoyed that bond without it spilling over into sexuality, but, meeting properly for the first time in their twenties, their union was compelling and catastrophic.

It was easy to understand why Jenny's arrival had knocked him for six. She was the niece he had never wanted to see because of the unthinkable possibility that she was both niece and daughter. He had poured his anguish and self-disgust into that final portrait: Jenny, the half-formed adult-embryo emerging from a dark exotic bloom. Each time it came into my mind I shuddered with revulsion. No wonder Jenny had stormed out of the studio in horror. No wonder Gus had ripped the canvas to shreds.

And what about the other paintings? Well, I could go on for hours about all the different reasons why he might have destroyed them, how it was to do with the way the transcendent light of his original vision was corrupted by the knowledge of what he had done, but I'd only be guessing, so I won't waste my time. And I'd risk a further guess, too, which is that Gus didn't really know, either.

Admitting that I didn't know, no longer struggling to find the reasons behind everything, was a novel experience, but it was one I was going to have to get used to.

Once Gus and Harriet and the others had gone and I stopped going obsessively over and over the same old ground, I began to enjoy my time at the Villa. The Inner Circle had obviously decided that rescuing Jenny and preventing Davy's abduction had more than wiped out my earlier sabotage with Tim. In fact, I had achieved a certain celebrity status which meant I was not required to do any work, though I was encouraged to join in group meditations and lectures and anything else that was going on. They made no attempt to get me to join their group permanently, but I no longer expected them to. The Heirs of Akasha were always going to be a small, select group, hard to join and easy to leave: only the truly dedicated were welcome.

I came to know Serafa quite well. It turned out that her reserved manner, which I had put down to arrogance, was only shyness. She was comfortable addressing an audience of fifty, but didn't like dealing with people face to face unless she knew them well. After I'd been a fixture at the Villa for a week or so, she began to relax with me. I learned that her name in the doomed outside was Dawn: her mother was half Irish and half West Indian and her father was from Taiwan. Not surprisingly, she had grown up with a deep feeling of rootlessness until she fell in with Ra and Palu. Now that Palu had been demoted, Serafa was the only person close enough to Ra to interpret his enigmatic silences, which obviously gave her huge power over the entire organisation.

My delaying tactics meant I was able to take part in the

ceremonies for the Oath of Loyalty at the full moon, an event so bizarre that I still don't know what to make of it. It was all nonsense, of course – lots of deluded people wandering about the Temple at sunset beating drums and chanting and leaping about until some of them actually fell down in some kind of fit. Dangerous and mad. But, if I'm really honest with myself, that ceremony was one of the most memorable things I've ever done. After listening to those complex drum rhythms for an hour or so, I felt as though a hard skin in which I'd been trapped for as long as I could remember was disintegrating and falling away, resulting in an incredible feeling of freedom. By that time we were all staggering around in the dark, embracing each other and exchanging the Loyal Greeting, 'After the Watershed!' and its formulaic response, 'Life will continue!' In a moment of what felt like inspired revelation I understood exactly what it's like to be a bee, both a separate entity and at the same time part of something far bigger and more complete. And the accompanying happiness, more powerful than anything I've known before or since, is impossible to describe, but I know it was real.

And then, at the beginning of November, Tim was brought back from the hospital. The damage caused by the massive electric shock was irreversible, drastically affecting his speech and movement. A couple of healers who, in the outside world had been physiotherapists, set up a programme of exercise, but they didn't hold out much hope that he'd ever walk again. It would have been terrible to see him reduced to such shambling helplessness if I hadn't remembered how close he'd come to killing me and Jenny, and that he had threatened to kill his own son rather than see him grow up with his grandmother and the Heirs of Akasha. Each time I started to feel sympathy for him, a sliver of ice near my heart made me think: it's better this way.

Katie tended him devotedly; it was as though her helpless baby boy had been restored to her. Davy seemed to enjoy climbing on his father's immobile knees and chattering merrily away without any response. What with Ra being mute and now his father, the child was growing up with a very odd perspective on male communication, I thought, but luckily there was no shortage of talkative men at the Villa to compensate.

It was time for me to leave. I'd talked briefly on the phone to both Brian and Gus to let them know I'd be returning to Sturford only long enough to wind up my affairs. Gus said he was putting Grays Orchard on the market and Brian told me that, if I had no objections, he intended to buy it so he and Jenny could live there after their marriage. Our old plan of applying for permission to build half a dozen houses in the lower orchard, the plan that had brought me and Gus together in the first place, looked like coming off after all.

On the evening before my departure I was informed by one of the helpers that Ra himself wished to have a private meeting with me. By this time I was so saturated in the attitudes of the group that I was almost overwhelmed by the honour: private audiences with Ra happened only once or twice a year, if that.

I was debating whether to unpack some smarter clothes than the jeans and sweater I was wearing and would be travelling in the next day, but the helper insisted that a summons from Ra had to be answered at once.

I followed the helper, a wiry ex-plumber from Boston who was responsible for general maintenance at the Villa, up a spiral staircase. The door at the top was ajar, and he pushed it open without knocking, then stood aside, gesturing to me to go in. I did so, and heard the gentle click of a latch dropping behind me.

There were windows on all four sides and the room was

filled with dazzling golden light from the sinking sun, so it was a moment or two before I could pick out Ra, who was sitting on what looked like a thin white beanbag to one side of the room. There was a blue beanbag about three feet in front of him, and he indicated that I should sit down.

Heaven knows what I'd been expecting: a weird laying-on of hands, perhaps, or a sexual overture. Certainly not the sound of his reedy voice asking, 'What d'you think then, Carol? You going to stick with Gus, or what?'

'What?' I asked. And then, stupidly, 'You spoke!'

He smiled and fiddled with his thin moustache. 'I can do it, you know. But the voice isn't really my best feature, if you know what I mean. It's not exactly what you'd call an asset, is it?' He was absolutely right. His voice made him sound more like a dodgy salesman than an incarnation of the Divine Spirit, but I didn't say so. He went on, 'Palu and me, we noticed years ago the way it turned people off, distracted them from the message. So we thought we'd give this muteness thing a go. We discovered people really got off on the silence – it's dead powerful. Now we're stuck with it, aren't we? But that's okay by me.'

'But what about the Akashic Record?'

'Oh, that's real enough,' he said, and he tapped the side of his head. 'All comes in up here, see. So, are you getting back together with Gus, or what?'

'No, that's finished.'

'Thought as much. Poor old Gus, he'll take it hard. Always was a soft-hearted bugger and he worships you. Still, it's his own fault. Can't help messing things up, that's his trouble. Too soft, really, though you'd never think so to meet him.'

'Don't,' I said. 'You'll have me feeling sorry for him and then—'

'No need for that, Carol. He's a big boy. That's been

your problem all along, hasn't it? You feel sorry for someone and they hook you right in. That's how the Fairchild maniac got his claws into you.'

'How do you know?'

'Oh, there's all sorts I know about you.'

The statement was made without menace but it made me uncomfortable all the same. There was such a discrepancy between that high-pitched, wide-boy voice and his eyes, so dark and lustrous and deep one could almost imagine he was in touch with other realities.

'Did you always know about me and Tim?'

He smiled. 'That's not important. No point going over old stuff. You've got to look forward and think what happens next.'

'I'm not going back to Sturford,' I said. 'Brian can run the business without me. I'd like to train for something, if it's not too late. I've always wanted a job that involved people, but I don't know if I'd be any good at it. Recently all my efforts to help have gone horribly wrong.'

'You get days like that sometimes, don't you? Still, you mustn't let it get you down. The thing is, you've got to know why you're doing it. Someone like you, for instance, you want to stop other people hurting because it's the only way you know to stop hurting inside yourself.'

'But—' I began to protest, then suddenly I realised he was absolutely right. Amazed, I asked, 'How do you know?'

'Told you, didn't I? There's lots I know about you.'

And there was. Swift and expert as a huntsman skinning a rabbit, he told me about my family and how I'd taken on the role of the one who took care of the others. How I'd stepped into my mother's shoes after she left and how I'd rejected the chance to go away and train for a job I wanted so I could stay behind to help my father with his business. How a major part of the attraction of both Gus and Tim had been their need of me.

'And there's no harm in that,' he said kindly. 'You just need to know what's going on. You probably won't change that much, but that's okay. You'd be brilliant in the right job. You might even decide to come back here one day, and you're always welcome.'

'Thanks, but I don't think I will.'

Just as I was wondering about this, Ra said suddenly, 'Did you know Gus had visions?'

'He told me about one.'

'In the orchard at Grays. That's right. I used to envy him that. Did he tell you we went round India together?'

'Yes.'

'Best mate I ever had. I wish he'd stayed, but I'm glad he came out anyway. Funny, isn't it? I spent years waiting for that lot to show up here, Gus and the others. I was dead certain that come the Watershed we'd all be together like we were at Grays. You build people up in your mind, don't you? Then they all arrived and suddenly I realised it's not important after all. He and Harriet are just a couple of ordinary punters, same as all the rest. Gus was the only one who stuck by me when the police tried to nail that murder rap on me. Evil they were. Still, I've got a lot to thank them for. That's what started me on my journey, probably brought me out here, if you think about it.'

'Do you know who killed Andrew?'

'I told you, all that past stuff is gone. Except what won't go away. It's all on the Record, anyway. Here, let me show you something.'

He sprang lightly to his feet and crossed the room to the enormous west-facing window. The sun had almost entirely dipped beyond the sea. Just a sliver of neon red showed above the dark line of the horizon.

'Morning and evening, those are the best times to see it,' he said, picking up a pair of binoculars that lay on the sill and putting them to his eyes. He searched for a while, then his smile faded. He said, 'It's not very clear today. See what you can find.'

'What am I supposed to be looking for?' I asked, taking the binoculars and adjusting them to suit my eyes.

'Just tell me what you see.' He was grinning now, like a child with a new toy.

'Well, I can see the hills, they're just starting to turn green. And a few trees. And the sea, of course, but no boats because it's too far away. And the last scrap of sun.'

'Nothing else?'

'Nothing else.'

He sighed, took the binoculars back, peered through them for one last look, then set them down again. 'It was there, all right, but it wasn't very clear. My eyes aren't as good as they were, that's the problem. I thought you might have more luck because Questers often have good vision. Usually they just see a tower or a spire, but sometimes it's the whole skyline.'

'Of what?' I asked.

'Atlantis,' he said simply. 'Don't get me wrong, Carol, I'm not saying it's physically out there, not so as you could take a boat to it or touch it or anything. But it's real, all the same. Like a tracing in the ether, you see, the important things never go away. I've seen it loads of times.' Then he added, with a touch of regret. 'Not so much recently, though. Shame, really.'

I walked down the broad steps of the Villa to my car. Katie had wheeled Tim round to the front of the house. She looked better than I'd ever seen her and, now that Tim was back from the hospital, she seemed genuinely happy. Much of the time while she went about her work she sang pop songs from the '60s and '70s. I was careful to avoid contact with Tim as much as I could and it was impossible to know what he was thinking, but sometimes there was a shadow in his eyes that suggested he wasn't too keen on a diet of Joni Mitchell and off-key Stones.

Katie and I hugged each other warmly, then I got into my car and drove slowly through the grounds, past the lunar vegetable plot and the Temple of Atlantis and the Hesperides and the main reception building. Mid-morning, and everywhere I looked people were working on the land, building and arguing and laughing and preparing for the end of the world and I thought, are they all mad, or is it me?

The gates opened and I drove through the Pillars of Hercules and on to the public road. There were no other cars about but instantly, though I know it doesn't make much sense, it felt as though I was breathing a different air – a safer air, but a duller one, too.

All the way back to Málaga, while I was in the airport and then all during the flight, I looked for answers, but without success.

You want neat endings, you want to know what really happened. So who can tell you? Not me. I used to think I could find the answers if I tried hard enough, but that was before I got caught up with the Heirs of Akasha, and before I discovered the secret that poisoned my life with Gus. I've learned a lot, but mostly I've learned how much I'll never know.

I've no idea if Tim's wife died accidentally or if she was an early victim of his murderous rage: it seems possible, but there'll never be any proof. Nor do I know if Palu deliberately gave him the wrong instructions for opening the gates or whether it was a genuine muddle. And I wouldn't pretend to know why Brian came out to Tartessus when he did: probably it was just a coincidence, but then again, who can say? And even after my solo meeting with Ra, I can't be certain if he's mad or a fraud or a genuine visionary or some strange mixture of all three. As I said, I used to believe you could discover the truth about things like that, but I'm learning to live with uncertainty.

A thin, gritty rain was falling when we touched down at Gatwick. In the railway station the ticket salesman was depressed and unhelpful, and behind me in the queue an expensively dressed woman muttered angrily as I fumbled in the bottom of my bag for some English money. I thought of a man who'd seen visions and whose world turned to darkness when he fell in love with the one woman he could never be with, and I thought of the man whose love I'd ignored until it was too late, and I thought of Invoking the Moon and AquaMed and the Akashic Clock. And I thought of the future, a life full of possibilities now that my days in Sturford were behind me.

Welcome back to the real world, I told myself wryly.

But all the way into London I was wondering, and wonder about it still.

The real world?